# BLUE BELLE

# BLUE
# BELLE

a novel by

## ANDREW VACHSS

ALFRED A. KNOPF   NEW YORK   1988

THIS IS A BORZOI BOOK
PUBLISHED BY ALFRED A. KNOPF, INC.

Copyright © 1988 by Andrew Vachss
All rights reserved under International and Pan-American Copyright
Conventions. Published in the United States by Alfred A. Knopf, Inc.,
New York, and simultaneously in Canada by Random House of
Canada Limited, Toronto. Distributed by Random House, Inc., New York.

Grateful acknowledgment is made to the following for permission to re-
print previously published material:

*Columbia Pictures Publications* and *International Music Publications:* Ex-
cerpt from "I Put a Spell on You" by Jay Hawkins. Copyright © 1956
(Renewed 1984) by UNART Music Corp. Rights assigned to SBK Cata-
logue Partnership. All rights controlled and administered by SBK
UNART Catalog, Inc. International copyright secured. Made in U.S.A.
All rights reserved. Used by permission.

*Stazybo Music:* Excerpts from "Heartlessly," "Body and Fender Man,"
and "A World I Never Made" by Jerome Doc Pomus. Reprinted by
permission of Jerome Doc Pomus for *Stazybo Music.*

Library of Congress Cataloging-in-Publication Data
Vachss, Andrew H.
  Blue Belle.
  I. Title.
PS3572.A33B57  1988    813'.54    88-45269
ISBN 0-394-57228-9

Manufactured in the United States of America
FIRST EDITION

FOR ABE, WHO I NEVER MET BUT HAVE ALWAYS KNOWN.
AND FOR NATHAN, WHO I KNEW.
TWO PIECES OF THE ROOT.
WATCHING ME FROM SOMEPLACE ABOVE THE JUNKYARD.

TECHNICAL ASSISTANCE:

R. Winslow Dennis
Dr. Loretta French
Dr. Richard Pitz
Jeffi Rochelle Powell
Larry Smyj
Dr. Walter Stewart
Woody Vachss
Roosevelt 10X Yamamoto
Anne T. Zaroff

# BLUE BELLE

1 || SPRING COMES hard down here.
The switchman was in the lo-
tus position—serenely posed on an army blanket he had neatly folded
into quarters before he assembled his tools and took up his post for
the day. A black man with glowing bronze skin, hair falling straight
and glossy down either side of his head like a helmet, framing a face
that was mostly skull.

He held a thick pad of graph paper open on his lap, carefully
filling a page with finely shaded symbols—a covert calligraphy all his
own. He didn't bother to hide his work from passing citizens. His
half-smile said it all—the simple slugs thought him insane; they could
never understand the difference between the messenger and the
message.

A pale-blue quilt covered his shoulders. He placed three identical
blue china bowls on the blanket around him. To his right, the bowl
sported a generous supply of fine-point felt-tip pens in different colors.
The bowl on his left held a heavy Zippo cigarette lighter and some
loose cigarettes—various brands. Directly in front was a bowl with
some coins, encouraging the passing citizens to make a contribution
to his mystical cause.

He had long tapering fingers, clean and smooth, the nails man-icured and covered with clear polish. I got a good look at his hands yesterday when I stopped to look over his shoulder and watch him work. He filled a quarter of the page with symbols, never using the same one twice, working in five separate colors, not acknowledging my presence. I helped myself to one of his cigarettes, lit it with his lighter. He never moved. I tossed some coins into his china bowl and moved on, smoking his cigarette. It tasted like it was about my age.

I didn't need the polished nails to tell me he was the switchman. The neighborhood is full of halfway houses for discharged mental patients—they disgorge their cargo into the streets each morning, but this guy wasn't part of that herd. He wasn't talking to himself and he hadn't tried to tell me his story. And he didn't look afraid.

The little piece of winter chill still hanging around in April didn't seem to bother him. He worked the same post every day—starting around eleven in the morning and staying on the job until about three. The switchman had a choice spot, always setting up his shop at the edge of a tiny triangle of dirt on West Broadway, between Reade and Chambers. The slab of dirt had a couple of broken backless benches and a runty tree that had been bonsai'ed by years of attention from pigeons, dogs, squirrels, and winos. An alley without walls. Down in this part of the city, they call it a park.

At eleven, he would still be in shadow, but the sun would make its move from the East River over to the Hudson past noon, and things would warm up. The switchman never took the quilt from his shoulders.

His patch of dirt was a border town: Wall Street was expanding its way up from the tip of Manhattan, on a collision course with the loft-dwelling yuppies from SoHo. Every square inch of space was worth something to somebody—and more to somebody else a few months later. The small factories were all being converted into co-ops. Even the river was disappearing as land-greed took builders farther and farther offshore; Battery Park City was spreading its branches into the void left when they tore down the overpass for the West Side Highway. Riverfront joints surrendered to nouvelle-cuisine bistros. The electronics stores that would sell you what you needed to build your own ham radio or tap your neighbor's phone gave way to sushi bars. Antique shops and storefront-sized art galleries shouldered in next to places that would sell you some vitamins or rent you a videotape.

People have always lived down here. The neighborhood used to be a goddamned art colony—it produced more pottery than the whole Navajo nation. The hippies and the artists thought the winos added just the right touch of realism to their lives. But the new occupants are the kind who get preorgasmic when you whisper "investment banking," and they didn't much care for local color. Locksmiths were riding the crest of a growth industry.

The Superior Hotel entrance was around the corner on Chambers Street, with rooms extending all along West Broadway. Mine was on the top floor, facing out over the park. Seventy-five bucks a week bought me a swaybacked single bed on an iron frame, a ratty old easy chair worn down to the cotton padding on the arms, and a metal closet standing against the wall. The room was painted in some neutral-colored stuff that was about half disinfectant. A heavy length of vinyl-wrapped chain stood against the wall, anchored at one end to U-bolts driven into the floor. The other end stood open, padlocked to nothing, waiting patiently. I hadn't gone for the optional TV at only two bucks a day.

Someone who had never lived in one might say the room looked like a prison cell. It didn't come close.

Almost one in the afternoon. Into my third hour of watching, I shifted position in the chair, scanning the street with the wide-angle binoculars, watching the human traffic flow around the switchman. A young woman strolled by with her boyfriend. Her hair was dyed four different colors, standing up in stiff spikes, stabbing the air every time she moved her head. Her hand was in the back pocket of her boyfriend's jeans. He looked straight ahead, not saying a word. A biker rolled up to a tobacco-colored Mercedes parked at the corner. The car's window slid down and the biker put his head and hands inside. He wasn't there long. The Mercedes and the biker went their separate ways. A young woman about the same age as the one with the spiked hair tapped her business-length heel impatiently on the curb, holding a leather briefcase that doubled as a purse, wearing a pin-striped skirt and jacket over a white blouse with a dark-red bow for a tie. Winos stretched out in the sun, sprawled across the benches— passengers on a cruise ship in permanent drydock. A diesel dyke cruised into view, her arm braced around the neck of a slender, long-haired girl, her bicep flexed to display a bold tattoo. I was too far away to read it, but I knew what it said: hard to the core.

Still no sign of the target. I had followed him for three weeks straight, charting every step of his lunchtime route. The calligrapher on the blanket had to be the switchman—it was the only stop the target always made. I rotated my head gently on the column of my neck, working out the stiffness, keeping my eyes on the street. Invisible inside the shadows of my room, I lit another cigarette, cupping the wooden match to hide the flare, and went back to waiting. It's what I do best.

**2** I was working in a dead-end hotel, but I'd gotten the job in the back seat of a limousine. The customer was a Wall Street lawyer. He dressed the part to perfection, but he didn't have enough mileage on his clock to make it seem like sitting in a hundred-thousand-dollar taxi was an everyday thing for him.

"It took quite a while for you to get back to me, Mr. Burke," he said, trying for a tone that would tell me he wasn't a man used to waiting for what he wanted. "I reached out for you yesterday morning."

I didn't say anything. I'm not in the phone book. You have to have a phone of your own to qualify for that. The lawyer had called one of the pay phones in the back of Mama Wong's restaurant. Mama always answers the same way: "Mr. Burke not here, okay? You leave message, okay?" If the caller says anything else, asks more questions—whatever—Mama just runs through the same cycle. She says it enough times, the caller gets the message: If it's *not* okay with you, it's too fucking bad.

The lawyer tried another ice-breaker. "My firm has a problem, Mr. Burke, and I was told you might be the ideal individual to assist us."

I shrugged my shoulders slightly, telling him to get on with it. He wasn't in a hurry—that's the problem with paying guys by the hour.

"Is there any particular reason why we had to meet out here?" he wanted to know, gesturing toward the Hudson River with an impatient sweep of his hand. He had a nice watch. Pretty cuff links.

"Who gave you my number?" I asked, stepping on his question.

The lawyer swallowed his annoyance, reminding himself he wasn't speaking with an equal. Time to put me in my place. "Do I have to say anything more than 'Mr. C.'?" he asked, smiling.

"Yes," I said.

He looked honestly puzzled. Since he was a lawyer, only part of that could be accurate. "I thought that would be enough. I was given to understand that a recommendation from Mr. C. would be all that you would require."

"Give the understanding back, pal. And tell me who gave you my number."

"I *told* you."

"You saying Mr. C. spoke to *you?*" I asked him, watching his face.

"The number came from him," he said, answering questions the way a lawyer does.

"Have a nice day," I said, reaching behind me for the door handle.

"Wait a minute!" he snapped, putting his hand on my sleeve.

"You don't want to do that," I told him.

He jerked his hand away, sliding into his speech. "I can explain whatever is necessary, Mr. Burke. Please don't be impatient." He shifted position on the soft gray leather seat, pushed a button, and watched proudly as the padded wall between us and the driver opened to reveal a well-stocked bar. "Can I get you a drink?"

"No," I told him, taking a single cigarette from my jacket. I put it in my mouth, reached the same hand back inside for a match. I kept the other hand in my pocket, where it had been since I climbed in the limo. The gesture was wasted on him.

"Would you mind opening the window if you're going to smoke? . . . I'm allergic."

I pushed the switch and the window whispered down, letting in the traffic noise from the West Side Highway. We were parked in the pocket between Vestry Street and where the highway forks near 14th. Cars went by, but not people. The limo had picked me up on Wall Street; I told the lawyer where I wanted to go, and he told the driver.

I lit the cigarette, inhaled deeply, watching the lawyer.

"Those things will kill you," he said. A concerned citizen.

"No, they won't," I promised.

He shrugged, using the gesture to say that some people are beyond educating. He was right, but not about me. He tried one more time. "Mr. C. is a client of our firm. In the course of discussing . . . uh . . . other matters, he indicated that you might be better suited to our immediate purposes than a more . . . *traditional* private investigator." He glanced at my face, waiting for a reaction. When he realized he'd have a long time to wait, he shifted gears and rolled ahead. "Mr. C. gave us certain . . . uh . . . *assurances* concerning your sense of discretion, Mr. Burke." His tone of voice made it into a question.

I drew on my cigarette. The breeze from the open window at my back pushed the smoke toward his allergic face.

The lawyer slid a leather portfolio onto his lap, deftly opened it into a mini-desk, tapped a yellow legal pad with the tip of a gold ballpoint to get my attention. "Why don't I write a figure down, Mr. Burke. You take a quick look, tell me if you're interested." Without waiting for an answer, he slowly wrote "10,000" in large numbers.

Reverently, like he was engraving a stone tablet. He raised his eyebrows in another question.

"For what?" I asked him.

"Our firm has a . . . uh . . . *confidentiality* problem, Mr. Burke. We occupy a rather unique position, interfacing, as we say, between the business, financial, and legal arenas. Necessarily, information crosses our desk, so to speak. Information that has a short but exceedingly valuable life. Are you following me?"

I nodded, but the lawyer wasn't going to take my word for it. "You're certain?"

"Yeah," I replied, bored with this. Yuppies didn't invent insider trading—information is always worth something to somebody. I was scamming along the tightrope between prison and the emergency ward while this guy was still kissing ass to get into law school.

The lawyer stroked his chin. Another gesture. Telling me he was making a decision. The decision never had been his to make, and we both knew it.

"Somebody in our firm has been . . . profiting from information. Information that has come to us in our fiduciary capacity. Are you following me?"

I just nodded, waiting.

"We know who this person is. And we've retained the very best professionals to look into the matter for us. Specialists in industrial espionage. People who are capable of checking things we wouldn't want to use a subpoena for. Still with me?"

"Sure."

"We know who it is, like I said. But we have been unable to establish a case against him. We don't know how he moves the information. And we don't know to whom he passes it."

"You checked his bank accounts, opened his mail, tapped his phones . . . all that, right?"

Now it was the lawyer's turn to nod, moving his head a reluctant two inches.

"Telegrams, visitors to the office, carrier pigeons . . . ?"

He nodded again, unsmiling.

"How much time would he have between getting the information and making use of it?"

"Ah, you *do* understand, Mr. Burke. That's exactly the problem. We deal with extremely sensitive issues. Nothing on paper. In a normal insider-trading situation, a profiteer would have a minimum of several days to make his move. But in our situation, he would have to act within a few hours—no longer than close of business on the same day the information comes in."

"And you've had him under surveillance every day for a while?"

He nodded.

"Drawing a blank?"

He nodded again.

"You call in the *federales*?"

"That wouldn't be our chosen scenario for this situation. The firm itself has its own interests, as well as the obligation to protect our clients. Perhaps you don't understand some of the complexities of our profession. . . ."

I gave him the closest thing to a smile I ever give citizens. I'd never heard the laundry business called a profession before.

"Why don't you just fire him?"

"We can't do that. He's a very well connected young man. Besides, our clients will demand some actual proof of his guilt before taking any action. They were very insistent on that, for some reason."

Sure. The "clients" wanted to make damn sure the problem was going to get solved for good. The only time humans like that are interested in the truth is when a mistake will cost them money.

"What do you want from me?"

"We want you to find out how this individual gets the information out. And we want *proof*. Something we can show our clients."

"And the only time he could possibly pass this along is during business hours?"

"Yes. Without question. After that . . . it wouldn't be of value to him or anyone else."

I lit another cigarette, thinking it through. It sounded like they had the wrong guy. Maybe the "clients" were setting them up. Maybe this lawyer was the one doing the stealing. It wasn't my problem. Money was. Always is.

"The only time I could watch him would be when he leaves the building, right?"

"Yes. Inside the building, he's completely covered."

"A grand a day. Until I find out how he does it or you call me off. Another ten if I get the proof for you."

"Mr. Burke, with all due respect, that's triple the rate charged by the finest security firms. And you'll only be working a couple of hours each day."

"In cash. In front. Nothing bigger than fifties. No consecutive serial numbers. No new bills," I told him. "You know how it's done."

The lawyer looked at me, watching my face for the first time since I'd climbed into the limo. "What makes you worth so much?"

"Ask Mr. C.," I suggested.

He dropped his eyes. "We won't need you every day. Just those days when something comes in. We'll call as soon as . . ."

"No."

"I don't understand."

"I need to work this guy *every* day, okay? I need to know him. I need to know when he's changed his pattern. You don't need to call me when the information comes in. I watch this guy long enough, *I'll* know."

"That could take weeks. . . ."

I nodded agreement. "Maybe longer. Who knows? I probably won't get him the first time he moves anyway. Depends on when you get something for him to trade."

"And you may not get him at all?"

"And I may not get him at all."

The lawyer pretended to think it over. Maybe he was better at pretending to be honest. "We need to get started on this. This is Friday; could you be on the job Monday?"

"Sure."

"All right, Mr. Burke. I am prepared to pay you one thousand dollars in cash right now. For Monday's work. In advance, as you requested. We will meet each evening—you'll give me your report and we will decide if you are to continue."

I just shook my head. Why they sent this fool to do business with me was a mystery: he was a pin-striped shark, but he couldn't bite people who never went near the water.

"You have another suggestion?"

"Yeah, pal. Here's my suggestion. You hand me twenty thousand dollars, like we agreed. Okay? That buys you twenty days, unless I pull it off quicker. I pull it off *before* ten days, you get a refund. Nothing jumps off in twenty days, we meet and see what you want to do. Got it?"

"That's outrageous," the lawyer said, his face a half-step out of sync with his words. "You expect me to just . . ."

"I'm tired of this. I'm tired of you. If Mr. C. really sent you out here to do business, you've got at least twenty large in that pretty briefcase of yours. And if you're a fucking little errand boy, go back and tell your boss that he sent the wrong messenger."

He sat there, staring. I lit another cigarette. "When this smoke is finished, so am I," I told him, waiting.

The lawyer tried to smile. "I'm no errand boy," he said, holding his head stiff. He opened another compartment in the briefcase. The money was neatly stacked, a paper band around the fifty-dollar bills. He counted off twenty little stacks, tossing them contemptuously on the broad seat between us, making sure I could see there was plenty left in the briefcase.

Telling me they would have paid more. That he had the last laugh.

"Can I drop you someplace?" he smirked.

I threw an empty pack of cigarettes back over my shoulder, out the window. "Thanks anyway," I told the lawyer, shoving the cash into different pockets of my coat, "I'll call a cab."

A battered gypsy cab rolled up next to the limo. The rusty old hulk was so filthy you couldn't even see through the windows. The lawyer's mouth dropped open. I nodded to him, backed out of the limo and into the gypsy. The driver dropped the hammer, and we moved out in a cloud of black smoke.

**3** ‖ I SPOTTED the insider when he was still a half-block away. Watching him for days tuned me in—I could pick him up in a crowd just by the way he moved. Heading for the switchman, like always. I zoomed the binoculars in on the switchman's hands. He was still working on his charts, face bent over in concentration. When the insider got close, I focused in on the three bowls, flicking past the one that held the pens to the second one—the one with the cigarettes. I locked into the last bowl in the triangle—the one with the coins. There was nothing else in my vision. I breathed gently through my nose, my elbows pressed into my chest.

Silver dropped into the switchman's bowl. Some coins. And a flat-folded piece of aluminum foil. I reached one hand up to the window shade and pulled it straight down. I dropped to the floor and raised the shade an inch at the bottom, so I could peek out without the binoculars.

A kid in a striped T-shirt shot around the corner on a skateboard. He lost control and spun out; the skateboard took off by itself and crashed into a parked car. The kid was ready for the crash: gloves on his hands, thick pads covering his elbows and knees. His head was hidden under a white plastic mask—the kind hockey goalies wear. He shook himself off, dazed.

Then he charged right at the switchman, snatched the coin bowl in both hands, and flew up the block, the bowl tight against his chest. The switchman started to come off his blanket when one of the winos stumbled into him from behind. The wino's long floppy raincoat blocked most of my view, but I could see the switchman whip an elbow into his chest, knocking him backward. The wino grabbed at the switchman to break his fall; they fell to the ground together. The switchman wrenched himself loose, stopping for a second to kick the helpless wino in the chest.

When he turned around, the kid was gone. I saw the gypsy cab pull away, heading for the river.

The switchman did a full circle, knowing he was too late. The wino crawled away, his hands wrapped around his ribs. The switchman pulled the corners of his blanket together, held it in two hands, and spun it around a couple of times to form a sack. He threw the sack over his shoulder and ducked into the subway.

It took me less than a minute to throw everything I had with me into the battered suitcase and head out the door.

I went out the side door on Chambers, and walked back through the park. The street was the way it was before the crash. Even the kid's skateboard was gone.

4 ‖ MY PLYMOUTH was parked on West Street, near one of the construction sites. The guy who built it years ago was trying to create the ultimate New York taxicab, but he died before he got it done. I threw my suitcase in the trunk and started the engine. The two-and-a-half-ton dull gray machine started right up, the way it always does. I hit the switch and my window slid down. Lit a cigarette and pulled away, heading for the pier.

I was there first. I backed in until the bumper tapped the base of the pier, shoved a Judy Henske tape into the slot, listened to "If That Isn't Love" for the thousandth time. Waiting again. If Linda Ronstadt is a torch singer, Henske's a flame thrower.

A couple of guys walked by, hand in hand, talking just to each other. An overmuscled beach boy posed against a burned-out abandoned car. A black man was adding a few touches to an oil painting of the riverfront. A man with a teenager's body cruised the scene on roller skates, wearing mirror sunglasses to hide the truth. The whores don't work this pier. Some zoning regulation the City Council would never understand reserved it for gays.

Nobody came near the Plymouth. I was into my third smoke, and Henske was breaking chops with both hands on "Good Old Wagon" by the time the gypsy cab pulled in at an angle next to me, its nose aimed at the Plymouth's trunk. The kid jumped out first, the goalie's mask gone, his baby face glowing with pride.

"Hey, Burke!"

"Keep it down," I told him, climbing out of the car.

"Did you see it? It went *perfect!*" He was bouncing up and down like he just hit a home run in Little League. Snatching money off the street was as close as Terry would ever get.

The Mole slowly emerged from the darkness of the gypsy cab. He was wearing a greasy pair of coveralls, a heavy tool belt around his waist, with another strap running over his shoulder. Something glinted off his Coke-bottle lenses—I couldn't tell if it was the sun. He walked into the shadow where our two cars touched and squatted on the ground, fumbling in his leather satchel. Terry hunkered down beside him, his hand on the Mole's shoulder, trying to peer inside the satchel. The Mole's pasty-white hands with their stubby fingers looked too awkward to open the clasp, but he had a touch like a brain surgeon. He pulled out the foil disk and dropped it in my palm, looking up at me with a question.

"Let's see," I told him, unwrapping it carefully.

In a neat, almost prim handwriting were the words "Maltrom, Ltd." Nothing else. I didn't need anything else.

"Nice work, Mole," I told him.

The Mole grunted.

"You drop Max off?"

He grunted again. Max the Silent didn't get his name because he moved so quietly. A Mongolian free-lance warrior who never spoke, Max made his living as a courier, moving things around the city for a price. His collateral was his life. He was as reliable as cancer, and not nearly as safe to play with. The wino who stumbled into the switchman had been Max. He'd taken the kicks to the ribs, even though he could have snapped the switchman like a matchstick. A professional.

The Mole was still hunkered down in the shadows. The kid was next to him. Waiting quietly now, like he'd been taught.

"I got about an hour," I told the Mole.

His face moved—the Mole's idea of a smile. "You don't want to call your broker first?"

I don't have a broker. I don't get mail and I don't have a phone. Maybe it's true that you can't beat them—you don't have to join them either.

"I have to see Michelle," the kid piped up.

I caught the Mole's eye, nodded okay.

"Give her my share," he said.

5 ‖ I WHEELED the Plymouth across the highway and started to work my way through the back streets of SoHo. Carefully, like I do everything.

Lily runs a special joint that works with abused kids. They do individual and group therapy, and they teach self-defense. Maybe it's all the same thing.

Max's woman works there. Immaculata. It wasn't so long ago that she tried to stop three punks from attacking what she thought was an old man on the subway. The old man was Max. He went through the punks like a chain saw through Kleenex, left them broken and bleeding on the subway floor, and held out his hand to the woman who stood up for him. Their baby was born a few months ago—two warriors' blood in her veins.

Terry watched me without turning his head, working on

what we'd been teaching him. But he was doing it for practice—he wasn't scared anymore. The first time I took him away in a car, he was a rental from a pimp. We were working a deep con, looking for a picture of another kid. We picked up Michelle on the street so she could watch Terry while we got ready to deal with his pimp.

I lit a cigarette, thinking back to that night. "Want one?" I asked him.

"Michelle doesn't want me to smoke."

"I won't tell her."

The kid knew better than to use the dashboard lighter in the Plymouth. I snapped a wooden match into life, held it across to him. He took a deep drag. We had a deal.

I watched him scan the passing streets with his eyes, not moving his head.

I was in Biafra during the war. It got bad near the end. Staying alive was all there was. No food, landlocked, soldiers pinching all four corners, planes spitting death—low enough in the sky to hit with a rifle. If you had a rifle. Too many ways to die. Some screamed, some ran. Nobody won. I saw kids lying like litter all through the jungle, their faces already dead, waiting. I had a 9mm pistol with three bullets left in the clip, half a pack of cigarettes, a pocketful of diamonds, and almost a hundred grand in Swiss francs. I left a sack of Biafran pounds back in the jungle. About a million face value, if Biafra won the war. It wasn't going to, and carrying a sack of money from a defeated country while you're running for your life is what they mean by "dead weight." I didn't even bury it—I wasn't coming back. Another big score gone to dirt. The gunfire stopped, and the jungle got dead quiet. Waiting. A young woman ran past me on my right, wearing only a pair of tattered men's shorts way too big for her, every breath a moan. I heard a grunting sound and hit the ground, the pistol up in front of me. A wounded soldier? If he had a rifle, maybe I could trade up. It was a little boy, about three years old, a tiny head on a stick body, his belly already swollen, naked. Alone. Past being scared. The woman never broke stride; she scooped the baby up on the run, shoving him up toward her slender neck, holding him with one hand. If she made it, the baby would have a new mother.

That's what Michelle did with Terry.

**6** I PARKED a couple of blocks away. Terry and I walked over to Lily's, not talking. The black guy at the front desk was reading a thick book through horn-rimmed glasses.

"Hey, Terry!"

"Hey, Sidney!" the kid greeted him. "Sidney's going to law school," he told me.

Somehow I didn't think Sidney would end up making deals with guys like me in the back of limos. "Is this your father?" he asked Terry. "The one who teaches you all that electronic stuff?"

That cracked the kid up. "Burke?" It was the Mole's thought, but the laugh was Michelle's. It's not just chromosomes that make blood.

Sidney waved us past. We walked down a long corridor to the back offices. The right-hand wall was all glass. On the other side, groups of kids were running, jumping, screaming their lungs out. Everything from disciplined martial-arts classes in one corner to some crazy game with kids taking turns trying to dive over a mound of pillows. Business as usual.

Immaculata burst out of one of the back offices, her long glossy hair flying behind her, a clipboard in one hand.

"Lily!" she yelled out.

"We're all back here," echoed a voice.

Immaculata saw us and spun in a graceful arc, her long nails flowing together as she pyramided her hands at the waist. She bowed gently to us.

"Burke. Terry."

"Mac." I bowed back.

Terry tried to bow too, but he was too excited to get it right. "Is Max here?"

"Max is working, honey."

"But is he *coming?* Maybe later?"

Immaculata's smile ignited the highlights in her eyes. "Who knows?"

"Max is the strongest man in the world!" the kid said, not inviting a dispute.

Immaculata bowed again. "Is strength so important? Do you remember what you have been taught?"

"Yes. Strength of character. Strength of spirit."

"Very good," the beautiful woman proclaimed, bending at the waist to give Terry a kiss. "And so . . . is Michelle strong?"

"She's so brave."

"And the Mole?"

"Michelle says he's the smartest man on the earth. That's what she says."

"And Burke?"

The kid looked doubtful, waiting.

"Burke is not strong like Max?"

The kid shook his head.

"Or brave like Michelle? Smart like the Mole?"

"No . . ." Terry said, reaching for it.

"So how does he survive?"

The kid knew all about survival. "He has strength too, right?"

"Right!" said Immaculata, giving him another kiss.

The kid was in heaven. Maybe he'd never see the inside of a prep school unless he went along on a burglary, but how many kids get to work a major-league scam, hang out with a lunatic, and get kissed by a lovely lady all on the same day?

"Come on," said Immaculata, reaching out her hand. I followed them down the hall to Lily's office.

7 || L I L Y  W A S seated at the screen of her so-called computer, playing some electronic game with the keyboard, a baby on her lap, balanced between her elbows. She was wearing a painter's smock over pink jeans; her hair was tied back. Her scrubbed face looked like a teenager's, animated with attention as she bounced the baby on her lap in time with a man running through a maze on the screen. Michelle sat on the desk, her flashy legs crossed, smoking a cigarette in a red lacquer holder. Her outfit was all black-and-white triangles. Even her nail polish was black. On a straight lady, it would have looked whorish. On Michelle, it was fashion.

"Mom!" Terry yelled, charging over to her.

Michelle pulled him close, hugging him, looking over his shoulder. "You spend a few minutes with Burke and you leave your manners in the street?"

Terry gave her a kiss, smiling, knowing she wasn't mad at him. "I greeted Immaculata," he said.

"And . . ."

The kid turned to Lily. "Hello, Lily."

"Hi, Terry!"

"Hello, baby," he said to the infant on her lap.

"Baby has a name," Immaculata reminded him gently.

"Hello, Flower," the kid said, taking her tiny hand and kissing it.

Immaculata clapped. "See! He learns his good manners from Burke."

Michelle laughed. "He'd be the first."

"Can I hold Flower?" Terry asked Mac.

"As I showed you," she warned him. Every female eye in the room was riveted on the kid, but he tucked the baby into the crook of his arm, sat down next to Michelle, and started cooing to Flower like he'd been doing it all his life. Like nobody ever did to him.

I gave Michelle the high sign. She tousled Terry's hair and slid off the desk. We left them in the office and walked down the hall, looking for an empty room.

8 ‖ WE DUCKED into a cubicle a few doors down. I didn't have much time.

"The Mole and I just did some work. He said for you to hold his share."

I handed her the cash. She snapped open her purse, divided the money into two piles, stowed it away.

"A little closer to Denmark, baby—to the real me," she said, blowing a soft kiss at the cash. Michelle had been talking about the operation ever since I'd known her. She'd been through the full-body electrolysis, the hormone injections, even the silicone implants in her breasts. But she had balked at the psychological counseling American hospitals required before they'd do a full sex-change operation.

"You'll take Terry back to the Mole?"

I nodded, checking my watch. "You go get him," I told her.

I dialed a number while I was waiting for her. The lawyer with the limo answered on the first ring.

"It's done," I told him. He started to babble. I cut him off. "You know Vesey Street, where it runs past the World Trade Center? Take it all the way west, right to the river. I'll meet you there in forty-five minutes." I hung up on him.

Michelle came down the hall, holding Terry's hand, calling good-bye to Lily and Immaculata over her shoulder.

**9** | TERRY SAT between us on the front seat. I lit a cigarette. "Want one?" I asked him.

"Michelle doesn't want me to smoke," the kid said, his angelic face giving nothing away. Michelle gave him a kiss. The Mole was teaching him science; I was teaching him art.

"I got to meet a guy, Terry," I told him. "You'll have to ride the trunk, okay?"

"Sure!"

"And when I'm finished, I'll take you back to the Mole."

"I can't go right back," he said.

I looked over at Michelle. "Why not?" I asked him, watching her eyes.

"Mole says he has work to do. Someplace else. He says for you not to bring me back until after six."

"How about if I bring you back to Lily's? I'll roll by in a few hours."

"Why can't I hang out with you?"

Michelle patted him. "Burke has work to do, baby."

The kid was hurt. "I do work too. I help Mole. Lots of times."

"I know you do, baby," she said. I shot the kid a warning glance. If Michelle wanted to think the kid helped out by holding the Mole's soldering iron, that was fine with me.

We rolled into the Wall Street canyon, following Michelle's directions. She had customers down there too. I pulled over to the curb.

She gave Terry another kiss and flowed from the car. We watched her make her way into the building. Watched men turn to look at her, thinking they had never seen a woman with so much style. I used to wonder what men would think if they knew the truth, but I don't anymore. The man waiting for her knew the truth.

**10** ‖ I WHEELED the Plymouth around the corner and slid along until I found an empty spot, just past the little park where they assemble crowds who want to visit the Statue of Liberty. A lot of people bring their cars down to the river to work on them. Guys were changing the oil, draining radiators, doing tune-ups. I pulled over and popped the trunk. The inside was lined with the padding that furniture movers use. A steel box in one corner covered the battery; a fifty-gallon fuel cell took about half the storage space, but there was plenty of room for a man to wait comfortably. A neat row of quarter-inch holes was punched through the tip of the trunk. I pulled the piece of duct tape away so air would circulate. "You know where everything is?" I asked the kid.

He looked at me the way the Mole does sometimes, his eyes shifting to the cable that would open the trunk from the inside and let him out. He knew he could also get out through the back seat if he had to. Two plastic quart bottles were bolted to the side of the trunk, one full of a water-and-glucose solution, the other empty. A man could stay there for a couple of days if he had to.

I pulled a thick roll of neon-red tape from the trunk, peeled off a precut piece, and handed the end to Terry. He pulled it taut, and we walked it over to the hood. It fit perfectly. Another piece went over the roof. One more for the trunk, and we had a distinctive racing stripe from front to back. Terry took the rubber block I handed him and smoothed out the little bubbles under the tape while I attached a foxtail to the antenna and snapped some blue plastic covers over the parking lights in the grille. I pulled another set of license plates out of the trunk and screwed them on over the ones I'd been using. In ten minutes we had a different car. With untraceable plates.

Terry patted himself down, making sure he had his butane cigarette lighter. Michelle didn't mind him carrying the lighter. It was a gift from the Mole. Loaded with napalm. The tiny Jewish star the kid wore on a chain around his neck gleamed dull against his pale skin. It was made of steel. "They took gold from our people's mouths to make their evil ornaments," the Mole once said, explaining it to me.

The kid made himself comfortable. I closed the lid and climbed back inside. On schedule.

11 ‖ THE LIMO was already there when I pulled up. I left the Plymouth a half-block away and walked toward the blacked-out passenger windows, hands in my pockets. He must have been watching my approach. The door swung open.

I handed him the foil-wrapped disk. Watched as he carefully opened it, smearing any fingerprints that would have been on it if I had left any. He held the paper away from me so I wouldn't get a look at the magic name. His hands shook. His tongue ran around his lips. He was looking at his ticket up the ladder.

"This is it," he said. Reverent.

"Good. Give me the money."

"Sure. Sure . . ." he said, almost absently, reaching in his brief-case, counting it out, not making a ceremony of it this time. Handing it over to me, not even watching as I buried it in my coat pocket.

I reached for the door handle. "Wait a minute," he said.

I waited, my hand wrapped around a roll of quarters in my pocket, measuring the distance to the spot just below his sternum, breathing through my nose, calm.

"How did you get this?"

"That wasn't our deal."

"I'm just curious."

I looked at his face until his eyes came up to mine.

"Ask Mr. C.," I advised him.

The limo was pulling away before I took three steps back to the Plymouth.

**12** ‖ I DIDN'T know if the lawyer had other eyes around, so I drove away slow, sliding through the maze of streets parallel to the river until we got back to the open piers a few blocks uptown. I stripped the tape off the car, pulled the foxtail, and popped off the parking-light covers. I tossed everything inside the trunk, reaching inside to get a screwdriver for the plates. Terry never moved, lost inside the darkness. "Want to get something to eat at Mama's?" I asked softly. His little fist tapped against the fuel cell once. Yes.

**13** ‖ THE PLYMOUTH pushed its anonymous nose past the entrance to Mama's restaurant, giving me a chance to read the messages. Mama used three identical dragon tapestries for a window display: one red, one white, one blue. Tourists thought it was patriotic. Only the white dragon stood in the window. No cops inside—no other trouble either.

I pulled around to the alley in the back. The alley walls were whitewashed, garbage cans neatly stacked, tightly capped. A calico cat the size of a beagle sat on top of one of the cans, marking his territory. A short set of Chinese characters in foot-high black letters stood stark against the white wall. Max's message to anyone who might have stupid ideas about asking Mama for a contribution to their favorite charity.

I popped the trunk and Terry climbed out, shaking himself like a dog coming out of water. The back door was steel, painted the same color as the building. You had to look close to see it. There was no doorknob. I pushed against it, and Terry followed me inside. We were in the kitchen. Half a dozen young Oriental men were scattered around. Two of them were tossing handfuls of meat and vegetables into a set of giant woks while a third man stirred, a flat wooden tool in each hand. He rapped sharply on the rim of one of the woks. Another man came forward, his hands wrapped in rags. He grabbed the wok by the rim, dumped the contents into a metal pot, and dropped the wok onto another burner. He tossed in a glassful of water, swirled it around, dumped out the water, and put the clean wok back in front of the cook. Handfuls of pea pods, water chestnuts, and some red stuff I didn't recognize flew into the empty wok. A vat of rice steamed against one wall. None of the workers gave us a glance. A fat man sat at the door connecting the kitchen to the restaurant, a tapestry the size of a tablecloth covering his lap. The tapestry rested on a wood frame, like a small table, the cloth reaching almost to the floor. The fat man's eyes were lost in folds of flesh, no more visible than his hands. I stopped in front of him, one hand on Terry's shoulder to show he was with me. The fat man's head held solid, drawing a bead. I didn't rush him. I knew what he was holding under the tapestry frame. Finally, he tilted his head a fraction of an inch. Okay. We went into the restaurant.

Terry and I took my table at the back. The place was empty except for a young woman and her date. She was wearing tinted aviator glasses, a string of pearls over a black silk T-shirt. A skinny, mean-faced woman with capped teeth. Her date had a neat, short haircut. The kind of tan you can buy without getting near the beach. He looked like a sheep that worked out a lot—taut lines, stupid eyes. She was asking the waiter a series of intricate questions about how the food was prepared. He answered every question with the same Cantonese phrase, reading her like a menu with only one dish on it. This went on for a couple of minutes, until Mama climbed off her stool by the cash register at the front and came over to them. She wore a bottle-green silk dress cut tight all the way up to the high mandarin collar and flowing loose from the waist down. Her hair was pulled back in a glossy bun, her broad face unlined. Only a fool would try to guess her age; only a fool with a death wish would ask her.

The waiter stood aside as she approached. She bowed gently to the woman and her companion.

"You have questions?"

"I certainly do. I have been *asking* this gentleman if you use MSG in the preparation of your food. Our diet doesn't permit . . ."

Mama stepped on the rest of the sentence. "Oh, yes. Plenty MSG. No problem."

"You don't understand. We don't *want* any flavor enhancers in our food. MSG causes . . ."

"MSG in everything here. Soup, vegetables, meat. Special stuff. Plenty MSG."

The woman gave an exasperated sigh. "Don't you have provision for preparing meals *without* MSG?"

"Why you want that? MSG in everything. Good for you. Make blood nice and thin."

The woman looked over at her date, a pained expression on her pinched face. I lit a cigarette, blowing the smoke in her direction.

"You have a No Smoking section, I presume?"

"You want cigarettes?" Mama asked, innocently.

"No. We don't want cigarettes. And we don't want MSG. Is that so hard to understand?"

Her date looked uncomfortable, but he kept quiet.

"Everybody smoke here. Even cooks smoke, okay? Plenty MSG. No American Express." Mama looked at her, smiling. "Not for you, right?"

"It certainly is not," said the woman, pushing her chair back. "Come on, Robbie," she said to the sheep.

"Have a nice day," Mama told her. She watched the woman and the sheep walk out the front door, giving their table a quick wipe. She looked around her empty restaurant and smiled. Business was good.

I slid out of the booth, bowed to Mama as she approached. Terry bounded over to her, his arms open. Mama clasped her hands at her waist, bowed to the kid. It stopped him like he ran into a wall, confusion overflowing his face.

"Easy. Move slow, okay?" She smiled down at him.

"I was just going to . . ."

"You going to kiss Mama?"

"Sure!"

"You see Burke kiss Mama?"

"No . . ."

Mama's face was calm. Set. "Mama kiss babies, okay? Not kiss man."

Terry stared at her face, figuring it out. Knowing by her tone not to be afraid. "I'm not a man," he said.

"What, then?"

He looked at me for help. I blew smoke out my nose. I didn't know the answer. He took a shot on his own. "A kid?"

"Only two pieces," Mama said. "Baby or man. No more baby, time to be a man."

"I won't be a man until I'm thirteen."

"Who says this?"

"Mole."

Mama glanced over at me. "Bar Mitzvah," I told her. "Jewish ceremony."

"Good. Not *official* man until thirteen, right?"

"Right," Terry told her.

"Start now," Mama said, bowing to him again. Case closed.

Terry bowed.

Mama sat down across from me. Terry waited, saw there wasn't going to be any more instruction, sat down too. Mama said something to the waiter. He disappeared.

"Soup first, okay?"

"Can I have fried rice?" the kid wanted to know.

"Soup first," Mama said.

The waiter brought a steaming tureen of Mama's hot-and-sour soup. Three small porcelain bowls. Mama served Terry first, then me.

Then herself. I pressed my spoon against the vegetables floating in the dark broth, taking the liquid in first, holding it above the bowl, letting it cool. I took a sip. "Perfect," I said. It was the minimal acceptable response.

Terry pushed his spoon in too deeply, covering it with vegetables. He carefully turned the spoon over, emptying it back into the bowl. Tried it again. Got it right. He swallowed the spoonful, tears shooting into his eyes. His little face turned a bright red. "It's good," he said, his voice a squeak.

Mama smiled. "Special soup. Not for babies."

I took another spoonful, swallowed it slowly. Let it slide down, breathing through my nose. Terry watched me. Tried it again. Smaller sips this time.

I threw a handful of hard noodles into my bowl. Terry did the same. He watched as I spooned off the top layer of liquid, mixing the last spoonfuls with the vegetables, not chewing any of it, gently breathing through my nose. The kid went right along.

When my bowl was empty, Mama spooned it full again. Terry was right behind me. Mama called for the waiter. He took the tureen away. Came back with a heaping plate of fried rice for Terry. The plate was beautiful—big chunks of roast pork, egg yolk, scallions— each grain of rice floating on top of another into a perfect pyramid. The kid's eyes lit up. He dug in without another word. I helped myself to a few forkfuls, bowing my acknowledgment of perfection to Mama.

Terry was halfway through the giant mountain when he looked up at Mama.

"What's MSG?" he wanted to know.

"Bad stuff. Special salt. Make weak food taste strong, okay? Chemical. Fake. No good for you."

Terry smiled at her, putting it together. "No MSG here, right?"

Mama smiled back at him. "Right."

I lit another cigarette. "How's business?" I asked her.

"Always same."

I put the money from the lawyer on the table. Split it into two piles. "For Max," I told Mama, touching one pile. "For the bank," I said, touching the other. Mama would hold the money for me. Her bank didn't pay interest. In fact, she took a piece for a storage fee. But her bank was open twenty-four hours a day and it didn't file federal paper every time you made a deposit.

Mama's long fingers flashed over the money, faster than a blackjack dealer's. The two piles became four. She pointed at each in turn. "For Max. For the bank. For Mama. For baby."

I nodded agreement. I knew the pile marked for Flower had some of my money and some of Mama's. Max knew nothing about it—it wasn't his business. Whenever Mama saw Immaculata, she would have a pink silk purse in her hand. "For baby," is all she ever said.

Down where we live, every day is a rainy day.

14 || WE WERE in the back room, the one between the restaurant and the kitchen, waiting for the cook to finish chopping up a pile of thick marrow bones, putting together a food package for me. Terry was in the kitchen, watching everything. Staying out of the way.

Three pay phones stood in a bank against the wall. The one at the end rang. Mama looked at me. I nodded. She picked up the receiver.

"Mr. Burke not here. You leave message, okay?"

I couldn't hear the other end of the conversation. It didn't matter what they said—Mama never went past the script.

"Not here, okay? Don't know. Maybe today. Maybe next week. You leave message?"

Mama listened. Wrote something on a scrap of paper. Hung up.

She handed me the paper. A phone number I didn't recognize.

"Woman. Young woman. Say you call this number before nine tonight."

"She say what she wanted?"

"A job for you."

"Anybody we know?"

"I never hear the voice before. Woman say her name is Belle."

"I don't know her."

Mama shrugged. Bowed goodbye to me and Terry. The steel door closed behind us. I turned the Plymouth north to the Bronx.

15 ‖ TERRY WAS quiet on the ride back. I let him have his silence— it's something a man has to learn. As he got older, I'd teach him not to give things away with his face.

I didn't fill the silence with the radio or my tapes. The radio works, but the faceplate is really just to disguise the police-band scanner built into the dash.

And all my tapes are the blues.

Kids can't sing the blues; when they try, it sounds wrong. They have the pain, but not the range.

We rolled over the Triboro to the Bronx. The kid watched as I tossed a token into the basket in the Exact Change lane. Learning. Don't call attention to yourself. When we pulled up to the junkyard, Terry made a circle with his finger. Go around to the back.

The back fence was heavy-gauge cyclone mesh, with three twisted bands of razor wire running across the top. Everything was two-tone: pollution-gray and rust.

A big dog the same color as the fence was basking in a patch of late-afternoon sunlight. His lupine face was impassive as we approached, but his ears stood straight up. Yellow eyes tracked the car, locking onto the target like a heat-seeking missile. An American Junkyard Dog. Best of a breed the American Kennel Club never imagined. City wolf.

I pulled the car parallel to the fence, Terry's door closest to the dog. The beast growled deep in his chest. Dark shapes moved behind the fence. Dots of light and flashes of white. Eyes and teeth, both ready.

"Tell the Mole Michelle has his money."

"Okay, Burke."

Terry climbed out of the Plymouth, flipped the door closed behind him. Walked over to the dog, talking in a low voice. The beast walked over to meet him. Terry scratched the dog behind his ear, standing next to him. I knew the dog wouldn't move until I did, so I wheeled the car in a tight circle, heading back the way I came. When I looked back, Terry was down on all fours, following the dog through a cut-out section of the fence. He had to twist sideways to get in.

**16** IT WAS dark by the time I turned into the narrow street behind the old paper-tube factory where I have my office. The garage is set into the building just past the sidewalk. When the landlord converted the joint into living lofts, he bricked up the old loading bay, where the trucks used to pull in, to make room for storefronts. The garage only has room for one car, right at the end of a row of little shops. I pulled in, hit the switch; the door rattled down, leaving me in darkness. I locked the car, took the steel steps up four flights, walking quietly past the entrance to each hallway. The doors lock from the outside and I keep them that way. There's another flight of stairs at the far end of each floor. If there's a fire, the tenants know which way to go.

When I got to the top floor, I let myself into the hall. I closed the door behind me. It looked like a blank wall.

There's no sign on my door. My name's not on the directory downstairs. As far as the tenants know, the fifth floor is sealed off. Most of it is.

I don't have a lease. I don't pay rent. The landlord's son did something very stupid a few years ago. The landlord is a rich man, and he spent the right money in the right places. The kid has a new name, a new face, and a new life. Home free. Until I found him. I wasn't looking for the little weasel, but I knew who was. They still are.

It's not a home, it's where I live for now. When the time comes I have to leave, I won't look back. I'll take everything I need with me.

And when I walk away, there won't even be a fingerprint left for them to play with.

**17** ‖ I TURNED the key, listening to the bolts snap back. Three dead bolts: one into the steel frame on the side, another at the top, the final one directly into the floor. The hall's too narrow for a battering ram. By the time anyone broke in, I'd have long enough to do anything I needed to do.

Another key for the doorknob. I turned it twice to the right and once to the left, and stepped inside.

"It's me, Pansy," I said to the monster sitting in the middle of the dark room.

The monster made a noise somewhere between a snarl and a growl. A Neapolitan mastiff, maybe 140 pounds of muscle and bone, topped with a head the size of a cannonball and just about as thick. So dark she was almost black, Pansy blended into the room like a malevolent shadow, teeth shielded, cold-water eyes unflickering. Pansy can't handle complex thoughts. She wasn't sure if she was glad to see me or sorry she wasn't going to get to tear some flesh. Then she smelled the Chinese food and the issue was settled. The snarl changed to a whine, and slobber poured from her jaws. I threw her the hand signal for "Stay!" and hit the light switch.

The office is one small room. Desk facing the door, one chair behind, one in front. No windows. Couch against one wall. To the left, there's another door, leading to the office where my secretary works. The door's a fake. So's the secretary. The other wall is covered with a Persian rug that never got closer to Iran than 14th Street. The floor is covered with Astroturf. I told my decorator I wanted low-maintenance modern.

I pulled the rug aside and stepped into another room, even smaller than the office. Tiny stand-up shower I installed myself, sink and toilet in one corner. Hot plate and refrigerator in another. A cot between them. The back door opens out to a landing. The fire escape rusted off years ago.

I opened the back door, calling for Pansy, and stepped out to the landing. Watched the Hudson River slime-flow to the west, patting my dog's head as she stood next to me. Three rooms, with view.

Pansy ambled past me, taking the stairs to the roof. She's been dumping her loads up there for years. There's stuff growing on the roof I don't even want to think about.

Pansy came back downstairs as I was putting away the food Mama packed for me. I pulled a big slab of roast pork from a container, held it in front of her. Every fiber of her dim brain focused on that pork. An icicle of drool formed in one corner of her gaping mouth, but she didn't move. She wouldn't take the food until she heard the magic word. It's called poison-proofing.

"Speak!" I yelled at her, tossing the slab of pork in a gentle arc toward her face. It didn't last as long as a politician's promise. I tried a big fat egg roll. One chomp, and Pansy was swallowing in ecstasy, pieces of egg roll all over the floor. "You're a slob," I told her. She nodded happily.

Pansy's food-supply system is against the wall. A pair of hollowed-out cement cinder blocks with a forty-pound sack of dry dog food suspended above one and a tube connected to the sink above the other. When either bowl is empty, she pushes against the tube with her snout and it fills again.

I filled a big ceramic bowl with three quarts of Mama's cooking and told her to make a pig of herself. She buried her face up to the eyes in the steaming mess, making noises Stephen King never dreamed of. I threw some of the marrow bones into a pot and put them on the hot plate to boil.

I went inside to my desk. It was almost seven-thirty, and the woman Mama had spoken to said to call before nine. There was a phone on my desk. It never rang, and I never got a bill from Ma Bell—the Mole had it connected to the trust-fund hippies who lived downstairs. I could use it early in the morning, when the sensitive artists were still recovering from trying to find the light at the end of the marijuana tunnel they'd explored the night before, but not otherwise.

I'd had the phone for years. No problems. I never used it for long-distance calls. That's why God made other people's credit cards.

The office looked the same way it always does. I don't get clients coming here much. The last one was Flood. The day I let her in, she came in too deep. I lit a cigarette, not wanting to think about the chubby little blonde head-hunter. She came into my life, got what she came for, and left me empty.

I didn't want to think about Flood. She came too often in my sleep. "I'm for you, Burke," I can still hear her saying. The way only a woman can say. And only say it once, if it's the truth.

It was.

Part of the full bloom I was still waiting for.

I went out to make my phone call.

**18** ‖ ALMOST EIGHT by the time I found the pay phone I wanted. Near the river, just a couple of blocks from the Yuppietown the developers had built by reclaiming a piece of the Hudson. Within eyeshot of the bullshit "security lights" flanking the high-rise but safe in a pool of darkness.

Like I was.

I don't like cold calls. My phone number's circulated all over this city. The phone's listed to Juan Rodriguez, and the address is the back end of a junkyard I own. The old man who runs it draws me a paycheck every two weeks. I cash it and give him back the money. It makes me a citizen—I pay my taxes, build up my Social Security, all that. Having a citizen's name is important. The name opens the door to all the goodies: legit address, driver's license, Social Security card. I don't lose any sleep worrying about the FBI, but the IRS is another game. I have a birth certificate too. It's so phony it even has a father's name on it.

My credit with Ma Bell is excellent. Never miss a payment. Never make any toll calls. I never make any calls at all. Anyone who calls the junkyard number activates the call diverter I have set up. The signal bounces over to one of the phones at Mama's.

I unscrewed the mouthpiece of the pay phone and slipped in the flat disk the Mole gave me. It changes my voice just enough to throw off the machines, in case anyone's listening. I pulled the tiny tape recorder from my coat and hit the switch; the booth was flooded with the background noise from a bowling alley. The number had a 718 area code. Brooklyn or Queens. I dropped a quarter and dialed the number.

She answered on the third ring. A young girl's voice, with the hard twang that sounds Southern unless you've spent some time in Detroit.

"Hello?"

"Belle?"

"Who's this?"

"Burke. Returning your call."

"Oh. I didn't think it would be so fast. I'm doing a favor for someone. Someone who wants to talk to you."

"Who?"

"I'd rather tell you in person."

"I'd rather you tell me over the phone."

"I can't do that. I promised."

"What's in it for me?"

"Money."

"How much money?"

"That depends. You'd have to work it out with him. I just said I'd talk to you. Tell you about it. See if you're interested in getting together."

"You get paid win or lose?"

"Yes."

"Tell him I said no, and collect your money."

"You have to hear me out. Tell me to my face. That's the deal."

"That's not *my* deal."

Her voice shifted, dropped a note. "What *is* your deal?"

"Time is money. My time is your money, okay?"

"How much money?"

"How much time?"

"Fifteen minutes."

"Five yards."

"That's a lot of money."

I didn't say anything, listening to the silence at her end, the sound of pins falling at mine.

"Can you meet me? Tonight?"

"Is he there with you?"

"No."

"How do you know he'll go for the cash?"

"I don't. I have to make some calls. I work at . . ."

"I don't care where you work," I said, cutting her off. "Do what you have to do. Speak to the man. I'll call you tomorrow morning."

"Not before eleven, okay? I get in late."

"You have a car?"

"Yes."

"I'll call you tomorrow. Tell you where to come and meet me. You bring the money—we'll talk."

"Thank you," the young girl's voice said, and she broke the connection.

**19** WHEN I called her the next morning, her voice sounded the same. Not breathy, or trying to be sexy. Short-winded.

"I got the go-ahead."

"And the money?"

"Yes."

"What kind of car do you drive?"

"A Camaro. A red one. With a T-top."

"You know Metropolitan Avenue?"

"In Queens? By the cemeteries?"

"Yeah. Take it west. Like you're going to the city, okay? Just keep going until it crosses over into Brooklyn. You'll come to a little drawbridge. Go over the bridge and look for a gas station on your right. Just pull up to the pumps—I'll meet you there."

"What time?"

"Three."

"How will I know you?"

"I'll be the man asking for the money."

**20** I TOOK the Delancey Street Bridge out of Manhattan, hooked back around to Metropolitan Avenue. I cruised past the gas station. At two in the afternoon, it looked the way it always does—a wino asleep in the sun, a dead bottle of T-bird half out of a paper bag next to him. A pair of red-brown dogs that had never been pets swept the empty concrete, all legs and ribs, looking for food. A black guy wearing a winter coat, tattered cowboy hat on his head, pushing a supermarket basket full of cans and bottles, checking the alleys for more nuggets. Grayish dust from the concrete plant on the other side of the draw-bridge settled over everything. The sun hit hard. The wino was half in shadow—he'd been sleeping a long time.

I parked the Plymouth a few blocks away, backed in against the metallic strip of water that carried the ore barges under the drawbridge. It took me less than five minutes to get back to the gas station. I found myself a comfortable spot against the wall and sat down to wait.

The skinny dogs circled, watchful. I reached into the paper bag next to me and took out a piece of cheese. I unwrapped it slowly, watching them from beneath the brim of my battered felt hat. I tossed the cheese in their direction, arcing it gently so they'd know it was no threat. The bigger dog moved in, sniffed it quickly, and took it into his mouth. He moved away, chewing slowly. I unwrapped another piece, tossed it the same way. The big dog's partner dashed in, snatched it, and moved back to where the other one was standing.

I lit a cigarette, watching the dogs sniff the air, trying to do the same. From where I sat, there was no way to approach the gas station without me seeing it. I wasn't worried about customers—the only gas in the place was in the plastic bottle in my paper bag.

Almost an hour passed. I'd gone through several smokes, and the dogs had exhausted my supply of cheese. They wouldn't come close enough for me to touch, but the big guy sat about ten feet away, watching me; his partner stretched out next to him.

I was completely in shadow when the red Camaro pulled up to the pumps. The windows were down. A woman in the front seat. She turned off the engine. The dogs left me, ambling over to the car. Trucks rumbled by on Metropolitan.

She got out of the car. A big woman. Honey-taffy hair, hacked off near her shoulders, bangs covering her forehead almost to her eyes. She was wearing a peach-colored sweatshirt over a pair of loose white pants. Hands on hips, she turned one complete circle, sweeping the area.

I came to my feet quietly, moved to her. She saw me coming, a wino with a paper bag in one hand. She stood her ground.

"Hello, Belle," I said.

"You're Burke?"

I nodded, watching her eyes to see if she was expecting company of her own. Her eyes were small, dark, set close together. Her face was round, smooth—unformed except for a tiny pointed chin. She was as tall as I was, wider through the shoulders and hips. I glanced at her feet. White running shoes, small, like her hands. No watch. No rings.

The back seat of the Camaro was empty. "Would you open the trunk?" I asked her.

"Why?"

"I want to see if you've got a spare."

She bobbed her head like she understood. Bent inside the car to pull the keys from the ignition. Her hips flexed under the loose white pants. She handed me the keys. The trunk held only a blue overnight case.

I motioned her to get in the car, climbed behind the wheel, and started it up. She walked around the front of the car, opened the passenger door, turned her back to me, swung her butt inside, and dropped it into the seat. Pulled her legs in and closed the door. She filled the seat. Sat there, tiny hands in her lap. Waiting.

I drove aimlessly around the area for a few minutes. Nothing out of place. The second time I passed the spot where I'd parked the Plymouth, I pulled in next to it, nose toward the water. I got out, walked around to the back of the car, leaned against the trunk. Belle followed me. Stood next to me. Put her hands behind her, palms against the trunk. Hoisted herself up. The trunk bounced a few times with her weight. If the hot metal was burning into her backside, she didn't show it.

"The man who wants to meet you . . ."

I held up my hand like a traffic cop. "We had a deal."

She pulled up her sweatshirt. A bunch of bills was folded into the waistband of her pants. Green on milk. She pulled the sheaf of bills out, handed it to me. All fifties. Ten of them. Used. I slipped them into my shirt pocket.

"Fifteen minutes," I told her.

"There's a man who wants to meet with you. He doesn't want you to get the wrong idea."

"This man have a name?"

I watched her face in profile. Her nose was barely a bump—lost on her broad, round face. A bead of clear sweat ran down one cheek. "Marques Dupree," she said.

I took a drag on my cigarette. "I already have the wrong idea," I told her.

"You said you'd hear me out."

I took another drag.

"He has a problem. A big problem. He said you're the man to help him—you'd know what to do."

"I know what to do. Why should I do it?"

"He said this is something you'd want to do."

"You know what it is?"

"No."

"So what's there to talk about?"

"Marques wants to meet with you. He said you wouldn't come if he called."

"He's right."

"He sent me to show you he's on the square. It's a job, okay? That's all."

"I don't work for Marques."

"He said you'd say that too. All he wants is for you to meet with him."

I bit into the cigarette, thinking. Marques was doing this the right way. He wouldn't be stupid enough to just roll up on me—he didn't have the weight for that. If Marques Dupree was coming to me, he had to have real troubles.

"You one of his ladies?" I asked her.

Her tiny chin came up. She turned full-face to me. Her close-set eyes were almost black; I couldn't see the pupils. "I'm not a whore." She wasn't mad—just setting it straight.

"So why you doing this?"

She reached out a tiny hand, patted my shirt pocket. Where the money was.

"I'll think about it, okay? Where can I find you?"

"Me?"

"Yeah. You. I *know* how to find Marques."

"I work at The Satellite Dish. Out by JFK."

"That's a strip joint," I said.

Something must have shown in my face. Her tiny rosebud mouth made a quick kissing motion. "You think I'm overqualified?"

I shrugged.

"I work every night except Tuesday."

I put my hand on her wrist. Gently, holding her attention. "Tell Marques not to call me. If I want to meet him, I'll come and tell you first."

"What if you don't want to see him?"

"Then I won't," I told her, guiding her back into the driver's seat, motioning for her to take off.

I started walking in the opposite direction. The Camaro drove off. I watched over my shoulder as she turned the corner; then I went back to the Plymouth.

21 THE WAREHOUSE off Division Street in Chinatown looked like it always does. Empty. Deserted. I pulled in, turned off the engine. Waited. When I heard the door close behind me, I knew Max was home.

The warehouse was furnished with dim shadows. I followed Max up the back stairs to the second floor. He usually went to the back room, where we'd work on our life-sentence gin game. Something different today. Max stopped on the landing. His temple was upstairs. The dojo where he practiced, the teak floor marked with a white-pine border. The sacred ground where Flood met a freak who called himself the Cobra. The killing floor.

Immaculata was sitting in a low chair in a corner of the white room. A black lacquer table covered with books and papers at her elbow. The baby sat across from her, wearing only a diaper, her little face grave as she watched her mother work. A butcher-block table ran the length of one wall, with hardwood straight-back chairs at each end. Max gestured to one of the chairs. I sat down as Immaculata put her notes aside and rose to her feet.

"Hello, Burke."

"Hi, Mac. How's Flower?"

"She is a perfect child," Mac said, as though she'd carefully considered all the other possibilities. "Some tea?"

"Thank you," I said, knowing what she meant.

Mac started to walk into the next room. The baby made a sound, less than a cry, maybe a question. Mac knelt next to her child, speaking quietly, her voice steel-cored. "Mother will come back, baby. *Always* come back, yes? *Never* leave you." She kissed the infant gravely on the forehead. Waved a goodbye gesture to the child. Again and again, patiently, until the child moved her hand too. "Smart baby!" Immaculata clapped.

I took out a cigarette, held it up for Max to see, asking if it was okay to smoke near the child.

Max pointed to an ashtray the size of a dinner plate, aluminum on the outside, glazed red ceramic on the inside. He lit a cigarette of his own, blowing the smoke toward the ceiling. Spreading his arms to say the whole world smoked and the baby wasn't going to spend the rest of her life in the house.

Immaculata came back inside. She had a pot of tea with two cups, a glass of iced ginger ale for me. "I have your mail," she said, handing me a stack of letters. I use a P.O. box over in Jersey. One of Mama's drivers empties it for me about every two weeks, leaves the letters in Mama's basement. Max picks them up when he has the chance and holds them for me. I shuffled through them. Nothing from Japan. Nothing from Flood. I put them in my coat.

Immaculata pulled up a chair, joined us, one eye on her baby. Flower was gurgling happily to herself. It sounded like singing.

Max held up one finger, catching my eye. Pay attention.

He moved off his chair without a sound, crouched behind the

baby. Suddenly he slapped his hands together. It sounded like a gun-shot. The baby jumped, trying to turn her head in the direction of the sound. Max scooped her up and held her against his chest, nuzzling her, his horn-callused hands now soft as a cloud. The baby's tiny hands searched—found one of his fingers, grabbed, and held.

Max carried the baby back to his chair, held her on his lap. Smiling.

Immaculata stood watching him, hands on hips. "Max!" she snapped, stamping her foot. He ignored her, watching me.

Immaculata sighed. "When I was pregnant, he'd do that all the time. He said the baby could hear him. When she came out of my body, he made everyone be quiet. He waited until she was nursing. . . . Then he clapped his hands like that. When she moved—when she *heard* him—I thought he was going to burst, he was so happy."

"She recognized his voice," I said.

"Sure. That's what *he* said."

"What else could it be?"

"I think"—she looked at her husband—"I think he was afraid our baby would be born deaf."

"Was Max born deaf?"

"I never asked him," she said, a slight warning tone in her voice.

He was my brother. I had earned the right to know. Earned it in a prison cell. I pointed at Max. Made a gesture as if I was rocking a baby. Pointed at him again. At my ear.

His face went hard, eyes slitted, mouth a straight line. He shook his head. No.

I opened my hands. "How?"

Max gently picked up his baby, carried her back over to the floor, put her down. Kissed her. He stood between Immaculata and me. Pointed to himself again. A fist flashed into his palm so quickly I only saw the vapor trail. A sharp crack. He pointed to his ear. Held his palm thigh-high. A little child. His hand became a claw, snatched something, lifted it off the ground. Threw it against the wall. Walked away. Pointed to himself again.

He wasn't born deaf.

I tapped my heart twice, bowed my head. My eyes felt funny.

Max pointed at Flower, playing by herself on the floor. Reached his hand across the table. Immaculata put her hand in his. He circled his thumb and forefinger. Okay. Okay, now.

Yeah. He was ahead of the game.

I took a sip of the ginger ale. Lit another smoke. I held my palms close together, not touching. A meeting.

Max did the same. The palms became fists.

I shrugged. Maybe. Who knows?

I pointed at him. At myself. Waved a pointing finger. A meeting outside. In the street.

He looked a question.

I rubbed my first two fingers and thumb together. Money. Maybe a job.

Max hissed an inhale through his nose.

I shook my head. Not cocaine. I made the sign of injecting something into my arm. Shook my head again. Not heroin. Held an imaginary joint in my mouth, triple-inhaled fast. Shook my head again. Not marijuana.

Max took a dollar from his pocket. Held up three fingers.

I shook my head again. Not funny-money.

Immaculata watched us, like a spectator at a tennis match. Waiting for the punch line.

Max pointed a finger, cocked his thumb. I told him no again. Not guns. I weaved my fingers in the air, making an hourglass. Women.

His face went hard again as he held his hand chest-high, asking.

I put my palm to my forehead, like a salute, measuring for him. Not kids. I made a gesture like I was talking to someone, negotiating. Showed money changing hands. I took some cash from my pocket, put it on the table. Made one big pile with a single bill off to the side. Pocketed the pile. Pushed the remaining bill across the table to my left. Made the hourglass sign again. Her share.

Max circled his hands around his head, tilted a hat brim forward.

I nodded. A pimp.

Max smiled. He made a gesture like he was pulling a wristwatch off. Pulled rings off fingers. Reached inside his shirt for a wallet.

I shook my head. Not a shakedown. Not a rough-off. I held my palms together again, not touching. Just a meeting. Okay?

He nodded.

I pointed at my watch. Made an "I don't know" gesture. I'd let him know when it was going down.

The baby cried. Immaculata went over to her, picked her up, and sat her down on her lap to nurse. I bowed to Max, to Immaculata, to my brother's baby.

I went down the stairs to my car, thinking of Flood. Back to being alone.

22 ‖ I WENT through the mail back in the office. The usual stuff. Congenital defectives replying to my ad promising "south of the border" opportunities for "qualified adventurers." Most of the mercenary action is in Central America now; the Cubans have made it real clear that Africa isn't the promised land. The good scams concentrate on "training exercises." There's decent money in stinging maladroits who want to dress up in camouflage gear and run around the New Jersey swamps learning how to "survive." I don't run one of the camps—I don't want to meet any of my customers face to face. But, for a reasonable fee, I'm always happy to process their applications.

The pedophile letters always have P.O. boxes of their own for return addresses. One was neatly typed on creamy bond paper, the monogram "CX" engraved in one corner. "I'm always interested in the real thing. Especially discipline, golden showers, and snuff. I hope we can be friends." I put the letter aside. If it wasn't from a Postal Inspector, I had a genuine freak—the kind who expected to pay for his fun. Scumbags. They always manage to get what they pay for. Sometimes I get lucky; then they pay for what they get.

The rest of the mail was replies to our new series of personal ads. We run them everyplace—from literary journals to hard-core slime-sheets. Variations on the same theme: young girl, serving a prison sentence, getting out soon. Lonely, broke, needs a friend.

Honey Blaine is the sweet young girl's name. If any of the suckers bothered to write directly, they'd find an "H. Blaine, #86-B-9757," doing time at Bedford Hills. Just the way it said in the ad. Honey would set them straight right away. She'd explain that she couldn't write the kind of letter she'd *really* like to: the prison censors wouldn't permit it. Honey had a secret P.O. box, though, and if a sincere man was willing to be a little patient, well . . .

I screened the letters. Michelle answered them. We had a few dozen different photos we used. All Polaroids ("That's the only kind they let us take here, darling"). Whatever the suckers wanted, that's what they got. Honey could be a nineteen-year-old victimized by a cruel pimp. A lesbian whose lover informed on her in a drug deal. A car thief. Anything but a scam artist. She could be the answer to an old man's prayer or the bottom of a minister's ugly fantasy. A very flexible girl, this Honey. All it took was Michelle's never-miss instincts and some creative writing. Honey would play the sucker, work the hook in deep, turning up the heat to full boil. Then the poor girl would start to have problems: a bull dyke hitting on her, demanding her body or her life; a threatened transfer to another section of the prison, where she wouldn't be able to correspond. Overdue rent on the P.O. box. A nice piece of cash needed to bribe the Parole Board. Gate money. And the money orders would start to come in.

After a while, the sucker would get his last letter returned. Unopened. An official prison stamp on the outside. Black-bordered. "Return to sender. Inmate deceased." The suckers always bought it—if it was a scam, why wouldn't sweet Honey have cashed the last money order?

H. Blaine, #86-B-9757, wasn't allowed visitors. Good thing. The name and the number were legit, but Hortense Blaine is a fifty-five-year-old, three-hundred-pound black woman. She raised three generations of foster kids. From babies dropped down incinerators who didn't die, to kiddie prostitutes who never lived. She never had a kid of her own, but she was mother to dozens. Her boyfriend raped one of the kids. A twelve-year-old girl named Princess.

I have a copy of the trial transcript. I got it from the lawyer who's working on the appeal. A hard-blues lyric they'll never put to music.

DIRECT EXAMINATION
BY MR. DAVIDSON:

Q: What, if anything, did you do after Princess told you about the rape?

A: I told the child he was never going to hurt her again. I carried her into my room. Put her in my bed.

Q: The same bed you shared with Mr. Jackson?

A: He wasn't going to be using it no more.

Q: And then?

A: I waited for Jackson to come home. He was out gambling someplace. He comes in the door, sits at the kitchen table. Tells me to get him a beer.

Q: Did you get him a beer?

A: Yeah.

Q: Tell the jury what happened next.

A: I asked him why he did this. I said . . .

Q: Excuse me for interrupting you, Mrs. Blaine. You asked him *why* he raped the child? Not *if* he did it?

A: There was blood in the child's bed.

Q: I see. Please continue.

A: I asked him why he did what he did. He tells me Princess going to be a woman soon. Won't hurt her none. Get her ready for what life's all about, he said. He said she was walking around in her nightgown when I was out working. Said she asked for it.

Q: Did you see the expression on his face when he said this?

MR. HAYNES: Objection. Calls for a conclusion of the witness.

MR. DAVIDSON: An observation of demeanor is not a conclusion, Judge.

MR. HAYNES: Your Honor, counsel for the defense is trying to introduce blatant hearsay. This is an attempt to impugn the character of a dead man.

MR. DAVIDSON: This Court has already heard the testimony of the child Princess. The character of this rapist is already in evidence.

MR. HAYNES: Objection! Mr. Jackson is not on trial.

MR. DAVIDSON: That's right. He's already been tried.

THE COURT: Gentlemen, that will be quite enough. The objection is overruled.

Q: I ask you again, Mrs. Blaine. Did you see the expression on his face when he admitted to you that he raped Princess?

A: Yeah. He was smiling. Like it was nothing.

MR. HAYNES: Objection.

THE COURT: Overruled.

Q: Did he say anything else?

A: He said the little bitch got what she deserved.

Q: What happened then?

A: I picked up the kitchen knife and I stabbed him in his heart.

Q: Did you mean to kill him?

A: Yes.

Q: Why?

A: So he'd never hurt my baby no more.

MR. DAVIDSON: Your witness.

Defending a murder charge wasn't a job for a courthouse gonif. Too many of our people had spent time with Hortense when we were coming up. Like the Prof. Short for "Professor." Or "Prophet." A tiny black omen-master who'd been on the hustle since before I was born, he talked rhyme and he walked crime. The Prof only stood as high as my chest, but he always stood up.

"Cutting up slime ain't no crime," was all he said, dealing himself in on whatever we had to do to raise the cash.

Davidson was the man for the job. A husky guy with a full beard, he plays the game hard. I first heard about him when he defended one of the UGL gunmen years ago. Davidson told us the only way to roll on this one was to do what he called a "psychiatric autopsy" on the dead man.

And he pulled it off. When he was finished, the jury knew Jackson had been a piece of living scum before he died. They came back with a verdict of Manslaughter, Second Degree. You could feel the weight lift—murder carries a twenty-five-to-life top in this state. But Davidson slammed his fist down on the defense table hard enough to break it. He never raised his eyes.

One of the jurors walked over to him. A fat guy in a brown suit. Said Davidson did a great job, asked him for his card. Davidson raised his face to look at the juror. His eyes were wet. "I'm particular about who I defend," he said, turning his back on the juror's outstretched hand.

The judge hit Hortense with two-to-six upstate. Only child molesters get probation in New York. One of her foster sons stood next to her when she got the sentence. All grown up now, he works in a bank, lives in the suburbs. When he heard she was going down, he started to cry. Hortense put a big hand on his shoulder. She had to reach up to do it.

"Be a man," she told him. Not giving an inch.

She gave Davidson a kiss on the cheek and held out her hands for the cuffs.

Davidson's working on the appeal. Working hard, the way he always does. While he's working on the appeal, we're working on putting together some cash for when Hortense walks out. Once a month, the Prof visits her at the prison, bringing a batch of money orders for her to sign. There's a check-cashing joint in the Bronx that doesn't ask a lot of questions. Hortense gets half the money; Michelle and I split the rest. It was supposed to be a four-way split, but the Prof gives his piece to Hortense. "Not *all* payback's a bitch," he said when we asked him.

Michelle doesn't work the streets anymore. I thought it was AIDS, but she said she couldn't risk a bust now. Now that she's a mother.

So she does phone jobs, suckers letting their credit cards run wild while she talks them over the top. Or she visits her clients indoors.

It was only right that she and Hortense would work a sting together. Walking different sides of the same one-way street.

**23** ‖ I FELT bad, and I didn't know why. I was some cash ahead, for a change. The last job went down like sweet syrup, and maybe there would be some more of that kind of work down the road. Nobody was looking for me.

I didn't spend time thinking about it. I used to do that. I used to do time. A couple of bad habits.

Pansy ambled over to where I was sitting, put her huge head on my lap. She made a noise that sounded like a growl, but I knew what she wanted.

"Not today, girl," I told her, scratching her head between her eyes. Max and I were training her to stay low when she hit. Most dogs leave their feet when they attack, some deep instinct forcing them to go for the throat. That doesn't work on people: human throats are too far off the ground. We take Pansy over to this vacant lot in Brooklyn. Pay some kid ten bucks and talk him into putting on the agitator's suit—leather covered with padded canvas. I hold Pansy on a snap leash, facing the agitator. Max stands to the side with a long bamboo pole. When I send Pansy, Max brings the pole down. Hard.

If she stays low, about groin-height, she can nail the kid wearing the suit. If she leaves her feet, Max cracks her in the head. Lately she's been getting through most of the time. I call her off as soon as she gets a good bite.

I have to get a different kid each time. The suit feels like it's armor-plated, but Pansy can turn a leg into liquid right through it.

I flipped the channels on the TV until I found a pro wrestling match. Pansy's favorite. I gave her one of the marrow bones and stretched out on the couch, opening the racing sheet. Maybe I'd find a horse I liked. Make my own kind of investment.

The last thing I remember before I fell asleep was Pansy grinding the marrow bone into powder.

**24** IT WAS past ten when I woke up. On the TV, a private detective was getting hit over the head with a tire iron. I lit a smoke. Opened the back door for Pansy. When I walked back inside, the private eye was wide awake and looking for clues.

I took a shower. Looked at my face in the mirror. Deep, past the image. Looked into myself, breathing through my nose, expanding my stomach, exhaling as my chest went out.

When I came out of it, I felt clear. Centered. Ready to go to work.

I shaved carefully. Combed my hair. I put on a pair of dark-gray slacks and a white silk shirt. Alligator boots. Custom-made, but they were a pretty good fit on me anyway. I moved aside some shirts in the bottom drawer of my dresser. Looked at a whole pile of rings, watches, bracelets, gold chains. The spoils of war.

I held a smuggler's necklace in my hand. Each link is a one-ounce gold ingot; it comes apart one piece at a time. Too classy for this job. I pawed through the stuff until I found the right combination:

a thick gold neck chain, a gold bracelet, and a gold ring set with a blue star sapphire.

Checked myself in the full-length mirror on the door of the closet. Something missing. I found some gel in the bathroom. Ran it through my hair until it looked thicker and a bit greasy. White hair shot through the black just past my temples. It didn't bother me—the only thing I ever posed for was mug shots.

I slopped some cologne all over my face and neck. To throw the dogs off the scent.

A few hundred bucks in my pocket, one of the Mole's butane lighters, a wallet I stripped of bogus credit cards, and I was ready to visit a strip joint.

**25** ‖ JFK AIRPORT sits at the end of Queens, near the Long Island border, sticking out into the bay. The surrounding swampland is slashed with two-lane side roads running off the expressway. Warehouses, light industry, short-stay motels.

The Highway Department keeps the roads in good shape, but they don't waste any money on streetlights. A bandit's paradise.

I found The Satellite Dish easily enough. A one-story blue stucco building, standing alone on a slab of blacktop. Two long, narrow windows framing a set of double doors, the dark glass covered with fluorescent promises: Go-Go Girls. Topless. Bottomless. Exotic Dancers.

I nosed the Plymouth through the parking lot. General Motors must have held a white-on-white sale: Eldorados, Buick Regals, Oldsmobiles. Vinyl tops, tinted glass, hand-painted monograms on the doors. I left the Plymouth at the edge of the blacktop, dull paint fading into the shadows. It looked abandoned.

I stepped through the double doors into a square foyer. White walls, red carpet. Hawk-faced guy in a powder-blue double-knit suit sitting at a little table to one side. The joint wasn't classy enough to have a hat-check girl—and not hard-core enough to shake you down for weapons.

"Ten bucks cover, pal. And worth every penny," the hawk-faced guy said. His heart wasn't in it.

I paid, went through the next set of doors. The place was bigger than it looked from the outside, so dark I couldn't see the walls. A T-shaped bar ran the entire width of the room, with a long perpendicular runway almost to the door. Small round tables were spread all over the room. Two giant screens, like the ones they use for projection TV, stood in the corners at each end of the long bar. The screens were blank.

The tables were empty. Every man in the place was seated at the bar, most of them along the runway. Hard-rock music circled from hidden speakers. Three girls were on top of the bar. Two blondes and a redhead. All wearing bikini bottoms, high heels, and sparkle dust. Each girl worked her own piece of the bar, bouncing around, talking to the customers. The redhead went to her knees in front of a guido with a high-rise haircut and diamonds on his fingers. She spun on the bar, dropped her shoulders. The guido pulled down her panties, stuffed some bills between her thighs, patted her butt. She gave him a trembly wiggle, reached back and pulled up the panties, spun around again, ran her tongue over her lips. Danced away.

It was somewhere between the South Bronx shacks where the girls would blow you in the back booths and the steak-and-silicone joints in midtown where they called you "sir" but wouldn't screw you out of anything more than your money.

I found an empty stool near the left side of the T. A brunette wearing a red push-up bra under a transparent white blouse leaned over the bar toward me. She raised her eyebrows, smiling the smile they all use.

"Gin-and-tonic," I told her, putting a fifty on the bar. "Plenty of ice. Don't mix them."

She winked. I was obviously a with-it guy. No watered drinks for this stud.

She brought me a tall glass of tonic, jigger of gin on the side. Put four ten-dollar bills back in front of me. Class costs.

"My name is Laura," she cooed. "I go on after the last set. You going to be here?"

I nodded. She took one of the ten-spots off the bar, looked a question at me. I nodded. She stuffed it between her breasts, winked at me, and went back to work. I left the money on the bar.

I sipped my tonic, waiting.

The music stopped. A short, stocky guy in a pink sport coat over a billowy pair of white slacks stepped to the intersection of the T. The lights went down. The house man hit the stocky guy with a baby spot. He had a wireless microphone in one hand.

"Here's what you've been waiting for . . . the fabulous . . . Debbie, and the Dance of Domination!"

The bar went dark again. Most of the men moved to the back tables. A door at the right of the T opened, and two dim shapes walked to the intersection. The music started. No words, heavy bass-lines and drums. One of the shapes went off the stage.

A hard white spot burned the center of the T, making it into an isolated island. A black straight-back chair stood by itself, thick high posts on each side. The giant TV screens flickered into life. The camera zoomed in on the chair, filling the picture.

A blonde in a black sheath came into the light. Black spikes on her feet, black gloves up to her elbows. A black pillbox hat on her head, a black veil covering her face. She sat down on the chair, crossed her legs. She tilted her chin up, waiting.

I could hear the humans breathing under the music, but there was no conversation. Topless waitresses were working the darkness, stopping at the little tables, taking orders for drinks. Business was booming.

It was like no strip act I'd ever seen. No playing to the audience— they were all watching through a window. Quiet. Lost and alone in their ugliness.

The stage went dark. The music stopped. Herd sounds from the crowd.

Nobody moved.

When the spot came on again, the blonde was on her knees, facing the crowd. She ran her hand across her thighs, into her crotch, as the music built. Then she lifted the veil slowly. The pillbox hat came off. The camera came in on her face. She licked her lips, her eyes wide. As she opened her mouth, the stage went dark again.

It stayed dark for a couple of minutes. Cigarette lighters snapped in the crowd. Tiny red flares.

Flood came into my mind. I saw her struggling to work skin-tight pants over her hips, shifting from toe to toe, flexing her legs. Bending over another chair, in another place, the fire-scar on her rump dark against the white skin. I put the image down—those bodies were buried.

The lights came up again, blaring rock music came back through the speakers, the TV screens went dark. Three different girls were working the top of the bar, gesturing for the men to come away from the little tables and get closer.

I poured the gin into the empty tonic glass, mixing it with the ice. The bargirl came back to where I was sitting, bringing me another set; she put my empty glasses on a little tray.

"You like that stuff?"

"Not my taste," I said.

"Maybe later you'll tell me what you like," she whispered, sweeping the rest of my money off the bar, doubling her tip.

I reached in my pocket for another fifty. Waiting for Belle wasn't a cheap job.

## 26

I FIGURED Belle must work as one of the back-table waitresses, but I didn't want to ask for her by name. The tables stayed empty while the girls worked the top of the bar, so I'd have to wait for the next number, move into the darkness by myself, look around. I sipped my tonic, lit another smoke.

I watched the girls spread themselves on the long bar, as turned-on as a gynecologist.

It was a good twenty minutes and another half-century note before the guy in the pink jacket took center stage again. "Cassandra," was all he said. The stage went dark again. I could see shapes moving around, setting things up. This time I went back to a table near the back wall. I took the tonic, left the gin.

When the spot hit the stage, a girl was seated on a padded chair, looking into a mirror. The camera came in on her face. Belle. A mask of makeup making the soft lines hard, a white bathrobe around her shoulders, a white ribbon around her hair.

The speakers fired into life. Nasty music, zombie-swamp blues, voodoo drums.

Belle was taking off the makeup, patting her face with cream. She shrugged her shoulders and the robe dropped to her waist. Her breasts were enormous, standing out straight, defying gravity in a white D-cup bra. The camera watched them in the mirror.

She rose to her feet, holding the robe in one hand at her waist like a skirt. The spotlight widened: she was in a bedroom, white ruffled bedspread, white shag rug on the floor. Belle stalked the white room, a young girl getting ready for bed. Running a brush through her thick hair, maybe humming to herself. She opened her hand and the robe dropped to the floor. Belle hooked it with one foot, delicately tossed it onto the bed.

With the robe off, it was a different Belle on the screen. She faced the crowd in the white bra and plain matching panties, bending slightly forward, as if she was looking out into the night. The big woman wasn't fat; she was wasp-waisted. When she turned sideways, the stinger was a beauty, standing out by itself, straining against the fabric.

The music came harder. Her hips wiggled, like they had a mind of their own. She paced the room, stretching the way a cat does, bending to touch her toes, working off the restlessness, too wired to sleep.

The speakers spit out the music, sliding from the voodoo drums into words. Words I'd never heard before. A man's voice, gospel-tinted

blues now. Warning. Blood moon rising. Slide guitar climbing on top
of the drums, picking high notes, bending them against the black
fabric of the bass. The words came through at the bottom of my brain;
my eyes were locked on Belle.

*The swamp gets mean at night.*
*Bloody shadows eat the light,*
*Things that snarl,*
*Things that bite,*
*Things no man can fight.*

The music stayed dense, but the tempo picked up. Belle cocked
her head, listening. She unsnapped the bra, carefully hung it on the
bedpost. Her huge breasts didn't sag an inch. She raised her hands
high above her head, touching them together, standing on her toes.
She made a complete turn that way, a tiny smile on her face. Not a
muscle twitched in the smooth skin. Her body was as seamless as an
air-brushed photograph. Her shoes were gone. She stalked the little
room again, listening to the throbbing music, rolling her head on the
column of her neck, working out the kinks. A nurse, tired from a
hard day's work? A waitress, finished with her shift?

The camera ran the length of her body. Only the white panties
on her hips, a thin gold chain around her neck, a gold cross resting
between her breasts. Some kind of blue mark on the front of one
thigh. Even with the camera zooming in, I couldn't make it out.

She rolled the panties over her hips, down past her butt. It took
a long time, but not because she was teasing the audience—the panties
had a long way to travel. Belle picked them off the floor, fluffed them
out, went over to the bed, and hung them on the bedpost. On top of
the white bra.

The music drove harder.

Belle dropped to her knees in front of the low bed. She clasped
her hands. A little girl praying. The camera moved from her broad
shoulders, past her tiny waist, down to the giant globes of her butt.
The seamless skin was sweaty in the burning spotlight.

The words pushed back the music.

*Yes, boy, you better beware,*
*You better walk with care.*
*You can carry a cross,*
*You can carry a gun,*
*But when you hear the call, you better run.*

*There's worse things than gators out there.*
*Worse things than gators out there.*

Belle's whole body was shaking now. Trembling as the spotlight blended from white to blood-red and back to white. She got to her feet and turned to face the crowd. She pulled back the covers, slid into the bed. She fluffed the pillow, pulled the covers to her shoulders, lying on her side. The mound of her hip was as high as her shoulders. The music faded down. The lights dimmed.

The music wouldn't let her sleep. Her body thrashed under the covers. Drums working her hips, guitar plucking her soft breasts. A blue spot burned down on her face buried in the pillow, turning her taffy-honey hair a ghostly white. The spot turned a softer blue, widening to cover the whole bed. The warning voice came back, soft, demanding. Telling the truth, the way the blues always does.

*There's worse things than gators out there, boy.*
*Much worse things than gators out there.*

Belle threw back the covers, the music pulling her from the bed. She looked out into the night, shook herself. She reached for her robe, put one arm into a sleeve. Then she dropped the robe to the floor.

The blue spot played over her body as she walked into the darkness.

**27** ‖ WHEN THE lights came up, I saw I had two more drinks in front of me. I hadn't touched them. The pile of ten-spots in front of me was lighter.

I went back to my spot at the end of the bar, no closer to talking with Belle than I'd been. Laura came over to me, her little tray loaded with another gin-and-tonic in separate glasses. She leaned over the bar.

"You like that act better?"

I felt a hand on my shoulder. "He sure does," said a little girl's voice.

I didn't turn around. I knew who it was.

"Is this yours?" Laura asked Belle.

"All mine," Belle said.

"I thought you didn't like men," Laura said, a nasty little smile on her face.

"I don't like boys."

Laura looked past me. She reached her hand over to my pile of tens. Took one. Stuffed it in her cleavage, looking over my shoulder.

"Take two," Belle told her, razor tips on her breathy voice.

Laura shrugged, pretending she was thinking about it. She pulled another bill off the bar and walked away.

I felt Belle's face close to mine in the darkness. Smelled her little-girl sweat.

"Where's your car?" she whispered in my ear.

I told her.

"Finish your tonic. I'll meet you outside in ten minutes."

I felt her move away.

**28** || I WAS still on my first smoke when I saw the floating white shape moving through the parking lot toward the car. Belle. In a white shift a little smaller than a pup tent.

She opened the door and slid into the front seat. "Got a cigarette, big boy?" she asked, her voice a parody.

I gave her one. Snapped off a wooden match, watching her face in the glare. It was scrubbed clean again. She inhaled the way you take a hit off an oxygen tank. Her breasts moved under the shift. Her thighs gleamed in the night. The blue mark was a tattoo. A tiny snake, coiled in an S shape.

She saw me looking. "You like my legs?"

"They look like, if you squeezed them, you'd get juice."

"Want to try?"

I put my hand on her thigh, fitting the snake tattoo in the web between my thumb and finger.

"Not that one," she said.

I moved my hand. Squeezed. Felt the baby skin on top, the long, hard muscles beneath. I watched her face.

"No juice."

"Not there," she said, shifting her hips on the car seat.

I took my hand away. Lit another smoke.

"How long were you watching?" I asked her.

"How'd you know?"

"You knew where to find me in the dark."

"Maybe I worked my way through the joint."

"You knew I wasn't drinking the gin."

Belle took another deep drag. "Maybe you *are* a detective," she said, a little smile playing around her lips. "There's a strip of one-way glass that runs all around the place. So we can see who comes in."

I didn't say anything, watching the snake tattoo.

"You know why it's set up like that?"

"That joint can't be making money. The strip acts cost a lot to package. The projection TV, the music system, all that. You're running a low cover charge. You don't sell sex. Even with the guidos paying grope-money and the watered drinks, the boss couldn't break even."

"And . . ."

"And the building's a hell of a lot bigger than the bar."

Belle took a last drag. Threw her cigarette out the open window. "What's that tell you?"

"Who knows? You got space enough back there for trucks to pull in?"

"Sure."

"The airport's real close. . . ."

My pack of smokes was sitting on top of the dashboard. Belle helped herself to one. I lit it for her.

"Marques *said* you were a hijacker."

"Marques is a pimp."

"I know. Not *my* pimp. I work for me. That's why that bitch made that crack about me not liking men. I don't sell sex."

"If you did, you'd be rich."

That bought me another smile. Then, "You came out here to tell me you're going to meet with him?"

"Tuesday night."

"Why Tuesday?"

"That's your night off, right?"

"So?"

"So you're coming along."

"Says who?"

"That's the deal, Belle. Tuesday night. Pier 47. Marques knows where it is. Eleven o'clock. Tell him to bring two grand. Tell him that's mine. For the talk."

"That's a lot of money for talk."

"You get paid for your work—I get paid for mine."

Belle took another drag. "What time will you pick me up?"

"I won't. Tell Marques it's gunfighters' rules—we each bring one person with us. He gets to bring you."

"I don't use guns."

"Neither does the guy I'm bringing with me. Tell Marques what I said. He'll get it."

"I don't want Marques knowing where I live."

"Tell him to meet you someplace."

"And after . . ."

"I'll take you home," I told her.

"Should I call you and tell you if he . . . ?"

"Don't call me. I'll be at the pier. Just tell him if he doesn't show not to call me again."

"You take me home anyway."

"Yes."

Belle leaned against me. A big, sweet-smelling girl with a snake tattoo on her thigh. She pushed her hand against my chest, holding me against the seat. Kissed me hard on the mouth, saying, "See you Tuesday," at the same time.

I watched the white shift dance in the dark parking lot until it disappeared behind the blue building.

**29** ‖ MAX WAS already dealt in on the meeting with Marques. I could get a message to the Mole easy enough, even if he didn't answer his phone. That still left me a few days to find the Prof.

It might take that long. The little man could be sleeping in doorways or prowling hotel corridors. He could be working the subway tunnels or the after-hours joints. He never had an address, but you couldn't call him "homeless." I asked him once why he didn't find himself a crib somewhere—why he lived in the street. "I got the balls, and I don't like walls," he told me. He didn't have to explain any more than that—we'd met in prison.

I think "Prof" was once short for "Professor," because he always seemed so much older and smarter than the rest of us. But somewhere along the line, he started telling the kind of truth they never write down in books, and now it stands for "Prophet."

A citizen couldn't find the Prof, but I knew where he picked up his paycheck. A few years ago, I'd fixed him up with SSI. Psychiatric disability. His official diagnosis was "Schizophrenia. Chronic, undifferentiated." The resident at Bellevue noted the Prof's grossly disorganized thought pattern, his grandiose pronouncements, his delusion that he was getting his marching orders from the dead spirit of Marcus Garvey. A typical microwave case. They tried medication and it did what it usually does—the Prof got sleepy. It was worth the thirty-day investment. When they discharged the Prof, they gave him a one-week supply of medication, a standing appointment at the clinic, and what the little man called his "crazy papers."

Once a year, the *federales* would send a letter to the Prof demanding a "face to face." He had to make a personal appearance at the clinic. Not to prove that he was still crazy, just that he was still alive. Uncle Sam likes to keep a close watch on his money.

It was a two-sided scam. Not only did the Prof get a disability check every month, but the diagnosis was a Get Out of Jail Free card in case he ever went down for something major. Nothing like putting an insanity defense together before you commit the crime. The government mails him the check to General Delivery, at the giant post office on Eighth Avenue, right across from Madison Square Garden. There are so many homeless people in New York that the General Delivery window does more business than most small towns.

I addressed a postcard to the Prof. Wrote "Call home" on the back, and dropped it in the box.

**30** | By late Tuesday evening, I had everything in place. I ate dinner at Mama's, working over my copy of *Harness Lines*, looking for a horse that would make me rich. Max came in, carrying his baby, Immaculata at his side. Mama snatched the baby from Max and pushed him toward my booth. She took Immaculata into a corner of her own. I saw a flash of pink as the purse changed hands.

I explained to Max that there'd be five hundred apiece for us no matter what Marques wanted. We weren't going to rough off any extras unless the pimp got stupid. He pointed at the racing sheet I had spread out in front of me, looked a question. I shook my head—there was nothing worth an investment.

Max held up five fingers, looked a question. He knew Marques was paying four times that—where was the rest of the money going? It wasn't like Max to ask. Maybe a baby changes everything. I held one hand chest-high, waving the other in sweeping gestures. The Prof. Then I made goggles of my hands, held them over my eyes. Max looked a question. I made the sign of pushing a plunger with both hands, setting off an explosion. The Mole. He looked another question—why all these people for a meeting? I spilled salt on the table, drew a circle. I put two coins inside the circle. Marques plus one coin. He was bringing somebody with him. I put down two more. Me and Max. Then I added the Prof, tapping the side of my head. I didn't know what Marques wanted and I might have to give him an answer right there. The Prof knew the hustling scene—he'd be more on top of Marques than I would.

I picked up one more coin, gesturing that it was the Mole. Put it on the table, deliberately outside the circle. Patted my back. Insurance policy. Max nodded.

Immaculata came over to the table, put her hand on Max's shoulder.

"Burke, is this dangerous?"

"Not a chance, Mac," I said, making the sign of steering a car. "You think I'm going to let Max drive?"

She laughed. Max looked burned. He thought he could drive the same way he walked: with people stepping aside when they saw him coming. But weasels who wouldn't meet his eyes on the street get big balls when they're behind the wheel. Driving a car, he was a rhino on angel dust.

Max kissed Flower goodbye. Mac held the baby's little hand at the wrist, helping her wave goodbye to her father.

31 WE FOUND the Prof where he said he'd be, standing by a bench at the east end of the park in Union Square. When he saw the Plymouth pull up, he hoisted a canvas sack over one shoulder and walked to us. The Prof was wearing a formal black tuxedo, complete with a white carnation in the lapel. The shiny coat reached almost to his feet, like a cattleman's duster. Some chump was going to be poorly dressed for his senior prom.

"Yo, bro', what you know?" he greeted us, climbing in the back of the Plymouth like it was the limo he'd been waiting for.

I turned west on 14th, heading for the river. The Prof poked his head between me and Max, linking our shoulders with his hands. "What's down, Burke?"

"Like I told you, Prof. Marques Dupree wants a meet. He went to a lot of trouble to get to me—walking around the edges. He's supposed to bring two G's with him. Four-way split. All we have to do is listen to his pitch."

"Who's the fourth?"

"The Mole will be there. Off to the side."

"You want me to ride the trunk?"

"No, we go in square. I don't know what he wants, okay? I may need a translator."

"The street is my beat," said the Prof.

Max looked straight ahead.

We got to the pier around ten-thirty. I pulled the Plymouth against the railing, parked it parallel. The pier was deserted except for a dark, boxy sedan parked about a hundred feet behind us.

We all got out. Max was dressed in flowing black parachute pants and a black sweatshirt. Thin-soled black leather shoes on his feet. He disappeared into the shadows. The Prof stood next to him. I leaned against the railing a few feet away. We waited. Max and the Prof took turns smoking, Max bending forward every time he took a drag when it was his turn. A watcher would see the little red dots, murky shapes. Two people.

Headlights hit the pier. A big old Rolls-Royce, plum-colored, with black fenders. I could see two heads behind the windshield. The Rolls parked at right angles to the Plymouth. Two doors opened. The Prof and I stepped into the outer fringe of the headlights, letting whoever was in the car see us.

Two people came toward us. Belle was a shapeless hulk in a gray sweatsuit. Even with sneakers on her feet, she was as tall as the man next to her.

Marques Dupree. A chesty mahogany man with a smooth, round face. He was wearing a dove-gray silk suit with a metallic pinstripe. Deep-slashed lapels over a peach-colored shirt. Sprayed in diamonds. He and Belle stopped in front of me.

"You're Burke?"

"Yeah."

"Who's this?" Indicating the Prof.

"My brother."

"You don't look like brothers."

"We had the same father."

Marques smiled. I caught the flash of a diamond in his mouth. "I never did time, myself."

I didn't want to swap life stories. "You want to do business?" I asked him.

Marques put his hand in his pocket, pulled out a roll of bills. A car door slammed. He didn't turn around. "What's that?"

"Just checking your car. Making sure you didn't bring friends."

"You said one friend apiece."

"You said you never did time."

Another door slammed. I lit a cigarette. Two more slamming doors. A bright burning dot of light fired where the dark sedan was parked. Okay.

"Your trunk is locked," I said. "I don't need to open it. Let's walk over this way."

I moved to my left, farther away from the parked cars. Marques kept his cash in his fist.

"Here it is," I said. "If anyone opens your trunk, there's a big bang. Okay? Everything goes right here tonight, goes like it's supposed to, my friend takes the package off your trunk. Understand?"

"No problem. You said two large?"

I nodded.

Marques peeled hundreds off his roll, letting me see the two thousand was nothing. I pocketed the cash.

Marques turned to Belle. "Go sit in the car."

She turned to go, nothing on her face. "Stay where you are," I said.

Marques shrugged, his face showing nothing. I knew what was in his mind—if Belle was a hostage, she was a worthless one.

I lit a cigarette. Max materialized out of the night. Marques jumped, his hands flying to his face. Max reached out one hand, picked up the Prof by the back of his jacket, and hoisted him to the railing.

Marques slowly dropped his hands. "You got a lot of friends, huh?"

"A lot of friends," I assured him.

He adjusted his cuffs, letting me see the diamond watch, getting his rap down smooth before he laid it out. Pimps don't like talking on their feet. "I paid for some time."

"Here it is."

Marques took a breath through his nose. It sounded hollow. Cocaine does that. His voice had that hard-sweet pimp sound, promise and threat twisting together like snakes in a basket. "We never met, but we know each other. I know what you do—you know what I do. I have a problem. A business problem."

I watched his face. His eyes were narrow slits in folds of hard flesh. I backed up so the Prof could put his hand on my shoulder.

"I'm listening."

"I am a player. A major player. I got a stable of racehorses, you follow me? All my girls are stars. All white, and all right."

The Prof laughed. "You got nothing but tire-biters and street-scarfers, my man. One of your beasts sees the front seat of a car, she thinks it's the Hilton."

Marques looked at me. "Who's this, man? Your designated hitter?"

"No, pal. He's a polygraph machine."

"You know my action or not?"

I felt the Prof's hand on my shoulder. A quick squeeze.

"Yes," I said.

"Then you know I don't run no jail bait, right? No kiddie pross in my string?"

Another squeeze from the Prof. I nodded agreement.

"I am an *elevated* player, you understand? That ride cost me over a hundred grand, and I got a better one back at my crib. I wear the best, I eat the best, and I live the best. I don't associate with these half-ass simps who think they can run on the fast track. I don't hang around the Port Authority snatching runaways. I don't wear no leopardskin hats, I don't flash no zircons, and that ain't no Kansas City bankroll in my pocket. My ladies are clean machines, and they're all of righteous age. I got lawyers, I got a bondsman, and I got my act together, all right? I don't *make* trouble, and I don't *take* trouble."

The Prof spoke up, his voice a near-perfect imitation of the pimp's. "Okay, Jim, you ain't Iceberg Slim. We got the beat, get to the meat."

Marques smiled. "You got some rhythm, man. The little nigger does the rapping, you just stand there."

"I talk the talk, Burke walks the walk," the Prof told him.

Marques wasn't a good listener. "What's the chink do, man? You going to send out for Chinese food?"

The Prof's voice went soft. "This is Max the Silent, pimp. You hear the name, you should know the game."

Recognition flashed in the pimp's eyes. "He's the one . . ."

"That's right, fool," said the Prof, cutting him off. "Max ain't Chinese, but he sure as hell does take-out work."

"You done with the dozens?" I asked.

"Yeah, man, let's drop the games. I know you're a hijacker, I know you run guns, I know you do work on people. I need some work done."

"I don't work for pimps."

"I *know* that, man. You think everybody on the street don't know who shot Merlin?"

"I don't know any Merlin."

"Yeah, right. 'Course you don't. But I know Merlin was no player, man. He was a stone rapist—that's what he was. Jumping on those little girls like an animal. Whoever shot him did all the real players a favor."

"So?"

"So you got no beef with me, man. I know you used to rough off trollers in Times Square—take them down right in the bus station. I know you chase runaways. See what I'm saying? I *know* you. That's why I didn't call myself. Didn't want you to get the wrong idea." He waved his hand at Belle. "I paid this bitch real money just to put you and me together."

"That lady don't look like no bitch to me," the Prof said. "Don't look like one of yours either."

Belle stepped slightly to the side, flashing a tiny smile at the Prof.

"She don't need to be mine to be a bitch, man. They all sell their time."

"I didn't know you were a philosopher, Marques," I told him.

"And I don't give a fuck. The only time you bought here is mine. And you've about used it up."

Marques locked eyes with me. "You know the Ghost Van?" he asked.

The Prof's hand bit into my shoulder.

I nodded.

The pimp went on as though I'd said no. "Big smoke-colored van. No windows. A few weeks ago, it comes off the river on Twenty-ninth. I got ladies working that block. Van pulls past the pack. Stops. One of the baby girls, not mine, she trots over. The doors swing open and she drops in the street. Nobody heard a shot. The other girls get in the wind. Papers say the little girl was fourteen. Shot in the chest. Dead."

I lit another smoke. Beads of sweat on the pimp's smooth face, his hands working like he didn't know where to put them.

"The next week, two more shootings. Two dead girls. One fifteen, one nineteen. I move my girls over to the East Side, but the pickings too slim there. This van must come off the river. The girls say it's like a ghost. One minute everything's cool; the next this gray thing is on the street. Taking life.

"Last week, one of the little girls gets in a blue Caddy. The Caddy goes up the street. One of my ladies gets curious; she pokes her head around the corner. Two guys get out of the Caddy, holding the girl. She's kicking and screaming. They throw her into the Ghost Van. The Caddy drives off and the van just fucking disappears.

"My ladies don't want to work. The street's like a church social, man. I move the girls again. Way downtown. Brooklyn. The Bronx. Everyplace, man. Three more girls been shot, one more snatched. All near the river. But even out of the city, working girls be saying they seen the van. Like a hawk coming down. The girls see the shadow, they run."

"What do you want from me?"

"Cops is all over the street. My ladies got to work someplace. If they can't work near the river, I got a serious deficit, you follow me? Between the Man and the van, I'm up against it. Until they take that van off, my girls are running scared, jumping at shadows. That hurts me, man."

"In the pocket."

"Yeah, okay, Burke. You a good citizen, right? You look down on me—that's your business. But this is your business too, the way I hear it."

"How's that?"

"The van is full of shooters and snatchers, man. And babies is what they hit. Right up your alley, right?"

"Wrong."

"Look, man, let's all be telling the truth here. The word's been out a long time—you got a kiddie problem, you call Burke. I know you ain't no social worker. You an outlaw, like me. You just work a different side of the street."

"I work for money."

"You think I'm here for myself? The players got together. This is bad for *everyone*, not just Marques Dupree. We put up a kitty."

"Pussy put up the kitty," said the Prof.

"Call it like *you* see it, it make you feel better. I call it what it is."

I waited.

"A bounty. Fifty thousand bucks. Dead or alive. The van's got to go. Goes to Attica, goes to Forest Lawn, makes no difference to us."

"Hire a private eye."

"I said a bounty, man. I look like a fucking trick to you? We not paying anyone by the hour."

"Put the money out on the street."

"Can't do that."

"Why?"

"We can't wait for some faggot to drop a dime. And we can't be sure the Man will do the work anyway."

"Why not?"

"We heard the van's *protected*. That's all I know. But the word is out, all over the street. Uptown, downtown. The van has to have a parking place, you got it?"

The Prof's hand worked on my shoulder again.

"Yeah," I said.

"It's good money, Burke. I'll work out any collateral you want."

"You're carrying your collateral."

Marques looked puzzled. "My jewelry?"

"Your head," I told him.

He took another deep breath. "You'll do it?"

"I'll think about it."

"You need to know anything else?" he asked.

"When the van goes down, we'll be around," said the Prof.

"Let's go, bitch," Marques said to Belle.

"She'll go with me," I said.

Marques Dupree smiled. "You like cows?"

"Go home and play with your coat hangers," I told him, waving to the Mole. So Marques could open his trunk later without losing his collateral.

32 ‖ THE ROLLS moved off. "Wait in the car," I told Belle. She waggled her fingers at the Prof in a goodbye. "Good night, pretty lady," he said. Max stood stone-still.

I watched her walk away.

"Prof, you know what he was running down?"

"The van's for real, Burke. It's been all over the street for weeks."

"You know something?"

"Something. When I know it all, I'll give you the call."

I gave Max his five hundred, a thousand to the Prof. "Take care of the Mole—he'll drop you off."

Max bowed. I shook hands with the Prof. "Watch yourself," I told him.

I got into the Plymouth. Belle was sitting against the passenger door, looking out at the river through the open window.

"Where to?" I asked her, watching the dark sedan pull away.

**33** | BELLE REACHED into the waistband of her sweatsuit, pulled out a pack of smokes. I handed her my little box of wooden matches, waiting. She inhaled deeply. It was like watching the Alps shift.

"You know Broad Channel?"

"Sure."

"I'll show you once we get on to Cross Bay Boulevard."

I pointed the Plymouth downtown, heading for the Battery Tunnel.

"How'd you meet Marques?"

"When I first came to New York. I was working at Rosie's Show Bar."

"Dancing?"

"I was a barmaid."

"He try and turn you out?"

"He thinks I'm a lesbian. Okay?"

She knew the score. Plenty of lesbians turn tricks, but a smart pimp doesn't want one in his stable. One day he turns around and he's missing two girls.

"They think the same thing at that joint you work at?"

"The boss doesn't care one way or the other."

"So why did Marques pick you for a messenger?"

"It's one of the things I do. I carry stuff, drive a car, deliver a message . . . like that, you know?"

"You carry powder?"

"No."

"That's where the money is."

"The fall's too far."

"You ever been down?"

"Just overnight a couple of times. Once for a week. In West Virginia."

"What for?"

"The cops thought I drove on a bank job. They didn't want me—I was just a kid—they wanted the gunman."

"They only held you a week?"

She caught something in my tone. "I stood up, Burke. The P.D. got bail for me and I caught a bus north. I know how to do it—if I go to jail, I go by myself."

"You never did time—where'd you learn the rules?"

Belle smiled in the dark. Slapped the side of one thigh. "Maybe I'm too heavy to roll over."

I looped the Plymouth onto the Belt Parkway, heading east to Queens. A red panel truck ahead of me changed lanes suddenly, cutting me off. I tapped the brakes, flicked the wheel to the right, touched the gas. The Plymouth flowed around the panel truck like a shark passing a rowboat. Belle wiggled her hips deep into the seat, testing her balance.

"This car's a lot more than it looks."

"So are you."

Her smile flashed again. A prim smile, showing just the tips of her teeth.

I wheeled the Plymouth off the Belt, picking my way through Ozone Park. No reason for Marques to have the car followed, but Belle said she played by our rules—she wouldn't want the pimp knowing where she lived. We stopped at a light. An abandoned factory stood to the side, waiting for a developer to finish the job a fire started years ago. It was wallpapered with graffiti except for a broad rectangle in the center that somebody had carefully whitewashed. On that white canvas was a message, lovingly slash-scripted by a gifted graffiti-writer. Day-Glo orange letters, shadowed in black so they screamed off the wall.

*DISS AT YOUR OWN RISK!*

Belle read the message, fascinated, going over every word, biting her lower lip. "What does it mean. 'Diss'?"

"It's short for 'disrespect.' This is a border town. Black and white."

She didn't say another word until we turned onto the Boulevard. I followed her directions into Broad Channel. Mostly little bungalows, set close together, right on the water. Years ago they were summer shacks, but most of them had been fixed up now, and people lived there year-round.

The cottage was at the end of a short block. White with blue trim around the one window, the dark roof almost flat across the top. Her red Camaro was parked in front.

"This is me," she said.

34 ‖ I SLID the Plymouth to the curb, killed the engine. The block was quiet, every house dark.

"Come in with me?" Belle asked.

The cottage was set close to the sidewalk, the path to her front door only a few feet long. She turned her key in the door, pushed it open, stepped aside. The inside of the house was in shadow; a soft light coming from the back. Belle motioned me to go ahead of her.

"You first," I said.

A little smile. "You being polite? Or scared?"

"Scared."

She walked in ahead of me. I watched from the doorway, gently pushing the door back and forth with my left hand, feeling for resistance. Belle bent from the waist in the shadows. I heard a click. A lamp came to life. She moved a few feet. Another.

"Close the door behind you," she said.

The cottage was one big room. A long modular couch took up

one wall, side tables with lamps on either end. The kitchen was strung out along the opposite wall, Hollywood-style, everything half-size. The side walls were blank, no windows.

"You want coffee?"

"No, thanks."

I lit a cigarette, walking toward the couch. The back of the house was still dark. I could see a triple-width window next to a door on the far left, a bed on the right.

Belle pulled the top of the sweatsuit over her head, tossing it into a white plastic basket next to the refrigerator. Her black bra was some kind of jersey material, the straps crossing behind her back so her shoulders were bare. She stepped out of the sweatpants. Underneath she had what looked like a pair of men's white boxer shorts.

She took her coffee cup in one hand, a pack of cigarettes in the other. Walked to the back door.

I opened it for her, followed her outside. A wood deck stretched out in the black water, a waist-high railing on both sides. The other cottages had decks too. I saw a small sailboat tied to one, a rowboat with an outboard to another. Belle walked out to the end, carefully balancing her coffee cup.

"Hold this," she said, handing the coffee and cigarettes to me. She turned her back to the water, one palm out to each side, and vaulted herself onto the railing. I put the coffee cup on one side of her perch, handed her back the smokes. She kicked one out, leaned forward, one hand on my shoulder for balance. I lit it for her.

I could feel the night air's chill through my jacket. Belle didn't seem to notice. I leaned my elbows on the railing next to her, watching the harbor lights a half-mile away. I felt her hand on my shoulder again.

"Did you really do all that stuff?" A soft voice, loaded with her breath. A girl's voice. The twisted snake tattoo stood out sharply on her thigh, inches from my face.

"What stuff?"

"What that guy said tonight."

"No."

She giggled the way kids do when they know you're playing with them.

"Yes, you did," she said.

I shrugged.

"I have something you might be interested in," she said, her voice quiet.

"You got something *anybody'd* be interested in."

She giggled. "I didn't mean *that*. Business. Can I tell you about it?"

"Not here."

"Why?"

"Sound carries over water."

She put an arm around my neck, pulling her face close to mine. Whispering. "You think I don't know that? I was raised on the water. Inside."

"Okay."

I turned toward the house, slipping an arm around her waist. She slid off the railing against me, her legs pointing straight out. I threw up my other arm instinctively, grabbing her thighs. Belle nestled into my arms. "Carry me," she said, soft-voiced.

"I'll get a double hernia," I growled at her, leaning against the railing for support.

"Please."

I would have shrugged again, but I needed all my strength.

She ducked her head into my chest as we went through the door, pushing it closed with her toe. I tried to put her down on the couch gently, but I dropped her the last couple of feet.

I flopped down next to her. "I love to be carried," she said, leaning over and kissing my cheek.

"Don't get used to it."

Belle bounced off the couch. She came back in a minute. Put her coffee cup in the sink, lit two cigarettes off the gas burner, walked over, and handed one to me.

"You first," she said.

I dragged deep on the cigarette, wondering how she knew.

"That music . . ."

"In my act?"

"Yeah. Swamp blues. I never heard it before. Louisiana?"

"Florida. It's an old record. I don't even know the singer. I found it in a store in the city."

"How do you know it's from Florida?"

Belle got off the couch. Walked over to the darkened bed. She hit a light switch. The bed was low, covered in white, a white rug on the floor. It was the bed in her act.

She came back to the couch, pulling her bra over her head as she walked. Turned off the two lamps on the end tables, one by one. She stretched out full-length on the couch, her head in my lap, facing up at me, eyes closed. Even with her arms at her sides, her breasts stood straight up at me, carved in flesh.

Her face was indistinct in the soft light, her eyes lost in the sheaf of taffy-honey hair. No lipstick on her mouth. Only the tiny chin with its sharp point moving.

"I'm from Florida. When I heard that song, I knew it was a home call. Understand?"

"Yeah."

She took my hand, pressed it to where her breast covered her heart. I could feel the beat. Strong, slow, steady.

"What did you think of my act?"

"I never saw anything like it before."

"Each girl gets to design her own. As long as our clothes come off before the lights go out."

"It's a psychiatric mirror."

"A what?"

"A psychiatric mirror. You do your act—people watch it—they all see something different—if you knew what they were thinking, you'd know them."

"Like that inkblot test?"

"*Just* like that."

Belle sighed. A tiny slash of white across her face where she chewed her lower lip. "It's true. Men send notes backstage."

"You ever answer them?"

"No. I'm like you."

"What does that mean?"

"I don't work for pimps either."

"You could work for yourself."

"I do work for myself—I'm not for sale."

She reached for my cigarette, ignoring her own. Put it in her mouth, took a deep drag. The smoke shot out her nose. I watched her stomach muscles flex.

"Did it work on you?"

"What?"

"My act—did you think of something?"

I bit into the cigarette filter. "I saw it like a play. Young girl coming into herself. Things pulling at her. Evil calling."

"Tell the truth—you saw a play?"

"*Like* a play. It all meant something."

"Not what you think."

"Yeah, *exactly* what I think. That's the way the mirror works."

Belle pulled herself into a sitting position, her back to me. She got to her feet, took my hand. "Come on," she said.

She walked over to the bed. Put a hand against my chest. "Stay here," she said. She hooked her thumbs into the waistband of the shorts, pulling them over her hips, dropping them to her feet. She stepped out of the shorts and padded to the bed. She fell to her knees, bent forward onto the bed, her hands clasped in front of her.

"Tell the truth," she said again, her little-girl voice almost hissing. Demanding. "What did you see?"

I looked at the shadows play over her body. "I saw a young girl. Praying."

"What did it make you want to do?" she whispered, looking back at me over one shoulder, wiggling her butt.

I took a breath. Telling the truth. "Answer your prayers," I told her.

Her little chin came up, smile flashing.

"Come on," she said.

**35** | SHE STAYED on her knees, watching me over her shoulder. She cocked her head to one side, listening as my clothes hit the floor.

"Where's your gun?"

"I don't have one."

"Marques did."

"I know—in his left-hand pocket," I said, standing next to her, my hand on her shoulder.

She came to her feet, facing me. Without the heels, she was maybe a half-inch shorter than me. Her eyes were set so close together it was hard to look into them. I ran two fingers along her jawline, feeling for bone lost in the soft flesh, cupping her little chin. I kissed her softly, feeling her lips swell. Her teeth clicked against mine.

"How'd you know he had a gun?" she asked, her tongue darting out, whispering into my mouth.

I moved my hands to her waist, and down to her sculptured butt, feeling the soft skin, squeezing the hard muscles beneath the surface. She locked her hands behind my head and fell backward, pulling me down with her.

The bed was hard. No springs squeaked when our weight came down. I landed on top of her, but she slid out from underneath me slick as an otter leaving a rock in the water. She snuggled into my chest, nudging me onto my back with her shoulder, one hand trailing across my stomach, throwing a thigh over mine. She burrowed her face into my neck, her whole body quivering.

"You have to tell me," she whispered. "I have to know those things."

"Why?"

She reached her free hand between my legs, wrapping it around me, rubbing the tip with the pad of her thumb. "You think this is the answer to my prayers?"

"I had hopes," I said.

"Come on, honey. How'd you know?"

"When you walked up with him, he didn't want you on his left side. When you moved away, he was more relaxed."

"So?"

"So either he was carrying on his left side or you were holding a piece for him."

"How'd you know I wasn't?"

"You kept your hands free. The clothes you had on—that sweatsuit—you couldn't get to it in time. Besides, you weren't his woman."

"Because I said so?"

"The way you carried yourself."

She stroked me gently, her mind somewhere else. Mine wasn't.

"What if you were wrong?"

"Huh?"

"What if I *was* carrying?"

"You're not fast enough to make it work."

"Not fast enough for you?"

"For Max."

"Which one was Max?"

"The guy that didn't speak."

"He was ten feet away from me."

I shrugged.

She shifted her weight, holding her head in one hand, her elbow cocked against the bed. Her breast was an inch from my face. The dark nipple looked tiny against the white globe. I kissed it. Her hand pulled against me in response.

"He's really that fast?"

"Faster."

Belle moved her head into my chest again. Her hand slid down the shaft, cupping my balls, lifting them gently, like she was trying to guess their weight. Her voice was all soft curves, hardness flexing underneath, the same as her body. "Tell the truth. When you saw me in the club—in the play—and you wanted to answer my prayers?"

"Yeah?"

"What did you want to do?"

"I'm not sure. . . ."

"Tell me!" she whispered hard against my chest, her hand closing on me.

"I wanted to rescue you," I said.

She moved her hand back to the shaft, shifting her body on top of mine, fitting me inside her. She was wet—I slid in like a bullet being chambered. Her hands were on either side of me, taking her weight, her breasts brushing my face. I moved my hands to her butt as she started to grind against me.

Her mouth came down to mine. "Rescue me," she said.

**36** WHEN I woke up a while later, Belle's face was on the pillow next to mine, her body still covering me. I couldn't see my watch. I flexed my shoulders to see if I could slide from under her without waking her up.

"You want a cigarette, baby?"

"I didn't know you were awake," I said.

"I never went to sleep. I've been here all along."

"How come you didn't get up?"

"I was guarding you," she said, her face close to mine. "I knew the only way you'd sleep is if I didn't move."

She padded over to the kitchen, opened a door next to the refrigerator. I heard water running. Belle came back with a big glass ashtray, cigarettes and matches inside, a washcloth over one shoulder. She bent over me, set the ashtray on the far side. She put a cigarette in her mouth, fired it up, handed it to me. Lit one for herself.

She smiled down at me in the darkness. "Are you my boyfriend now?"

I thought I was going to laugh—it came out kind of a snort. "Your boyfriend?"

"Yes, my boyfriend."

"What does that mean?"

"I don't know. I never had a boyfriend. But if you rescued me, you have to be my boyfriend, right?"

"If that's what it takes to rescue you, there must have been a thousand applicants for the job."

She bent to kiss me. "You're a sweet man. But that was a down payment. I'm not rescued yet."

She ground out her cigarette, pulled the washcloth off her shoulder. Started to clean me off, not being that gentle about it. The washcloth was wet, warm. I felt myself growing in her hands.

I finished my cigarette. Belle was still scrubbing me like she was going to use my cock for surgery, kneeling on the floor, her body at right angles to mine. I lit another. She tossed the washcloth aside, climbed on the bed, her knees next to my chest. She bent forward and took me in her mouth, her butt in the air, blocking my view of the rest of the world.

She took her mouth from me, peeking back over one shoulder, licking her lips. "Put out your cigarette."

"Why?"

"I don't want you to burn me."

"I wouldn't burn you."

She caught the warning in my voice. "I didn't mean on *purpose*, honey," she whispered. "I know you're not like that."

I held the cigarette in my left hand, took a deep drag, my right hand stroking her outside thigh.

"Just don't keep it in your mouth," she said, bending forward again, nibbling at my cock. She swallowed the engorged tip, sucking hard. I put the cigarette in my mouth, dragging deep, letting the smoke bubble out my nose, lost in the feeling.

Belle moved her inside foot against me, sliding it onto my chest.

I shifted the cigarette to my left hand as she threw her leg over, straddling me, her butt still in the air, now squarely in front of me. She wiggled her rear, sucking, working her tongue. I took another drag. Her butt came down, moving toward my face. I flashed my right hand hard against her cheek, a sharp crack in the quiet room.

She pointed her butt in the air again, pulling her mouth off me. "Was that a message—or did you just want to see what it felt like?"

"A message," I told her.

"Why didn't you just tell me?"

"There wasn't time."

She pivoted on her knees so her face was close to mine. "You don't want to taste me?"

"No."

"Why not, honey? Don't you think I'd be sweet?"

"It's not that."

"You think a man doesn't do stuff like that?"

I snubbed out the cigarette. "I don't think that. It's just not me."

"Prison?"

"It's not that simple. There's no code against it." I laughed. "The only cons who swear they've never eaten a woman are pimps."

Belle rubbed her face against my chest. "Wouldn't you do something to make me happy?"

"Some. Things. You understand?"

"I'd do whatever you want."

"The only way it works is if you do what *you* want, Belle. That's the only thing that goes the distance."

She lit a cigarette for herself.

"Do you have a woman?"

"Yes."

"With you?"

"No."

"Where is she?"

"I don't know."

The tip of her cigarette flared. "But you love her—you're waiting for her?"

"Yes."

"She's coming back?"

"I don't know."

She ran her hands through her hair, holding it in a bun on top of her head, looking down at me.

"Will you love me?"

"I never thought I would love her," I said.

She held the cigarette to my mouth. Her face was intent in the light it threw. She didn't have to ask me to tell the truth—she knew it when she heard it.

"I'm going to love you, Burke. And you're going to rescue me." She moved her hand away from my face, leaving the cigarette in my mouth.

"If I try to sit on your face again, you going to give me another smack?"

"You want me to tell you another way?"

She spun on her knees again, bending her face down again. She looked back over her shoulder. "No, send me another message. I like the way you did it."

Her mouth locked onto me again. I went hard in her mouth. She rubbed her thighs together. My hand stroked her butt. Her thighs opened. I stroked my fingers against the back of her knees. A liquid drop fell into my hand. I felt the pinpricks of pressure in my balls, tightening into a thick mass. I hooked my hand around the front of her thigh, pulling her toward me. She wouldn't move, sucking harder now. Strega flashed into my mind—Strega and her witch games. I jerked her thigh hard, trying to pull her face off me. It was rigid as a cell bar.

"Belle," I whispered. "Come here."

She didn't move. I cracked her hard against the same cheek I'd hit before. She made a humming noise but stayed where she was. I hit her twice more, feeling the sting in my palm, wondering what she felt.

Her mouth came off my cock. She crawled forward on the bed, throwing a leg over me. She pushed her butt between my legs until

I was smoothly inside her, moved to her knees, straddling my body, her back to me.

"Come on!" she said, her voice hard, bucking until we both got there.

**37** SHE SLEPT then. On her stomach, one arm flung across my chest. I slipped under it, found the bathroom. It was small-scale, like the kitchen. Cheap black-and-white tile covered the floor and ran halfway up the wall from the tub. The hot water came up right away; the pressure was good that time of night. I took a quick shower, used some of her Brand-X shampoo, toweled myself off. The little medicine cabinet was empty except for a toothbrush and a bottle of aspirin. A plastic hairbrush and a bottle of green mouthwash stood on the sink. I wondered where she kept all her makeup . . . maybe on the dressing table near her bed.

The bathroom was full of steam, the mirror cloudy. I wiped it off, looked at my face. Whatever she wanted, she hadn't seen it there.

My foot hit something under the sink. A black metal box with a latch on the front, carry-handle on top. I popped it open. Sterile bandages, individually wrapped. A roll of gauze. Elastic tape. Three scalpels with different-sized blades. A pair of surgical scissors. A bottle of iodine. Two more of sulfa powder. A pair of matching plastic vials, both full, unlabeled. I opened them. Penicillin. Percodan. There was no tag on the metal box, but I knew what it was. Bullet-wound kit.

The refrigerator had a half-empty carton of milk, a lump of cream cheese, and a head of lettuce under a plastic wrap. I found some ice cubes, filled a glass, let it get cold while I got dressed.

I sipped the water in the easy chair near her bed, smoking, trying to think it through. A Ghost Van in my mind.

Belle rolled over on her side as her eyes came open.

"This time you guarded me," she said.

"I've got to go," I told her.

"Let me take a shower first." She didn't wait for an answer, shoving past me to the bathroom. It was still dark outside—my watch said it was almost four-thirty.

She came out of the bathroom brushing her hair, her body gleaming wet.

"Why do you have to go?" she wanted to know, stepping close to where I was sitting.

"There's something I have to take care of."

"What's her name?" she asked, a mock-growl in her voice.

"Pansy."

She pulled back. "You better be kidding."

"Pansy's a dog. My dog."

She giggled. "You have a dog named Pansy? You tie ribbons in her hair and all that?"

"She's about your size."

"I'd like to see that."

"You will."

"Can I come with you?"

"Not this time," I said, getting to my feet.

She put her arms around my neck, pushing her nose so close to mine that my eyes went out of focus. "You'll be back here tonight?"

"I thought you had to work."

"I'll call in sick. Most of the girls do that after their night off—it's no big deal."

"Okay," I said, running my hands down her smooth back to the swelling of her rear.

"What are you thinking?"

"I was thinking if I pressed a quarter against your back and let it go it would fly off your ass like it was a ski slope."

She slipped her hand between us, patting my crotch. "You got a quarter in there someplace?"

"No," I said, pushing gently against her. "I have to go—no joke."

She put her hand in mine, walking me toward her door. "Burke, you know when you didn't want to taste me? You said that wasn't you, right?"

I made a yes noise, walking with her.

"That's okay. You can be you. It's okay that I keep dancing?"

"If that's what you want to do."

"I'm telling the truth now, Burke. I'm going to love you. And you're going to love me too, when you see how I am. But I have to be me while I do it, understand?"

"I'm not arguing with you, Belle."

She put her mouth on my ear, whispering in that little-girl breathy voice, holding my hand tight. "I'm me. You don't change for me—I don't change for you. But I wouldn't let you dance."

"That means what?"

Her voice was pure and sad in my ear. "If Pansy's a dog, like you said, I'm going to pat her. If she's a woman, I'll kill her."

She kissed me on the cheek, pushed me away, stood to the side while I stepped out the door.

I looked back at the cottage as I climbed into my car. It was dark.

**38** ‖ THE PLYMOUTH tracked its way back to the office, its monster motor barely turning over. The all-news station was talking about Kuwaiti ships flying the American flag in the Persian Gulf, mine-sweepers guarding the point. I flipped to the oldies station. Screamin' Jay Hawkins. "I Put a Spell on You." Growling his love-threats to his woman and to the world.

*I don't care if you don't want me, I'm yours*
*Right now.*

Belle would know he was telling the truth.

Most of the traffic was trucks, highballing it toward the city. A customized van passed on my right. Big glass doors cut into the side, a plastic bubble on its roof. As it went by, I saw a narrow metal ladder running from the bumper up to the roof. A mural was painted on the back—some religious scene.

I lit a smoke. The van I was looking for was a custom job too. I knew that meant something, but I couldn't lock in on it. It would come.

If Marques was right, the van had been working for a few weeks now. Time enough for the police to be on the job. I flicked my cigarette out the window, wondering if McGowan was working nights.

Bob Seger came through the radio. "Still the Same." Motor City blues. Somebody once said it was about a guy catching up with his old girlfriend, but it never sounded like that to me.

It sounded like a kid catching up with his father.

**39** I LET Pansy out to her roof. Picked up the phone on my desk, checked for hippies. All quiet.

I dialed a number.

"Runaway Squad, Officer Thompson speaking." A young woman's voice.

"Is McGowan around?"

"Hold on."

I lit a smoke, waiting. Any other detective bureau in the city, they ask you who's calling. The Runaway Squad knows most of the callers won't give their names.

"McGowan," said the voice on the phone. The same hard-sweet voice pimps use, but McGowan did it different, giving you your choice.

"It's Burke. We're working the same case. Got a few minutes to meet with me?"

"I'm off at eight. Breakfast at Dino's? Eight-fifteen, eight-thirty?"

"I'll be there," I told him, and put down the phone.

Pansy ambled in, rested her head in my lap. I patted her. "You're always glad to see me, aren't you, girl?"

She didn't answer me.

I pushed her head off my lap, helped myself to a drink of ice water from the refrigerator. I took out two hard-boiled eggs, cracked them against the wall, peeled off the shells.

"Wake me in an hour," I told Pansy, handing her the eggs.

I closed my eyes so I wouldn't see the mess she made.

40 | WHEN I opened my eyes, it was seven-thirty. I took another shower, changed my clothes. I let Pansy out again, watching her run around while I took a deep slug of Pepto-Bismol. Eating at Dino's on an empty stomach was dangerous.

I drove north on the West Side Highway, moving against the snarled rush-hour traffic. Dino's was on Twelfth Avenue, about ten blocks south of Times Square. Yuppies in New York are heavy into diner food now, but Dino's wasn't going to make the list.

McGowan's unmarked cruiser was parked right out front, empty slots on either side. I pulled in, not wasting my time trying to spot him through the greasy windows.

He was sitting in a booth near the back corner, hat tipped back on his long Irish face, cigar in his mouth. Wearing a dark suit, a shirt that had once been white, a blue tie that had never been silk. I sat across from him, my back to the door. We'd known each other a long time.

He shook his head sharply before I could open my mouth, tilting his chin up. Somebody coming.

It was only three hours into her shift, but the waitress was already tired, her broad face lined with strain. Still, she had a smile for McGowan. They all did.

"Good morning, lovely Belinda," he greeted her. "How's the play coming?"

"It comes about like I do, McGowan. Not too often."

"Nothing good comes easy, my little darling," he said, turning aside gloom like a bullfighter. He took one of her hands, holding it in his, patting her.

"Belinda, it was your choice. A lovely young girl like you, the boys would be all over you and they had a chance. But it's not the life of a housewife for my girl, is it now? Your play will come. Your day will come."

"Ah, McGowan . . ." she said, trying to sneer at his blarney. But the smile came out, like they both knew it would.

"Give me two of your finest eggs, sunny-side up. Bacon, toast, and some Sanka, will you, girl?"

She wrote it down, turned to me.

"Two eggs, fried over hard, break the yolks. Ham, rye toast, apple juice. Burn everything."

"You got it," the waitress said, moving away, the bounce back in her walk.

McGowan puffed on his cigar, knowing we wouldn't talk until the food came.

"How's Max?"

"The same."

"I heard he was a proud papa."

"That's on the street?"

"Sure," he said, watching me closely. "Any problem with it?"

I shrugged. No point asking McGowan where he got it—maybe from one of the little girls he brought to Lily's program, maybe . . .

The food came and we ate.

It didn't take either of us long. Swallowing it wasn't as bad as looking at it. The Senator's Motto.

Belinda cleared our plates. McGowan settled down over his second cup of Sanka, relighting his mangy cigar.

"So?"

"The Ghost Van—you know it?"

"Everybody knows it."

"Any more than what's been in the papers?"

"A bit. What's your interest?"

"Some people want me to find it."

"And take it off the street?"

"It's just an investigation. The people who want me to do this job don't have anything personal at stake. For all they care, I find it, I could call the cops."

McGowan leaned across the table, his Irish blues going cop-hard. "It's personal to me, Burke. The swine shot one of my girls."

"When?"

"The second shooting. Little girl named Darla James. Fifteen years old, and on the stroll for the last two. I was close to taking her off the track. Real close, Burke. They put two into her chest at twenty feet—she never had a prayer."

I lit a smoke, watching his face. McGowan had been working the cesspool for twenty years and he'd never fired his gun. He won some and he lost a hell of a lot more, but he always kept coming. He played the game square, and we all respected him.

"You want me out of it—I'm out of it," I told him.

"I want you *in* it, pal. In fact, I was going to put it out on the wire last week for you to come around. These are bad, bad people, Burke."

"How do you make it?"

He puffed on the cigar, his eyes still hard, but not looking my way. "Has to be a vigilante trip. One of those sicko cults. They're shooting the poor little girls to fight the devil. Or maybe they're sacrificing bodies to Satan. It all comes out the same."

"You sure?"

"I'm not sure of anything. I'll tell you what we have—it's precious little enough."

I kept my hands on the table, where he could see them. McGowan would know I don't write things down, but he looked upset enough to forget.

"Tell me," I said.

"There's been five girls shot, not the three the papers reported. And two snatched—not just the one everybody knows about. Ballistics says they were all shot with the same piece. Military hardware, probably an M-16, or one of those Russian jobs. High-speed ammo. Ballistics says the slugs were twenty-two-caliber."

"They mean 5.56-millimeter. About the same thing."

"Whatever," McGowan snarled. He wasn't a forensics man. "The girls were all torn up inside—ripped to pieces. Dead before they hit the ground."

"You ever find either of the girls who were snatched?"

"Not a trace."

"Were all the girls underage?"

"Either that or they looked it."

"You sure it's random?"

"We thought of that. Questioned half the pimps in Times Square. We can't make a connection."

"Who's 'we'? The Commissioner got a task force working on this?"

McGowan's laugh was too ugly to be cynical. "Task force? Sure, and why would they be doing that? It's not like it was citizens getting killed."

I sipped my apple juice, thinking out loud to draw him in. "Seems like a strange piece to use. . . ."

McGowan's eyes snapped into focus. "Why?"

"It's not an assassin's weapon. Doesn't have the shock power of a heavier slug. That high speed's a waste at such close range. The bullets fly so fast that they tumble around as soon as they hit something. That's why the girls were so torn up inside. And it makes a hell of a bang—real hard to silence."

I took another drag, thinking it through. I wasn't playing with McGowan: it really didn't make sense. "Automatics jam," I told him. "You know that—that's why they don't let you guys carry the nine-millimeters you want. So why risk an automatic when you're only going to fire off a couple of shots? And if it was so random, why didn't they just sweep the street? With an M-16, they could chop down a dozen girls just as easy as one. You check with ATF?"

"They're too busy looking for Uzis. The guy I talked with said what you said. Doesn't even have to be a military piece—there's all kinds of semi-auto stuff floating around—AK-47s, AR-15s. Takes ten minutes to convert them to full auto, he said."

"It's still the wrong gun for killing at close range. A heavier piece, even if you hit someone in the arm, you'd blow it right off. They'd be dead before the ambulance got there."

"Maybe it's all they have?"

"Doesn't add up. This is an expensive deal, McGowan. And for what?"

His honey voice turned sour. "Couple of bullets and gas money—it don't sound so expensive to me."

"You ever find the van?"

"No. So?"

"So they didn't dump it after the shootings. So they have to have a place to stash it. They got to have at least a driver, a shooter, and another guy to fling open the doors. And the snatch . . . they had a switch-car for that, right?"

"Where'd you hear that?"

"Out there," I said, pointing vaguely out the greasy window.

"Yeah. We found the switch-car. Took it apart, piece by piece. We got some decent prints, but no match."

"Anything else?"

"There's no pattern. No thread. The girls didn't know each other. Two were on the runaway list, but that doesn't mean anything. Half the little hookers out there were on the list one time or another."

"Any mail?"

He knew what I meant. Some serial killers have to tell the cops how clever they are.

"No letters. No phone calls. Blank fucking zero. It's so bad the pimps aren't even afraid to be seen talking to us—they want these guys off the street too. I even heard talk about a bounty. . . ." His eyes locked on mine. "You hear anything about a bounty, Burke?"

I met his stare. "No."

It didn't impress the cop. He knew where I'd been raised.

"People like that . . . who knows what could happen if they were arrested. A smart lawyer . . . maybe some kind of NGI deal . . . drop a few dimes. Maybe they'd make it a goddamned miniseries."

NGI. Not Guilty, Insanity. "Better they don't get arrested," I said quietly.

His eyes were ball bearings.

41 || I HEADED back to my office, weaving through the West Side blocks, checking the action. It looked the same to me. If the Ghost Van was trying to keep baby pross off the street, it wasn't working. I couldn't pick up the scent—you have to work close to the ground to do that. If it was out there, the Prof would find it.

Called Mama from a pay phone. Nothing.

Back at the office, I let Pansy out to her roof. I had a few more calls to make, but they'd have to wait until the afternoon.

Pansy ambled over to the desk, where I was working on the racing form, making that snarling noise she does when she's trying to tell me something. I knew what she wanted. "I was at Dino's," I told her, explaining why I hadn't bought her a present.

There was a trotter I fancied in the fourth race at Yonkers. Mystery Mary, a five-year-old mare, moving down from Canada. She'd been running in Open company at Greenwood, finishing pretty consistently in the money, but no wins. She had a lot of early speed, which is unusual for a mare, but she kept getting run down in the deep stretch. Greenwood is a five-eighths-of-a-mile track—a long run from the three-quarter pole to the finish line. Yonkers was a half-miler— a longer launch and a shorter way home. She was moving up to higher purses in New York, but I thought she had a shot if she could get away clean. I checked the last eight races. Mystery Mary was a sure-footed little trotter—no breaks on her card. The morning line had her at 6–1. Most of the OTB bettors would use the *Daily News* as a handicapping form. All that would show is her last three outs: two thirds and a fifth-place finish. I made a mental note to call my broker before the close of business, flipped on the TV, and kicked back on the couch. The last thing I remember before falling asleep was Abbott telling Costello that paying back rent was like betting on a dead horse.

It wasn't a good sleep. Dark, fleshy dreams. Flood facing the Cobra, the snake on his arm turning into the tattoo on Belle's thigh. Strega licking her bloody lips, crazy eyes full of ugly promises. The Ghost Van zoomed up a narrow street, a silent gray shark. Max at the end of the block, waiting, shielding Flower in one arm.

I woke up before the crash, sweating like when I'd had malaria. Sergeant Bilko was on the TV. A little past three o'clock.

I took a shower, changed my clothes. Pansy jumped on the couch as I was walking out the door.

Mama still had nothing for me. I dropped another quarter, called Maurice. He answered in his usual breezy style.

"Yeah?"

"It's Burke."

"This a social call, or what?"

"Yonkers. Give me the two horse, fourth race. A deuce to win."

"At Yonkers. Horse number two, race number four. Two on the nose, is that right?"

"Right. How you doing, Maurice?"

"You want conversation, play fucking Lotto," he said, hanging up.

I changed phones, fed another quarter. I don't know why they make dimes anymore. I rang the direct-line number of a reporter I know.

"Morelli."

"It's Burke. You got anything outside the clips on this Ghost Van?"

"Bullshit gossip. Cop talk. Nothing good."

"The cops think they're close?"

"They're waiting for the van to get a parking ticket."

"Can you pull the clips for me?"

"You looking?"

"Looking *around*, anyway."

"You'll clue me in front?"

"If I can."

"I'll pull the clips, leave them downstairs by six. Okay?"

"Yeah. Could you do a NEXIS spin too? See if there's any more van jobs around the country?"

"You think it's a group?"

"No, but check anyway."

"You got it."

One more call. Belle answered on the first ring, sounding like she ran a hundred yards to snatch it off the hook.

"Hello?"

"It's me. Want to get some dinner?"

"Oh, I'm *starved*. There's nothing in the house."

"I know. Why didn't you go out?"

"I knew you were going to call."

"I said . . . never mind. I'll pick you up in an hour, okay?"

"Hurry up," she said.

I put the phone down, moving fast to beat the charge out of the city.

42 I PULLED in behind the red Camaro a little after five. The door opened as my fist came down to knock. A hand came around my neck, pulling me inside. Belle mashed her face against mine, kissing me hard, firing her hip at the door to close it.

She pulled her face back a couple of inches, still holding on to me.

"That was a cold kiss. Didn't you miss me?"

"I was working, Belle."

Her mouth went down at the corners. "I'm sorry," she said. "I didn't mean to push you."

I put my hand on the back of her neck, working the tight muscles, keeping my voice quiet.

"You're not pushing me. You don't know me, okay? I don't show a lot on the surface—it's not my way."

"You *did* miss me?"

"I did miss you."

She twirled away, flashing a smile. Her face was all made up, the blue eye shadow making her eyes look bigger, bright lipstick smeared on her teeth. She was wearing a fire-engine-red T-shirt big enough for a linebacker. It fell to mid-thigh, just covering the tattoo.

"I'm just about ready, baby. Give me a minute. I have to find my shoes."

She scooped a pair of glasses from the dressing table. Big round lenses with a light-blue tint, sitting in a thin black plastic frame. "Here they are," she said happily, dragging a pair of red spike-heeled shoes from under the bed.

"Belle."

She was bending forward, slipping on the shoes. Black panties that didn't have a prayer of covering her rump peeked out as the T-shirt rose. "What, honey?"

"You're going out like that?"

Her face fell. "You don't like it?"

Damn. "It's not that," I said quietly, walking over to her, taking her chin in my hand. With the spikes on, she was taller than me—I had to look up into her eyes.

"You go on the street like that, every man that's not brain-dead is going to remember you."

"So?"

"So it's not my game to attract attention, girl. The places I have to go—I don't make reservations, understand?"

"You like me better when I'm all covered? When I look like a big fat cow?"

"I like you the same. It's *you* I like, yes?"

"Yes?"

"Yes!" I said, slapping her rear.

She grabbed my hand, pulled it around to her butt. Held it there. "You like this big fat thing?"

I looked deep into her eyes, watching a tear run down her cheek. Keeping my voice quiet: "Belle," I told her, "it works on me like a hormone shot."

She never took her eyes off mine. "Burke, I'd do anything for you."

"Will you put on a pair of pants?"

"Sure, baby. I've got just the thing."

She rummaged through a chest of drawers, throwing clothes on the bed. Finally, she pulled out a pair of white overalls, the kind with suspender straps. She kicked off the high heels and stepped into the overalls, pulling the straps over her breasts. She wouldn't disappear in a crowd, but at least she wasn't flashing a hundred yards of skin.

"You look beautiful," I said.

She threw me a smile, lacing up a pair of dirty white sneakers. "I'm ready," she announced, bouncing off the bed to me. She wasn't the only thing bouncing.

"Belle . . ."

"What now?"

"Could you put on a bra too?"

She took off her glasses, unsnapped the suspenders, pulled the red T-shirt over her head. She found a white bra with heavy shoulder straps. Slipped into it, hooked it in front.

"I didn't know they made them that big," I said, watching her.

"Boobs?"

"Bras."

She slapped me on the arm, smiling, pushing me to the door with her hip.

**43** ‖ I HELD the car door open for her. She slid across and flicked the in-side handle to let me in. I wheeled the Plymouth in a tight U-turn and headed back to the city. When we hit the highway, I shoved a cassette into the dash. Belle sat with her back against the door, feet on the seat between us, hands clasped around her knees. Smoking and listening. Charley Musselwhite's harp barking its challenge on "Stranger in a Strange Land." Buddy Guy driving his mojo north to Chicago, Junior Wells riding shotgun. Lightning Hopkins being sly about grown-up schoolgirls and John Lee Hooker threatening anyone with an eye for his woman. Paul Butterfield riding the mystery train.

The tape looped over to the Brooklyn Blues. One group after another slipped through the speakers and surrounded us. The Jacks, the Chantels, the Passions. When I heard Rosie and the Originals, the clear, high voice of the girl singer hitting "Angel Baby" like no one else ever could, I kicked out the cassette.

I felt Belle's eyes on my face. "Remind you of something?"

"Yeah," I said. Dancing with Flood in the warehouse garage, helping her pull it back together before her last fight. I should have erased the fucking thing.

We were heading toward the Midtown Tunnel. I pulled into the Exact Change lane, tossed a two-dollar token into the basket, and slid into the right lane. When we pulled up outside the magazine on Second Avenue, it was already past six.

"Go inside and tell the guard you're there to pick up a package from Mr. Morelli," I said.

She didn't ask any questions. She was back in a minute, tossing a thick manila envelope on the seat between us.

"Where're we going, honey?"

"You wanted to meet Pansy," I said, pointing the car downtown.

**44** I TUCKED the Plymouth into the garage, showed Belle the back stairs, motioning her to go ahead. Her swaying hips narrowed the staircase.

She knew how to act—didn't make a sound on the way up. When we got to the office door, I gently pushed her to one side while I worked the locks. I went in first, saying "Pansy, jump!" as soon as I did. She hit the floor, paws out in front, her monster's head tilted up to watch Belle.

I made the hand motion that said everything was okay, and told Belle to come in.

"This is Pansy," I said.

Belle stood on the threshold of the office like she was rooted. "Good sweet Jesus! That's a *dog*? He looks like a swamp panther. What kind is it?"

"*She's* a Neapolitan mastiff. The most beautiful Neapolitan mastiff in the world, aren't you, girl?" I asked Pansy, rubbing her head. Pansy growled agreement, her tongue lolling in happiness. Belle hadn't moved.

"Go sit on the couch," I told her. "It's okay."

Belle obediently went to the couch, sat down like she was in church, knees pressed together, hands in her lap. I spread my arms wide, telling Pansy she was released. The beast plodded over to Belle, sat in front of the couch, cocked her head.

Belle didn't move. Pansy rammed her head into Belle's lap, shoving at her hands, demanding a pat. Or else.

"She won't hurt you," I said.

Belle gave Pansy a halfhearted pat on the head. The beast made a rumbling noise in her chest. Belle jerked her hand away. Pansy shoved her head back in Belle's lap.

"She just wants to be friends."

"Burke, I swear to God, she's scaring me to death."

"That's her happy noise," I assured her.

"How much does she weigh?"

"About the same as you."

"I'd kiss you for that if I wasn't scared to move off this couch."

I went into the next room, pulled a couple of strips of steaks out of the refrigerator, tossed one at Pansy, saying "Speak!" as I did. The steak disappeared. I threw the other piece on the floor and watched Pansy drool over it.

"Why won't she eat it?"

"She's waiting for the word."

"What you just said?"

"Yep."

Belle looked at Pansy, said "Speak!" in the same tone I'd used. Pansy ignored her. "It only works when you say it?"

"That's right."

"Well, *say* it, then. The poor dog's dying for the meat."

Pansy flashed Belle a grateful look as I gave her the word. As soon as she polished off the steak, she came back to the couch. Belle patted her with a bit more confidence. "I think she likes me, Burke. Does she do any more tricks?"

"Those aren't tricks," I told her. "Pansy works. Just like you and me."

I threw Pansy the signal and she came over to the door. I opened it and she disappeared into the dusk.

"Where's she going?"

"To the roof."

"It must be beautiful—can we go up there?"

"Belle," I said, "trust me. That roof's one place you never want to go."

"Can I get up?"

"Sure. It's okay—Pansy understands."

I showed Belle the rest of the office. I let her poke around by herself while I laid out the clips Morelli got for me on the desk, thinking I should have heard from the Prof by then.

Belle walked in, put a hand on my shoulder. "Pansy will know me from now on?"

"Sure."

"So if I came here by myself . . . if I had a key . . . she'd let me in?"

"She'd rip you to pieces, Belle."

"Oh," she said in her little-girl's voice, watching as Pansy came back inside and curled up in a corner.

I stubbed out my cigarette, anxious to get in the street, see if the Prof had called in.

"Want some dinner?"

"If you do, baby."

"I thought you were starving."

"I can wait for what I want," she said, her voice still too small for her body. "I waited for you."

So she went through a lot of résumés looking for the ideal hi-jacker. Big deal. "Let's go," I told her.

Belle was still rubbing my shoulder, watching the dog. "Will she get jealous if I kiss you?"

"She couldn't care less."

"That's my kind of girl," Belle said, and kissed the side of my mouth.

45 ‖ THE JOINT I took her to just says "Bar" over the green metal door. A hustlers' hangout off West Street, it serves decent food in the back room, all the tables set aside in booths so people can do business.

I left Belle in the booth to call Mama from one of the pay phones in the bar. I dialed the number that rings at her desk, in the front of the restaurant. She said something in Cantonese.

"Anything?" I asked.

"No calls," she said, recognizing my voice.

I hung up, went back inside. A redheaded waitress was talking to Belle. I recognized her as I got close. MaryEllen. She'd been working there for years. It was a nice quiet joint, no grab-ass drunks, all business.

"What'll it be?" she asked, like she'd never seen me before. My kind of place.

"You order?" I asked Belle, watching her settle into the booth. Sitting down, she was shorter than me—I guess most of her height was legs.

"I waited for you, honey."

I looked up at MaryEllen. There's no menu, but the food doesn't vary much.

"We have some real nice shell steaks."

I looked a question at Belle. She nodded. "One medium and one . . ." I looked at Belle again. "Rare," she said. I ordered a ginger ale. "You have beer on tap?" Belle asked. MaryEllen shook her head no.

"What brand?"

"Cold," Belle said, smiling at her.

Maybe she had been starving—Belle TKO'd her steak in the first round. She had two more beers and half my potatoes before I was halfway through. "You want another one?" I asked her, joking. She nodded happily. Even with the head start, we finished about the same time.

MaryEllen cleared the plates off. I lit a smoke.

"Don't they have dessert?" Belle asked.

"Not here," I told her. "You want coffee?"

"Can I have ice cream later?"

"Sure."

I was smoking my cigarette, thinking about the Prof. Belle sipped her coffee, watching me quietly. I felt a hand on my shoulder, a lilac-and-jasmine smell. Michelle. Wearing a wine-colored silk sheath, a black scarf at her throat. She looked a question at me. I moved over so she could sit down next me. She gave me a quick kiss as she slid in, turned to look at Belle, talking to me out of the side of her mouth.

"Hi, baby. Who's your friend?"

"Michelle, this is Belle."

Michelle held out a manicured hand. "Hi, honey."

"Hello," Belle said, shaking her hand. Holding on to it too long, watching my face.

Michelle took her hand back, figuring it all out in a split second. "Don't look at me like that, girl. This ugly thug's my brother, not my lover."

Belle's mouth twitched into a half-smile. "He's not so ugly."

"Honey, *please!*"

Belle laughed. "He's got other fine qualities."

"I know," Michelle said.

Belle's face went hard. "Do you?"

Michelle stiffened, her claws coming out. "Look, country girl, I say what I mean. And I mean what I say. Let's put it all out, okay? I never had a brother until Burke came along. I love him—I don't sleep with him. Wherever you go with him, I don't want to go. And where I go with him, you *can't* go. Get it?"

"I get it."

"Get this too. You want to be my friend, you come with the best recommendation," Michelle said, patting my forearm. "You want to be a bitch, you came to the right place. I'll be here after you're gone, girl."

"I'm not going anywhere," Belle said.

"Then let's be friends, yes?" Michelle said, her sculptured face flashing a deadly smile.

"Yes," Belle said, reaching over and taking my hand.

Michelle took one of her long black cigarettes from a thin lacquer case and tapped the filter, waiting for a light. I cracked a wooden match. She cupped my hand around the fire, gently pulling in the smoke. Belle watched Michelle as if she had the answer to all her questions.

Michelle fumbled in her huge black patent-leather purse. She pulled out a sheaf of photographs. Terry. In a blue blazer with gold buttons, wearing a white shirt and a striped tie, his hair slicked down. "Isn't he handsome?" she asked me.

"A living doll," I assured her.

Michelle jabbed me in the ribs with her elbow. "Pig," she snapped. She held the photos out to Belle. "My boy."

Belle took the pictures. "He *is* handsome. Does he go to boarding school?"

I laughed. Michelle jabbed me again. "He most certainly does, honey. One of the most exclusive in the country, I might add. And if it wasn't for certain people teaching him bad habits . . ."

"Don't look at me," I said.

"The Mole does not smoke," Michelle said, ending the discussion.

"How old is he?" Belle asked.

"He's almost twelve."

"He's going to be a heartbreaker when he gets older."

"Just like his mother," Michelle said, ready to talk about her favorite subject for the next few days.

"I can't find the Prof," I told her, bringing her back to the real world.

"Well, honey, you know the Prof. He could be anywhere."

"He was supposed to call in, Michelle. We're working on something."

"Oh."

"Yeah. Will you . . . ?"

"I run on a different track now, baby. But I still have my associates in the right spots. I'll throw out some lines, okay?"

"Tonight?"

"I have a late date—I'll make some calls before I start. If you don't hear by tomorrow, give me a call and I'll take a look myself."

"Thanks, Michelle."

She waved it off.

I got up to call Mama again. She answered the same way.

"Anything at all?"

"Nothing. You worried?"

"Yes."

"Call later. Leave number, okay?"

"Okay."

When I got back to the booth, Michelle and Belle were yakking it up like old pals. Michelle had Belle's face in her hand, twisting it different ways to catch the light. The big girl didn't seem to mind. I sat down, lit another smoke, listening to Michelle rattle on.

"You draw the eyeliner *away* from the center, honey. *Separate* those eyes. And we use a sharper line *here*"—drawing her fingernail across Belle's cheekbone—"for an accent. Are you with me so far?"

Belle nodded vigorously, not trying to talk while Michelle was grabbing her face.

"Now the mouth . . . we use a brush, yes? We paint a *thin* line just past the lips, then we fill it in with a nice dark shade. Widen that mouth a bit. Then we . . . Oh, come on," Michelle said, standing up, dragging Belle by the hand. "We'll be back in a minute," she said to me.

I ignored her. I knew what a minute meant to Michelle. I knew what it meant when the Prof didn't call in.

It was two ginger ales and a half-dozen cigarettes before they came out of the ladies' room, Michelle still leading Belle by the hand. They both sat across from me. I had to look twice. Belle's soft face was sharpened, different. Her eyes looked set farther apart, bigger. Her cheekbones stood out, her tiny mouth was more generous. And her hair was pulled over to one side, tied with Michelle's scarf.

"You look beautiful," I said.

"You really like it?" she asked.

"Honey, face it, you're a traffic-stopper," Michelle told her. "All it takes is a little work."

"Michelle, you're a doll," Belle said.

"They all say that." Michelle smiled. "Don't they, Burke?"

"Among other things."

Michelle was in too good a mood to pay attention to me. "Stripes," she said to Belle. "Vertical stripes. You're big enough to be *two* showgirls, sweetie. And watch the waist—you cinch it too tight, your hips look huge."

"He likes my hips," Belle said, smiling at me.

"All lower-class men like big hips, honey. Don't pay attention to him."

Belle looked at me. "You've got some family. A little black brother and a big Chinese one. And a gorgeous sister."

Michelle flashed her perfect smile. "It's the truth, girl."

She gave each of us a kiss. "I've got to go to work—my baby needs violin lessons."

Belle kissed her back. "Thanks, Michelle. For everything."

"Fry their brain cells, honey," she said, "and watch the walk."

A quick over-the-shoulder wave and she was gone.

**46** I WAS stopped at a light at 43rd and Ninth when Belle's baby voice poked through the mist in my brain.

"Honey . . ."

"What?"

"We've been driving around for two hours. Around and around. You haven't said a word to me—you mad at me for something?"

I took a breath, glanced at my watch; it was past eleven. I was just going to make one quick sweep of the city, see if I could spot the Prof. I replayed the path in my head: both sides of the river, Christopher Street to Sheridan Square, across Sixth Avenue to 8th Street, back downtown to Houston, across to First, through the Lower East Side to Tompkins Square Park, outside the poolroom on 14th up to Union Square, across to Eighth Avenue and up into Times Square, working river to river into midtown. And back again. Driving through the marketplace, somebody selling something every time the Plymouth rolled to a stop. Crack, smoke, gravity knives, cheap handguns, watches with Rolex faces and Taiwan guts, little boys, girls, women, men dressed like women. Cheap promises—high prices. Murphy Men selling the New York version of safe sex—the hotel-room key they sold you wouldn't open the door, and they wouldn't be standing on the same corner when you went back to ask for better directions. Islands of light where flesh waited to take your money—pools of darkness where wolf packs waited to take your life. And vultures to pick your bones.

Something else out there too. Something that would make the wolves step aside when it walked.

I looked over at Belle. She was facing out the windshield as though she didn't want to see my face, twisting her hands together in her lap. It hurt my heart to watch her—it wasn't her fault. "You're a good, sweet girl," I told her. "It has nothing to do with you; I'm looking for my friend."

"The little black guy?"

"Yeah."

"I've been looking too," she said, her voice serious. "You think we should get out? Ask around?"

I patted her thigh. She was down for whatever it took—knew I had to do this. I couldn't explain how it worked to her. Asking around for the Prof could get him in deeper than he already was.

I drove back to the river, turned downtown until I saw a pay phone. Mama still had nothing for me. If the Prof had been swept up by the cops, he'd get a call out sooner or later. Nothing to do but wait.

I sat on the hood of the Plymouth, feeling the warmth of the engine through my clothes, watching the Jersey lights across the river. I felt compressed. Things were moving too fast—not like they were supposed to. Belle was inside my life without the preliminaries. We'd made some deals without talking them over—she'd been in my office, Michelle was showing her baby pictures and giving her makeup advice. I was going to help her hijack some hijackers. All too fast.

The Prof was lost somewhere in the freak pipeline under the city, and I couldn't go after him without spooking the shadows.

I got back into the car, started the engine.

"I'll take you home," I said.

"Will you stay with me?"

"I have to leave a phone number. Where I can be reached tonight."

"Why don't we go to your house?"

"There's no phone there," I told her. She hadn't put it together that I live in my office.

She lit a smoke, watching me, her voice soft. Not pushing. "What if I don't want my number given out?"

"It's okay. I'll drop you off. See you soon, all right?"

"No!" It sounded like she'd start crying in a minute. "You can leave my phone number. I know it's important, Burke. I'm sorry, okay?"

"Yeah."

"Can't we go to your house first?"

I looked a question at her.

"So you can pack a suitcase."

I tried to smile at her, not knowing if I pulled it off. "I can't stay with you, Belle. Not while this is going down."

"But when it's over . . . ?"

"Let's see what happens."

She moved close to me, gave me a quick kiss. "*Whatever* happens," she said.

I pointed the Plymouth out of the city.

47 | IT WAS past two when I called Mama from Belle's phone. I gave her the number where I'd be, told her I'd call when I went on the move again. She didn't tie up the phone lines telling me not to worry.

"Where's the nearest pay phone?" I asked Belle.

"About four blocks down. Outside the grocery store on the right."

"I'll be back in a few minutes," I told her.

"Honey, why don't you use this phone? If it's none of my business, I can step outside on the deck until you're finished."

"It's you I'll be calling. Make sure your phone works, okay?"

She watched my face. "Whatever you say."

I found the pay phone, called Belle's number, listened to her answer, hung up.

The walk back didn't help—I could work it out in my head easy enough, but the answers were no good. The Prof was dead reliable. If he hadn't called in, he was in trouble, or he was dead. Either way, I had a debt.

Belle let me back in. I checked the phone; the cord was long enough to reach anyplace in the little cottage, even out onto the deck. I asked Belle for a fingernail file. Then I flipped the phone over, opened it up, checked the contact points, making sure the bell would work. I closed it back up, turned the dial on the underside to the loudest setting. I put the phone back on the end table near the couch, watched it.

Belle's voice came through the fog. "You can do everything to phones but make them ring, huh?"

The room came back into focus. Her face was scrubbed clean, but the glow was gone. "What is it, Belle? You look like you're afraid of me."

"I'm afraid of you shutting me out."

"This isn't yours," I told her, my voice flat.

Belle's hands went to her hips. Her little chin tilted up, eyes glistening. "What kind of a woman do you think I am?" she demanded.

I shrugged, knowing it was cruel, locked into my own course.

She moved closer, taking up all the space between us. "I said I was going to love you, Burke. You think I'd make you tell the truth and not do it myself?"

"No."

"You think I told you the truth?"

"Yes."

"You know what I want?"

"Sure."

She bent down to where I was sitting, pulled the cigarette out of my mouth, pressed her nose against mine.

"Tell me what I want."

I didn't move, didn't change expression. "The back of the joint where you work—it's like a suitcase with a false bottom. Plenty of room back there. Armored car gets hit at the airport—the hijackers take off running. But they don't go far, right? They pull in the back of the joint, stash the getaway car, and walk into the club. When the cops come looking, they've been there for hours. An alibi and a hideout all in one. Easy to come back in a few weeks. Move the cash out." I took the cigarette out of her hand, leaned back, took a deep drag. "How do they get rid of the getaway car—chop it down? repaint it back there? drive it into the back of a moving van, dump it in the swamp one night?"

She didn't answer me. Just watched.

"All that money just sitting there. Clean, unmarked bills. Probably two or three good jobs stashed in one place. Couple of hundred grand, minimum. Wouldn't be the first time somebody turned around and hit the syndicate. Hijackers aren't like numbers runners—that's why they don't make good employees."

I took a last drag, stubbed out the butt. Feeling her eyes burn on my skin.

"Whoever set this up, it's a big operation. Costs a lot of cash to front. The syndicate probably takes a piece from every hijacking at the airport. That's the way they'd do it. I know how things work. All the young mob guys want to do today is move product. They leave the armored cars and the banks to the independents."

I lit another cigarette, thinking back to the way I used to be. Telling the truth, the way she wanted it.

"A good thief, he can't stand to see a big lump of cash sitting around. Just a matter of time before some crew takes a shot."

Belle took the cigarette away from me again, put it to her lips. A red dot glowed in front of my face. Two more in her eyes.

"You didn't answer me, Burke. Tell me what I want. Tell me the truth."

"You want me to hijack the cash."

I saw her right shoulder drop, but I kept my eyes on her face. Her hand came around in a blur, her little clenched fist catching me high on the cheekbone just under the eye. She drew back her fist again. "That's enough," I said.

Her mouth trembled. The firelights went out of her eyes. She pulled away from me, fell face-down on her big white bed. Cried softly to herself as I pulled some ice cubes from the refrigerator. I wrapped the ice cubes in a towel and held it to my face. Sat by the phone.

**48** W H E N I woke up, it was past four o'clock in the morning. My jacket was soaking wet on the left side. I snatched the phone. Dial tone.

"It didn't ring." A soft voice from the bed. "I've been listening since you fell asleep."

"Thanks."

"I'll stay by the phone now. When you get where you're going, you can call me. If you don't get your call by then, you can switch the numbers, okay?"

"Yeah."

"I've got an electric heater: it gets cold by the water in the winter. You can dry your clothes first."

I pulled off my jacket, unbuttoned my shirt. Belle came off the bed. I handed them to her. "Your face is swollen," she said, her voice a breathy whisper, the way you tell a secret.

"It's no big deal. Nothing's broken."

"My heart is broken," she said. Like she was saying it was Wednesday morning.

"Belle . . ."

"Don't say anything. It's my fault. I made a mistake. I wanted a hard man. A hard man, not a cold man."

I lit a smoke. She came back over to me, her voice sad now. Sad for all of us. "Not a cold man, Burke. Not a man who wouldn't take my love."

"I just . . ."

"Yeah, I know. You think telling the truth's not a game for a woman to play."

"That's not it."

"No?" she challenged, her little-girl's voice laced with acid. "You think I couldn't find a cowboy to stick up a liquor store for me? You don't think I could pussy-whip some guido into picking up a gun? Sweet-talk some cockhound into showing me what a big man he is?"

"I know you could."

Belle stalked the room, unsnapping the suspender straps, pulling the T-shirt over her head, unhooking the bra. She worked the zipper, pulled the white pants over her hips. She sat down on the bed. Unlaced her sneakers, threw them into a corner. She went over to the kitchen corner, where my shirt and jacket were stretched on coat hangers, baking in the glow from the electric heater. She picked up my shirt. "It'll dry better this way," she said, slipping into it. She tried to button it; it wouldn't close over her breasts.

She fell to her knees beside me, hands on my thigh, looking up at my face.

"Can we have another chance?"

"Who's 'we'?"

"You and me."

"To do what?"

"To tell the truth. Let me tell you the truth. The real truth. I swear on my mother," she whispered, one hand making an X on her breast. "That's my sacred oath."

"Belle . . ."

"Don't hurt me like this, Burke. I'd never hurt you. You don't know what I want. You don't have any idea. Let me say what I have to say."

She got to her feet, held out her hand.

I took it.

She pulled me to her bed. "Sit down," she said. She took a fat black candle, grounded it in a glass ashtray, positioned it on top of the headboard of the bed. "Light it," she said.

I fired a wooden match. I heard a click—the electric heater snapping off. Belle laid back on the bed, her hands behind her head. I sat next to her, watching the tiny candle flame.

"This is the truth," she began. "I grew up in a little place you never heard of. In South Florida. Just me, my father, and my big sister. Sissy. We lived on the edge of the swamp in a tiny house. Not much bigger than this one. My father did a little bit of this, a little bit of that. Like everyone there. Grew some vegetables out back. Made some liquor. There was a mill nearby—he'd work when they had work. Shoot him some gator for the hides. Fix boats. We lived poor, but nice. When my father would make a good score, he'd always buy something for the house. Had a big old freezer, nice color TV. Good boat too. Mercury outboard." Her voice trailed off, remembering. I lit a cigarette, handed it to her.

"I was always told my mother died giving birth to me. Sissy really raised me—took care of me—my father never paid me any attention."

She took a drag on the cigarette, looking at the dark ceiling.

"I was a big, tall girl, even when I was real young. And skinny too—you believe that?"

"Sure."

"I was. Like a board. Ugly old skinny girl with no kind of face at all. Sissy was pretty once. You could tell by looking at her in the morning light. Sissy was hard on me. I had to do my chores *sharp*, or she'd let me know it. Homework too. We had a school, all the kids together in one class. Sissy made sure I did my homework. Always sent me to school clean, no matter how things were at home. She never had a new dress in all the time I knew her. Said it didn't matter to her. She had nice nightgowns, though. She caught me trying one on once and she took a switch to me so hard I didn't want to sit down for a couple of days. Anything she had, she'd give to me. Except those nightgowns. Or her perfume."

She took another drag.

"My father never much bothered with me. Once in a while, I'd do something to make him notice me. Pay some attention to me. He didn't care if I did my homework, but he had to have his coffee just so: dark coffee with a big dollop of cream across the top; he never mixed it.

"I talked back to him once. He grabbed my arm, pulled off his belt to give it to me. Sissy jumped in between us, kitchen knife in her hand. The devil was in her face—you could see it. You never put a hand on that child, she told him.

"He backed off. Told her I had it coming, but he wouldn't look her in the face. Sissy said if I had something coming *she'd* be the one to give it to me. Go ahead, my father said, give it to her.

"Sissy ripped the belt out of his hands, dragged me outside to the back. You better yell now, she told me. *Loud!* She whipped me something fierce that time. Brought me back inside by the hand, told me to get to work on my chores and keep my mouth shut. My father was watching us when we came in. Sissy went back in the bedroom. I saw her taking one of her nightgowns out of her drawer. My father went back there too."

She drew on the cigarette again, the flame close to her hand.

"My father was real drunk one day. Late in the afternoon, swamp shadows across the back of the house. I heard him fighting with Sissy when I came back home. I swear I'll kill you, Sissy told him. He just laughed at her. Slapped her hard across the face. I went after him. He threw me off, but I got up again. Sissy and me fought him until he was out of wind. He just lay there on the floor, looking up at us. I'll be back tonight, he told Sissy, I'll be back, and I'll take what's mine.

"He staggered out the door. Sissy grabbed me, took me to the back of the house. Your time has come, she told me. She took out a suitcase. I didn't even know she had one. Put all your clothes in this, she told me. Don't argue. I helped her fill it up. I thought we were going to run away together. We snuck out the back, into the swamp. Sissy showed me a marker on a cypress tree, where she'd cut it with her knife. She gave me a shovel and told me to dig. Deep. I found an old mason jar, wax-sealed. Found two more. Sissy broke the jars open. There was near a thousand dollars in the jars."

Belle yelped—the cigarette had burned into her fingers. I held out the ashtray and she dropped it in, put her fingers in her mouth for a second to suck on them.

"Sissy sat me down at the table. He'll be back in a couple of hours, she said. You take that suitcase and get into the swamp. I'll fix the boat so he can't go after you. You take the back trail all the way through, to where it catches the highway. The late bus to town comes past there about nine—you got plenty of time to make it."

Belle's face was wet with tears, but her voice was the same quiet whisper.

"Where am I going? I asked her.

"You go to the bus station. Take a Greyhound north, and don't stop until you're out of this state. Go north and keep going, Belle, she told me. You're going to be on your own.

"I didn't want to go—I didn't understand. Sissy wouldn't listen to me. You're grown now, she said. Almost fifteen years old. I held him back as long as I could, baby, but now your time has come. You got to mind me, Belle, she said. This one last time. You got to mind me—do what I say. She took her nightgowns out of the drawer, threw them in the suitcase too. Your nightgowns . . . I said. I won't be needing them anymore, she told me. I think I knew then. For the first time."

Belle was crying now, working hard to keep her voice steady.

"I grabbed on to her. Hugged her tight. Don't make me go, Sissy, I begged her. She pushed me away. Looked at me like she was memorizing me. Then she slapped me across the face. Hard.

"Why'd you slap me, Sissy? I asked her. Why'd you slap me? You never slapped me in the face in all my life."

Belle took a deep breath, looking straight at me in the dark.

"I slapped you so you'll never forget my name, baby. Don't you ever call me Sissy again, not even in your dreams.

"I was standing there, crying. Sissy rubbed my face where she'd slapped me. So tender and sweet. She kissed me to take away the pain, like she used to do when I was little.

"We heard my father's car pull in. Sissy was calm. I'm not just your sister, Belle. I'm not Sissy. I'm your mother.

"I couldn't move. Go! Sissy said. Go, little girl. I'm your mother. I kept you safe. Now run!

"I ran into the swamp, but I didn't go far. I hid down in a grove,

so scared I couldn't make my legs work. I heard my father yell
something at Sissy. Then I heard this explosion; flames shot up. The
boat. You stay right there, bitch! I heard my father yell. Then I heard
his gator-gun blast off. Once. Twice. He yelled my name. Screamed
it out into the night. I ran through that swamp. My mother wasn't
lying there dead by the boat—she was inside me—running with me—
keeping me strong. She's always inside me."

Belle grabbed me, holding me tight, her arms locked around my
back.

Crying the truth.

**49** I DON'T know how long we were
like that. Belle loosened her hold.
She drew back from me, reaching out a hand to touch my face.

"Does it hurt?"

"No."

"I didn't mean to hurt you. I just wanted you to remember my
name," she whispered.

"I do."

"Will you get in bed with me, honey? Lie down with me?"

"Sure."

She propped herself on one elbow, reached across my chest for
the cigarettes. "I have to tell you the rest," she said.

"You don't . . ."

"Yes. Yes, I do. You still don't know what I want from you."

I fired a match for her and watched the smoke drift out her pug
nose, not pushing her.

"How old do you think I am?" she asked.

"Twenty, twenty-two?"

"I'm almost twenty-nine years old," she said. "It was fourteen
years ago when my mother saved me. I went running. Even when I

was a young girl, they only looked at my chest, not my face. There's always young folks running in this country. I found them—they found me. I made some rules for myself, promises to my mother. I never turned a trick, but I let my tits hang over plenty of bars. I could always make men buy drinks. I never let a man beat me—there's some who wanted to try—big girl like me makes them feel small, I guess. I drove cars too—I'm real good at it. Getaway cars sometimes. I ran 'shine over the mountains in Kentucky. Drove stolen cars from Chicago to Vegas. I thought I was going to be a showgirl there. I've got the size and the body for it, but my face . . ."

"You have a beautiful face, Belle."

"No, I don't. But I know it's the truth to you. Just listen to me, don't talk."

I nodded, rubbing her shoulder.

"I saved my money. I read a lot of books, teaching myself. I'm an incest child. You know what that means? I have my father's blood and my sister's too. That's why my face is so . . . like it is. My eyes close together and all. I have bad blood, Burke. Bad blood. Only the Lord knows what's gone on in my family before I was born. Or what happened to Sissy's mother. My grandmother, I guess. I saw a doctor. At New York University. I told him the truth. He did some tests, but he couldn't tell me anything without testing my father too. I'm all messed up inside. I'm missing a rib here"—she pressed my hand under her heart—"and one leg's a bit shorter than the other. The doctor wouldn't tell me that much, but I made him say the truth."

She smoked in the dark while I waited.

"I can never have a child. Never have a baby of my own, you understand? My father's bloodline has to stop with me."

She felt the question.

"He's down to Raiford State Prison. In that drawer over there, I have all the papers. I was busted once with a station wagon full of machine guns. I rolled over on the people who hired me," she said, watching my face. "They told me it was stolen watches when they asked me to drive."

"They didn't tell the truth," I said.

"Yeah, you understand. They didn't tell the truth. I got a free pass out of it—no testimony, just the names. And one of the feds, he looked up my father for me. He's doing a ten-year jolt for manslaughter; he gets out this Christmas."

"How come he's still in on a ten-year hit if it happened fourteen years ago?"

Belle's face twisted—I saw her teeth flash, but it wasn't a smile. "He never did a day for killing my mother. He shot a man in a dispute over some gator hides."

She pointed her toe in the air, flexing her thigh, drawing my eyes to the tattoo.

"Look close," she whispered. "Look real close. What do you see?"

"A snake."

"When I was running through the swamp that first night, I stopped in a clearing. A snake hissed at me. Cottonmouth, maybe. I couldn't see him in the dark. He had me rooted—too scared to move. Then my mother's spirit came into me and I knew I had to go. No matter what. I threw a branch at the noise and it stopped. A gator wouldn't stop. I was dancing in this club in Jersey. All of the girls had tattoos. Butterfly tattoos. Their boyfriends' names. A rose on their butt. They told me where they got it done. I had the man do a snake. Right on my thigh, pointing at my cunt. A poison snake—that's all the men saw."

I looked hard at the tattoo, knowing there was more. Seeing it. "The snake, it's the letter 'S'."

"Yes. For 'Sissy.' For my mother. It's the only gravestone she'll ever have."

I lit a cigarette. "That's where your dance comes from."

"Tell me," she whispered. "Tell me you see it."

"I see it. There's worse things than gators out there," I told her. "But not as bad as what's in the house."

She kissed my chest. "That's what I wanted," she said, talking fast now, like I'd cut her off before she finished. "That's what I wanted from you. Marques told me he wouldn't meet you without a cut-out. He told me you were a dangerous, crazy man. Said you used to be a hijacker and now you're a hired killer."

"Marques doesn't . . ."

"Ssssh . . ." she said, putting her finger to my mouth. "He said you killed a pimp just because he had a little girl on the street. He said everyone knows you lose your mind when people fuck kids. He said you took money to bring back some runaway girl. You got her away from the pimp, then you shot him anyway."

"And you wanted . . ."

"I wanted you to *rescue* me. I told you the truth, honey. I told you the truth. It's my soul that's lost. My spirit. My mother saved my life—I need someone to save the rest."

"The hijacking . . ."

"I deserve to have my ass beat for that. I played it wrong. I wanted a hard man. I knew I couldn't hold you with sex. I wanted you to rescue me—I wanted to be your partner. I thought if I brought you a solid-gold score, handed it to you on a platter . . . you'd know I was worth something. I didn't want the money."

"Damn."

"Burke. I don't care if you take off the back room. You want to do it, I'll drive the car. And I'll leave the engine running until you come out the door, I swear it."

"And if I don't?"

"I'll go inside and pull you out."

I took a deep drag. "I mean, if I don't want to pull the robbery?"

"I just want you to want me," she said, her voice grave. "I never meant anything more in my life."

I took another drag, feeling so tired.

"I can't rescue you, Belle."

"You let me help you. Help you with your friend. Find that van. Then decide."

I sat quietly, watching the shadows.

"Please, honey."

"Go to sleep, Belle," I said, stroking her back. "If the Prof's okay, you can help."

She closed her eyes on the promise.

**50** ‖ SHE SLEPT with her face against my chest. I brought the Prof's face into my mind, keeping him alive. Seeing the Prof made me see prison. Where we met. I never knew what sent him down that time. Any time the subject came up, the little man made it clear what he was about. "I didn't use the phone, and I came here alone," is all he'd say. It was enough.

The first time I went down, I was a kid. In New York, sixteen years old, you're too far gone for another bit in reform school. I came in with a good jacket: attempted murder. But it wasn't enough. One thing good about all that time in reform school—I knew the rules. I did the thirty days on Fish Row by myself. The Prof rolled up on my cell one day—he was the runner. Said, "This is from a friend," and tossed a couple of packs of smokes and an old magazine in my cell. I wanted a smoke bad, but I left everything on my bunk, waiting for him to come around again. I grabbed him through the bars, pulling him close.

"Take this stuff back where you got it," I said to him, nice and quiet. "I got no friends here."

The little man looked up at me. His eyes had a yellowish cast. No fear in them.

"Here's the slant on the plant, son. Don't play it hard when you not holding no cards."

"I'm holding *myself*," I told him. "You tell whoever gave you this stuff for me that I'm sending it back, okay? And if he don't like it, tell him I'll send it back with interest when I hit the yard."

The little man smiled, not even trying to pull away. "Jump back, Jack! I ain't no wolf, and that's the truth."

I looked over at the cigarettes. "From you?"

"From me, fool. You never heard of the Welcome Wagon?"

"I thought . . ."

"I know what you thought, youngblood. Here's a clue—don't play the fool."

"I can't pay you back," I told him. "I got no money on the books."

"Look here, rookie. I've got more time behind the Wall than you've got on the earth. In prison, first you learn, *then* you earn."

"Learn what?"

"Here's your first case, Ace. Don't smoke the butts. Don't read the magazine. Let it all sit. Don't trust me. When you get into Population, keep your ear to the ground, ask around. People call me the Prophet. I don't stand tall, but I stand up. Take a look before you book."

I let go of him. The little man made his way down the tier, rhyming the time away.

When I got into Population, I moved slow. Asked around, like the man said. The Prophet had some rep. Guys knew him going back twenty years—this was at least his fifth time behind bars. He once did four years straight in solitary for smuggling a gun inside. He hooked up with a guy doing three life sentences, running wild. They took a guard hostage. Got all the way to the front gate when they ran out of room. The guy with him got blown away. The hacks broke half the bones in the Prof's body.

In solitary, they kept at him. Every day, every night. He kept telling them the gun came to him in a vision. Every con in the joint knew where the gun came from . . . where it *had* to come from. A guard. And the Prof was too much of a man to give up even one of them.

It took a few weeks, but I finally saw the Prof on the yard. I rolled up on him, keeping both hands where he could see them. The group of men around him pulled up close. The Prof made a motion with his head and they peeled off, giving me room.

"What's the word, rookie?" he challenged me.

I took the two packs of smokes and the magazine from under my shirt.

"You handing them back?" he asked.

"No. I wanted you to see for yourself," I said, opening a pack, taking out my first cigarette in seven weeks. "Smoke?" I asked him, holding out the pack.

"Much obliged, Clyde," the little man replied, a smile shining.

I hunkered down against the wall with him, my back to the yard, watching. Speaking out of the side of my mouth, looking straight ahead.

"I'm sorry for what I thought."

"That's okay, gunfighter. You just a schoolboy in here."

I wasn't looking at him, but he must have felt the question.

"I glommed your jacket."

"How'd you pull that off?"

"You don't have to pay if you know the way," the little man said.

I did three years on that bit. Not a day went by that the Prof didn't teach me something. When it was near my time to leave, he schooled me about how to act in front of the Parole Board. When the Board set a release date for me, he gave me the hard stuff. Straight.

"You're short now, schoolboy. You know what that means? Thirty days to wait, and you walk out the gate. They'll come at you now. Punks you backed down before, they'll get bold, knowing you don't want to fuck up the go-home. You got two plays: hide or slide."

"Break it down."

"First guy fucks with you, you can go to the Man. Take a PC for the rest of your bit."

"No."

"Yeah, that only works for the citizens. The guys who're never coming back here. That ain't you. So we got to slide. I got people here—leave it to me."

"Which means?"

"Which means young blood is hot blood. You got to be cold if you want to grow old. Someone moves on you, tell them 'later' with your eyes, but don't do nothing right away, okay?"

"Okay, Prof."

By the end of the week, it happened. A big fat jocker named

Moore who'd moved on me early in my bit. I showed him a shank and he backed off. Went looking for easier game—there was a lot of it around. I was sitting at my table during chow when I felt him looking down at me.

"You lost four crates on the Series, Burke. When you planning on paying?"

"You're dreaming, pal. I never bet with you."

"I say you did. You got till Monday. Then I want my four crates or I take it out in trade."

I pushed my chair back, knowing everyone was watching. The Prof made a growling noise in his throat. I looked up at Moore.

"I'll see you before Monday," I promised him, my voice under control.

He walked away, slapping five with one of his buddies.

Late that afternoon, we were on the yard. A pair of bikers broke from their group and came our way. Monster bodybuilders both, their arms were so choked with muscle they had to cock their elbows to walk. I reached for my sock. A bluff—I wasn't carrying so close to parole, but I wanted to give the Prof time to run. He chuckled. "Take a hike, Mike," he said.

I wouldn't disrespect him by arguing. When I glanced back over my shoulder, he was deep in conversation with the gorillas.

Sunday morning, the cafeteria was buzzing when I came in. A black guy I knew slightly from boxing walked by my table. "Right on, man," he whispered. I lit a cigarette to mask my face.

Bongo pulled up a chair across from me, an old buddy from reform school. His trick was using his head as a battering ram in a fight. He'd done it too many times.

"Burke, you hear what happened in the weight room last night?"

I shook my head no.

"You know Moore? That big fat faggot? He decides he's going to bench-press four hundred and fifty pounds, can you dig it?"

"That's a lot of weight."

Bongo giggled his crazy laugh. "Too *much* fucking weight, man.

His spotters musta been bigger punks than he was—they dropped the weight right on his chest."

"What?"

"Yeah, man. Square business. The hacks found him on the bench. Crushed his chest like it was cardboard."

When the Prof finally walked out the gate, I was there.

**51** I LIT another smoke, keeping the Prof alive in my mind. Belle stirred in her sleep. I patted her, saying, "Ssssh, little girl," but it was no good.

"I can't sleep, honey. What time is it?"

"About five."

She pulled her body away from me, shifting her hips so they were against the headboard, her face still on my chest.

"Help me go to sleep," she whispered, rubbing her face on my stomach.

"Belle . . ."

She squirmed lower, gently licking my cock, taking me in her mouth, making soft sounds to herself. I felt myself stir, but it was like someone else.

"Pull my pants down," she said, taking her mouth off me.

I got them past her butt, but that was as far as they could go. A black ribbon across her thighs. I went semihard in her mouth.

"I don't . . ."

"Don't do anything, honey. Please. I'm lonely for you—you're far away. Let me just hold you till I fall asleep."

She put her mouth back on me. In a minute, she was asleep again.

**52** I PATTED her rump, drifting in and out. At least it was a hell of a lot more than time on my hands. Time. Back to prison, where time is the enemy and you kill it any way you can. It was the Prof who got me into reading books. The first time he laid it on me, I laughed at him.

"They don't write down everything in those books," I said.

"Just because you locked in a dump, you don't have to be no chump, bro'. Pay attention. Hear the word. What you going to do when you hit the bricks, get a job?"

"Who'd hire me?"

"You gonna hook up with a mob—kiss some old asshole's pinky ring?"

"No way."

"That's the true clue. You ain't Italian anyway, right?"

"I don't know."

The Prof's face flashed sad for just a second. "You really don't?"

"No. I did the State Shuffle. Orphanage to foster homes to the gladiator schools. To here."

"And you always knew you were coming."

"I always knew."

"Okay, bro', then know *this*. You can't score if you don't learn more, got it? One way or another, you got to steal to be real. And I know what's in your schoolboy head: pick up the gun and have some fun. Right?"

I smiled at the little man, thinking about guns. And banks.

He grabbed my arm, hard. I was always surprised at the Prof's powerful grip.

"You got to go on the hustle, schoolboy. There ain't no fame in the gun game—play it tame, the money's the same."

"I'm no hustler. I don't have the rap."

"Man, I'm not talking about no Murphy Man shit. Or pimping off some little girl either. The magic word is 'scam,' my man. *Use* this time. Study the freaks in here. Watch them close. Learn. How. Things. Work. That's the key to the money tree."

I started reading books just to show the Prof respect. It was his advice—it had to stand for something. I read it all. Everything I could get my hands on. When the prison library ran low, I joined the Book-of-the-Month Club. I scored a couple of dozen books before they threatened to garnishee my salary. I wrote to religious organizations— they sent me books too. I covered hundreds of pages with notes, calculations. Figuring the odds.

When I got out, things didn't work like I planned. It took me another couple of falls to get things down to where I have them now. But I always kept reading, listening. Watching for the crack in the wall.

It was during my second bit that I started reading psychology. I never knew they had sweet words for some of the freakish things people did. The Prof said, if I read the books enough, one day they'd talk to me. I knew what I wanted to be, just not what to call it.

Ice-cold.

Stone-hard.

And I worked at that too.

One day, I was reading a psychology book and a word jumped out at me. "Sociopath." It called to me. I read it over and over. "Sociopath. The essential characteristic of this disorder is a lack of remorse, even for violent or criminal behavior. The sociopath lacks the fundamental quality of empathy."

I ran to the battered old dictionary I kept in my cell. "Empathy: the intellectual identification with or vicarious experiencing of the feelings, thoughts, or attitudes of another." I puzzled it out. A sociopath thinks only his own thoughts, walks his own road. Feels only his own pain. Yeah. Wasn't that the right way to live in this junkyard? Do your own time, keep your face flat. Don't let them see your heart.

A couple of weeks later, I watched the hacks carry an informant out on a stretcher, a white towel over his face. A shank was sticking out of his chest. "That's a nice way for a rat to check out of this hotel," I said to the guys around me. They nodded. I knew what they'd say— Burke is a cold dude.

I kept my face flat. I never raised my voice, never argued with anybody. Practiced letting my eyes go slightly out of focus so I could look in a man's face for minutes without turning away.

Sometimes, alone in my cell at night, I'd say the word softly to myself. "Sociopath." Calling on the ice god to come into my soul. Willing to be anything but afraid all the time.

I listened to the freaks. Listened to Lester tell us how he broke in a house, found some woman taking a bath. Put his gun to her head, made her suck him off. Then he plugged in her hair dryer, tossed it in the water. I kept my face flat, walking away.

Lester grabbed a young boy who'd just come in. "Shit on my dick or blood on my knife," he told the kid, smiling his smile. I took him off the count the next night. He never saw me coming. I hooked him underhand in the gut with a sharpened file, ripped it upward all the way to his chest. I dropped the file on his body, walked away. A few guys saw it—nobody said anything. I let them think it was over a gambling debt.

I read the psychology books again and again. They have some of us pegged. Michelle is a transsexual. A woman trapped in a man's body. *The Diagnostic and Statistical Manual of Mental Disorders* even has a special coded number for it—302.50.

But I never got it to feel right for me—never found the name for what I was. And the number they gave me upstate didn't tell me a thing.

**53** THE PHONE woke me. I snatched it off the hook on the first ring.

"Yeah?"

"Your friend call," Mama said. "He say come to Saint Vincent's Hospital. Room 909. Visiting hour at nine o'clock. You ask for Melvin, okay?"

"Thanks, Mama."

Belle was awake, still twisted like she was when she fell asleep, looking up at me.

"He called?"

"Sure did." I got up. "I'm going to take a shower, okay?"

"Let me use the bathroom for a minute first."

She padded off. I lit a smoke. Melvin was the Prof's brother, a semi-legitimate dude who worked the post office. He must be in the hospital for something or other. If we had to meet in the daytime, Saint Vincent's was as good a place as any.

"All yours," Belle said, giving me a kiss.

I didn't sing in the shower, but I felt like it. Pansy's the only one who likes my singing.

I slipped into my shirt. It smelled of Belle. She was bustling around the little house, a smile on her face. "You're going?" she asked.

"Yeah. I got to be downtown at nine."

"It's not quite six, honey."

"I got to hit my office, grab a shave, change my clothes."

Belle went over to the bed, bent from the waist, looking back at me, her big beautiful butt trembling just a little bit. "You've got some time," she said.

I went over to her.

"This has got to make you think of *something*," she said, her voice soft and sweet.

I slid into her smooth. She dropped her shoulders to the bed, pushed against me. "Come on."

Belle locked her elbows tight as I slammed into her from behind, my hands on her waist. I was lost in her.

"I'm coming," she said, her voice calm.

"Try not to get so excited about it," I told her.

She giggled. Her whole body shook. "I mean I'm coming *with* you. To the hospital . . . oh!"

I blasted off inside her, fell on top of her on the bed. I lay there, catching my breath until I got soft and slipped out of her. "You want a smoke?" I asked her, lighting one for myself.

"No, I have to get dressed," she said, bouncing off the bed.

I didn't argue with her.

**54** THE MORNING was bright and clear. Like I felt. We pulled off the West Side Highway just past the Battery Tunnel. I motored quietly up Reade Street, heading for the river and my office. A mixed crew of blacks and Orientals were taking a break from unloading a truck. The black guys were eating bowls of steaming noodles, working with chopsticks like they'd been doing it all their lives. One of the Orientals yelled something in Chinese to a guy standing in the doorway with a clipboard in his hand. The only word I caught was "motherfucker."

Pansy was glad to see me. She always is, no matter what's in my hands. I love my dog. Guys doing time promise themselves a lot of things for when they hit the bricks. Big cars. Wall-to-wall broads. Fine clothes. Who knows? I promised myself I'd have a dog. I had one when I was a kid and they took him away from me when they sent me upstate. I'll never go to prison again over anything money can buy. Wherever I have to run, I can take Pansy.

The beast took my signal and let Belle inside. I gave her a couple of the bagels we'd brought with us and went inside to shave. When I came out, Belle was sitting on the couch, holding her paper cup of coffee with both hands, her arms stiff as steel. Pansy was lying on the couch, happily slurping from the cup, spilling coffee all over Belle.

"Pansy, jump!" I yelled at her. She hit the floor, spilling the rest of the coffee in the process. "You miserable gorilla," I told the dog.

Belle looked at me, appealing. "I didn't know what to do—I was afraid to push her away."

"It's not your fault—she's a goddamned extortionist."

Pansy growled agreement, always eager for praise.

Belle's white sweatshirt was soaked. She pulled it over her head. "I'll wear something of yours," she said, smiling.

I knew none of my shirts would fit her, but I kept my mouth shut. I found a black turtleneck sweater in a drawer, tossed it to her.

I pulled out a dark suit, nice conservative blue shirt, black knit tie. A pair of black-rimmed glasses and an attaché case and I was set.

Belle looked me over. "I didn't know you wore glasses."

"They're just plain glass—they change the shape of your face."

"That's what I wish I could do," she said bitterly.

"I like your face," I told her.

"It doesn't look like his," she said. "But I still see him in the mirror sometimes."

"If it hurts you, maybe you should fix it."

"You mean like plastic surgery?"

"No."

"Oh. You think . . . ?"

"Now's not the time, little girl."

She nodded. A trusting child's face watching me. Listening.

Just about time to go. I let Pansy out to the roof, blanking my mind. No point speculating—the Prof would have something for me and I'd find out when I saw him.

Pansy strolled downstairs and flopped down in a corner. She wasn't into exercise.

"You want a beer?" I asked Belle.

"Who drinks beer at this hour?"

I pulled the last bottle of Bud from the refrigerator, uncapped it, and poured it into a bowl. Pansy charged over—made it disappear.

**55** SAINT VINCENT'S is in the West Village, not far from my office. "Just act like you know where you're going," I told Belle.

The information desk gave us a visitor's pass and we took the elevator. Room 909 was at the end of the corridor. I walked in first, not looking forward to shooting the breeze with Melvin, hoping the Prof was already on the scene.

He was. In the hospital bed, both legs in heavy casts, suspended by steel wires. A pair of IV tubes ran into his arm. His face was charcoal-ash, eyes closed. He looked smaller than ever—a hundred years old.

My eyes swept the room. Empty except for a chair in the corner. I came to the bed quietly, images jamming my brain.

The Prof didn't move, didn't open his eyes. I bent close to him.

"Burke?" His voice was calm. Drugged?

"It's me, brother."

"You got my message?"

"Yeah. What happened?"

His eyes flicked open. They were bloodshot but clear, focused on my face. His voice was soft, barely a whisper. "I was poking around. On my cart. Scoping the scene, you know? I was working Thirty-sixth and Tenth. By the Lincoln Tunnel."

The Prof does this routine where he folds his legs under him and pulls himself along on a board with roller skates bolted to the bottom. It looks like he has no legs at all. Sometimes he carries a sign and a metal cup. Working close to the ground.

"You want to wait on this? Get some rest?"

His eyes hardened. "They gave me pain, but I'm still in the game. The nurse'll be around in a few minutes to give me another shot. You need to know now."

I put my hand on his forearm, next to the IV tubes. "Run it," I said, my voice as quiet as his.

"You ever hear of this freak karate-man they call Mortay?"

"The one who's hitting all the dojos? Challenging every sensei?"

"That's him. You know Kuo? Kung-fu man?"

"He teaches dragon-style, right? Over on Amsterdam?"

"He's dead, Burke. This Mortay hits the dojo, slaps Kuo in front of his own students. Kuo clears the floor and they go at it. Mortay left him right there."

I let out a breath. "Kuo's good."

"He's good and dead, bro'. It's been going on for a while. This Mortay's been selling tickets—says he's the world's deadliest human. The word is that he was kicked off the tournament circuit—he wouldn't pull his shots. Hurt a lot of people. He fought a death-match about a year ago. In the basement under Sin City."

"I heard about it."

"Every player on the scene was there. They put up a twenty-grand purse, side bets all over the place. He fought this Japanese guy from the Coast. The way I heard it, Mortay just played with him before he took him out. Now he's hooked on it. Death. He finds a dojo, walks in the door. The sensei has to fight him or walk off the floor."

"He's got to be crazy. Sooner or later . . ."

"Yeah. That's what everybody's been saying. But he's still out there."

The Prof took a deep breath. "He does work too."

"For hire?"

"That's the word."

"He did this to you?"

"I'm on my cart, talking to a couple of the working girls, handing out my religious rap. Like I'm the man to deal with the van, you know?"

"Yeah."

"Car pulls up. Station wagon. Spanish guy gets out. Short, heavy-built dude. Big diamond hanging from his ear. Tells me he has someone wants to talk to me. I tell him that I bring the Word to the people, so the people got to come to me. The Spanish guy don't blink an eye. Pulls a piece right there in the street. Tells me he has to bring me, don't matter what condition I arrive in. I tell him not to get crazy— how am I supposed to go, walk? He calls to another guy. They each grab one end of my cart, put me in the back of the wagon. The girls just faded. They're hijacking me off the street, nobody's paying attention."

The Prof's voice was the same quiet flow, his eyes focused on someplace else.

"They take me to one of the piers. Past where they have the big ships. I'm not blindfolded or anything. They haul me inside this old building at the end of the pier. Place is falling apart: big holes in the roof, smells like a garbage dump.

"Guy's waiting for us. Tall, maybe six two, six three. Couldn't weigh more than one and a quarter."

"That thin?"

"Skinny as a razor blade, man. Arms like matchsticks. You'd look like a weightlifter next to him."

"Mortay?"

"Oh, yeah. Mortay. No mystery—he *tells* me who he is. Like his name is supposed to stand for something. He got this weird voice. Real thin, high-pitched. He says that he heard I been asking around. About the Ghost Van. He says that's a bad thing to do. Could make him mad, I keep doing that.

"I rap to him. Try my crazy act. He don't go for it. He says he knows me too. Calls my name—the Prophet. Asks, if I know the Word, why I can't cure myself. Fix my own legs.

"I tell him no man can change the will of the Lord. He comes over to me, kneels down, starts on me with his hands, pressing spots on my face, watching me. Then he says, You lie. Just like that. You lie. He slaps me right off the cart, tells me to stand up. For a minute,

I thought my legs stopped working for real . . . but I got to my feet.

"He says he's going to have to show me it's a mistake to ask questions. I know bodywork's coming up. I got no place to go. I fucked up, brother," the little man said, his voice shaking. "I was scared. You know I don't spook easy, but this freak . . . It was like he was sending out waves. Hurting me inside, and he wasn't even touching me."

I felt Belle behind me. "Wait outside," I told her. I didn't know what was coming, but it wasn't for her to hear.

"It's all right, Prof," I said to my brother, squeezing his arm.

His voice went sad. Shamed. "No, it ain't all right. I lost control, Burke. I put Max's name out. I told this freak the Silent One was my brother. I ran the whole rap. Told him the widow-making wind would tear down his house if he messed with me. I figured if he knew I was hooked up with Max . . ."

"It's the truth. And he's not the only one."

The Prof's face was deep-down sad. "You know what he did? He *smiled*, man. He said he *wanted* Max. In a match. Said he made me walk, he could make Max talk. The freak said he had word out for months that he wanted to meet Max—that Max was dog-yellow.

"I went dumb. It wasn't no act. It was the devil talking to me, standing right there. He said he's been looking for Max's dojo. When he finds it, he's going to take it for himself.

"And then he asked me where it was. Smiling at me. Saying since Max was my *brother* and all, I *had* to know.

"I told him I didn't. I know when a man is lying, he says. Looks at me. Right through me.

"The Spanish guy says something. Mortay flicks his wrist at the Spanish guy's face like he's brushing away a fly. Blood jumps out on the Spanish guy's face.

"Then the freak says to me he sees I don't know where Max's dojo is. So he wants me to give him a message.

"I say okay—tell me the message. He takes this fucking machete from someplace. Hands it to me. Test the blade, he says. Big smile on his face. I touch the edge—it goes right into my hand, draws blood.

"Sharp enough? he asks me. For what? I say.

"I'm going to fix your legs, he says.

"I try and stall him. Put the blade down, take off my coat. Like I'm getting ready to duel with him. I pick up the blade, swing it in both hands. Like I'm testing it? I check the door where they brought me in. Spanish guy standing there, holding the gun. No place to go.

"I was scared, Burke. But shamed too. I knew I put Max's name out. Broke the rules. I'm a man. I never cried when they broke me up in the joint. I have a name too."

"Your name is gold, Prof."

The little man wasn't listening; tears on his face.

"I pulled it together. I called his name: Come on, pussy! He came at me. I hit the floor, flipped onto my back, flashing the blade up at him with both hands—hard. Going to cut his balls off."

The Prof's arm trembled in my hand.

"He *floated* right over me. Musta been six feet off the ground. He comes again. I step to him, blade going side to side, razor-circle. No way in for him. He comes *inside* the blade, chops me on the wrist. The blade goes flying.

"Fun's over, nigger, he says."

The Prof's eyes closed.

"I grab for his eyes. White mist comes. I hear a crack—I know it's my leg. I go down."

His eyes opened.

"When I come around, I'm in the back of the station wagon. Mortay—he's sitting like Max sits. Against the back door, facing me. Taking you to the hospital, he said. Put you in a nice private room—everything's on me. Tell Max *I* did this. Says his name real slow. Two pieces. Like More-Tay. Get it right, he said. Give him my message."

The Prof bit into his lip, reaching inside for what he needed. "You're the only one I called," he said.

"I know."

"I fucked up. Fucked up bad."

"You did the job, brother. This Mortay . . . he's got to be locked into the van somehow."

"But Max . . . ?"

"He *knew* about Max before he ever grabbed you, Prof. That's his own scene. You gave him nothing he didn't already have."

"Burke . . . I never saw nothing move so fast in all my life."

I patted his arm, feeling the little man's fear vibrate through to me.

"I need you on this one, brother," I told him.

"I won't be running no races for a while," he said, looking at his legs.

"It's your brain I need. Knife-fighters are a dime a dozen."

The ghost of the Prof's old smile showed. "If you got a plan, I'm your man."

"They still have the death-matches in the basement under Sin City?"

"They move them around, what I heard."

"Who'll know?"

The Prof thought a minute. "Got to be Lupe, brother. That dude's a battle-freak. Cockfighting, pit bulls, rope-dancing . . . it's a good bet he'll be on the set."

"Where's he hang?"

A bigger smile this time. "Your favorite place, Ace. Every week-night, he's at the end grandstand at Yonkers."

"Which end?"

"Way past the finish line . . . where it looks like bleachers?"

"Yeah, I know it."

"Every night. He sets up matches. Takes a piece."

The little man's eyes moved into stronger focus. Working again. "Light me a smoke."

I fired one for him, held it to his lips. He took a deep drag.

"Lupe's about fifty. Greasy 'do, wears it in an old-style D.A. Pachuco cross on his hand. Short, fat dude. Bad teeth. Got him?"

"Yeah."

The Prof looked up at me, eyes clear. "All the faggot broke was my legs, Burke."

"I know."

"No rhyme this time. This is the true word: he'll be sorry."

"For breaking your legs?"

"For not killing me when he had the chance," the little man promised. Back to himself.

I heard loud voices in the corridor. Pushed open the door a crack. A big black nurse was trying to push her way past Belle and not having any luck.

"It's okay," I told Belle, holding open the door.

The nurse came in, pushing a cart with a metal tray on it. "Time for your medicine," she told the Prof, a West Indian tang to her voice.

The little man winked at her.

"You better hope that ain't no dope," he said, pointing his chin at the hypo on her tray.

"And why is that?" she said, a smile creeping onto her broad face.

"Dope makes me sexy, Mama. I couldn't trust myself around a fine cup of Jamaican coffee like you."

"Never mind with a smart mouth, mahn," she snapped, still smiling, loading the syringe.

The Prof looked at me and Belle. "Look here, fools, can't you see me and this lady want to be alone?"

I waved goodbye. Belle bent over and kissed him.

He was already deep into his rap with the nurse by the time we got the door closed.

**56** BELLE RESTED her hand lightly on my arm as we waited for the elevator, not saying a word. She stayed quiet until we got in the car.

"What happened to him?"

"He was in an accident."

Her face went sulky. "I told you the truth. I told you my secrets. You don't have to tell me yours." She lit a cigarette. "But don't lie to me—I'm a big girl, not a baby. It's none of my business, just say that. Don't tell me stories, you want me to trust you."

"It's none of your business," I said.

She didn't say another word until I hit the highway and she saw where I was headed.

"No."

"No what?"

"No good. What happened to your friend—it's none of my business, okay. But you're going to do something now. I know you have to."

"And?"

"And *that's* my business. I'm in too."

"No, you're not."

"Yes, I *am*. Don't you tell me I'm not. I can do things. I can help."

"Look, Belle . . ."

"*You* look. You think I'm just a piece of ass with a sad story? I'm a woman. A woman who loves you. You don't want my love, you say so. Say so right now."

"I . . ."

"Just shut up. I don't sell my love. I never gave it away before. I said I was going to love you. That *means* something. My love is worth something—you have to give me a chance to show you."

"You'll get your chance."

"How? Coming to see you on visiting day?"

"If that's what it comes down to."

"No! I love you. I swear I love you. I pay attention when you talk. I learn things. You want to mistreat me, I'll still love you. I play for keeps. But you can't disrespect me. Like on that wall you showed me."

"I'm not disrespecting you."

"No? You've got work to do, I should stay at home, right? I'm too fat for an apron, and I don't know how to cook."

I lit a cigarette, blew smoke at the windshield, driving mechanically.

Belle moved in close to me, her hip against mine, both arms around my neck, talking softly into my ear. "You *have* to love me. And you won't . . . not *really* love me . . . unless you let me in. I won't get in the way—I'll just do my piece. You say what it is. But you have to let me in or you'll never see what I am . . . you'll never love me, Burke."

I took a deep breath. Let it out slow.

"You won't free-lance? You'll do what I tell you?"

"I swear."

"I'll pick you up tonight. Around seven."

"Where're we going?"

"The racetrack."

"I thought . . ."

"That's not the deal," I reminded her.

She gave me a kiss, nuzzled against me for a minute, moved back to the passenger side.

"You're the boss." She smiled.

Sure.

**57** ‖ WHEN WE got to her house, Belle bounded out of the car like she was going to a fire sale on salvation. I wheeled the car around and shot back to the city. Lots of work to do.

I pulled in behind Mama's. Grabbed the *Daily News* from under the register and sat in my booth. The waiter brought me some hot-and-sour soup, not even pretending I had a choice. I read the paper, waiting for Mama. Nothing about any new Ghost Van murders. I flipped through to the back. The race results. Mystery Mary came out on top. Wired the field, trotting the mile in 2:00.3. She was three lengths up at the top of the stretch and held on by a neck. Paid $14.20. I was up almost a grand and a half. I couldn't remember the last time

I figured a race so perfectly. I waited for the rush. It didn't come.

Mama moved into the booth. Greeted me, her eyes shifting to the newspaper.

"You win?"

"Yeah."

"I tell Max pick up the money?"

"Yeah. And tell him to lay low for a few days. Stay off the street, okay? I'm working on something—a nice sweet score. Let people think he's gone away for a while."

Mama looked at me, waiting.

"I got to go," I told her.

She didn't say anything.

**58** ‖ I HIT the post office. Told Melvin where the Prof was, gave him the phone number of the private room. Anyone comes around asking for the Prof, he should call me at Mama's, leave the word.

The City Planning Office had the detailed grid maps I needed. I paid for them in cash.

I spent another couple of hours at the library, groping around, not sure what I was looking for.

I drove to the junkyard. Turned around before I got there. It wasn't time for the Mole yet.

I went back to the office. I put the grid maps of the city on the wall. Spread out the clips Morelli got for me. I couldn't make them work.

I went into myself, deep as I could go. I came back empty.

Pansy and I shared some roast beef.

When I looked at my watch, it was time to go.

**59** THE DOOR opened before I could knock. "Close your eyes," Belle said. "Keep them closed."

She led me over to the couch, pushed me into it. "Just sit for a minute, honey—I'm not done yet."

I lit a smoke, looking around. The whole place was a mess—boxes and paper all over the floor, bed not made, ashtrays overflowing.

Belle came out of the bathroom, prancing on a pair of shiny black spikes. Her hair was swept to one side, held together with a black clip. Her face was so different I had to look twice: dark eye liner pulled her eyes apart, sharp lines over her cheekbones. Her mouth was a wide, dark slash. She was wearing a black silk top over a pair of skin-tight pants in a wide black-and-white stripe. Two heavy white ropes tied loosely around her waist. She twirled before me, as pretty-proud as a little girl in her first party dress.

"See. Just like Michelle said."

I stared at her.

"Burke. Say something!"

"Damn!"

"What does that *mean?*" she demanded, moving closer.

"I think my heart stopped. You want to try some mouth-to-mouth?"

The smile lit up her face. "Isn't it great? Michelle's so smart." She twirled again. Stood hip-shot, her back to me. "Vertical stripes," she boasted, patting her hip.

The black-and-white stripes were vertical all the way up her legs. But when they got to her butt, they stopped going parallel and ran for their lives in opposite directions. Flesh stomps fashion every time.

"You're the loveliest thing I've ever seen in my life," I told her, reaching out my hand.

She slapped it away. "No, you don't." She laughed. "I didn't put all this on for you to pull it off."

I got to my feet, reaching in my pocket for the car keys. Belle moved in close to me, holding the lapel of my jacket with one hand. Dark-red polish on her nails.

"Burke, I was only teasing. You want to stay here, it's okay."

I patted her on the rear. "I wish we *could* stay here. We're working, remember?"

"Then why'd you say . . . ?"

"I lost my head."

She gave me a quick kiss. "Wait till later," she promised.

## 60

I ROLLED onto the Belt Parkway, taking it past the crossover for the airport, heading for the Whitestone Bridge. When I saw a break in traffic, I pulled over on the shoulder. Turned off the engine. Belle sat quietly, black-and-white-striped legs crossed, waiting patiently.

"Were you really a driver?" I asked her.

"Oh, yes," she said, her eyes opening wide, watching me close.

"Want to show me?"

She was behind the wheel in a flash, almost shoving me out the door. I went around to the other side, let myself in. Lit a smoke, watching her.

Belle kicked off the spike heels, wiggling her hips in the seat. She wasn't playing around, just getting the feel of the machine. "Can I move the seat back a bit?"

I showed her where the lever was. She took it back an inch or two, extending her arms toward the wheel, looking another question at me. I threw a toggle switch and the wheel dropped into her lap. "Move it to where you want it and I'll lock it in place."

She played with the wheel for a minute, getting it just the way she wanted it, squirming around in the seat, checking the mirrors, rolling her shoulders to get the stiffness out. "Anything I should know?" she asked.

"Like what?"

"Do the brakes grab? Does it pull to one side?"

"No. It tracks like a train. Stops straight. But watch the gas—it's a lot stronger than it looks."

She nodded. Turned the key. Blipped the throttle a couple of times. "No tach?" she asked.

"It's built for torque, not revs. You want to drop it down a gear, just kick the pedal. Or you can move the lever down one from D."

Belle gave herself plenty of room, waited until the traffic was quiet in the right lane. She came down hard on the gas, adjusting the wheel when the rear started to slide, and pulled out onto the highway hard and smooth. She merged with traffic and flowed along, getting the feel.

"Where's the flasher for the headlights?"

"Flick the turn signal toward you. But be careful—the high beams are real monsters."

"Horn?"

"There's two. The hub on the wheel is the regular one; the little button near the rim—see it?—that's for moving trucks out of the way."

She flicked a glance over her right shoulder. "Okay to play?"

"Go," I told her.

She spotted an opening, mashed the gas, shot all the way across to the far-left lane, blew past a dozen cars, backed off the gas, and rolled into the center lane. She pulled the Plymouth so close behind the car in front that it looked like we were going to hit. Kept it right there until the guy in front of us pulled over.

"Follow the signs to the Whitestone Bridge," I told her.

Belle handled the big car like it was part of her, cutting through traffic, moving from one clot of cars to another, staying in the pack each time. When we got to the bridge, she pulled into the Exact Change lane without me saying a word. I handed her a token. She flicked it into the basket without looking. We motored along the Hutchinson River Parkway, Belle still putting the Plymouth through its paces, not talking to me. We came to the last toll before the hook-turn to the Cross County. A guy in a white Corvette was in the lane next to us, coming out of the chute at the same time. Belle goosed the Plymouth, heading for the left lane. The 'Vette jumped out ahead of us. Belle kicked it down—both cars were flying to the same lane, the 'Vette a half-length in front. Belle kept coming. The gap got narrow. I heard the scream of rubber—the 'Vette's driver stood on the brakes as we shot through.

A minute later, the 'Vette steamed by in the right lane, cutting sharply in front of us as soon as he passed. Belle flicked the brights, punching the horn button at the same time. The sky lit up. The twin air horns under the horn blasted the warning call of a runaway semi. The 'Vette ducked out of the way as we went by. Belle slashed over into his lane. I heard the shriek of brakes again.

Belle brought it down to about seventy. We were in the right lane, heading for the hook-turn at Exit 13. Bright lights flooded the back window. Belle reached up, turned the rearview mirror to the side. She hit the hook-turn with the 'Vette boiling up behind us.

"Come on, sucker," she muttered as the 'Vette pulled into the outside lane behind us. She nailed it around the sweeping turn, holding the inside track. The 'Vette roared behind us, closing fast. Belle's mouth was a straight line. She slid the Plymouth into a piece of the outside lane, but this time the 'Vette was ready for her—he darted back to the inside. Belle slashed the wheel back to the right, carrying the 'Vette right off the road onto the grass. She pulled the Plymouth together for the straightaway, swept under the overpass, and slid into the new traffic stream as smoothly as a pickpocket working a crowd.

She patted the steering wheel hard—like you'd do a horse who'd run a strong race. "Good girl," she said.

"You took the words out of my mouth."

She flashed me her smile.

We exited the Cross County and hooked back to the racetrack. I showed her where to pull in: around the back, near the stable area.

Nobody parks there except the horse vans—it's a long distance to the entrance. I gave Belle the buck and a half for the guy collecting the entrance fee, and we motored slowly through, stopping for grooms to walk their horses across the road.

"Park over there," I told her, pointing at a blacktop road that runs behind the paddock. "Leave the nose pointing out."

There are a couple of hundred acres of gravel behind the road. Pitch-dark. Belle turned off the road, stomped the gas, blasting straight into the darkness. She floored the brakes, feathering the gas at the same time, spinning the Plymouth into a perfect bootlegger's turn right into the spot I'd pointed to. She turned off the engine. A whirlwind of dirt and dust flew outside the windows, settling on the car.

"What'd you think, honey?"

"You're a natural," I told her.

Her face went sad. "No. No, I'm not."

I took her hand, squeezed it. "Don't disrespect your mother," I told her.

She gulped. Took a breath. "You always know what to say, Burke."

"I know what to do too," I promised her.

I walked her past the paddock, holding her hand. The black-and-white stripes swayed in the night. I bet some of the mares were jealous.

**61** I PAID our way past the turnstiles. Stopped in the open area to toss a dollar at the guy selling programs from behind a little desk. There was a box of tiny pencils next to the stack of programs. Belle reached past me and took one.

"That's a quarter for the pencil, lady," the guy called out.

Belle looked at him like he was deranged. "For this little thing?" She tossed it back into the box.

"Behave yourself," I told her, taking her hand to lead her outside. A booth about the size of a one-bedroom apartment was set up outside, open along the sides, canvas across the top. Barbecue grill inside. "Want something?" I asked her.

Smart move. She ordered four hamburgers with everything, two beers. The guy behind the counter finally stopped staring and barked the order over his shoulder, not moving his eyes from her chest.

"What're you getting, pal?" the counter geek asked me.

"He gets it later," Belle assured him.

The guy's jaw went from gaping to unhinged.

I paid the money, carrying a beer in each hand, motioning for Belle to climb the stairs ahead of me, admiring the view. We found seats in the outside grandstand, right near the top of the stretch.

Belle put her hamburgers on one seat, took some napkins, and thoroughly cleaned off two more. She took a slug of beer, then handed it back to me to hold for her while she worked on the burgers.

"You see that guy's face?" she asked innocently. "Michelle was right about the makeup."

When she finished eating, I stowed the refuse under our seats, lit a smoke, and opened the program. Belle slouched against me, her head on my shoulder, holding the last beer in one hand.

"What do all those little numbers mean?"

"They all mean something different. You really want to know?"

"Yes," she said, sounding injured.

I went through it quickly, just once over lightly. Showed her how you could tell the horse's age, sex, color, breeding, all that kind of thing. I was up to the comparative speed ratings at the different tracks and she was still paying attention.

"What's the most important?" she wanted to know.

"What d'you mean?"

"Like, all that stuff. It can't all mean the same thing."

"Belle, that's the trick of it. It all means different things to different people. Some people like speed, some people like breeding, some people . . ."

She cut me off. "What about you? You think breeding is important?"

I looked at her face against my shoulder. "Class is what's important to me. Heart. Going the distance. Breeding don't mean a thing."

"But breeding has to count for something, right? Or they wouldn't put it there," she said, pointing to the program.

"They put *everything* on the program, girl. Because the gamblers want to know, see? What possible difference could a horse's color make? That's on there too."

"But it must . . ."

"It does mean something, Belle. I've been looking at horses since I was a kid—I'll tell you what it means—you want to tell if a horse has real class, you look at its mother."

She tilted her head up to me, a smile growing. "Truly?"

"That's the way nature made it, girl. You can never know for sure who the father of a baby is, but there's never a doubt about the mother."

"Never a doubt," she agreed, patting my thigh.

The P.A. system blared into life; the horses were on the track for the first race. Belle watched as they paraded in front of the grandstand behind the marshal. She lit a cigarette, watching everything, leaning forward in her seat, her hand on my knee.

The tote board said two minutes to post time. "Are you going to make a bet, honey?"

"Not this race," I told her, watching.

Belle sipped delicately at her second beer. The very image of a lady, about ten percent past life-size.

The race wasn't much. If I'd had binoculars, I would have looked for Lupe.

Belle finished her beer. "Who's going to win the next race?" she demanded.

I studied the program. Same class, same crop. Mostly older horses on the way down. But there was one four-year-old, a Warm Breeze mare; Hurricane was her name. I pointed her out on the program.

"This one's getting stronger all the time—maybe she's a late bloomer."

Belle lit a smoke. "I like this," she said, watching the horses come out for the post parade. "Which one is ours?"

"The five horse," I told her. "The one with the white blanket."

"She's pretty. Kind of small, though."

At five minutes to post, Hurricane was up to 15–1.

"Let's bet on her," Belle said.

"Okay. I'll be right back," I said, getting up.

"Can't I come too?"

"Come on," I said, ripping the front and back covers off the program and folding the pages into the rungs of our seats to mark them as ours.

She held my hand as we walked to the windows. A group of Latins were standing against a pole, arguing about the race in Spanish. One blurted out *"Mira, mira!"* as we walked by. Belle stiffened. "It just means 'Look at that!' " I said to her, squeezing her hand. "Must be those vertical stripes."

I threw a double-sawbuck down on the mare.

Back in our seats, Belle squirmed, swiveling her head so she wouldn't miss anything. I lit a smoke as they called the horses to the gate. As the car pulled off, the horses charged into the first turn, fighting for position. Hurricane didn't get off quickly—she was pushed to the outside, deep in the pack.

"Oh, she's losing!"

Hurricane moved wide on the paddock turn, gaining a little ground. The three horse was in front, the six next to him, Hurricane running behind the six.

Belle was pounding her fist on my knee, bouncing a little in her seat. "Come *on!*"

Hurricane fired on the back stretch, going three-wide around the horse in front of her, collaring the leader. But she couldn't pull ahead, and the three horse looked fresh. The two of them ran away from the pack into the final turn and pounded for home, not giving an inch.

"Don't quit, baby!" Belle yelled.

The three horse pulled a neck ahead, but the mare wouldn't give it up. She reached down and found something, shot forward again. The crowd roared—the three horse was the odds-on favorite. They crossed the finish line together—too far down the track for me to see who came out on top. "Photo" shot up on the board.

"Did she win?"

"I don't know, Belle. It was close—we have to wait for the photo."

"She didn't quit, though, did she?"

"Sure as hell didn't."

The crowd buzzed. The "Photo" came down and the numbers went up: "5–3–4."

Belle stood up, her hands on the railing, leaning out into the night. "Good girl!" she shouted to the mare. Heads turned toward the sound; the male heads stayed turned. I grabbed her hand, pulled her back into her seat.

Hurricane drove past us, heading for the stable. Belle stood up again, clapping her hands. "Oh, she's beautiful!" she said, happy as a kid at Christmas. The kind of Christmas the Cosby kids have.

I lit a smoke. Almost $350 to the good. With Mystery Mary last night, I was on the longest winning streak of my career.

"Burke, it's just like you said. Heart. She had heart—she went the distance."

## 62

"ANYTHING YOU want to bet in the next race?" I asked her, keeping my voice as neutral as possible under the circumstances.

"No, honey. I don't want to bet anymore. Let's just watch, okay?"

"I'll be right back," I said.

I cashed in the ticket. "Nice hit," the teller congratulated me. The money made a sweet roll.

I sat down next to Belle. "Now, listen—I have to go and see someone. On the other side of the track. You stay here. Don't get out of your seat. Okay?"

"Yes."

"The next race is going to start soon. I'll get up like I'm making a bet. I'll be back as soon as I can."

"Okay."

"Now, *listen*, Belle. And don't tell me anything. If I'm not back by the end of the seventh race, you get up and leave." I pressed the car keys into her hand. "Drive to your house. Call the number you called me at the first time. Ask for Mama. Tell her I met with a man named Lupe. Tell her everything you know."

"When will you be back?"

"I don't know. I'm going down a tunnel. If you don't hear from me in a couple of days, call Mama again. She'll tell you what to do."

"Burke . . ."

I held her face in my hand, grabbing her eyes. "You want to be my woman?"

She nodded.

"This is part of what it costs," I told her.

I didn't look back.

**63** I WENT to the betting windows, put down ten to win on the six horse, slipped the ticket into my pocket. I hadn't looked at the program. I made my way through the track until I was past the finish line. Then I went downstairs, paid an extra buck, and went into the Clubhouse area. I stayed outside, climbing into the dark grandstand at the end, working my way to the top row.

I spotted Lupe in a couple of minutes, sitting by himself in the far corner, wearing a neon-green jacket with some writing on the back. I moved down until I was across from him, making sure. The Prof's description was right on the money.

I lit a smoke, stuck it in my mouth, and moved over to him, both hands in front of me.

"Lupe?"

"Who wants to know, man?"

"Name's Burke," I said, sitting down.

He grinned, showing me his lousy teeth. "I know you, man. I heard of you. You got that monster dog, right? You want to put her in the ring?"

"Only if you get in there with her," I said, keeping my voice even.

"I got no beef with you," he said quickly.

"I got no beef with you either. I heard you were the man to see about a match, that's all."

"What you got?"

"I got nothing. I want to get down on some action."

"You know Van Cortlandt Park?"

"I don't mean dogs, pal. Or roosters either."

"So?"

"I heard this guy Mortay—he's been doing some duels. Heavy action."

"*Mucho* action, man. But this motherfucker Mortay—he only had that one match."

"With the Jap?"

"Yeah! You saw it?"

"No, just heard about it."

His eyes glittered, crazy-cold eyes. "You got someone wants to meet Mortay, man?"

"Yeah. Me."

Lupe laughed. "With what, man? A machine gun?"

"I don't want to fight him—just have a talk. I figured you could set it up."

"No, man," he said, sadness in his voice. "I don't find him—he finds me. He's got this guy, Ramón. He's the one who makes the meets."

"How'd he find the Jap?"

"The Jap found *him*, man. Guy rolls in from the Coast, puts the word out. I hear this Mortay totaled his brother out there. He was looking for payback."

"Didn't have much luck, did he?"

"Man, Mortay don't take prisoners. He *earned* his name. Mortay, man. You get it? *Muerte*. Death. He deals death, man. Eats it alive."

"You don't know where to find him?"

"Man, I don't *want* to know where to find him."

"Yeah. Okay. This Ramón comes around, you tell him I'd like to meet Mortay. Public place, no problems. Just want to talk to him for a minute."

Lupe shrugged. "He comes, I ask him, man. Where you gonna be?"

"Just give him my name. I'm in the phone book," I told him, walking off.

64 || I was back next to Belle before the start of the fifth race.

"Not so bad, huh?" I asked her.

"I waited here, just like you said."

"Good girl."

"But if you hadn't come back, I was going looking."

"That's not what I told you to do."

"I wasn't going to make trouble. Just poke around."

"Yeah, you got a great disguise all right. Nobody'd remember seeing you."

"Burke, I love you. I had to . . ."

"You had to *listen*. Like I told you to. Like you promised. Stupid bitch."

"Honey!"

"You don't want to listen, you can walk. We made a deal."

"I'm sorry, baby. I am. I just . . ."

"Just. Fucking. Nothing. I'm not going to tell you again."

She leaned into me, her hand near the inside of my thigh, whispering. "You want to take me home, beat my ass, teach me a lesson?"

"I thought you said no man ever hit you."

"It'd be worth it," she whispered. "You know why?"

"Why, dopey?"

"You'd have to be there to do it," she said.

I stood up, held out my hand. She took it, meek as a lamb, a little smile on her face.

**65** I DROVE the Plymouth on the way back. Belle was quiet. "You mad at me?"

"I'm not mad at you—I'm not *going* to be mad at you. That's not the way I work. You want to be with me, I have to trust you. That's all there is."

I turned to look at her. A tear rolled down her cheek, tracking through the makeup.

"Okay?" I asked her.

"I swear," she promised, lying down on the front seat, curling up next to my leg. She didn't say another word all the way back to her house.

**66** WHEN I pulled in behind the red Camaro, Belle was still lying across the front seat, her head against my leg. She put her hand on my thigh, grabbed hard enough to hurt.

"You have to come in with me."

"Pretty bossy, aren't you?"

She looked up at me, her face wet, the lovely makeup ruined.

"Just come inside, honey. Come inside—you can be all the boss you want to be, but don't go away now."

I opened my door, got out. Walked around to her side of the car to let her out. I held my hand out to her. "Come on," I told her.

She piled out of the Plymouth faster than I thought she could move.

67 ‖ "DON'T TURN on the lights," she said, pushing me to the couch. She patted my pockets, found cigarettes and matches. Lit one for each of us. The little flame shot highlights into her hair.

"I don't know what to do," she said, sounding lost.

"About what?"

"I want to wash my face. Take these tears off. But if I do, the makeup won't stay."

"Wash your face."

"But you liked the way I looked. You *said* so."

"I like the way you look in those pants too—does that mean you'll never take them off while I'm around?"

"It's not the same thing," she sniffled.

"Yeah, it is," I told her. "Exactly the same thing. Underneath whatever you put on there's still you."

"But . . ."

"But what?"

"That's not the way it is, honey. All my life . . . it's been the same thing. I have to take off my clothes to make a man forget my face."

I held her against me, her face pressed into my chest, talking softly into her ear.

"Listen to me, Belle. You said you'd listen to me, yes?"

Her head nodded against me.

"*You're* the one who doesn't like your face. Because you don't understand it's your *own* face. I know whose face it is, okay?"

She nodded against me again.

"Go take off the makeup," I said, patting her gently.

While she was in the bathroom, I called the Prof. His voice sounded much stronger.

"I'm on the line with plenty of time."

"It's me."

"Back from the track?"

"Yeah. I spoke to the man."

"So we got a plan?"

"No. Not yet. I want to see the guy you talked with. Square the beef. Drop the case. Walk away."

"He's got to pay, but not today?"

"Right. And we don't want anyone else in the game—just you and me."

"He's not going to stop till he gets to the top."

"I'm not sure that's right, Prof. I think this dueling shit isn't the real story—he was riding shotgun on this other thing, and you stumbled into the line of fire."

"Could be, man. But . . ."

"No names, we'll talk later. I'll come and see you. On the first shift, okay?"

"I can't run, son."

I hung up.

68 ‖ BELLE CAME out of the bathroom wearing a black bra over the striped pants, a doubtful look on her freshly scrubbed face. She lit another of her fat black candles, propping it on the sink.

"I'm ugly again," she said.

I gave her a hard look but she didn't flinch. "I looked for myself," she said, her voice sad.

I took a drag of my cigarette. "You want me to fix it?"

"How? Put a bag over my head?"

"Come here," I said, keeping my voice even.

She walked over to the couch.

"Take off those pants."

She reached back to unhook her bra. "Just the pants," I told her.

She stepped out of her spike heels. Even with the zipper all the way down, getting the pants off was a struggle. She stood there in her bra and panties, hands on her hips. "You want these off too?" she asked, her thumbs hooked in the waistband.

"Yeah."

She did, watching me every second. "Now what?"

"Come with me," I said, taking her hand. I led her back to the bathroom, posing her in front of the sink. The candle's flickering glow carried through the open door.

"Lean forward," I told her, my hand on her shoulder. "Look into the mirror."

"I still think . . ."

"Shut up. Just do what I tell you, okay?"

"Okay."

"I'm going to ask you some questions," I said, sliding my hand down to her waist. "Soon as you get the right answer, I'll stop. Got it?"

"Yes."

"Look in the mirror—tell me what you see."

"An ugly old girl."

I slid my hand to her butt, took a plump cheek in my right hand, gave her a hard, sharp pinch.

"Ow!" she yelped.

"Wrong answer," I told her. "What do you see now?"

"The same thing," she snapped, her voice set and stubborn.

I pinched her harder.

She yelped again. "Take another look," I told her. She tried to rub herself—I slapped her hand away.

"I don't care if you pinch it right off, I'm not . . . Burke!" she squealed as I pinched her again. My hand was getting tired.

"I see a beautiful young girl," I whispered to her. "You *sure* I'm wrong?"

Tears rolled down her face. "You mean it? You swear you mean it?"

I squeezed her butt, gently this time. "I've got all night," I promised her.

"This isn't fair," she said, a smile peeking out from beneath the pout.

"Tell me what you see," I said, still holding her in the same place, tightening my hand. "Last chance."

"I see a beautiful young girl," she said. Like a robot.

I pinched the sweet flesh hard. She tried to push past me but I blocked her way.

"Okay!"

I stroked her butt gently. "Tell me."

"I see a beautiful young girl."

"Me too," I said, kissing her.

She came into my arms, baby-soft. I kissed her for a long time. "I'm going to be black and blue," she said against my chest.

"I'm sorry."

"I'm not," she said, pulling me toward the bed. "It's a lot better than being just blue."

**69** $\|$ SOMETHING FLICKED at my brain just before I drifted off to sleep. Something about a letter. I made a grab for it, but I went under before I could pull it close.

When I came around, it was still dark. Belle was lying crossways on the bed, her breasts flattened against my chest, her face buried in the pillow next to mine. She was awake too—I could tell from her breathing.

"What, baby?" I asked her.

She turned her head, propping herself on an elbow. "Baby . . . I'll never have a baby."

"Sure you will. Someday."

"No, I won't. I fixed it. I had a real ugly harelip—you know what that is?"

"Yeah."

"Well, I had a bad one. Pulled up so bad you could see my teeth all the time. I saved some money—went to a plastic surgeon. You know what, Burke? He told me he could fix the whole thing, give me a different face. A real nose instead of this little pig's snout, cheekbones, anything I wanted."

"So what happened?"

"I started on it. He did the harelip first. Did it real good too. But then I went on a job with a couple of boys. It got nasty right in the middle—the wheels came off and we had to fly. We got away, but one of the boys got himself shot up pretty bad. There's this old doctor, back in the hills. We went by his place, stayed there for damn near a month. Cost us every dime we had between us, but he pulled Rodney through."

She fumbled around the night table, looking for a cigarette. Her body gleamed in the flame from the match.

"This old doctor—he was an outlaw. Like us. I don't even know if he was a real doctor and all, but he had good hands. I was pregnant— maybe two, three months gone. I found out while we were holed up. I was just a big dumb old girl—never figured on getting pregnant. When the doc told me, I told him to go and get the baby. Take it.

"He wanted to know was I sure. So I told him. I told him the truth. He said I was right—I was doing the right thing. He said he saw a lot of babies like I was gonna have—said they never did too well. Trying to make it gentle for me, but I knew what he meant."

She took a deep drag off her cigarette.

"He said he could fix me up inside when he went to get the baby. Tie my tubes. I didn't have to think a minute."

Her voice was soft in the night. "I could love a baby—I know I could. But I figured, if I loved a baby, I'd never have one. You understand?"

"Yeah."

"How come you never worried about it?"

"About what?"

"Making me pregnant."

I laughed. "I can't make babies, Belle."

"You tried? With that woman . . ."

"No. I never tried. Never thought about it when I was young. Spent most of my time in places where you couldn't make a baby anyway. I got jumped once. Long time ago. It wasn't a personal thing— I was in the wrong place. Or maybe I was just the wrong color. Doesn't much matter. Anyway, they really did a number on me. When the ambulance dropped me at the hospital, the pain was so bad . . . there's no way for me to describe it to you."

"What'd they do?"

"Broke some ribs. Fractured my jaw. But the real hurt . . . they kicked me in the balls so many times I thought they were going to fall off. The doctor said it was a testicular torsion."

"A what?"

"A torsion . . . like a twist." I held my two fists together in front of her face, twisted one sideways. "Like that."

"Ugh!"

"Yeah. I looked down at myself—the whole sac was black. Before they put me out, the doctor said the blood supply was pinched off— they'd have to cut me open and stitch a new wall inside to hold the balls in place."

"God!"

"I remember telling them, could they do a vasectomy while they were at it. . . . The doctor thought it was funny—like, as long as they were in the neighborhood and all. But they did it. No babies from me either."

"Does that hurt you?"

"No. It's not for me. I don't think about it. But I never told anyone before."

Belle kissed me. "You can tell me anything," she said.

I reached past her. Lit a smoke for myself. My watch said it was past four in the morning.

"Go back to sleep," I said, rubbing her back, pushing against her shoulder.

"I have to sleep on my stomach," she said, a smile playing around her lips.

"You're breaking my heart—I didn't pinch you that hard."

"You *did!*"

"Give it a rest, Belle. I'd need a set of vise grips to do a job on all this," I said, patting her butt.

"I looked in the mirror. While you were asleep. You made a big mark."

"It'll be gone soon."

"I know," she whispered. "That's why I'm sleeping on my stomach. I want to see it again before it goes away."

She put her face in my chest. I felt the tears.

"What?"

"It'll fade away. You will too."

"I'm right here."

"For now."

I took a last long pull on the cigarette, tangling my hand in the hair at the back of her neck.

"It's like you said before, Belle. We're outlaws. Tomorrow's for citizens. For us, it's always now."

"I love you," she mumbled into my chest.

"Go to sleep, little girl," I told her, holding her, kissing her hair. Waiting for daylight.

**70** | I was back up a couple of hours later. I lit a cigarette, walked out onto the deck. A big seagull sat on the railing. He didn't fly away as I walked closer to him, just shifted his head so he could watch me close. He knew he had the whole sky to run to.

I felt Belle behind me. "You better go back to sleep," I said.

"Why? I'm awake now."

"You already missed a couple of nights' work. You're going to be wiped out if you don't get some rest."

"I'm not going back. In that business, girls come and they go. It happens all the time."

"Yeah, but . . ."

"I'm in this with you, Burke. I know you could walk away from me anyway. When it's over. But I got to take this shot. Show you what I can do . . . so you'll want to be with me."

"Look, Belle . . ."

"You promised. Maybe you didn't say the words, but you promised. An outlaw's promise—I'm in on this. I've got some money put away. You won't have to take care of me."

"Hell, I'd have to rob a bank just to feed you."

She slapped me hard on the arm. "I *mean* it. Don't joke around."

She slipped her arms around my neck from behind, pressed against me, talking only for my ears. "I'm going to be with you. I don't want men looking at me anymore the way they do. You made it too late for that." Her grip tightened. "I want a man who looks at my face."

I let out a breath. "Get dressed," I told her.

**71** WE WERE back in my office by seven-thirty. I let Pansy out to the roof, called Mama. No messages came in for me, but she got mine out to Max. One more quick call. The Prof was a little blurred on the phone—I guess they were still shooting him up.

"How you holding up, brother?" I asked him.

"If the Board don't call, it's time for the Wall."

One of his old sayings—if you can't scam the Parole Board, it's time to start working on an escape plan. I guess he was pretty sick of the hospital.

I spread out the street maps on the desk again, stared at them.

Belle's hand on my shoulder. "What're you looking for, honey?"

"I don't know yet."

Pansy came back downstairs. One glance told her the situation. I was working—no point in trying to extort food. Then her beast's brain came as close to an idea as she was ever likely to get. She butted her massive head against Belle's leg, pushing her back a few feet. Belle headed for the couch, but Pansy cut her off, butting at her again.

"What does she want?"

"Food," I said, not looking up.

I heard the refrigerator open. "Well, what suits you?" Belle asked. Pansy growled. "Can I give her some of this brown rice?"

"Heat it up first," I told her, keeping my eyes on the maps.

Belle came back inside. "Honey, is there a store around here?"

"What kind of store?"

"Like a supermarket or a grocery?"

"Not far. Why?"

"I need some stuff."

"Later, okay?"

"But I want . . ."

"Belle, I'm trying to figure something out. Just be quiet for a while, okay?"

She leaned over the desk, her breasts in my face, one hand slipping into my lap. "Maybe you should put something in my mouth . . . shut me up good."

I looked up at her, holding her eyes. "If you won't let me work with you here . . ."

Her eyes went soft and sad. "I was playing."

"Now's not the time."

She leaned closer, watching my eyes. "I know. I thought you'd give me a slap. Where you pinched me last night."

"What good would that do?"

"I have to feel you. You won't let me help. . . . I just want-ed . . ."

"I *will* let you help. But if you don't shut up, I'll never figure out how."

I patted her rump. Gently. "Okay?"

"Okay."

72 ‖ WHEN I looked away from the map, she was curled up asleep on the couch, Pansy was lying parallel to her on the floor.

I snapped my fingers. Pansy's head swiveled. I pointed toward the far corner of the office. She moved with the speed of a runaway fire hydrant. As soon as she was at her post, I went over to the couch. I kissed Belle on the cheek. She came awake. "What is it, honey?"

"I got something for you to do—you awake?"

She rubbed her eyes. "Sure."

"When you spoke to Marques, he call you or did you call him?"

"Both."

"So you have a phone number for him?"

"Sure."

"I want you to call him. Tell him I came by the club and saw you. Asked you to get in touch with him—set up a meeting. Tell him I said any time, any place. About what we talked about the last time."

"What if he has to call me back—where do I tell him?"

"Don't tell him anything. If he can't give you a time and a place right then, tell him to call my number. The one he gave you the first time."

"The Chinese woman."

"Yeah."

"Burke, is she the one? The one you . . . ?"

I ruffled her hair, kissed the back of her neck. "Come on, Belle. We got a lot to do today."

**73** ON THE way to the hospital, I asked her about Marques.

"You know the best time to call?"

"What difference does it make?"

"He's a pimp. He goes off the street before four, five in the morning, the other players will think he's losing a step. Best time to catch him at his crib is early afternoon."

"Sometimes, when I come off my shift, I can't sleep. Maybe I could try him now."

"Yeah, okay. When I go up to see the Prof, you take the car. Find a pay phone, take a shot." I looked at my watch. Almost ten-thirty. "I'll meet you in the parking lot around noon. If you haven't reached him by then, we'll try again."

I pulled up outside Saint Vincent's. "The registration papers are in the glove compartment. You get stopped by the cops, tell them you borrowed the car. It's not on any list."

I showed her the papers.

"Juan Rodriguez?"

"That's me. I met you at the club. Told you you could borrow the car any time you wanted. You've never been to my house. I told you I wouldn't need the car for a couple of weeks 'cause I'd be on vacation."

I gave her a slip of paper with a phone number on it. The phone would ring at the junkyard I own a piece of in the Bronx. The old man who made out my paycheck would tell anyone who called I was on vacation. In Puerto Rico someplace. Juan Rodriguez was the ideal employee—he never showed up for work, but he cashed his paycheck and gave the boss back the money. Fuck the IRS.

"Drive the car like it was hot. Don't call attention to yourself. But if you get pulled over, don't run. If you get a ticket, just take it. Don't say anything."

"All right, honey."

The Plymouth pulled away and disappeared in traffic. Smoother than I ever drove it.

74 ‖ THE PROF looked stronger already. I pulled my chair to the head of the bed and we talked like we used to on the yard. Quiet, each looking in a different direction. The West Indian nurse came in.

"I smell smoke in here," she said, like she'd caught us stealing.

"Smoke don't have a prayer against your own sweet smell, Mama," the Prof sang out.

"There's no smoking in the patients' rooms. Now, you know that *very* well. I have told you before."

The Prof spread his hands to the heavens, seeking divine guidance. "Lord, what must I say to make this woman give me a play?"

The nurse's broad face creased as she fought off the smile. "You smart-mouth little man—I'd break the rest of your bones."

"You don't mean a word of it, a goddess like you."

The nurse had a pill and a plastic cup of dark liquid. "You going to take this medicine with no more of your speeches?"

The Prof regarded her, his fine head cocked to the side. "You know why a man climbs a mountain?"

She sighed, used to this by now.

"So, then. Why does a man climb a mountain?"

" 'Cause the air's so sweet when you get to the top," the Prof said, and popped the pill in his mouth, holding the glass like a toast. "You going to give a poor man a reason to live?"

"You keep messing with me, you *have* no reason to live," she warned him, then waited patiently for the Prof to finish drinking his medicine. Snatched the glass from his hand and stalked out.

"A little more time and she's all mine," the Prof said. He was right—all Mortay broke was his legs.

I lit another cigarette, pulling the half-filled water glass we used as an ashtray from under the bed.

"I went to the track. Saw the man. Like I told you."

"And?"

"He can't put me in touch. Says this Mortay's a death-dealer for real. That duel with the Jap—it really went down."

The Prof dragged deep on his cigarette. "Yeah. But he's no warrior. Not like Max. He's a junkie for it."

"It connects, Prof."

His eyes flashed. "Run it down, home."

"You weren't looking for this freak, right? Just poking around . . . asking about the van."

"Right."

"And this guy's no bodyguard. You must have stepped on his turf by accident."

"It's not enough. We need to know more if we going to score."

"I'm working on it. I told this Lupe . . . the guy who makes matches . . . I want to meet."

"You not going to bring Max?"

"Max is out of this one, Prof."

He reached his hand across the bed. I squeezed it.

"That seals the deal," he said.

"Right. You getting anything over the wire?"

"Not yet. It'll come, though. I got a lot of hooks floating."

I stood up to leave. "You need anything?" I asked.

"I need a nurse," he said.

**75** BELLE WAS behind the wheel of the Plymouth as I came through the parking lot, reading a newspaper spread over the steering wheel. She had the car moving before I closed the door.

"Very nice," I told her.

"This is some lovely car."

"You're some lovely woman. You call Marques?"

"No answer. Can't we try him from your office?"

"That phone's no good past eight in the morning. You can't stay on the line more than a minute anyway. I'll show you where to pull over."

We found an open pay phone by the river. I handed Belle a quarter. She took one of those premoistened towelettes from her purse, ripped off the foil, wiped down the mouthpiece.

She dialed the number. Waited. Somebody picked up. I only heard her end of the conversation.

"Could I speak to Marques, please?"

.   .   .

"Belle."

We waited a couple of minutes. I opened my palm to show her I had another quarter ready.

"Hi. Remember that man you wanted me to call for you? Burke?

He came by the club. Said he wanted to meet with you. About what you talked about the last time."

.  .  .

"He said it was up to you. Any time. Any place."

.  .  .

"No, he didn't seem mad at all. He just said he needed information about the scene, and you were the best person. . . . He didn't want to poke around without checking with you, he said."

.  .  .

"Okay. Wait, let me write this down," she said, signaling to me. I nodded. "Go ahead," she said into the phone.

.  .  .

"Junior's? Where's that? Oh, he'll know."
I nodded to her again.
"What time?"

.  .  .

"Eleven. Okay. And tell him not to bring his friends? Sure. Okay, thanks. I'll tell him—he said he'd call me before I go to work tonight."
She put down the phone.
"Good girl," I told her.
She tossed her head, smile flashing in the sun. "You just wait and see," she promised.


**76** ‖ I TOOK the wheel. As I pulled out, I noticed the back seat full of cartons. "What's all that stuff?" I asked her.
"Stuff I needed," she said. Case closed.
"You hungry?"
She made a noise like Pansy does when you ask her the same question.
I pulled in behind Mama's, taking Belle by the hand as we walked

through the kitchen. Mama's collection of thugs watched us impassively—they'd seen stranger things come through the back room.

The joint had a few customers—no way to keep them all out at lunchtime—but my booth was empty, the way it always is.

The waiter came over to us, blocking Belle's side of the booth, looking a question at me with his eyes. I shook my head, telling him Belle wasn't trouble. He flicked his eyes toward the front of the room. I nodded—send Mama over.

Mama's dress was a deep shade of red. Opal earrings matched the ring on her hand. She returned my bow, face a mask.

"Mama, this is Belle," I said. "Belle, this is Mama." I said it carefully. Nice and even, same tone of voice. Mama was stone-solid reliable when it came down to a crunch, but she was funny about women.

She bowed. "Friend of Burke, friend of Mama."

Belle started to reach out her hand, thought better of it. Bowed gently. "Thank you, ma'am." Polite as a little girl in church.

Mama slid into the booth next to me, barking something in Cantonese over her shoulder.

The waiter brought the soup. Mama served me, then Belle, then herself. Watched carefully, smiling with approval as the bowl emptied. "You have more soup?"

"Yes, please. It's *delicious*."

Mama bowed again. "Very good soup—good for strength. Special for my people. Always here."

Belle looked a question.

"Burke my people," Mama said. No expression on her face, nothing in her tone. But a low-grade moron would have caught the warning.

Belle quietly worked her way through beef in oyster sauce, snow-pea pods, water chestnuts, fried rice, hard noodles, paying no attention to us.

Mama took a look at the empty plates, raised her eyebrows, called the waiter over again. Belle had a portion of lemon chicken, washing it all down with some Chinese beer. She patted her face with her napkin. "Oh, that was *good!*"

"You want more?" Mama asked.

Belle smiled. "No, thank you."

"You come back sometime. When no more trouble, okay? See my granddaughter, yes?"

"You have a granddaughter?"

"Why not?" Mama asked, her face hardening.

"You don't look old enough."

A smile flashed. Disappeared. "Plenty old enough. Burke explain to you sometime."

"Do you have pictures of her?"

Mama scanned Belle's face, taking her time. "Many pictures," she said, tapping her head. "All in here."

Belle walked past the warning like she hadn't heard it. "What's the baby's name?"

"Flower."

Belle sipped her tea, prim and proper. Her eyes were soft. "If I was a flower, I know what kind I'd be," she said, half to herself. "A bluebell."

Mama bowed, as though she understood. The way she always looks.

## 77

"I HAVE to go in the street for a while," I told Belle as we climbed in the Plymouth. "I'll call you when I'm done with Marques. Late, okay?"

"Can't I wait at your office?"

"It's only a little after two now—I'll be coming back there to change around eight. It's a long time to be cooped up."

"I won't be cooped up."

"Yeah, you would. I could leave you there with Pansy, but she wouldn't let you out."

"It's okay."

I drove back to the office, helping Belle carry her boxes up the back stairs.

"I'm not playing, girl. Pansy lets people in, but they're always there when I come back, understand?"

"Sure. Go ahead. I'll just take a nap."

"Don't use the phone. And don't open any of the file cabinets."

"O-*kay!* I got it."

I gave her a kiss.

**78** ‖ I FOUND Michelle at The Very Idea, a transsexual bar on the East Side. I walked through a jungle of hard looks until I got to her table, feeling them fall away when she kissed me on the cheek.

"Hi, handsome." She smiled. "Looking for me?"

I sat down next to her, lit a cigarette, waiting patiently for her two girlfriends to leave. Michelle didn't introduce me.

"The Prof's in the hospital," I told her.

"What's the rest of it?"

"His legs are broken. Somebody did it to him. For poking around, asking questions."

"You know who?"

"Guy named Mortay."

Her big eyes went quiet, two long dark fingernails flirting with her cheekbone, meaning she was thinking. "I don't know him . . . but it seems like I heard the name. . . ."

"It's Spanish for 'death.'"

"Honey, you know my language is French."

I didn't say anything, looking straight ahead. Michelle's hand grabbed my wrist. "Honey, I'm sorry. But it's business, right? The Prof was poking around, like you said. It's not the first time he stepped on a nail."

"The guy didn't have to do it, Michelle. It was a message. He's some kind of freak—wants to fight Max. That's why he worked the Prof over."

"He wants to fight *Max?*"

"That's what he said."

"He should change his name to 'death *wish*.'"

"Yeah, great. Thanks for your help." I got up to leave.

"Burke!"

"What? You think I came here to listen to your snappy dialogue? The Prof's my brother. Yours too. I know you're off the street—I didn't think we were off your list."

Michelle grabbed my arm, her talons biting deep. "Don't you ever say that!" she hissed, pulling me closer. She got to her feet, hooking her arm through mine. "Let's get out of here—too many ears."

We walked out into the daylight. I let her lead me down the street to another joint—a singles bar that wouldn't come alive for a couple of hours. We grabbed a pair of stools near a corner. Glass tinkled; a brittle edge to the juiceless, anorexic laughter of the patrons. The bartender brought Michelle her white wine and me my ginger ale.

"Tell me," she said, not playing now.

"You know the Ghost Van?"

"Just the rumors. The gossip off the street. But I know it's for real—somebody's shooting the working girls."

"There's a bounty on it. I talked with some people. Made a deal to track it down. The Prof was in on it. That's what he was looking for when he ran into this Mortay."

"So they're connected?"

"I don't know. When Mortay leaned hard, the Prof pulled out Max's name. Thinking to put some protection on himself. It backfired. Mortay *wants* Max—that's what he said. Wanted to know where his dojo was. The Prof didn't know. Mortay snapped his legs."

"How'd you find him?"

"They brought him right to the hospital. Like I said—a message."

"Where are you now?"

"I did some digging. There's this guy Lupe. Works out of the Bronx. Sets up matches. You know: cockfights, pit bulls, crap like that?"

"Yes?"

"He said this Mortay fought a duel. A bunch of the players got together, put up this purse. Twenty grand. Mortay killed the other guy in front of the whole crowd."

"I can see it. Regular prizefights are too tame for the freaks. Too much cocaine, too much filth . . . After a while, they have no nerve endings at all. It takes a superjolt to get their batteries started. They want the real thing."

"I told this Lupe I want to meet Mortay."

"Burke, that's not like you, that macho foolishness."

"Not fight him, Michelle. Meet him. Just to tell him I'm walking away. No hard feelings."

"Baby, I've known you forever. *All* your feelings are hard feelings."

"I have to turn him away from Max."

"It doesn't sound like . . ."

"I don't know what it sounds like. If he's free-lance, it doesn't matter. He can't find Max."

"So?"

"So, if he's tied up with this Ghost Van, maybe he's tied up with people who *could*."

The bartender brought us another round. I felt a flesh-padded hip bump my arm. A girl in a pink leather skirt, moving onto the stool next to me, talking to her girlfriend. Secretaries prolonging their lunch hour to look around.

Michelle sipped at her wine. "What do you want me to do?"

"Ask around. About the van. I'll check out this Mortay the best I can. See if it all catches up."

"I thought you were going to walk away."

"If I can, I will. I don't like any of this. If this guy's really fighting duels, he can't last forever. There's no old gunfighters."

Her big eyes pinned me over the rim of her glass. "I may be a sweet young thing, honey, but I go back a ways, remember?"

"Ex-gunfighter," I said, quietly.

"Yeah, we're all X-rated, aren't we, babe? I'm an ex-streetwalker, and you want me back on the stroll to listen to the beat. And you're ready to pick up the gun again—I can hear it in your voice."

"It'll be all right. I'll talk with him, square it up."

The girl in the pink skirt leaned into our conversation, her hard-pointed breasts brushing my arm. "Excuse me, honey," she said to Michelle, "could I ask your boyfriend a question?"

Michelle gave her an icy smile. "He's not my boyfriend—he's my lawyer."

"Oh, perfect!" the girl said, pulling her pal into the scene. She looked at me, flicking her tongue over her lower lip. "Do you think prenuptial agreements take the romance out of marriage?"

I blew a jet of smoke across the bar. "Rubbers take some of the romance out of sex," I said, "but they beat the hell out of AIDS."

I tossed a couple of bills on the bar. Michelle followed me out.

**79** I DROVE Michelle over to her hotel. She was quiet on the drive, her eyes on the street. I pulled up down the block from her place.

"I can't explain it to you," I told her. "I wish I could—it's somewhere inside my head—I have to work with it until it makes sense."

"Not everything makes sense."

I lit a smoke, shook my head. "It's just a feeling . . . but I know this whole thing is bad for us. For all of us. I'm not looking for trouble."

"Okay, honey. I'm with you."

"Thanks, Michelle."

She lit one of her long black cigarettes like she does everything else. Elegantly.

"You still with that big girl?"

"Yeah."

"That's a very fine woman, Burke. Believe me when I tell you. Nobody's ever been nice to her."

"I'm nice to her."

She smiled. "Are you?"

"Yeah, I am. She took your advice."

"Vertical stripes."

I laughed. "You should have seen them on her."

Michelle slapped my arm with unerring instinct in the same spot Belle always used. "You work with what you have, baby. You're looking at the expert."

"I know."

"Okay. You got some cash on you?"

"Yeah."

"Then let's do some shopping."

"Shopping? For what?"

"For a *present*, you idiot. For your girl."

"I have to . . ."

"Drive down to the Village," she ordered me, not willing to discuss it further.

Michelle found what she wanted in a little basement dive on Sullivan Street. A necklace of small dark-blue stones. The old Turk who ran the place had been a chemist before he fled some border war a hundred years ago. He'd been one of the Mole's first teachers.

"How much for this old thing, Mahmud?" Michelle asked, holding the necklace up to the light.

"That is pure lapis lazuli, young lady. Very fine. Very special."

"Sure, sure. About a hundred bucks retail, right?"

"A hundred dollars? For Old World craftsmanship? The stones alone are worth many times that."

"Since when is Taiwan the Old World, Mahmud?"

The old man's eyes gleamed. "Lapis lazuli. The mineral is called 'lazulite.' Very rare. You will not find it in the Far East. This perfect crystal comes only from Madagascar."

"Does the geography lesson cost extra?"

Mahmud and I exchanged shrugs. "Even a hurricane eventually passes, leaving the calm," he said.

Michelle wasn't moved. "You take American Express?"

Mahmud laughed so hard, tears ran down his face. "From him?" he said, pointing at me.

Michelle moved in for the kill. "Okay, so how much of a discount for cash?"

Mahmud moved to center ring, gloves up. "This necklace is worth one thousand two hundred dollar."

"Get out of town! Do I look like I'm on medication?"

"You look lovely, as always, Michelle. One thousand two hundred dollar."

"Four hundred. And you don't have to gift-wrap it."

"For you, because you are so beautiful, because such a beautiful necklace should have a beautiful home . . . a thousand."

"It's not for me, you old bandit, it's for Burke. For his girlfriend."

"This is true?"

I nodded.

"He just brought me along for protection," Michelle said, smiling sweetly.

"Ah, I see. Eight hundred, then."

"Did you say five?"

"Seven hundred dollar, and only because I respect your good taste."

"Can we split the difference?"

"Seven hundred dollar," the old man said. He meant it.

"Give him the money," Michelle ordered me.

I handed it over. Mahmud slipped the necklace into a soft leather pouch, handed it to me. "You take this too," he said, rummaging around under the counter. He came up with a tiny round wood box.

He unscrewed it, holding it out to me. It was filled with a fragrant paste, colorless in the dark wood.

"Jasmine," he said. "Just a touch on the lady's finger, then . . . here"—touching his chest. "The lapis takes its fire from the earth; it will blaze all the brighter if there is fire in the heart."

I bowed to Mahmud. Michelle gave him a kiss. When we hit the street, it was past six.

**80** "WHERE TO?" I asked Michelle.

"Take me back to my hotel. I need to change my clothes before I get to work."

"Michelle . . . you'll look?"

"I'll do better than that, baby. There's plenty of those little girls out there that know me. Like the Prof would say, if they know me, they owe me."

"Debts."

"Debts all come due, Burke. You know I love you. And even if you were still nothing but a rough-off artist like you used to be, I'd still love you." She lit a smoke, her face dead serious. "I'd love you because you're right . . . sometimes you have to go down the tunnel even if you don't know what's at the other end."

She blew the smoke at the windshield. Reached over and squeezed my hand. "I don't know what you're doing half the time. I don't think you do either. You're a hard man trying to be a hustler, and you don't always make it. I don't know why you went into that house last year— all I did was make a phone call like you asked. I don't know why you started that whole mess."

"It doesn't matter now," I said. Thinking of the witch-woman, Strega. "It's all over now."

"It doesn't matter why you did it . . . but I know this. You brought me my son. And I'll never forget."

She leaned over to kiss me as the Plymouth pulled to the curb. "If it's out there, I'll find it," she said.

"Michelle . . ."

"What?"

"Use a telescope, okay?"

She just waved a goodbye and moved down the street. Heads turned. Her walk didn't make men want to bite into their palms like Belle's. It pulled at a different piece, but it pulled just as hard.

**81** ‖ I T W A S almost seven-thirty by the time I got back to the office. I had the key in the lock when the smell hit me. A hard-sharp smell. I stepped inside. Pansy was at her post, tail wagging, even happier to see me than usual. All the furniture was against one wall. The fake Persian rug was off the wall. The smell was stronger inside.

Belle came in from the back room. Barefoot, wearing only a bra and pants, her hair tied on top of her hand, a rag in one hand.

"You came home too early."

"What in hell is this?"

"It's *almost* a clean office, honey. Lord, this place was dirty—I damn near had to use a chisel on the floor in the back."

"Belle . . ."

"I couldn't get that rug up. And you don't have a vacuum—I should've known. It's some kind of plastic, isn't it? I had to scrub it down. . . . It's still damp—watch where you put your feet."

I walked over to the couch. Sat down. Slowly. Pansy leaped onto the cushions, pressing against me. I patted her head.

Belle came over to me. "That old beast—she followed me around everywhere. Big busybody, poking her nose into everything. She wouldn't hardly let me work."

"I . . ."

"Honey, don't you like it?"

"Yeah. I mean, it's great. I just . . ."

"Take a look," she said, reaching out her hand to me. "Come on."

The bathroom sparkled, the back window gleamed. The floor glistened. The walls were a color I had never seen before. Even the hot plate looked new.

"Damn!"

"It's *good*, huh?"

"It's unbelievable."

"I thought there was another room. Behind the rug on the wall."

"That's what people are supposed to think," I said, half to myself. The surfaces of the file cabinets looked like someone had worked them over with a power sander. My old desk was oiled—you could even see the grain in the wood.

"How'd you do all this?"

"I'm a working fool—always have been. I was raised on work."

"I don't know what to say." It was the truth.

The big girl moved in against me, sharp sweat-smell blending with her natural juices into something way past sweet. "Say what I want to hear," she whispered.

I slipped both hands inside her pants, pulling her tight against me. "Go take a shower," I said.

She ground her hips against me. "That isn't it," she said.

"Trust me."

"I do."

"Well . . . ?"

She pulled back from me, walked toward the back room, shaking her butt like she was on the runway. Pansy shook her head in amazement. "You want out?" I asked her, opening the back door. The beast turned away in disgust—I guess she'd been on the roof a few times since I'd been gone.

I had most of the furniture back in place in a few minutes. I was rehooking the rug on the wall when Belle came out. Nude, beads of water covering yards of pink flesh. She had a towel around her head, holding it in place with her hands.

"I'm all clean."

"Come here," I said, reaching into my jacket pocket.

She came over to the desk, giving her hair one final rub with the towel, then tossing it over to the couch.

"Just stay there for a minute," I said, signaling Pansy to come with me. I dumped everything in the refrigerator into her giant bowl. I added some chocolate-chip cookies and a pint of vanilla ice cream. "Speak!" I told her. It would keep her occupied for a good five minutes.

I went back inside. Belle was standing by the desk, the soul of patience. I stood close to her, holding her face in my hands, looking into her dark eyes.

"Turn around," I said.

She turned her back to me, bent over so her elbows were on the desk, butt in the air.

I stepped in against her, grabbed her shoulders, pulled her back so she was standing up again. "Just do what I tell you," I said.

"I thought . . ."

"Sssh. Close your eyes."

"Okay, I . . ."

"And be quiet."

She stood with her back to me, hands at her sides. So quiet I could hear her breathing.

I took the necklace out of the leather pouch, unhooked the clasp, and slipped it around her neck. I hooked it closed. "Turn around," I told her.

Her eyes were still closed, but her mouth was trembling. The lapis was blue fire against her, falling down just to the top of her breasts. I kissed her on the lips. "Take a look," I whispered to her.

Belle kept her eyes closed, working the necklace with her fingers, feeling the heat. Her eyes came open; she lifted it in her hands, bent her head.

"It's the most pure-beautiful thing I've ever seen in my whole life," she said solemnly. Tears on her face.

"What're you crying about—you don't like it?"

"Don't be such a hard guy," she said, ignoring the tears; "you *know* why."

I kissed her. "Okay. Be a baby if you want to."

"It's *your* baby I want to be," she said, pushing me to the couch.

She dropped into my lap, sprawling across me, covering me, knowing she wouldn't fit and not giving a damn. I snaked a hand around her hip and pulled out the jasmine box. Handed it to her.

"What's this?"

"Open it."

"Oh, it's perfume!"

"Paste, not spray. Here," I said, touching my finger to it, rubbing it between her breasts.

She pulled my head down to her. "How do I smell?" she asked.

"Like juicy flowers," I told her.

She rolled off my lap, pulling at my belt. "I've got some juice for you, baby. Come on, come on!"

**82** IT WAS after nine when I looked at my watch. Belle was lying half on top of me on the couch. Pansy was spread out on the floor, looking glum. I rolled off, sliding away from Belle.

I took Pansy to the back door, jumped into the shower, dressed fast. Junior's at eleven, Marques had said.

I leaned over to kiss Belle on my way out. "You going to be okay here?"

"I do love you," is all she said.

The Plymouth hummed, a fast horse on a short rein. Maybe it missed the way Belle drove. Junior's was over the border. Uptown. A players' joint, it wouldn't even start to roll until past midnight. The bar was in shadow, Billie Holiday on the jukebox. "God Bless the Child."

I wasn't going to pull a house-to-house search through the booths. The bartender came over. Slash of white skin across his dark face like a scar.

"Can I help you, Officer?"

"I'm not the Man. I'm looking for Marques. Marques Dupree."

"Nobody by that name here, friend."

"Yeah, there is. He's expecting me. Ask him."

"What name should I call?"

"How many good-looking white men you see in this bar?" I asked him.

He looked me full in the face. "None," he said, moving away.

I lit a cigarette. Felt a tap on my shoulder. Slim blonde woman in a bottle-green sheath. "Burke?"

"Yeah."

"Marques is over this way," she said, moving off.

I followed her to a horseshoe-shaped red leather booth. Marques was sitting at the center, another blonde to his left. The one I had followed moved to his right. I sat facing him.

"My man!" Marques said, not offering his hand. "How's the hijacking business?"

I nodded to him, not answering.

"You come by yourself?" he asked, not looking around, sure of himself on home ground.

"Same way I came into this world," I assured him.

"You packing?"

I let out a breath, disgusted with his bullshit games. "Yeah, I got a machine gun in my pocket."

"Mind if Christina takes a look?"

"Whatever it takes to get on with this."

The blonde who had come over to the bar moved next to me, running her hands over my body. She reached into my crotch, squeezed. "Nobody home, huh?"

I didn't answer her, my eyes on Marques.

She slid back next to him. "He's got three packs of smokes, two lighters, bunch of keys, some folding cash. . . . He's empty."

I watched Marques's teeth flash. "Can't take chances with you gunslingers."

"Ready to talk now?"

"Fire away."

I looked deliberately at the blonde on his left. Turned my head, looked the same way at the one on his right.

"My ladies are cool—you can talk in front of them."

I shrugged, putting a pack of cigarettes and a butane lighter on the table in front of me. I lit another smoke, snapping off a wooden match. He didn't pay attention. That's why he was a pimp and I was what I was.

"You know a man named Mortay?"

"The fighter?"

"Yeah."

"I don't know him. Man, I don't *want* to know him. He's not on my list—I don't let my women mess with no freaks."

"What's that mean?"

"I saw him do his thing, man. It was unreal. He fought this other dude. . . ."

"The Japanese guy. In the basement under Sin City?"

"Right on. I didn't even know what the entertainment was going to be, but it was on the wire that it was a big thing, you know? I had to make the scene. Get down, be around. When you set the style, you got to show it off."

"Yeah, right. You saw the whole thing?"

"The whole thing. This Mortay, man, that's a scary dude. Moves like a fucking ghost."

"That may be the connect, Marques."

"I'm not reading you, man."

"Read this: One of my people was looking around. On that job you and me talked about?"

"Yeah?"

"And he met Mortay. I don't know if it was just a territory thing, wrong guy in the wrong place . . . maybe so. It happens to all of us."

"So?"

"So Mortay warned him off. Maybe he's front-ending the thing. Guarding the van."

Marques snapped his fingers. The blonde on the left pulled a vial from her purse, tapped out some white powder on a mirror. She cut it into four lines with a gold razor blade, put it in front of Marques. He rolled a bill into a tight straw, snorted a line up each nostril. Each of the blondes took a remaining line for herself. The pimp looked across at me, letting the coke rush around inside his head.

"I can't see it, man. You're off the wall."

"Could be. What if I'm not?"

"Look, man. We had a deal. You're working for *me*. I pay, you play my tune."

"Watch your back, Marques," I said, starting to get up.

"Hey! Hold up, I'm not downing you. Just lay it out, okay? Why you here?"

"I'm here because you know things I don't know. And you can find out things I can't. I don't want any more to do with this Mortay than you do. But if I'm going to do the job on the van, I need to know if he's in the play."

"How would I know?"

"I'll find that part out myself. What I need is whatever you can find out about Mortay. *Anything* could do some good—I won't know till I get it. He's out there—he has to live someplace, hang out someplace. I'm not asking you to walk the wire, just listen to what you hear, okay?"

"I don't know, man."

I felt like breaking his face. I lit another cigarette, centering myself, coming to what would work. I kept my voice quiet, letting another pitch take over, working the corners. "Marques, there isn't another player in this town with your weight. You want to take the Ghost Van off the streets, protect your women—I respect that. You know your game—I know mine. That's why we got together, right? We're partners on this thing. Now I need your help. That's why I came here. This Mortay, he had people with him. Guy named Ramón, for one. If they show anywhere on the set, somebody'll scope them out. All I want is for you to use your network—you don't have to get out of your Rolls-Royce—just let it come to you. And pass it along."

The pimp sat like he was considering, basking in the praise. "I'm the one that can get the lowdown, no question about it."

"None at all," I agreed.

"All right, hijacker. I don't promise nothing, but I'll get back to you if something comes up."

"Thanks," I said, getting up to go again. Putting the butane lighter back in my pocket. I don't use it to light cigarettes.

The blondes never said a word. Good bitches. Whores in their hearts. Renting out what they never owned.

**83** I SLIPPED the Plymouth through Times Square on the way back. Sin City was a monster building squatting in the middle of a long block. It stood four neon-faced stories high, towering over the storefront-sized sleaze shops on either side. I stopped at the corner. A black stringbean sporting a red porkpie hat was hunched over a folding table covered with gold chains. Cesspool Specials: the chains were broken, so the suckers would think they'd been snatched on the subway. The hustler breaks the chains himself—nobody snatches gold-plated junk. "Check it out!" he called to the passing pack of slugs. He wouldn't be there tomorrow.

I motored slowly around the block—couldn't see the back of Sin City from the other side. The buildings were packed tighter than the crowd at a lynching.

The Prof felt the pain before Mortay ever touched him. That kind of power leaves a scent.

But only to those he marked.

Tenth Avenue was quiet. Eleventh was alive with working girls. The river was only a block away. A black woman in a blond wig strolled up to the Plymouth. Red spandex pants, a matching halter top, red heels. All yesterday's stuff, like she was.

"You want some action, baby?"

I let her come close, watching the other girls through the windshield, trying to get the feel of the street. It felt calm—didn't make sense. The Plymouth sat through the green light; the pross took it for a signal. She leaned into the window, folding her arms under her breasts to poke them forward.

"What you say, honey. Fifty takes you around the world."

I looked in her face, keeping my voice low.

"You got a room?"

"We just drive around the block, honey. Nice dark places to park—take all the time you need."

"Around here? Haven't you heard about the Ghost Van?"

She laughed. Hard and bitter. "The Ghost Van don't eat no dark meat, baby."

It started to hit me then. I feathered the gas pedal and the Plymouth moved off, leaving the whore alone in the street.

## 84 ‖ PAST MIDNIGHT. I found a phone, rang Mama's.

"It's me."

"Nobody call."

"Okay."

"Max has your money."

"You keeping him close?"

"Yes. Keep close. Waiting for you."

"I'll call you tomorrow."

"Burke?"

"What?"

"Nice girl you bring here. Nice big girl."

"Yeah."

I put the phone down. Dialed the Mole. I heard the phone being picked up, nothing on the other end. The way he always answers.

"It's me. I need to come see you tomorrow night—talk something over. I'm bringing someone with me—someone you need to meet. Okay?"

"Eight o'clock," said the Mole, hanging up.

**85** IT HIT me as soon as I stepped out of the back staircase into the hallway. The electricity started at the base of my spine. It shot upward in little jolts, forming a T-bar at my neck, firing out to my shoulders. My hands trembled. I knew what it was—an old friend. Fear.

I opened the door. The office was pitch-dark. Pansy was standing at her post, wire-tight, eyes glowing. The hair on the back of her neck was standing straight up. I closed the door behind me, hit the light switch.

Belle was on the couch—on her knees, a butcher knife in her hand.

"What happened?" I asked her.

"Somebody rang the bell downstairs. It buzzed up here. Maybe twenty minutes ago. I didn't answer it. I killed all the lights, turned off the radio. Then those strobes, the ones above the door, they started flashing."

"Somebody coming up the stairs."

"That's what it was. Pansy, she ran right over to where she is, making these ugly low sounds. Like a gator eating a pig. I got scared."

"Anybody try and get in?"

"No. They just pounded on the door. Real loud. I thought the dog would bark, but she just stayed where she was. Like she was waiting."

"She was."

"They rattled the doorknob—you know, just shaking it, like they were mad. There were at least two of them; I could hear the talking."

"You hear what they said?"

"No. I was scared to move from here—I didn't want to get in the dog's way—she looked crazy. But one had like this Mexican accent."

"How long'd they stay?"

"Just a minute, maybe—but it seemed longer. The strobes went off again. It's been quiet since then."

"And you're still on the couch?" I asked, as I walked over to her, put my hands on her shoulders.

She looked up at me. "Burke, I don't know much, but I know about men. You learn to tell. From little things. The guy talking— the Mexican—he was one of those nasty men you see in the club sometimes. The way they look at you—like screams would make them smile."

"I know. You did the right thing." I gave her a smile, my thumb under her chin. "What were you going to do with that knife?"

"I didn't know what to do . . . but I could see the dog knew. Where she was standing, they'd walk in right past her. I figured they come toward me, and Pansy'd just blind-side them."

"That's what she'd do all right. But she'd do the same thing if you hid in the back room."

"I was going to give her a hand," Belle said, her hands still shaking but no tremble in her voice.

I cupped a breast. It overflowed my hand. "There's a big heart under this big thing," I said.

"It's yours."

"Which?" I asked, squeezing her breast.

"Both. But only one's for playing with," the big girl said, eyes locked on mine.

I kissed the bridge of her nose, between her eyes. She put her face against my chest. I held her for a minute, making up my mind.

I let go of Belle, threw the signal to Pansy to pull her away from her post. Opened the back door to let her out to the roof.

"Get ready to go," I told Belle, opening drawers, filling my pockets.

**86** ‖ IN THE garage, she watched quietly as I lifted the rubber floor mat, spun the wing nuts, and put the pistol inside the hollowed-out space near the transmission hump.

"You remember how to get to your place from here?"

"Sure. I couldn't tell you how to do it, but I can take the car there."

I checked the back of the garage. The street was quiet. Belle backed the Plymouth out. I hit the switch and the door closed behind us.

The Plymouth tracked through the empty streets. Belle handled it like it was a baby carriage. I lit a cigarette, putting it together. Any fool could get into my building from the front—just press the hippies' bell in the middle of the night and they'd buzz you in. It wasn't a customer—they'd come in even when my bell hadn't been answered. Spanish accent. Pounding on the door, but they hadn't tried to break in. Lupe would have told them about my dog.

"Anybody with us?" I asked Belle, not looking around.

"No," she said, her eyes flicking to the mirrors. "Not since we pulled out."

**87** ‖ AS SOON as we walked in the door, I grabbed the phone. Mama answered like it was noon.

"They called, right?"

"Yes. Man say playground, behind the Chelsea Projects. Midnight tomorrow."

"Spanish accent?"

"Yes. Nasty man. Whisper on phone, like those men who call women, you know?"

"Yeah, I know. You say anything to him?"

"Nothing to say. You want Max now?"

"No! Mama, this is a bad play. You keep him close, like we said."

"If . . ."

"Mama, listen. Listen to me. If Max comes in now, it could be trouble for the baby, okay?"

She said something in Chinese. I didn't need a translator. "Later, Mama," I told her, hanging up.

Belle came over to the phone as I was lighting a smoke. "Me too," she said, holding my hand, guiding the match. She was wearing a white T-shirt that came halfway down to her thighs, the blue necklace around her neck.

"I'll be right back," I told her, reaching for my car keys.

"Let me . . ."

"Stay here," I told her.

She dropped to her knees, holding her hands out in front of her, bent at the wrists like dog's paws.

"Don't be so fucking smart," I said. "I'll be back in a couple of minutes—I need a pay phone."

88 || I THREW in a quarter, listened to the woman say something in Spanish.

"Dr. Pablo Cintrone," I said. Waited patiently for a long rap about how the doctor wasn't in at that hour of the night, but if it was an emergency . . .

*"Attention!"* I barked into the receiver. "Dr. Cintrone. Burke. *Teléfono cuatro.* Ten o'clock tomorrow morning, *por favor.* Okay?"

The voice never changed tone. "Burke. *Teléfono cuatro.* Ten o'clock tomorrow morning."

*"Gracias."*

She hung up.

When a citizen's scared, he calls the cops. Where I live, you call a terrorist.

## 89

THE FRONT door was unlocked. I shut it behind me, walked through the cottage. Belle was out on the deck. I leaned on the railing, looking across the black water. Belle moved in next to me, fingering the necklace.

"You know why I danced in front of men?"

"Yes."

"I know you do. You're the first man who ever looked at my face after I took my clothes off." She pulled the cigarette from my mouth. Took a drag, handed it back.

"Nothing on this earth means anything all by itself. You know those orchids they sell in fancy flower shops? They grow wild in the swamp near where I was raised. And gator hide . . . It costs so much to make a little purse out of it, but the big old things are out there thick as mosquitoes. You know about gators?"

"Not much."

"Baby gators, they ain't got much of a chance. It's easy to find the eggs—the mama gators just bury 'em and they walk away. Most of them don't make it even if the eggs do hatch. When they're born, they're only a couple of inches long. The big birds grab them up. Bobcats, panthers, coons, damn near everything in the swamp feasts on them. Baby gators, they're not like puppies or kittens. You know the difference between a six-inch baby gator and a six-foot bull?"

"No," I said. Her face was turned in profile, tiny flat nose just a bump.

"Five and a half feet. They don't grow, they just get bigger, you understand?"

"Yeah."

"What they say about gators . . . Most of the little ones, they never get to be big ones, what with everything out there trying to eat them and all. The ones that do get their full growth—they spend the rest of their lives getting even."

"I know people like that."

"I thought I was like that too, once. But it's not the whole world I need to get square with."

"I know."

She moved against me, hip bumping gently. "There's things inside me. Bad things. In my blood and in my bones. I'll never have babies and I'll never get old. You're good with words, but there's things you don't like to say."

"I don't understand."

"Yeah, you do. Remember when I wanted you to taste me? When we first came together? I've met plenty of men good at romance, but I never met one any good at love. You're what I want, and you can't do things but one way. Your way."

"Belle, I . . ."

She pressed her fingers against my mouth. "Don't say anything. You already said all I need you to say. I'm with you to the end. Just make me one promise?"

"What?"

Tears rolled down her face, but her voice was steady. "I know you have people. I don't have anybody. If my time comes, you settle my debts. Pay them off."

"I will."

"One more thing. Just one more thing, and I'm going to give you my life, Burke. I'll never take my clothes off for another man again. And I'll never take this necklace off either. You see that I'm buried in it."

"Cut it out," I said, smacking her on the rump, trying for a smile.

She turned her face to me, holding my shirt with both hands. "Now's not the time for that. You can't change what's going to happen. You *promise* me. Promise me right now. I married the outlaw life— I've got a right to be buried in my wedding dress."

"I promise, Belle."

She pulled me close, her mouth butterfly-soft against mine. "My mother saved my heart for me. She died to do it. I waited a long time. I'm giving it to you now. And I'll die to do it too."

I held her against me in the dark. For that little piece of time, I didn't have to call on the ice god of hate to fight the fear.

## 90

BELLE FELL asleep holding me in her mouth. The bedside clock said four. I set it for six, stubbed out my last cigarette, and drifted off.

When the alarm went off, I was sleeping on my side. Belle was wrapped around my back. I slapped the clock to shut off the buzzer. The morning light was just coming through. Belle reached down for me, holding me in her hand, whispering in my ear.

"When I went shopping . . . to buy all that stuff to clean your office . . . I bought something else. A surprise for you. Something to give you nobody else has ever had. I was going to give it to you last night, when you came back. But you came back with my necklace. And all that other stuff happened. It's still here for you. Special. But not now," she said, stroking me, "not now. When your blood's up."

I felt myself grow in her hand. "Seems like it's up to me," I said.

She laughed, a rich laugh from her belly, moving against me. "When your *blood's* up, honey. I'll know. But as far as this other thing . . ." The big girl pushed against my shoulder, shoving me flat on my back, swinging one huge leg over me, her hand guiding me inside. "Come on, now," she whispered, her teeth in my shoulder.

**91** A N  H O U R later, we were moving into the city. I had to be at the pay phone in the lobby of the Criminal Court before ten. The last phone in the long bank near the back wall. *Teléfono cuatro.*

There were only two places in the city I could go for what I needed. This freak I had to meet could call himself "death" if that's what got his rocks off, but I knew a guy who earned the title. A guy we did time with years ago. A guy who let the ice god into his soul like I'd wanted to. A guy named Wesley. Even saying his name in my mind made my hands shake. The other choice was the UGL.

Una Gente Libre—A Free People. Puerto Rican terrorists to the *federales*, hard-core *independentistas* to their people. The FBI had been trying to get a man inside for years—they'd have better luck getting Jimmy Hoffa to testify. The UGL didn't blow up buildings. They didn't write letters to the newspapers. Some of them fought in the mountains of their home, some in the city canyons of America. Their New York territory stretched from East Harlem to the Bronx. They kept their plate clean. You try to sell crack on their streets, you *get* cracked. You come back again, you get iced. The Colombians didn't like that much. One of their honchos sent a crew into UGL turf. Sprayed the streets with machine guns. Dropped five people, one of them a pregnant woman. The next day, the crack salesmen were back, stopping the BMWs and Mercedeses full of mobile slime on their way to the suburbs. Smiling. Three days later, the first salesman who showed up pushed his way through a crowd packed around a fire hydrant. The honcho's head was sitting on top of the fireplug like a bust in a museum display case. Whoever hacked it off hadn't been a surgeon. The last thing the salesman left on that street was his puke.

Dr. Pablo Cintrone was a psychiatrist. *New York* magazine did a profile on him once. Harvard Medical School graduate who returned to the mean streets to minister to his people. It made him sort of a hero to the upscale crowd for a couple of weeks. Not too many people in Spanish Harlem or the South Bronx read the magazine, but they knew El Jefe of the UGL.

**92** ∥ INSIDE THE office, I let Pansy out to the roof while I checked the security systems. Nobody'd made a move on the place last night.

I changed into a dark pin-striped suit, grabbed a leather attaché case. It wouldn't get anybody's attention if I stood by the pay phone in the Criminal Court waiting for it to ring.

When Pansy saw the leash, she spun in a circle, dancing for joy. I hooked her up and we all went down the back stairs.

First stop was the hospital. I left Pansy in the back seat, taking Belle's hand.

"Is she going to be all right back there?"

"What could happen to her?" I asked, reasonably enough.

The Prof was sitting up in bed, half a dozen pillows propped up behind him. His legs were still in casts, but lying flat on the bed. A metal bar ran between the casts. I looked a question.

"To make sure they stay straight until the casts come off," he said.

"How you doing?"

"Not as sweet as drinking wine, not as bad as doing time."

"We got something," I said, moving close to the bed.

The little man's eyes shifted to where Belle was standing against the wall. I held out my hand behind me, not turning my head. She came up and took it. "She's with us," I told him. "She's in this."

He flashed his smile at her. "This your man, little girl?"

Her smile blazed back. "He surely is."

"That makes me your brother-in-law, darlin'. Soon's we finish this fight, I'll show you the sights."

She leaned over and kissed him. "I'll be waiting."

Belle sat on the bed. It didn't shift more than half a foot. I pulled up the chair, keeping my voice down.

"Mortay called. We got a meet tonight."

"Where?"

"Playground back of the Chelsea Projects."

"Skinner heaven."

"I know."

"I don't like it. If he don't buy the play, how you gonna walk away?"

"I need a shooter. With a night scope. On the roof."

"The only one I know is . . ."

"Not Wesley. I'll get someone else—I got it covered." The Prof didn't know about my connect to UGL.

His voice dropped even lower. "You going to dust him?"

"No way. Just make sure he gets the word—I want to tell him we got no beef. Walk away. The shooter is in case he wants to try and send another of his freakish messages."

"Burke, I'm telling you, this Mortay . . ."

"I got it covered," I told him again. "You hear anything?"

"Got some promises, but no product."

"I'll see you tomorrow."

He put his hand on mine. "Burke, listen to me like you used to on the yard. You want to roll the dice, make it nice."

"I got it," I said, throwing him a salute.

**93** I HELD the door for Belle to get into the car. "He's really so much better, isn't he?"

"He's better, but he's not back to himself yet."

"You'd expected him to be dancing by now?"

"Not the physical thing. The Prof, he's like two people. Half is this rhyming-time, upbeat thing you see, okay? The other half is how he got his name. Like a religious thing—I don't have a name for it. He got his name because he can *see* things."

"Like what's going to happen?"

"Sort of. Like I said, I can't really explain it. But he can preach, square business. Talk that religion like he means it. Strong enough to make you buy a piece sometimes, when he really gets on a roll. That's what's missing now."

Belle tapped fingernails on one knee, paying attention, listening close. She turned to look at me. "Maybe he don't like what he sees comin'," she said, the Southern-swamp tang strong in her voice.

**94** I PULLED the Plymouth into the parking lot across from the Criminal Court. The parking lot where I met Strega for the first time. The court where I first saw Wolfe in action. It was nine-forty-five—all the spaces were taken.

"Cruise around the lot like you're looking for a place to park," I told Belle. "You find one, pull in. Watch for me—I'll be coming down those steps," I said, pointing across Centre Street. "You see me coming, catch my eye. We may have to move out right away."

I gave Pansy the signal. She flopped down in the back seat, filling it to capacity.

I crossed the street, grabbed the phone I wanted. I picked up the receiver, holding down the hook, and acted like I was listening to someone on the other end, glancing at my watch.

I knew my watch was accurate, because it read ten o'clock just as the phone rang. I released the hook.

"Can I see you? Today?"

*"Muy importante?"*

*"Sí."*

"Handball court closest to Metropolitan. One o'clock."

"Thanks."

I was talking to a dead line.

**95** I CAME down the steps, spotted the Plymouth making a slow circuit. I caught it on the second pass, opened the door. Belle rolled out to Lafayette Street, turned south, in the direction of the office.

"I don't have to get moving until around noon," I told her. "But I need the car when I do."

"I'll go with you."

"No, you won't. And get that pout off your face."

She didn't. "Make a right," I told her as we came to Worth Street. "Head down to the river."

Pansy poked her head over the top of the front seat. "Want to run, girl?" I asked her. She growled.

I showed Belle where to pull in. There were only a few cars on the broad strip of concrete, the usual collection of humans minding other people's business. I opened the back door, hooked Pansy's leash, and we strolled along the river. Her snout wrinkled at the smells, but she held her position. On my left side, slightly ahead. Every time I stopped, she sat. When we got to the deserted pier, I let her off the lead, making a circle with my hand, telling her not to roam far. Freed of the restraint of the leash, she did what comes naturally to her. Lay down.

"You lazy old thing," Belle said. She looked around, her eyes sweeping the Jersey shore on the other side. "Sure doesn't smell like any water I ever saw."

"It's not water—just a liquid toxic-waste dump."

"You can't swim in it?"

"No. But on a good day, you could walk on it."

"Ugh!"

A sailboat went by, loaded with yuppies in yachting gear. Sailboats down here make about as much sense as No Smoking sections in L.A. restaurants, so you see a lot of them.

Belle pointed to one of the round beams that held up the pier. "Boost me up," she said, one foot in the air. I cupped my hands and she stepped in, reaching to the top of the beam. I heaved, and up she went. It wasn't as bad as loading trucks, and the view was a lot better. I lit a smoke, handed it up to her. The breeze pulled at her hair, pulling it off her face. She turned to the side, sucking in a deep breath. I took one of my own—no Viking ship ever had a prouder figurehead.

Two teenagers pulled up, riding those little motor scooters you see everyplace. They stopped a decent distance, watching Pansy.

"What kind of dog is that?" the taller one asked.

"One that bites," I told him.

"He looks like a giant pit bull."

"Close enough."

"Where could I get one?"

"You can't."

The shorter one piped up. "He looks like a big lump to me. That ain't no pit bull."

"Pansy, watch!" I snapped at her.

She came slowly to her feet and strolled toward the kids, making her noises. I never heard an alligator eat a pig, but I knew what Belle meant. She pinned the boys with her ice-water eyes, one skull-crusher of a paw pulling at the concrete.

"Jump!" I yelled at her. The kids took off before she hit the deck. She looked over at me, bored to death. I made a circle sign again. This time she took off, loping the length of the boards, peering over the edge into the water. She jogged back, stopping at the beam where Belle perched. The beast leaped up, her paws locking into the wood a foot below Belle. She reached down and patted her. "Does she want me to come down?"

"I think she wants to come up."

"There's no room."

"Maybe that's a message."

Belle jumped down from her perch, landing next to me. "What message?" she said, bunching a small fist.

"That they should make those beams bigger."

"Or these smaller?" she asked, smacking herself on the rear.

"Wouldn't be my choice," I assured her.

She took my arm and we walked around some more, Pansy hanging close.

"She's so beautiful. She really is like a panther, the way she moves. So smooth."

I lit a smoke, thinking it was the truth.

"Burke, how come you got a female dog?"

I shrugged.

"Well, she's for protection, right? A guard dog? I thought they were all males. I thought they were tougher, you know? A man I knew once, he had a German shepherd. Wouldn't have a female dog around him—said a bitch would turn tail and run from a fight."

"He's a moron. Male dogs, they smell a bitch in heat, you know what they want to do?"

"Sure."

"No, you don't. What they want to do is fight every other male dog around. In the wild, they run in packs. The way the pack stays alive, they only let the strongest bulls mate with the bitches. So the litters are strong too. The way they see who the strongest dog is they fight it out."

She put her head against my shoulder. "Maybe they're right."

"They're right for dogs. Not for people. I grew up like that. It took me a lot of years and a lot of scars before I snapped that a good woman won't make you fight over her."

"I worked with girls like that. Fire-starters. Blood makes them come."

She swayed against me, pulling me to a stop along the pier. "Is that why you have a girl dog? So she won't want to fight other dogs and all?"

"Males are just no good. Any kind of male. A man'll fuck a chain-link fence."

She patted my pockets, took out a cigarette. I cupped a wooden match against the wind for her. She sat on the bench. Pansy jumped up next to her. I sat on the other side.

Belle looked at the water. "The man who said a bitch would turn tail—that's what he wanted me to do. I never had much of my own. Things you buy . . . they're not really yours. But I own what I do. He found out too."

"What happened?"

"I cut him. Cut him good."

We walked back to the Plymouth. "You want to wait at the office for me?"

"Me and Pansy," she said.

**96** BACK AT the office, Belle looked at the street maps rolled up in a corner. "Can I tack these on the wall?"

"Sure. I was going to do it anyway. Why?"

"I want to learn the city."

"Okay. I'll be back in a couple of hours, maybe more."

I moved to the door.

"Honey?"

"What?"

"Come here for a minute. Sit with me."

I sat on the couch. She put her head in my lap, looked up at me. "Can I ask you something?"

"Sure."

"What I told you, about my mother and my father and all? Is that the worst thing you ever heard?"

I thought about kiddie porn. About selling little boys in Times Square. Rapists. Child molesters. Snuff films. The tape looped inside my head. I hit the stop button. "It's not close," I told her. "Everybody's pain is the worst thing in the world for them. Your mother really loved you. *Died* for you—you always have that."

"You think I'm . . . sick."

"No. I think you're hurt. And, one day, we'll fix that."

"I love you."

I bent to kiss her. "I've got to go," I said.

She pressed her head down against me. "Tell me something worse. Tell me something worse than what he did."

"It'd be worse for someone else, baby. Like I told you. Everybody has their own. Good and bad."

She came to her knees next to me. "Tell me the worst thing. The worst thing you know."

I looked in her face, talking quietly. I'd had enough of this crazy game. "People steal babies, Belle. Little tiny babies—they steal them from their parents. And they never bring them back."

"What do they do with them?"

"They sell most of them. Some of the pretty white kids, they sell them to nice rich folks who want a baby of their own. Black-market adoption."

"What about the others?"

"You know what a chop shop is?"

"Where they steal cars, break them down for parts?"

"Yeah. They have them for babies too. They sell the white babies. The other ones, they're not worth too much for adoption, so they cut them up for parts."

"Burke!"

"Rich baby needs a heart transplant, a new kidney, you think they care where the organs come from?"

"I don't believe you!"

"The world I live in, it's a lot deeper underground than any subway. It's a world where you can buy a baby's heart."

I held her against me. "Don't ask questions so much, little girl. I only got ugly answers."

She pulled back from me, dry-eyed. "You saw this? You saw this yourself?"

"Yeah. Guy's kid was in the hospital. Dying. Needed a transplant. It was in the papers, on TV. Looking for a donor. Baby only had a few days to live. He got a call. They promised him a baby's heart. Fresh. All packed and ready for transport to the hospital. Twenty-five thousand, they wanted. He made some calls—a lot of calls. A cop I know sent him to me. I went down the tunnel."

"What happened? Did they have the heart?"

"Just like they promised."

"You took it? The baby was saved?"

"Yeah."

She nodded. "Damn their souls to hell."

"I don't do souls," I told her. "Just bodies."

97 ‖ THE HANDBALL court was in the shadows of Metropolitan Hospital, just off 96th Street near the East River. Once the tip of Spanish Harlem, it was now liberated territory—the yuppie land-grab machine wouldn't be satisfied until gentrification ate the South Bronx. I liked it better the old way, when the human beings lived in the tenements

and investment bankers lived in the suburbs. Now we got plenty of rehab apartments for tomorrow's leaders. And more people living in the streets than they have in Calcutta.

I parked under the East Side Drive overpass and walked over to the court. Ten minutes to one. I watched people playing: handball, paddleball, basketball. No stickball. People working too. Working the cars. Selling flowers, newspapers, clean windshields. Ninety-sixth Street was the DMZ when I was coming up. North was theirs, South was ours. Now it all belongs to someone else—they just let us play there while they're at work downtown.

"These chumps can't play no basketball." A voice behind me. Pablo. The lack of a single Puerto Rican in the NBA makes him crazy.

He was wearing his white doctor's-coat over a black turtleneck, his round face looking the same way it did when he walked out of Harvard fifteen years ago.

"*Gracias, compadre,*" I said, thanking him for coming.

He shook hands the way he always does, using both of his.

"Something bad?" he asked me, standing close.

"I have to meet a man. Tonight. He hurt one of my brothers. He said it was a message. I don't know what's on his mind. I want to walk away—tell him I got no beef with him. But he might not go for it."

"You have Max."

"Can't use him for this, Pablo. It may be Max he wants. He's a *karateka.* Been going around the city, challenging sensei in their own dojos. Max, I think his name may be in the street over this. You know Lupe? The guy who sets up the cockfights?"

Pablo spat on the ground. "I know him. *Mamao.* A punk. Tough talk—no *cojones.*"

"He set up a match. Between this guy I have to meet and a Jap. Duel to the death."

"I heard about that. In Times Square?"

"Yeah. That's what I mean. Seems like everybody's heard about it. Max fights this guy, he's got no win. Probably have cops in the audience."

Pablo looked at me. "Max wouldn't walk away from a challenge."

"So he doesn't get to hear one."

"I see. You want your back covered when you meet this guy . . ."

"Mortay."

*"Muerte?"*

"Yeah. I don't know how he spells it, but it means the same thing."

"He's not a problem for us?"

"Not for you. Not now. I'm working on something, and I just bumped him accidentally. How he's tied in—*if* he's tied in—I don't know for sure."

"You chasing a missing kid?"

"Dead kids. The Ghost Van."

Pablo's round face went hard. His eyes were dark, flat buttons behind his round glasses. "Baby-killers. That van comes into our *barrio*, we'll *make* it a ghost."

"It just works off the river, near Times Square. I got a lot of threads, but no cloth."

"This Mortay . . . he knows?"

"I don't know. I'm not gonna ask him. He lets me walk, I'm gonna promise him I won't come his way again. He wants me off the van, I'm off the van."

"That's what you'll *tell* him."

"Yeah," I said, lighting a smoke.

"What time is your meet?"

"Midnight tonight. The playground behind the Chelsea Projects."

"How many people do you need?"

"Just one," I told him. "El Cañonero."

Pablo's lips moved. Just a tic. Nothing else showed in his face. "He only does our work."

"I don't want him to take anybody out. Just be around, break a couple of caps if he has to. He can do it from a distance. I figure maybe the roof . . ."

"He only does our work. He is not for hire. My people are soldiers, not gangsters."

"They do what you say."

"They follow me because they follow the truth. My personal friendship is with you, *hermano*. I can commit only myself."

I put my hand on his shoulder. "I understand what you say. I respect what you say. But there are two reasons why he should do this."

"Yes?"

"He does only your work. More than once, I have also done your work, this is true?"

"True."

"El Cañonero does this work tonight for UGL, it is UGL I owe. *Comprende?*"

He nodded. Rubbed the back of his neck like it was stiff. A young Hispanic woman in a blue jogging outfit stopped her slow circuit of the courts and trotted over. He took her aside, speaking in rapid-fire Spanish. She took off, running hard now, heading for the street.

We watched the basketball game. It wasn't in the same league as the semipro action at the court on Sixth Avenue in the Village, but it was intense. I asked him about his kids. Pablo's got a lot of kids— the oldest one's in college, his baby girl's still in diapers. He's never been married. Takes care of all his children. He never seems to make anybody mad with all his tomcat stuff, not even the women who have his babies. Most of them know each other.

I met Pablo in prison. He wasn't doing time—he was doing his residency in psychiatry. His supervisor was a wet-brain who did five-minute interviews with the cons before they saw the Parole Board. And handed out heavyweight tranquilizers any time they shoved the Rx pad under his nose. I was the wet-brain's clerk—a scam artist's dream job. Five crates of cigarettes and you got the prescription of your choice, twenty crates bought you a "fully rehabilitated" write-up for the Board. It only took Pablo a month to read my act, but he never said a word. I was on to him faster than that. He wasn't studying mental illness among convicts—he was recruiting.

The woman in the jogging suit ran back to us, pulled Pablo aside. Pablo turned to me. "You parked close by?"

"Under the overpass," I said, pointing.

"Sit on the hood. Smoke one of your cigarettes. See you in ten minutes."

He walked off with the woman.

**98** THREE SMOKES later, a black Lincoln sedan pulled up. Dark windows, M.D. plates. The front door popped open and I stepped inside. The woman was driving. I glanced in the back seat. Pablo. And El Cañonero.

"*Vete*," Pablo said. The Lincoln moved off.

Pablo's voice came from the back seat. "Turn around, *compadre*. My *hermano* needs to memorize your face."

I turned full-face to the back. El Cañonero was a short, stocky Hispanic, not as dark as Pablo. He had straight, coal-black hair. Pablo once told me Puerto Ricans were a mixture of all the world's races. Looking at the two men in the back seat, I could see the African in Pablo, the Incan in El Cañonero. The shooter's face was featureless except for heavy cheekbones. But I'd seen his eyes before. On a tall, lanky man from West Virginia. Sniper's eyes—measuring distances.

The Lincoln worked its way downtown. We pulled to a stop across from the playground.

Kids were running everywhere. Little kids screaming, chasing each other, bigger kids in a stickball game. Teenagers against the fence, smoking dope, listening to a giant portable stereo. Pablo jerked his thumb. We got out, leaned against the car.

The gate to the park would be closed at midnight. Wire mesh—it wouldn't keep anybody out.

El Cañonero's eyes swept the scene. He said something in Spanish to Pablo, who just nodded.

I saw the man against the wire mesh. A medium-sized white man with a baseball cap on his head. Watching the kids play. He was wearing a yellow sweater, the sleeves pushed up almost to his elbows.

I focused in on him, lighting a smoke. He had a heavy rubber band around one wrist. He pulled at it again and again with his other hand, snapping it against the inside of his wrist. I nudged Pablo, pointing at the man with a tilt of my head.

"Aversive therapy," I sneered.

His face went hard. "They should've tied the rubber band around his throat."

El Cañonero grunted a question. Pablo explained it to him. I couldn't follow the words, but I knew what he was saying. They have programs where they try "conditioning" on child molesters. The idea is to show them a lot of pictures of kids—then blast them with an electric jolt when the freaks get aroused. Nobody believes it works. When they discharge one of the freaks, they tell him to wear a rubber band around his wrist. When he feels himself getting excited over a kid, he's supposed to snap the band—reactivate his conditioning.

The shooter's eyes bored in on the man in the yellow sweater. *"Maricón!"* he snarled. Pablo launched into another speech. A child molester isn't a homosexual; most gays hate them too. El Cañonero listened, flat-faced. I heard my name. The shooter nodded. Then he held out his hand. I shook it. Pablo must have told him what I did.

Pablo leaned over to me. "We're going around the back, take a look. You stay here with Elena."

"I want to talk to the freak. Just take a minute."

*"Sí."* He gestured for the woman to move close. "Elena, that man over there, he is a molester of children. He is the wolf, stalking the baby chickens. My *compadre* wants to approach him, get a good look at his face, so *el gusano* will know he is known to us. Perhaps threaten him with violence, okay?"

She nodded. Pablo and El Cañonero moved off.

"Do you speak any English?" I asked the woman.

"I *teach* English," she said, nothing on her face.

"I didn't mean to offend you."

"You could not offend me. Just say what you want me to do."

I told her. I held out my hand. She took it, moving smoothly against me as we crossed the street.

Elena left me and moved off behind the freak. He stayed glued to the fence. I wrapped my hand around the roll of quarters in my pocket, moving my shoulder against the freak, slipping my left hand behind his back.

"Kids are cute, huh?"

He jumped like he'd been stabbed. "What?"

I snatched a handful of his sweater, locking his belt from behind, shoving my face into his, my voice cell-block hard. "When did they let you out, freak?"

"Hey! I didn't . . ."

I pushed him against the fence, my face jammed into his. "Don't come back to this playground, scumbag. We've been watching you. We know you. We know what you do. You do it again, you're dog meat. Got it?"

The freak twisted his head away from me. I looked where he was looking. At Elena. Standing three feet from us in her blue jogging suit, hands buried in the pockets of the sweatshirt. She took out her left hand, pulled up the waistband. A little black pistol was in her other hand. The freak whipped his head back to me. I pulled him away from the fence, bringing my right hand around in a short hook to his gut. He made a gagging sound, dropped to the ground. I went down on one knee next to him. His face was against the pavement, vomiting.

"We know your face, freak," I said quietly. "Next time we see you, you're done."

I stomped my heel hard into the side of his face; it made a squishy sound. Nobody gave us a look. When we climbed back inside the Lincoln, Pablo and El Cañonero were already in the back seat. Elena took the wheel and we moved off.

The rifleman tapped my shoulder. I turned around. He nodded his head once, a sharp, precise movement.

The Lincoln dropped me off at my car. Pablo got out with me. He handed me a strip of cloth, Day-Glo orange.

"Tie this around your head when you walk into the playground tonight. Bring a couple of bottles of beer. Pull your car into the playground, put the bottles on the hood. You raise your hand, one of the beer bottles blows up. This Mortay, he'll know you're covered."

"Thanks, Pablito. I owe you."

"El Cañonero said to tell you he'll be on the roof by eleven."

"Okay."

"He said to ask you something. . . . If it gets bad . . . if this guy won't be warned off . . . if he comes for you . . . you want El Cañonero to drop him or just fade?"

"Drop him."

*"Bueno."*

**99** I HEADED back downtown, stopped at Mama's. She took a long time to come to my booth. When she did, Immaculata was with her. They slid across from me. Mac didn't waste any time.

"Burke, is there trouble for Max?"

"I don't know. I'll know soon," I told her, stabbing Mama with my eyes. She stared right back. I shouldn't have mentioned the baby.

"You'll tell me as soon as you know?"

"Will you give me a fucking *chance* to head it off first?"

She reached across the table, took my hand. "I will. And I'll keep Max close for a few more days. Don't blame Mama. She told him you were working on something and he keeps pushing her. He thinks it's you who's in trouble. She needed my help."

"No hard feelings," I told her, remembering Michelle's words. "Where's Max now?"

"He's home with Flower." She got up to leave. Kissed me. "Be careful," is all she said.

Mama gave me about thirty pounds of Chinese food to take with me. I bowed to her as I left. Her eyes asked if I understood.

"It's okay," I said.

**100** "ANYBODY COME calling?" I asked Belle, stepping past Pansy.

"Been real quiet," she said, taking the cartons of food from me. Pansy followed her into the back room, ignoring me. The bitch.

Belle cleared off the desk so we could eat. "What's all that?" I asked her, pointing to yellow legal pads covered with scrawls.

"Just some charts I made. I have to see the streets for myself— the maps don't do it all. But I wrote down some ideas."

"Is it easier for you to memorize directions if you're driving or if you're a passenger?"

"Driving is best."

"Okay," I said, digging into the hot-and-sour soup, "you drive tonight."

"Where're we going?"

"To a place you might have to come back to by yourself someday. A safe place."

She nodded, her mouth full of food. I tossed an egg roll over my shoulder, saying "Speak!" as I did. It never hit the ground.

I smoked a cigarette while Belle put the dishes away, playing with the few pieces I had. I put the thoughts down—after tonight, I'd have more pieces.

Six o'clock. I let Pansy out to the roof, went to the back to put things together. Steel-toed boots with soft rubber soles. Black cotton pants. A black sweatshirt. I took a white jacket from the closet, checked the Velcro tearaways at the shoulders. Slipped the orange headband into a pocket. I put a clean set of papers together: driver's license, registration, Social Security card, all that crap. Six hundred bucks in used bills, nothing bigger than a fifty. A cheap black plastic digital wristwatch.

I let Pansy back inside. Took a shower. Put on a terry-cloth robe.

When I came out, Belle was lying on the couch, her hands locked behind her head, long legs up on the backrest. Wearing one of my shirts over a pair of little red panties. She couldn't button the shirt.

I sat down. She dropped her legs across my lap.

"Burke, this is it, isn't it?"

"What're you talking about?"

"This place. This office. That's all there is, right? This is where you live."

"Yep."

She rolled over on her stomach, pushing her hands against the couch until her hips were across my lap. There's a new kind of stove they make. Induction coil, they call it. You don't have to turn it on—the burner stays cold until you touch it with a copper-bottom pot. I knew how the stove felt.

Belle leaned her head on her folded arms, talking back over her shoulder at me. "I thought you had a house. I thought you wouldn't take me there . . . wouldn't let me sleep in your bed. Because you had a woman there. The woman you talked about."

I lit a cigarette, watching my shirt move on Belle's rump every time she readjusted herself.

"But she's gone, isn't she? Like you said. You told me the truth."

"Yeah. I told you the truth."

"I'm a bitch. I know that's not all bad—it's what I am. But I should have believed you, there's no excuse."

"Outlaws only lie to citizens."

"No, I met plenty of outlaws who lie. But I know you don't. Not to me."

She wiggled her hips, snuggling tight against me, feeling the heat. "Is she dead?"

"I don't know, Belle," I said, my voice hardening. "I told you all this before. There's no more to tell."

"Are you mad at me?"

"No."

"I'm sorry, honey."

"Forget it."

She pulled the shirt off her hips. "Why don't you give me a smack? You'll feel better."

"I feel fine," I said.

Belle wiggled again. "Come on, please."

I put my hand on her rump, patting her gently.

"Come on. Do it, just a couple of times. I swear you'll feel better."

I brought my hand down hard. A sharp crack. "Do it again," she whispered, "come on."

I smacked her twice more in the same place. She slid off my lap to her knees, looked up at me. "Feel better?" she asked.

"No."

"You will," she promised, taking me in her mouth.

**101** WE WERE on the East Side Drive, heading for the Triboro Bridge. Belle took a drag of her cigarette, watching the road.

"How do I turn up the dashboard lights?"

I told her. She peered at the speedometer. "I can tell how fast we're going without it, but I need to know the mileage."

"There's a trip odometer."

"It's okay, I'm keeping count."

We motored over the bridge. I showed her the cutoff, led her through the twisting South Bronx streets, past the warehouses, past the burned-out buildings, into the flatlands. "Next corner, left," I told her. "That's the spot."

She pulled to the side of the road. No streetlights here—we were in darkness.

Belle turned to me. "You think I'm a freak?" she asked, her voice shaking a little bit.

"Why would I think that?"

"Don't play with me—you know why I asked you. I liked it

when you pinched me so hard—when you made me say what I saw in the mirror. I liked it when you spanked me before. I like it when you do that. Makes me feel like you love me. Special." She took another drag. "You think that makes me a freak?"

I lit a smoke of my own. "You want the truth?"

"Tell me."

"I think *you* think you're a freak. I think you believe your life is a damn dice game. Genetic dice, rolling down the table, and all you can do is watch."

"My blood . . ."

"Your blood may have done something to your face. Your blood tells you not to have babies. But it doesn't tell you how to act. You still have your choices."

"You don't understand."

"You're the one who doesn't understand, girl. You see it but you don't get it. Remember what you told me about alligators—the difference between a six-inch gator and a six-foot one?"

"I remember."

"What's the difference between a puppy and a dog? The same thing? Just size?"

"Isn't it?"

"How you raise the puppy, how you treat it, what you feed it—it all makes a different dog when it grows up. Two puppies from the same litter, they could be real different dogs when they grow up."

"Okay."

"Don't give me that 'okay' bullshit. You don't get it, we'll sit right here until you do."

"I get it."

"Then explain it to me."

She started to cry, her face in her hands. "I *can't*," she sobbed.

"Come over here," I told her. "Come on."

She unbuckled her seat belt, slid over against me, still crying. "I'm sorry. . . ."

"Shut up. Just be quiet and listen, okay?"

"Okay," she gulped.

"Telling you about dogs and puppies wasn't the way to do it. You think blood will out, don't you?"

She nodded. "Yes." Still crying.

"You know about Dobermans . . . how they're supposed to turn on their owners?"

"Yes, I heard that."

"It's a lie, Belle. People get Dobermans, they're afraid of them. They've all heard the stories. So they beat the hell out of them when they're still puppies. Show them who's boss, right? One day, the dog gets his full growth, the owner goes to hit him, the dog says, 'Uh uh. Not today, pal,' and he rips the guy up. So this fool, this creep who's been beating up on his own dog, mistreating him all this time, he says, 'Well, the son of a bitch *turned* on me.' "

Belle giggled. "He sowed his own crop."

"Sure did. There's nothing *genetic* about Dobermans' turning on their masters. What's genetic about them is that they don't take a whole lot of shit once they get their growth. That's the truth."

"I thought . . ."

"We're people, Belle. Not alligators. I know people so cold, so evil, you meet them, you'd swear they came out of their mothers' wombs like that. But that's not the way it is. All the human monsters have to be *made*—they can't be born that way. You can't be born bad, no matter what the fucking government thinks."

"But if he . . ."

I cut her off sharp—I knew who "he" was. "It was his choice, Belle. No matter how he was raised, no matter what was done to him. There's no law says he has to repeat the pattern. He's not off the hook. I came up with guys raised by monsters. Did time with them when I was a kid. They still had choices."

I lit a cigarette. "Hard choices. The only kind people like us get. But choices still . . . You understand?"

"I do. I swear I do this time." She nestled against me. "I knew you were going to rescue me."

She kissed me full on the mouth, stabbing me with her tongue. I pulled back from her, watching the lights dance in her dark eyes. "The man we're going to see, millions of his people died because some slimy little psychopath decided their blood was bad. The psychopath, he's in the ground. The maggots are eating his body, and if there's a god, his soul is burning. And there's a country called Israel where there used to be only desert."

I squeezed her gently. "Okay?"

She let the whole smile go this time. "Okay."

**102** I SHOWED Belle where to pull in. "Flash the high beams three times, then shut the lights off."

"Something's coming," she said, peering into the darkness.

"Dogs," I told her. "Just be quiet."

They came in a pack. Simba didn't wait to make his entrance like he usually does. There was a tawny flash and a light thump as he landed on the hood of the Plymouth, baring his fangs as he looked through the windshield. Belle looked back at him. "Is that a wolf?"

"City wolf," I told her. "And that's his pack"—pointing to the river of beasts flowing around the car.

"What d'we do?"

"Wait."

The kid came through the crowd, bumping dogs out of his way like the Mole does. He called to Simba. The dog jumped off the hood, followed the kid around to the driver's side. "Switch places with me," I told Belle. I hit the switch. The window came down. Simba's lupine face popped into the opening.

"Simba-witz!" I greeted him.

Simba sniffed, poking his nose past me to look at Belle. A low growl came out of his throat. The pack went quiet. "It's okay, Terry," I told the boy. "This is Belle—she's with me."

The kid was wearing a dirty jumpsuit, a tool belt around his waist. A regular mini-Mole. Michelle would be thrilled.

"I'll open the gate," he said.

I drove the Plymouth a few feet into the yard, watching the gates close behind us. "I'm going to get out now," I told Belle. "I'll come around and let you out. The dogs will be with us, but they're okay. Don't be scared."

"Too late for that," she muttered.

When I let her out, she stepped to the ground. The dogs moved in close. "Should I pat them?" she asked.

Terry laughed. "Follow me," he said.

I took Belle's hand as we moved through the junkyard. Simba flashed ahead of us in a Z pattern, working the ground. The dogs came close, barking at each other, not paying much attention to us.

The Mole was sitting on a cut-down oil drum a few feet from his underground bunker. He got up when he saw us coming, pulling a slab of something white from his overalls. He threw it in a loping motion, like it was a grenade. The dogs chased off.

Before I could open my mouth, Terry took over. "Mole, this is Belle. Belle is Burke's friend. She came with him. I'm Terry," he said, holding out his hand. Belle shook it, gravely.

The Mole didn't offer to shake hands, pointing at more of the cut-down oil drums like they were deck chairs on his yacht.

"I should stay?" Terry asked.

The Mole looked at me. I nodded. The kid reached in his tool belt, pulled out a cigarette, lit it with a wooden match. He gets something from everyone in his family.

"Mole, I brought Belle here because she may need a place to run to. Soon. She's our people. She's mine, okay?"

"Okay."

"I wanted you to get a look at her. She has to come back in a hurry, you'll know her."

He nodded.

"Can Terry take her around—show her the other ways in?"

He nodded at the boy. Terry came over to Belle, holding out his hand. "Come on," he said. She went meekly as a child, towering over the kid.

I moved my oil-drum seat closer to the Mole. "I'm working on something. The Ghost Van. The Prof was nosing around. Guy named Mortay caught him. Broke both his legs. Told him to stay away."

The Mole nodded, waiting.

"I don't know if this Mortay is fronting off the van or he's got his own list. He told the Prof he wanted Max. In a duel. He's been moving on other *karateka* around the city. I can't bring Max into this until I know what the score is."

The Mole watched me as if I was one of his experiments. Waiting for something to happen.

"I'm meeting him. Tonight. Midnight. I've got backup. I'll call you when I get back. You don't hear from me, you call Davidson. The lawyer. You know him, right?"

"Yes."

"If I don't call you, I'll probably be locked up. Tell Davidson I'm good for the cash. Tell him to call Mama if he needs bail money."

"Okay."

"Thanks, Mole."

"There's more?" he asked. I couldn't see his eyes through the Coke-bottle lenses.

"Maybe. Maybe a lot more. I got pieces, but they may be two different puzzles. After tonight, I should know enough to come and ask you."

He nodded. Terry came back, leading Belle by the hand. "She knows the way," he said, standing by the Mole.

"Take them back to the car," the Mole told him. Nodding good-bye to me and Belle.

## 103

WHEN WE crossed the Triboro, I told Belle to bear left.

"That's toward Queens."

"I know. You're going home. I need the car. I'll come back when it's over."

"I want . . ."

"I don't care what you want. It's way past nine and I'm meeting a man at midnight. You're not coming. And I'm not telling you again."

She drove in silence for a few minutes. "Burke, what's that orange cloth you put in your pocket?"

I lit a smoke. "A sign. So I'll be recognized."

"What's it mean?"

"Signs mean different things to different people, right? Middle-class kid, he's on his way to school. There's this bully waiting for him. Middle-class kid, he don't want to fight, but he don't want to look chicken. So he wraps his hand in bandages, says he cut himself. Understand?"

"Yes."

"You wear the same bandages in the places I was raised, just makes you an easier target. Different rules, okay?"

"Okay."

We pulled up outside her cottage. Ten o'clock. I followed her inside. She didn't turn on the lights.

"Burke, don't hate me for asking this. . . ."

"What?"

"Are you scared?"

"Scared to death."

"Then . . ."

"I'm more scared not to go. I have to find out. Get some answers."

"Let's run," she said, standing close to me in the dark. "Let's just go. We can be in Chicago by tomorrow. Or anyplace you want to go. I've got money stashed. Right here in the house. We can . . ."

"No."

She turned away from me. "What scares you?"

"This guy I have to meet—he's a psychopath. Behind the walls, being a psychopath is like walking a high-wire. Guys are scared of a man with eyes like an alligator's. That's good—makes people keep their distance. But it's no good to scare people too much. Just the *possibility* you might get hurt, that keeps you away. But if there's no doubt about it, if you know the guy's coming for you, you take him first. If you can."

"And that's what you need to find out?"

"That's it."

She moved close to me again, whispering in the dark room. "Why take a chance?"

"It's not that simple. I can't do anything until I find out. I don't know what else's out there."

"Burke, you come back here. You come back here to me."

"I will. As best I can."

I lit a last cigarette, pulled her to me. "You don't see me by tomorrow morning, drive back to the junkyard. The Mole will know who to contact, what to do."

"You'll come back. I've got something for you."

"I know you do," I said, giving her a kiss.

# 104

ELEVEN-FIFTEEN. I was parked down the street from the playground. Breathing deep through my nose, sucking the air into my belly, expanding my chest as I let out each breath. Fear snapped around inside me. I gathered it together in a spot in my chest. Worked my mind, putting a fluid box around the fear. Testing the box, pushing it in different directions. I concentrated on the box, shooting clean, cold beams at it. Breaking it into little pieces. Smaller and smaller. *Seeing* the fear-blob break up into little liquid pieces inside me. Like tears. I held my hands out in front of me, willing the little pieces of fear to come out the ends of my fingers. Feeling them come. Some came out my eyes.

I felt so tired. Closed my eyes for a second. My watch said eleven-forty. Time.

I nosed the Plymouth up on the sidewalk, up to the playground gate. I jumped out, holding the heavy bolt-cutters in two hands. The chain around the fence gave way with one squeeze. I pulled the Plymouth inside the dark playground. Got out and closed the gate behind me. I made a slow circle of the yard, stopped when the Plymouth was pointed back at the street.

I got out, taking a six-pack of beer with me. Glass bottles. Lined them up on the trunk of the car, all in a row. Parallel to the building where the shooter would be waiting. I popped the top off one, held it to my lips. Lit a cigarette. Slouched against the car to wait.

The tip of my cigarette glowed. The streetlights didn't reach the corners of the buildings ringing the playground, but it was bright enough where I stood.

"You're early, punk." A voice from the shadows.

I dragged on my cigarette, keeping both hands in sight.

Two men walked toward me from the left. One more from the right. I watched them, not moving. Well-built Spanish guy in a short-sleeved white *guyabera* shirt. Dark-haired white man in a leather jacket. And a tall man in a white T-shirt and white pants. He looked like a stick figure moving toward me. Mortay.

"Step away from the car," he said. His voice was a whisper-hiss, snake-thin.

The Spanish guy came to meet me. I held my hands away from my body as he searched. A diamond glinted in his ear. A fat diamond, not a stud.

"Empty," he said, stepping back.

Mortay stopped four feet from me. His face was at the end of a long, thin neck, so small I could have covered it with my hand. Hair cropped close—I could see the shine of his scalp. A heavy shelf of bone linked his eyebrows, bulging forward, a visor over his eyes.

"I don't recognize the school," he said. Meaning the orange headband. "Do you fight?"

"I'm just a student."

"You wanted to meet me?"

"Thank you for coming," I said, my voice gentle and low. "You had a dispute with a friend of mine. A small black man. On a cart."

He stood stone-still, waiting.

"The dispute was our fault, and we apologize. He wasn't looking for you. We don't know anything about you. We don't want to know."

"What was he looking for?"

"The Ghost Van."

"Don't look for the Ghost Van," Mortay hissed. "You wouldn't like it if you found it."

"I'm not looking for it. I'm off the case. I just wanted to tell you to your face. We have no quarrel with you—whatever you did, it was just business, okay?"

I turned to go.

"Stay where you are."

I faced him. He hadn't moved.

"I gave the little nigger a message. Didn't you get it?"

"I just told you we did."

"About *Max*. Max the Silent. Max the *warrior*. I called him out. I want to meet him."

"If I see him, I'll tell him."

"You know my name? You play with me, you play with death."

"I'm not playing."

"I know you. Burke. That's you, right?"

"Yeah."

"Max is your man. Everyone knows that—it's all over the street. Everyone says he's the best. He's not. It's me. Me. He wants to admit it, go down on one knee, he can live. Otherwise, we fight."

"You can't make him fight."

"I can make *anyone* fight. I spit on dojo floors. I killed a kendo master with his own sword. Everybody has a button." He opened his hands, a gambler fanning a handful of aces. "I push the buttons."

"Let it go," I said.

He moved in on top of me. Spit full in my face. I didn't move, watching his eyes.

"You're better than I thought," he whispered. "You're too old to jump if I call your mother a name. But you spit in an ex-con's face, he has to fight."

"I won't fight you."

"You *couldn't* fight me, pussy." I felt my face rock to the side, blood in the corner of my mouth. "Never saw that, did you?"

"No," I answered him, chewing on my lip, my mind back in an

alley when I faced another man years ago. Wishing I had a gun, glad I didn't.

"I'm the fastest man there is. Max, he's nothing but a tough guy. I'll kill him in a heartbeat—he'll never see what does it."

"You can't make him fight—he doesn't fight just 'cause you call his name."

"What if I snap your spine, leave you in a wheelchair the rest of your life? You think that'll bring him around to see me?"

"You can't do that either," I said, my voice soft. "I'm not alone here."

The Spanish guy laughed. "I don't see nobody," he said, pulling an automatic from his belt.

I raised my hands as though I was responding to the pistol. One of the beer bottles exploded. I took another step away from Mortay.

"There's a rifle squad on the roof. Night scopes and silencers."

Mortay was ice, watching me.

"Want to see it again?" I raised my hand. Another bottle exploded. El Cañonero was the truth.

"I don't want any beef with you. You scared me good. I don't want anything to do with you. This is a walk-away. You can't hurt me, and you can't make Max fight you. It's *over*, get it?"

Mortay's voice was so low I had to lean forward to catch it. "Tell Max. Tell him I know about the baby. Tell him I know about Flower. Tell him to come and see me. Come and see me, or the baby dies."

I threw myself at him, screaming. I felt a chop in the ribs and I was on the ground. A flash of white and Mortay was gone. Bullets whined all around the playground. The dark-haired white guy went down. His body jumped as more bullets hit. Pieces of the building flew away.

I crawled over to the car, pulled myself inside. I twisted the key, floored the gas, and blasted through the gate.

**105** THE PLYMOUTH thundered toward the river, running without lights. I grabbed the highway, sliding into the late-night traffic, willing myself to slow down. My shoulders were hunched into my neck, tensing for the shot that never came. No sirens.

A quick choice—my office or Belle's? My office was closer, but Mortay knew where it was. The Plymouth's license plates were smeared with dirt and Vaseline—nobody could call in an ID.

I slipped through the Battery Tunnel, staying with traffic, one eye locked to the rearview mirror. Clear. I pulled the sleeves off the jacket I was wearing. The Velcro made a tearing sound. One sleeve went out the window on the Belt Parkway, the other a few miles down the road. I slipped out of the body of the jacket, dumped that too. The orange headband was the last to go, slipping away in the wind.

Two blocks from Belle's. I stopped at a pay phone, pulling the pistol from under the floor mat. She answered on the first ring.

"Hello?"

"It's me. You okay?"

"I'm fine, honey."

"What's your favorite animal?"

She caught it. "An alligator. It's clear, baby."

I hung up, stepping back into the Plymouth. Her door opened as I was coming up the walk. I slipped into the darkness, the pistol in my hand.

**106** I WENT to the couch, set the pistol down next to me, reached for the phone. Belle sat next to me, reaching out her hand.

"Honey . . ."

"Get away from me, Belle. I got work to do and I don't have much left."

I punched the numbers, cursing Ma Bell for having different area codes for Queens and Manhattan. Mama picked up.

"It's me. No time to talk. You get to Immaculata. Get her to come and see you, okay?"

"Okay."

"She has to go out of town for a while. With the baby, Mama. That's the important thing. With the baby. Let her tell Max whatever she wants—visit friends, whatever. But get her out of here."

"Max too?"

"Can you do it?"

"Big problems for me. Business problems. In Boston, okay?"

"Okay. But keep him low to the ground. Work quiet."

"Tomorrow morning he goes."

"With the baby."

"With baby. Like you say. Come by, tell me soon."

"Soon."

"Plenty help here, okay? Nobody hurt baby."

"Get them out of here, Mama."

"All done," she said.

I took a deep breath. Belle was motionless next to me. I punched another number, taking the lighted cigarette she held out. The Mole's phone was picked up at his end.

"It's me. I'm okay."

He hung up.

I started to shake then. Couldn't get the cigarette into my mouth. Belle put her arms around me, pressing my head to her breasts.

"Let it go," I said, pushing her away. "Let it come out—I know what to do."

I let the fear snake its way through me, shaking my body, a terrier with a rat. I replayed the tape—back in the playground, down on the ground, a ribbon of killer bees death-darting between me and Mortay, El Cañonero on the high ground keeping me safe.

My body trembled in the terror seizure. Malaria flashes. Taking me back to the burned-out jungle in Biafra where fear grew thicker than the vines.

I couldn't make it stop—didn't even try. I stayed quiet and still. Careful as a man with broken ribs—the kind that puncture a lung if you cough.

Fear ran its race.

When it stopped, I was soaking wet, limp. Drained. I closed my eyes then, sliding my face into Belle's lap.

# 107

It was still dark when I came around. I turned my head. My face slid across Belle's lap, her thighs slick with sweat. Or tears. I pulled myself up, next to her.

"Can you get a duffel bag out of the trunk of my car? I need to take a shower—I don't like the way I smell."

"You smell fine to me."

"Just do it, okay?"

She got up without another word. I took off my clothes. They felt heavy in my hands. I dropped them on the floor, stepped into the shower.

When I came back out, Belle had the duffel bag on the couch. I toweled myself off, put on a fresh set of clothes. Belle's clock said two-fifteen. I took a pillowcase from the duffel bag, stuffed everything I'd been wearing into it, even the cheap watch.

"I don't have a washing machine here," she said, watching my face.

"This stuff needs an incinerator," I said, tossing it near the front door.

"You want a drink?"

"Ice water."

She cracked some cubes in a glass, ran the tap, brought it over to me. I lit a cigarette, watching my hands on the matches. They didn't shake.

I propped myself against the arm of the couch, sipping the water, smoking my cigarette. Watching the smoke drift to the ceiling. Belle stood a few feet away, watching me, not saying a word.

"Come here, baby," I said.

She sat on the floor next to the couch. I put my hand on the back of her neck, holding her. It was quiet and safe in the dark. Belle took the ashtray from me, put it on the floor where I could reach it. Lit a smoke of her own.

"When I was a young man, just a kid really, I had a place of my own. A basement, but it was fixed up like an apartment. I was raised in other people's places: the orphanage, foster homes, reform school. Nothing belonged to me. I got to thinking that place was real important."

I dragged deep on the cigarette, watching the glow at the tip.

"A man wanted my basement. I didn't know how to act then— there was nobody to tell me what to do—nobody for me to listen to. I got a gun and I went to meet him. In an alley. I was scared. I thought if I couldn't keep my basement I could never keep anything. Never have anything of my own.

"I had to meet the man. Like tonight. I can still see it—like I was right back there. I got ready to go. Ran Vaseline through my hair so nobody could get a grip. Wrapped my body with layers of newspaper in case he had a knife. Taped the handle of the pistol. So I wouldn't leave fingerprints . . . but really because I was so scared I thought I'd drop it when I took it out. I looked around that basement one last time. My basement. Left the radio playing as I walked out the door. It was Doc Pomus. A great old blues singer. Walking the line just before rock 'n' roll came. 'Heartlessly.' That was the song. I still hear it.

"He was there, waiting for me with his boys. I tried to talk to him. He just laughed at me—called me a punk. I showed him the pistol. He said I wouldn't pull the trigger—said I was scared to death. He was half right. I shot him."

"Did you kill him?"

"No. I didn't know it at the time. I just pumped a slug into him. The other people with him—they saw me do it. I just walked away. Back to my basement. I thought the word would be on the street. Don't fuck with Burke. He's a man now. Not a kid."

"What happened?"

"They came for me. I went to prison. I paid attention in there—found people I could listen to. I never wanted to be a hijacker. I'm not a gunfighter in my heart, I'm a thief. I never wanted to be a citizen—knew I never could anyway. But I didn't want to stick up liquor stores. I wanted to walk the line. Use my head, not my hands."

I stubbed out the cigarette.

"I've been waiting for full bloom all my life, Belle. It never worked out for me, Belle. I run some scams for a while, make a few good scores. But it seems like I always end up going back into that alley."

I took another hit of the ice water, Belle's hand on my chest.

"I thought it was all about that damn basement. I swore I'd never fight over a *thing*, never again. No matter what, I'd walk away. Travel light."

I lit another smoke.

"I cut the crap out of my life. I don't drink, don't play with dope. I learned to be careful. Real, real careful. I've got cut-outs inside cut-outs. Boxes inside boxes. Background tapes when I make telephone calls, phony license plates on the car. I got passports, birth certificates, driver's licenses. I sting freaks who can't sting back. I just wanted what the little ones want—what your mother wanted for you."

"To be safe?"

"Yeah. To be safe. The pattern I made for myself—it was like a ritual. Something you pray to. To keep you safe from demons. I was so scared before, when I was shaking on the couch. It made me think. Like you're praying your ass off and the devil shows up instead of God. It makes you stop praying. It's not a world out here, it's a junkyard. I grabbed a little girl once, maybe fourteen years old. Working the street. She spent her nights with her eyes closed and her mouth full. Turned over all the money to some dirtbag who beat her up and sent her back for more. I was taking her to this place I know, where they'd keep her safe, and I asked her about being a runaway. I thought you ran away to get to a better place. She told me she *was* in a better place."

"I know."

"I know you do. I've been thinking about it. Lying here. I wanted to live off my wits. Not beat the system, just take my little piece off to the side. Play it extra-safe.

"But I see it now. It was a pattern. The one thing you don't want to do."

"What pattern?"

"In prison, a guy who's thinking about going over the Wall . . . you can tell. You watch him, he falls into a pattern. Does the same thing every day. Maybe he stays in his cell instead of falling out for the movie. 'Cause he's working on the bars. Little piece at a time, putting dirty soap into the cuts to hide them. Waiting. Or you see him on the yard, watching the guard towers. Making schedules in his head. *Any* pattern marks you after a while. This South American dictator, he always went everywhere in an armored limo. Bodyguards in front, bodyguards in back. Safe as a bank vault. The other side, they blew up the car with a fucking rocket. See? The pattern taught them what to do. They didn't waste time with hijack stuff. Just blew the problem away."

"But . . ."

"It's me too, Belle. I've been at it too long. I play it safe, but I don't play it alone. You understand what I'm saying?"

"No, honey."

"I can walk away from that office and never look back. They'll never nail me fighting over my home again. I don't have a home. Remember when you said we should run? I can't run. I don't have a home, but I have people. My people. The only thing that's mine. That's my pattern."

"The little black guy?"

"The Prof is one. There's others. I don't know how it happened. I didn't mean for it to happen. I have these dreams. I was going to be a gunfighter. Live hard until I died. But I found out I didn't want to die. Then I was going to be a scam artist. But I kept running into kids. And they keep pulling me into what I didn't want to be.

"I wanted to use my head, Belle, and they make me use my hands. I was going to be a lone wolf. I even liked the way the words *sound*, you know? But it's not me. All my life, I never found what I am . . . just what I'm not."

Belle shifted her weight on the floor, looking at me. "I know what you are," she said.

"No, you don't. You know what you want. I do that too. I think I want something, I make what I have into whatever that is. It doesn't work."

She grabbed a handful of my shirt. "You better not be telling me a fancy goodbye, Burke."

"There's nothing fancy about it. There's not going to be any more basements in my life. I'm over the edge now. Past the line. This guy, the guy I met tonight—he wants my brother. And he knows how to make him come to fight. I can't let Max do it."

"If he's as good as you say . . ."

"It's not a duel, Belle. Max has a baby. He's an outlaw. Like us. But he walks his own road. He fights this freak, there's no win. It's like turning over a rock—you don't know what's underneath. This Mortay, he's started something. If they fight, maybe Mortay wins. And my brother is dead. Max wins, he won't win easy. And even if he does, he's out of the shadows and into the street. Don't you get it?"

"No!"

"Listen to me, little girl. Listen good. There's no more outlaw code. There's no rules for freaks. I've known this since I was a kid, but I never really dealt with it. When I went back to my basement, after I shot that guy?"

"Yeah . . ."

"The people who came for me, they weren't his friends. It was the cops."

"I . . ."

"Listen! It was the *cops*. I was a stupid fucking kid who thought he was going to be a gunfighter. I went back to my basement. I thought they'd come for me—we'd shoot it out. I didn't care if I lived or I died. If I couldn't have my basement, I didn't care. If they came for me and I won, I'd have a rep. Walk down the street, women would look at me, men would whisper my name. I thought they'd come with guns—they came with a warrant."

I lit a smoke. My hands were still steady.

"I'm telling you the truth now. Max can't win a fight with this freak. *Somebody's* coming for him after that. Sooner or later . . ."

"Burke . . ."

"I've got my debts too, Belle. You've never been a slut with your body; don't be one with your respect. But give me what's coming to me. I got no choice about this. I don't want to live here if I have to pay so high."

"You have to kill him," she said. It wasn't a question.

"I have to kill him. And I'm not good enough to do it and walk away."

"You've been to prison before. I said I'd wait for you. I'll wait for you even if you buy a life sentence."

"I'm doing a life sentence right now. It's time to stop playing with myself. I got a plan. I know how to take him out. But it'll never end up in court."

"Honey . . ."

"The Mole. The guy you met tonight? He's a genius. Like you wouldn't believe. I'll have him make me a jacket. Line it with the right stuff. I'll find Mortay. He'll do what he does. And when he hits, there's a big bang and it's over."

She was crying, her head on my chest. "No, no, no . . ."

"Don't take this from me," I said. "If I could figure out another way, I'd do it in a minute. But I looked in his eyes. There's nobody home there. I can't take a chance. If I try and I miss, my people will go down. And it'll be me who did it.

"I could live with jail again, Belle. But if I miss this freak, I couldn't live with myself. I'd have nothing to come back to."

"Why can't you . . . ?"

"What? Call the cops? Have us all move to the mountains? I'm going to *try*, okay? I don't want to die. I'm not good enough with my hands to take him out. For a minute, when I was in the shower, for just a minute, I let it run in my head. Thought the answer was there. There's a *reason* for this freak being connected to the Ghost Van. It's all patterns. If I could hook into his, maybe I'd have a handle to twist him with."

She pulled back, watching my face as if she could see past my eyes, big round tears on her face. Glass beads—they'd shatter if they hit the floor.

"You'll try?"

"I'll try, sure I'll try. I don't have much time. I have to put it together . . . but maybe it doesn't fit. Maybe there is no pattern."

"But you'll *try*? You swear?"

"I swear. But I'm cutting you out, Belle. Right now, nobody has you with me. You can be out of here in a few hours. I've got some money. I'll give you a number to call. It'll all be over in a few days, one way or another."

"Get some sleep, baby," she said, kissing me on the lips.

**108** I FELT the heat. My eyes snapped open. My head turned to the side. Belle stood naked in front of me, my eyes on a level with the triangle of her hips, the soft pelt between them.

"You think you're being a man?" she asked.

"I'm being myself. Trying to be myself."

"I won't stop you. I love you. But you can't stop me either."

"What're you talking about?"

"I'm in this. I'm with you. Whatever way it plays."

"I told you . . ."

"What're you going to do, big man? Beat my ass? I *like* that, remember?"

"Belle . . ."

"You know *why* I like it?" she whispered. "Yes. Yes, you do. I only let two people hit me in my life. Sissy. And you. She loved me, and I wanted you to love me too. Own me. Take care of me. Rescue me, like she did. You don't want to live in this world alone. I understand what you said. I listened to you. I'm not running away, make some fucking phone call, find out if you're dead."

"Do what I tell you."

"I'll take your orders. I'll take whatever you have. But only if I'm *yours*, understand? I'm in this."

"You're not."

"I'm *in* this, you bastard. You can't stop me. You let me in this, you let me help you, I'll obey you like a slave. I'll do whatever you say. But if you don't, I swear I'll go back to work tomorrow night. And I'll tell every man in the place that I'm your girlfriend. I'll tell my boss. I'll put it on the street. I'll take an ad in the fucking newspapers, I have to! You don't want me in the pattern, you have to let me in your life."

I propped myself on one elbow, looking straight ahead. "You big, stupid bitch." It was all I could say.

I wasn't watching her face, but I could feel the flash of her smile. "I'm a beautiful young girl," she whispered, "and you taught me that. I'm a woman. Your woman. And you're going to see just what a stand-up woman is all about."

I closed my eyes again.

**109** WHEN I came around again, Belle was standing in the same place, hands on her hips. "What time is it?" I asked her.

"Time to get up," she said, kneeling down next to the couch, pressing her mouth against me, hands fumbling at my belt. I stroked her back, smooth and moist, like she just stepped out of a bath. She smelled of jasmine.

She unbuttoned my shirt, her face against my chest. The necklace shone against her skin. She licked my chest, my belly. Then she took me in her mouth.

I knew what she was doing. I knew it wouldn't work. But I felt myself grow in her mouth. Swell to bursting. I looked at the ceiling. Shadows. I closed my eyes.

She took her mouth from me. "Almost ready," she whispered.

"I'm ready now."

"Not yet. Wait." She stroked me with something slippery in her hand, gently working it in from the root to the tip. She took my hand. "Come on," she said, pulling me from the couch, leading me to the bed.

She sat down on the bed, pulling me with her, pushing me onto my back again. She lit a cigarette, put it in my mouth. She lay down on her stomach, her face inches from mine.

"Will you do something for me?"

"What?"

"Never mind what—will you do it?"

"I . . ."

"Just listen to me, okay? Then decide. All right?"

"Yeah." I felt so tired. Like an old man starting another long sentence.

"Remember I told you about that man I was with once? That tough guy? The guy who wouldn't have a bitch dog?"

"Yeah."

"Remember I told you he said all bitches would turn tail? That's what he wanted me to do?"

I nodded, dragging on the cigarette.

"You know what he meant? He meant turn *my* tail. He wanted to fuck me in the ass."

"Uh."

"He said a real man could always find a piece of ass—said he'd been in prison and he even found some there." She reached over, took the cigarette from me, drew on it. Handed it back. "Did you ever do that?"

"What?"

"Fuck a man. In prison."

"No."

"What'd you do?"

"I went steady with my fist," I snorted. Close to a laugh, but not there yet.

"'Cause a real man doesn't do that?"

"I don't know what a real man does. It's like everything I know, Belle—I only know the dark side. I only know what a man doesn't do."

"Is that why you wouldn't taste me? The first time we made love?"

"I told you the truth then—it's the same truth. In prison . . . men do things. I don't put them down for it. Man wants to fuck another man, it doesn't say anything about him."

"What is it a man *doesn't* do, then?"

"He doesn't fuck someone who doesn't want to be fucked, okay? That's the only rule, the only real one. Fucking another man in the ass doesn't make you less of one. But *taking* it . . ."

"I know. It makes a man into a girl."

"That's bullshit. A kid who gets raped in prison, it says something about the guy who did it to him, that's all."

"But if the kid doesn't fight . . ."

"He *has* to fight. He doesn't have to win."

"What happens to a kid who's raped?"

"He can lock up, go into PC. Protective Custody. Or he can hang up. Take himself off the count. I guess he could even escape. But he can't walk the yard unless he squares it."

"How does he square it?"

"Kill the guy. Shank him, pipe him, poison him . . . it don't matter. Even it up. Get it back."

I sat up in the bed, lit another cigarette. "That's what I was trying to tell you. There's rules. For everything. They don't have to be fair ones. The first time I was in reform school, one of the bigger kids rolled on me. I never let him finish his pitch. We fought. He could beat me, but he knew he'd never turn me. The next time I went back inside, I was older. Smarter. They were running another game then. It was all gangs inside. They'd make one of the little kids run. Take off at night. Then they'd run out and catch him. Kick the shit out of him, drag him back. They used to get a go-home behind it. Just another way of being raped.

"When they came to me, I told this big guy I'd do it, but I wasn't doing it for nothing. He had to give me his radio. I watched his face— I could see he was thinking what a chump I was.

"He gave me his radio and I told him I'd run in a week. I spent a lot of time on the grounds. Looking around. Getting ready. When the night came, I took off. I told him I'd be waiting for him by this big tree. Made him promise not to hurt me when he brought me back. I kept watching his face—I knew he was lying.

"I took off. Climbed up in the tree with this cinder block I'd found. He came looking for me. Calling my name. Real quiet, so he'd be the one to bring me in. Get all the credit for himself."

I bit into the filter tip of the cigarette, feeling myself smile inside at the memory, my hand on Belle's hip.

"I dropped the cinder block right on his head. He went down. I jumped on top of him, stomped his face into the ground. I held the cinder block over my head and slammed it into his ribs a couple of times. Then I went back and told the Man that this guy had escaped and I'd stopped him, but he was too heavy for me to drag back.

"I got my parole. He went to the hospital."

"Good."

"Yeah, good. I know how things work. I had to pay for what I know, but I know."

"You can figure this out too, honey."

"I don't know. . . ."

"You're scared of this guy, but . . ."

"I'm always scared of *something*, Belle. The trick is not to let it get in the way. Like ego—ego gets in the way. I went there tonight to tell the guy I wasn't carrying a beef. Almost *begged* him to walk away, let it go. But it wasn't what he wanted."

Belle reached for me again. "How about what I want?"

"*What* do you want?"

She squirmed until she was next to me, one arm on my shoulder, still holding me in the other hand, slippery.

"I told you only two people hit me in my life. You and Sissy. I told you the truth—I told you why," she said, moving closer to me, whispering in the night. "I took my clothes off for men to watch. Everything I ever did with a man, I did with you. But special. From the very first time. I knew. Sometimes you just *know* something. I want you to do it to me. What he wanted. Nobody ever did."

Her voice dropped even lower, swamp-orchid soft. "I didn't know what I was saving it for, but I knew I had to save something. It's for you."

I kissed her cheek. "You saved it *all* for me, girl. Don't fuss about it."

"Burke, do it! Come *on*. I need you to do it. It's special. For you. Not for you to take . . . for me to give."

"Belle . . ."

Her mouth was against my ear, tongue darting inside. "Want me to get down on my knees and beg?"

I got off the bed, stood facing her. She was on her knees, taking me in her mouth. "Aagh!" she said, pulling her face away. "That stuff tastes awful."

"What is it?"

"K-Y Jelly. I bought it when I went shopping. It was supposed to be your surprise." She stroked me again, slathering the stuff on. "Yes?"

I nodded.

She turned, still on her knees, her backside to me. "Where's that stuff?" I asked her.

She handed it to me. I covered myself again. Patted her butt, squeezed a glob on my finger, worked it inside her. Softly, slowly. She wiggled her rear. "Uhmmmm . . ."

I put one hand on each side of her, gently pulling her apart. I felt the tip slide into her. Pushed forward.

"*Easy*, honey. A big house can have a little door."

I pulled out of her.

"Come on."

"I don't want to hurt you."

"I was just teasing, baby. Come on, now. Come on."

I slipped in her again, working the tip back and forth, a little bit at a time. She rammed herself back against me, grunting, maybe in pain. I looked at her in the dark, split by my cock, her palms flat on the bed, elbows locked. She looked back over her shoulder. "Nice and easy," she said, smiling. The blue beads swinging from her neck.

I found the rhythm. She moved with me, just a little, working me deeper into her. "Just for you," she whispered, as I shot off inside her.

**110** ‖ WE WERE on the move before it got light outside. I swung the Plymouth into the garage, led Belle up the stairs, the pistol cocked in my hand.

Everything was as I left it. I let Pansy out to her roof, poured some food into her bowl. Belle stood next to me.

"You're not worried he'll try this place?"

"I don't think he wants anything to do with rooftops after last night."

"What happened?"

"It doesn't matter," I said, popping open file cabinets, handing her papers to put on the desk.

Pansy strolled into the room. Belle patted her head. The beast ignored her, demolishing the food. I opened the floorboard in a corner of the back closet. Belle knelt next to me. "Take this stuff over there," I told her, filling her arms with death.

She dumped it all on the couch like it was laundry. A sawed-off .12-gauge holding three-inch magnum shells. Double-O buckshot in one barrel, a rifled deer slug in the other. A Sig Sauer .45—the closest thing to a jam-proof automatic they make. Six fragmentation grenades, little gray baseball-sized bombs. Four sticks of dynamite, wrapped together with duct tape. A heavy Ruger .357 magnum single-action revolver.

I went over to the desk, moved the papers to one side, reached for the phone. Belle was standing by the couch, watching.

"Come here," I said, watching her face. When she got close, I made one last try.

"I don't think he's coming here. But if he does, it'll take him a while to get through that door. He does, and this whole building's going up. You understand?"

"Yes."

"You *sure?* I can't use the guns. There's no way to shoot through that door, and if he gets inside, there's no room. No time. He's too fast. Mortay makes it inside here, there's no gunshots. Just one big boom."

"I know."

"You can work with me. I'll keep my promise. But I don't want you to stay here. You take the car, go back to your house. I'll call . . ."

"Forget it."

"I'll call you when I *need* you, okay? Not when it's over. Before that. When I need a driver," I said, trying my last hope.

She put her hands on her hips, her legs spread wide apart. "You want me to take Pansy with me?"

"No."

Her dark eyes were on fire. "One bitch is good enough to die with you, not the other, huh?"

"Belle . . . Pansy wouldn't go with you."

"That's bullshit. You could get her out of here. You just think she might do you some good."

I threw up my hands. "I give up," I told her.

"Burke, don't give up. I'm not asking you to give up. Let it play out, okay?"

"Okay," I said, reaching for her hand.

She sat on the corner of the desk, looking down at me. "Where do you think you go when you die? You think we all go to the same place?"

"I don't know."

"This guy comes here, we'll find out together," she said, holding my hand tight.


**111** I STARTED going through the papers piled on my desk. Smoking and thinking. Belle put her hand on my shoulder. "You want some paper, write stuff down?"

"No. I'm not used to working like that. I have to do it in my head."

"Can I help?"

"Not yet."

I went back to the files, working over the clips on the Ghost Van, sorting what I had into little boxes inside my head. Stacking them in rows, building a foundation. You work from the ground up, brick by brick. When you reach out your hand for a brick and it's not there, you've found the door. Whatever's missing, that's where you have to look.

The man who played with death wanted Max. I wanted him. He had all the cards, but I had one edge. I knew something he never would. How to be afraid.

The edge burned at the corners of my guts.

Seven-thirty. I picked up the phone. All clear. Dialed Mama. She answered in the middle of the first ring.

"Gardens."

"It's me. What?"

"Gone."

"All of them?"

"All gone. Maybe three weeks, okay?"

"Perfect."

"You have two calls. Man called Marques, couple hours ago. And the cop. McGowan. Maybe ten minutes ago."

She gave me the numbers. McGowan was calling from the Runaway Squad; I didn't recognize the other one.

"I'm off, Mama."

"You come soon?"

"Soon."

I lit a smoke. Ten minutes ago . . . I dialed McGowan. He answered himself.

"You called me?"

"We got to meet, pal. *Now*."

"I'm hot."

"Just say where."

"Battery Park. Where they park to go out to the Statue of Liberty. The benches facing the water."

"Thirty minutes?"

"I'll be there."

Belle was behind me, her hands on my shoulders. I told her the number Mama gave me for Marques.

"That the same one you have?"

She went into the back room, came out with her purse, fumbled around. Pulled out a little red leather book, thumbed through the pages. She looked up. "No."

I punched the number into the phone. A woman's voice came on the line.

"Mr. Dupree's office," she said, a coked-up giggle in her voice.

"Get Marques," I told her.

The pimp took the phone. "Yes?" Like an executive.

"You called me a couple of hours ago?"

"Who's this?"

"You called at the Chinese Embassy, okay?"

"Oh, yeah. I get you. Look, man, I got some dynamite stuff. This guy who hangs with him, he . . ."

"Hold up," I barked, listening hard. The phone didn't sound right. "Where you calling from?"

"From my ride, man. You ever see one of them car phones?"

"Yeah. It's a *radio* phone. It's not just me you're talking to now, get it?"

"It's cool."

"It's *not* cool. Give me a number to call you at."

"No way, José. I got business out here, won't be back to the crib for *hours*. Give me *your* number, I'll ring you in an hour."

I pulled a looseleaf book from the desk drawer. "East Side or West Side?"

"What?"

"Where you going to be in an hour? In your car. Where?"

"Oh. East Side, man."

I ran my finger down the list of numbers. "Make it nine o'clock, okay? Rush hour, nobody's paying attention. There's a pay phone in the gas station at Ninety-fourth and Second. Go there, fill up your ride, I'll ring you there."

"You'll call *me*? On a pay phone?"

"Yeah, don't worry about it. We set?"

"They got super-premium gas in that station, man?"

I hung up the phone.

**112** PANSY PUT her two front paws on the desk, making her noises. I scratched behind her ears. "Not now, girl." She licked my face. I'd have to use disinfectant for an after-shave.

One more call. The Mole. I heard the phone picked up.

"It's me. I need another car. Can I make the switch in a couple of hours, leave mine there?"

"Okay."

I pulled my first-aid kit out of the bottom drawer. "Belle, come over here."

She came over. Quiet and watchful. "I have to meet some people. Can you take a cab over to the hospital? See the Prof? Just stay there until I call—three, four hours?"

"Why can't I go with you?"

"There's a thin line between a brat and a bitch," I said, holding an aluminum splint against my forearm, measuring. "A little girl can't be a bitch, an old woman can't be a brat."

I pulled a three-inch-wide roll of elastic bandage from the kit, put it aside. Started cutting pieces off a roll of Velcro, working fast. "Woman your age, she can be either one. Or both. Big as you are, you can still act like a little brat sometimes. You want something, you put your hands on your hips. Pout, stamp your feet. It's cute, okay? Makes me want to give that big rump of yours a slap."

She smiled her smile.

"But when you try and go back on a deal, you're over the line. Makes me want to dump you someplace. Not come back."

Her face went hard. "You better . . ."

"Shut up, Belle. We made a deal, right? You're in this, but you . . . Do. What. I. Tell. You. That's what you said—that's what you do."

"I'm sorry."

"Don't be sorry. I don't have time for sorry."

"Honey . . ."

"Get me one of the grenades."

"These?" she asked, holding one of the metal baseballs like it was an orange.

"Yeah."

She handed it to me. I put it down on the desk, rolled up my sleeve, fitted the aluminum splint into place. "Hold this," I told her, wrapping the tape around until I had a thick pad. I put the grenade in my hand, wrapped my fist around the blue lever. Pulled the pin.

"Burke."

"Yeah. That's right. I let go of this thing, everything blows up."

I wound the Velcro strips around my fist, leaving a loose tab at the end. It looked like I broke my hand punching a wall and drew a ham-fisted intern when they brought me to the emergency ward. I swung my hand back and forth, testing the tape. I relaxed my fist. The lever stayed tight.

I got to my feet. "Help me on with my jacket," I said to Belle. She took the surgical scissors, slit the left sleeve neatly. I slipped my arm through.

"Honey, why . . . ?"

"It's safe. Unless I pull this tab," I said, showing her how the Velcro worked to seal the lever. I put the pin in my pocket, handed her a spare. "Tape this to the inside of your wrist—we might need it in a hurry."

"I don't . . ."

I put my arm around her waist, pulling her close to me. "You go to the hospital, like I said. I'm out in the street, I could run into this freak. I'm *trying* to put it together. Like I promised you last night. But if he comes for me before I'm ready . . ."

"It's crazy! If that thing comes loose . . ."

"Everything's already come loose," I said, holding her. Making her see it in my face.

**113** In the garage, I said goodbye. "I'm going out first. You wait a few minutes, then you slip out. Take a cab to the hospital. Wait for my call there. You won't see this car again until it's over."

She kissed me hard. "You be careful."

"That's what I do best."

She kissed me again, her hand rubbing my crotch. "Second-best," she whispered.

I backed out into the street, watching the garage door close through the windshield. I couldn't see Belle in the shadows.

**114** I parked the Plymouth near the Vista Hotel and walked to where I said I'd meet McGowan. The grenade felt heavy swinging at the end of my arm—I'd have to rig up some kind of sling when I got the chance.

I found the bench, sat down. I one-handed a wooden match out of the little box, braced it between my taped-up hand and my knee, fired it up.

McGowan's car swung in. He popped out the passenger side, walking toward me fast. I heard tires on the pavement, flicked my eyes to the side. Another dark four-door sedan. Whip antenna, two guys in front. About as undercover as a blue-and-white with roof lights.

"You're here," he greeted me.

"Like I said I would be. And all by myself too."

His smile was hard. "Volunteers. Not your problem. What happened to your hand?"

"I grabbed something I shouldn't of."

"Not the first time, huh?"

"Nope. What'd you want, McGowan?"

He fired one of his stinking cigars. "You trust me?"

"So far."

"I'm not wired. The other guys, they're backup. Not for you. For me."

"Go."

He looked straight ahead, puffing on his cigar, keeping his voice low. "A man named Robert Morgan got himself killed last night."

"Never heard of him."

"Nine-one-one call came in around midnight. Uniforms found a dead man. In the playground by the Chelsea Projects."

"So?"

"He had seven slugs in him, maybe a four-inch group, all in the chest. High-tech stuff. Whoever smoked him was a pro."

"So?"

"Nobody heard a shot. This was no punk kid running around on the roof with a .22—it was a hit."

"So?"

"The ground was all chewed up. Pieces of concrete ripped right out. The shooter had more than one target."

"This is real interesting, McGowan. Give me a light, will you?" I leaned close to his lighter. His hands were steady.

"Where were you last night, Burke?"

"With someone. Far away."

"You're sure?"

"What's the big deal?"

McGowan's cigar steamed in the morning air. It smelled as bad as his story.

"The guy had ID. That's where we got the Robert Morgan handle. Since it looked like a pro hit, they ran his prints. Nothing.

The lab guy's a good man—he was on the ball. I heard from him an hour ago."

"Heard what?"

"This Robert Morgan, his prints matched one we took off the switch-car. The one that snatched the baby hooker."

"Why tell me?"

He looked straight ahead. "You're good, Burke. I think they could wire you to a polygraph and you'd never bounce the needles." He tilted his head back, looking up at the sky. "This dead guy, he was in the Ghost Van. It's the first lead we got. I figure you left it there for us, but you didn't know it."

I dragged on my cigarette, waiting.

"I think you're already in the tunnel. We're coming from the other end. I don't want to meet you in the middle—somebody could get hurt."

I snapped my cigarette into the street. "Stay out of the tunnel," I told him, getting up to leave. "I'll call you."

I didn't look back.

**115** NOBODY FOLLOWED me to the Plymouth. I took the East Side Drive to 61st, hooked York Avenue, and kept on going uptown. I pulled over on 92nd, checking the clock in the window of a boutique that hadn't opened yet. Eight-thirty-five. Plenty of time.

I made a sling out of a loop of Ace bandage, holding one end in my teeth to tighten the knot. Smoked a couple of cigarettes. Mortay was tied into the Ghost Van now for sure. For dead sure. And maybe it wasn't just bodyguard work he was doing. I was in a box—I had to get him in there with me. And know where the back door was.

I watched the cigarette smoke puddle against the windshield, playing with it. I was in Family Court once, listening to Davidson sum up on a case, watching him for the UGL—they wanted to know what he was made of before they hired him for a homicide case. They had this baby in foster care for years. Kept him there while the social workers tried to make parents out of the slime who tortured the kid. In this city, a pit bull bites two people, they gas it. To protect the public. A human cripples his own kid, they give him another bite.

Davidson was representing the kid. They call it being a "law guardian." The parents had their own lawyers; the city's lawyers represent the social workers. I still remember what he said:

"Judge, this baby will only be a child for a little while. Then he's an adult. We only have a few years to help him. The parents, they've had their chance. More than one. But this baby's not in foster care, he's in limbo. What about *him*? Isn't he entitled to some end to this? All butterflies, no matter how beautiful, have to land sometime. Or they die. The parents started this mess. The social workers kept it going. It's up to you to stop it. Stop it now. Let this baby have a *real* family."

The judge went along with it. He let the butterfly land. The baby was released for adoption. The mother cried. For herself. Davidson makes a living keeping criminals out of jail, but that day he kept someone from going to jail years later. I know.

My thoughts floating like that butterfly, looking for a safe place to land, I got out of the Plymouth. The clock said eight-fifty-five.

I started walking to the pay phone on the corner, snapping away my cigarette.

**116** MARQUES ANSWERED on the first ring. "That you, Burke?"

"Yeah. I just wanted to make sure the phone was working at your end. I'll call you back in five minutes."

"Man, you think I got nothing better to do than to sit around here and . . ."

"Five minutes, Marques. No more. Then we'll talk. Be cool."

I hung up, started walking again.

I turned the corner, spotted the Rolls parked next to the pay phone. I came up to the driver's window from the back. It was open, a man's elbow resting on the sill. Diamonds on his wrist.

"Let's talk," I said.

Marques jumped. "What? How'd you . . . ?"

"Everything's cool. Just relax. I didn't want to talk on the phone. How about we go for a ride?"

"I ain't going *anywhere* with you, man," he said, eyes darting around.

"In *your* car, okay? Anywhere you want to go."

He got hold of himself. "In the back seat," he snapped to the blonde next to him.

I held the back door for her. One of the whores who'd been with him in Junior's. She didn't smile. I climbed in the front. Marques backed the car out of his spot, headed uptown, to Harlem. "What happened to your hand, man?"

"Nothing much."

"Yeah. Okay, look here, I . . ."

"You want to talk in front of Christina?" I asked him, tilting my head toward the back seat.

"I told you before, man. This is my bottom woman. Besides, she's the one got the dope."

I lit a smoke. The windows whispered up, sealing off the outside world. We stopped at a light. Two kids rolled up to the driver's side. Marques hit the switch. A black kid bent down. "You want your windows done, Mr. Dupree?"

"Later, baby," the pimp said, slapping a bill into the kid's hand.

We pulled away, cruising. I waited. If Christina wanted to listen to Marques, that was okay with me, but I wasn't adding to the conversation.

"Remember you asked about this guy with Mortay? Ramón?"

I nodded.

"He's a switch-hitter, man. Takes it up the chute from Mortay, hands it back the other way."

"To boys?"

"To girls, man. This Mortay, he pulls hard guys. Right off the street in Times Square. Takes the most macho guys he can find: rough-off boys, sluggers . . . you know what I mean?"

I nodded again.

"He's bent, man. Bent out of shape like you wouldn't believe. He takes the hard guys, makes them suck his cock. Turns them right around. Then he marks them. With that diamond in the ear. This Ramón, he's not the first. He had another boy. Guy they called Butcher. Mortay turns him over. One day this Butcher is shaking down street people, doing his thing—next day he's walking with Mortay, that diamond in his ear."

I opened my hand in a "What happened next?" gesture.

"He just disappears, man. Poof! He's off the street. And Ramón—he's wearing the diamond."

"And he's an evil freak too!" Christina snarled, leaning forward between me and Marques.

"Tell him, baby," Marques said.

The blonde's voice was ugly. "He was known before. He wasn't a player, but he'd grab some little girl, slap her around, take her money. Like Marques said, a rough-off artist. Always carried a gun, let you see it. Times Square trash."

"Tell him the rest."

"He does the massage parlors now. All the girls know him. He pays big, so he got a lot of play at first. But he's a pain-freak, man. He has to hurt a girl to get off. You know Sabrina? Big fat Sabrina?"

I shook my head no.

"She does pain-for-gain. Whips and chains. She used to work at Sadie's Sexsational? Just off Eighth?"

I nodded.

"This Ramón had a date with her. Goes in the back. Stays a long time. Manager comes back to see what's taking so long, Ramón's just walking out. Points a piece in the manager's face and just keeps going. Sabrina was a mess, man. He tied her up, put a ball-gag in her mouth, whipped her till she was nothing but blood. Left a whiskey bottle sticking out of her ass."

I bit into my cigarette. I'd seen it before. They start out mean, they end up evil.

Christina sat back in her seat. Marques snorted a fat line of coke off his wrist. "That's the story, man. Nobody knows where Mortay lives. This Ramón, he's on the street most every night. Meets Mortay different places and they go off together."

"You did good," I said, dragging on the smoke.

"I'm out of it now, man. These people are too heavy for me. I'm a lover, not a killer. That's why I came to you."

I didn't say anything.

"Drop you someplace, man?"

"Thirty-ninth, anywhere near the river."

"Man, that's only a block away."

"Downtown. Not a Hundred and thirty-ninth."

"Oh, yeah. Right," Marques said, flashing his pimp-smile. "I forgot you was white."

Marques rambled on during the drive downtown. It's expensive to keep good women working. The IRS just took a major player off the street for back taxes. Bail bondsmen and lawyers were eating him alive. Couldn't find a decent mechanic for the Rolls.

I mumbled just enough to keep him talking, my mind floating someplace else. Like a butterfly.

Hawks have to land too.

117 ‖ MARQUES DROPPED me off where I asked him. "I'm out of it," he said again.

I leaned into the window, keeping my voice low. "You're out of it when the Ghost Van's off the streets. You did your piece. But if I need to talk to you again, I'm going to call."

He wouldn't meet my eyes. "Yeah, man. Right on. You know where to find me."

I watched Christina let herself into the front seat.

"I always will," I promised him.

I watched the Rolls pull into traffic.

**118** HE ANSWERED the phone like he always does.

"Morelli."

"It's Burke. I need to talk."

"Talk."

"Not on the phone."

I heard the groan in his voice. "And you won't come to the office, right?"

"Take a walk downstairs. I'll meet you on the benches in front of the UN. Right across from Forty-first."

"Now?"

"Now."

**119** I HAD a good twenty minutes to myself, waiting for Morelli. My mind was a rat, gnawing at the corner of a warehouse full of grain.

The UN towered behind me. Useless piece of junk. I wondered how long it would be before somebody turned it into a co-op.

I spotted Morelli across the street. Tall guy, looks ten years younger than he is. Never wears a hat, even in the winter. Dressing better now that he's married, but not much. He doesn't look like an investigative reporter. Hell, he doesn't look Italian. But he's the best of both.

He was twenty feet away when it hit me. Money. Where's the money? I filed the thought like a bitch-wolf hiding her cubs.

I shook hands with Morelli. "Let's walk," I said.

We found a place by the railing. Tourists flowed by. Security guards. People late for work. Morelli didn't waste time asking about my hand—it wasn't his way.

"What've you got?"

"I may have this fucking Ghost Van," I told him, watching his eyes light up. A hound on the scent.

"Tell me."

"There's a pattern. A karate-freak's been fighting duels all over the city. Challenging the leaders of every dojo. Killed at least a couple. He had a death-match. In the basement of Sin City. Every player made the scene. Big purse, side bets, the whole thing. Like a cockfight, only with people. I thought he was fronting off the van. Bodyguard work. He warned one of my people off. Broke his legs. Some other things happened, and now it's me he's looking for."

Morelli glanced at my left hand.

"Yeah," I said. "Like that. We're off the record now. Way off, okay?"

"Okay."

"A man got killed last night. The cops matched his prints to the switch-car for the Ghost Van."

"Yeah . . . ?"

"The guy that was killed, this karate-freak was with him when he bought it. It won't make the papers."

"Where do I come in?"

"We got two pieces left. Why the Ghost Van in the first place? What's it doing out there? That's my piece. Here's yours: where's the money?"

"What money?"

"There's always money. Somewhere, there's always money. This whole operation cost a bundle—somebody's scoring."

"I read the clips myself. It sounds like a sicko trip to me."

"You're reading it wrong. I know it. Let me do that bit, it's not for you."

"What's mine?"

"Sin City. Who owns it? Who's watching it? There's something about that place that ties it up. This karate-freak. Mortay. Nobody knows where he lives. But that's where he fought the duel. I'll work it through. I'm close now. I know it."

"I have to sit on the fingerprint story?"

"Yeah. But you're in on the kill when it all comes down. My word on it. No matter what happens, you'll get the whole story."

"First."

"From the horse's mouth."

"How much time I got?"

"Less than I got. And I got none."

He shook hands again, moved off.

I watched the street for a minute. Then I stepped on the uptown bus.

120 | THE PLYMOUTH was where I left it. In some neighborhoods, I worry about amateurs trying to strip it for parts—in Yuppieville, the only danger is that some citizen will want it towed away as an eyesore.

I headed for the Bronx on automatic pilot, still working the puzzle in my head. Pulling the pain into a laser point to burn through the haze.

The junkyard looks the same, day or night. Terry walked past the dogs, motioning me to shove over. He got behind the wheel. "I know the way," he said, steering carefully through the mine field until we pulled up outside a row of corrugated-iron sheds. The kid drove right in. I stood to the side, watching him jockey a couple of wrecks back and forth, filling up the area. In five minutes, the Plymouth had disappeared.

We walked through the yard, heading for the Mole's bunker. Terry bummed a cigarette. "Shouldn't you be going to school?" I asked him, handing it over.

"I am," the kid said.

The Mole was waiting for us. "What kind of car do you need?"

"Something that won't make people look twice."

"Big car? Fast?"

"Doesn't matter."

He turned to Terry. "Get the brown Pontiac."

The kid took off.

I sat down next to the Mole. If I waited for him to ask questions, I'd do a life sentence in the junkyard.

"Thanks for the car, Mole."

He grunted, disinterested.

The kid rolled up. The Pontiac was a couple of years old. A chocolate-brown four-door sedan. A nice, clean, boring commuter's car. It had New York plates, a fresh inspection sticker.

"Registration's in the glove compartment. Insurance card too," Terry said.

"Good work." If I got dropped, I'd tell the cops I borrowed the car from a guy I met in a bar. The owner would never show up to claim it, and the Pontiac wouldn't be on any hot-car list.

I lit a smoke. "Mole, I need to talk to you for a minute."

"Talk."

"The kid . . ."

"He has to learn," the Mole said.

"I'm working on something. The wheels came off last night. This guy's looking for me—I'm looking for him."

The Mole tapped my left hand. "What's that?"

"Grenade."

"I have better stuff."

"It's okay for now. That's not what I need."

The Mole waited. Terry opened his mouth to ask a question, caught the Mole looking at him, shut it down.

"There's a tie-in to this whole mess I told you about before. I think it's inside a building. Times Square, on Eighth. Maybe the basement. I'm having some things checked out now." I dragged deep on the smoke. The Mole and the kid sat like twin toads.

"Can you get inside the building for me?"

Terry laughed. It was like asking Sonny Liston if he could punch.

"I'm hot. This freak, Mortay, he's got the area wired. He sees me, I'm gone. I'm not ready for him yet. I can't go in with you."

The Mole shrugged.

"And you can't use Max for backup. He's out of this until it's over."

"Why?"

"I met the freak. Face to face. He wants Max, says he'll take out the baby to make Max fight. Mama sent him out of town for a few weeks."

"He knows?"

"No."

The Mole wiped his hands on his greasy jumpsuit. "You want something from inside?"

"Just a look around. A good look."

"When?"

"I'll get back to you. But soon, okay?"

"Okay."

I stomped out my cigarette. "You can't take out the electricity. It's right in the middle of the cesspool. Takes a lot of juice to run all that neon."

The Mole turned to Terry. "Get the master-blaster," he said.

I followed the Mole to the entrance of his bunker. There's a network of tunnels under the junkyard, shored up with I-beams. He led me down some steps. Bright light ahead. Terry came up behind us.

The Mole pointed ahead. "Streetlight," he said. "Like they have outside. Turns on at night—goes off in the daytime. You know how it works?"

"Con Edison?"

"No. Infrared sensor. When it gets light out, the sensor reads it. Shuts itself off."

"So?"

We turned the corner. Terry handed the Mole a portable spotlight. The kind you plug into the cigarette lighter in your car. The Mole aimed the spotlight, pressed the button. A flash of white-hot light. The streetlight went out. We stood in the pitch dark. I counted ninety seconds in my head. The streetlight came back on. I followed the Mole outside.

"Car headlights, maybe seventy-five thousand candlepower on high beams. Cop's spotlights, maybe a hundred and fifty thousand. This throws a million. Tricks the streetlights—tricks motion sensors—anything."

"Damn! What happens if you blast somebody in the face with it?"

"They go blind for a few minutes. Too close, you burn the eyeballs."

"Mole, you amaze me."

"Let Terry drive the car out of the yard," he said.

121 BELLE WAS lying on her stomach across the hospital bed, chin in her hands. Her legs were bent at the knee, feet twirling behind her. Like a teenage girl talking on the phone. The Prof was in an easy chair, the casts on his legs still separated by the bar, propped on a footstool. He looked sharp—clean-shaven, bright-red robe.

"It's quiet?" I asked, stepping into the room.

"This is a hospital, fool."

"I mean . . ."

"We *all* know what you mean. Everything's cool. Too bad you showed so soon, I was just getting ready to show the lady your baby pictures."

I pulled up another chair. "You got something?"

Belle climbed off the bed, sat down on the floor between us, her hand on my knee.

The little man was back to himself. All business, but working in circles. "You remember J.T.?"

"Yeah."

He turned to Belle. "This J.T. was a real country boy when he came up here. A stone rookie. Wouldn't know a hoe-down from a throw-down. Couldn't decide if he was gonna be a yutz or a clutz. You follow?"

Belle tilted her chin to look up at me. "What's a throw-down?"

"A challenge. Or a fight."

"How do you tell the difference?"

"One you do with your mouth, the other with your hands. Now shut up—let the man finish."

Her lips turned into a perfect pout, like she'd been practicing all her life.

The Prof patted her arm. "Don't pay attention to this thug, girl. You can school a fool, but you can't make him cool. J.T., he's not what you call a mental heavyweight, but he's good people. A few years ago, he got into this beef over a girl. Working girl. He thought he was in love. Shot the pimp right on Forty-fourth Street. Girl starts screaming, J.T. starts running. I'm on my cart, see him flying. I told him to toss the piece. Buried it in my coat. The cops grabbed him a couple of blocks away, but they never found the gun. The pimp didn't die. We put together a package for J.T. Michelle talked to the girl, Burke talked to the pimp. Visited him right in the hospital. They held J.T. a few months, waiting for somebody to testify. Finally, they cut him loose. He's still a dumb-ass cowboy. Too dumb to hustle, and he's not cold enough for stickups. He's always out there, picking up spare change. You understand?"

Belle nodded, a serious look on her face. Like there was going to be a test later.

"Anyway, old J.T. hears what happened. Out there. He comes to see me. Like I said, he's good people, but he ain't swift. Wants to square the beef for me—take care of the people who busted me up. I tell him to back off, it's been handled. He gets a look on his face like I just downed him, you know? Like I think he ain't worth shit. So I give him this *assignment*, okay? Just do what he does, but keep his eyes open. Don't ask nobody nothing. Just watch. Last night, he walks in here. Brought me that radio," the Prof said, pointing to a suitcase-sized boom box sitting in the corner. "And he brought me this too."

He put it in my hand. An eight-sided gold metal coin. Embossed on one side was a nude woman, one hand behind her head, spike heels on her feet. I turned it over. On the other side it said "Sin City."

"It looks like a subway token," Belle said.

"It works the peep-show machines. Costs a quarter."

"So what's the . . ."

I chopped a hand in the air to cut her off, holding the coin in my fingers. "He say anything else?" I asked the Prof.

"Said he followed the guy—not Mortay, the Spanish dude—into the railroad yards. On Forty-third, off Tenth. Spanish guy disappears. J.T. figures, the hell with it, he'll go watch a movie. He goes right to Sin City, goes in the front door. Now, that's the *only* door, babe. And who does he see when he gets to the bar? The Spanish guy. J.T. says there ain't no way in the world that the Spanish guy could've got there first."

"So there has to be another way in?"

"Has to be."

"What time was this?"

"Like eleven in the morning, man. Broad daylight."

I lit a smoke. "He did good, Prof."

"When you cast bread upon the waters . . ."

"Yeah. You got anything else?"

"Just one more little piece. I reached out for Tabitha, asked her to make the run up to see Hortense, explain to her I was laid up. Now, you know Tabitha; she owes Hortense too. So she did it. Anyway, she comes back to see me. Said Hortense said she'd whip her ass when she got out, Tabitha didn't do something for me now. So Tabitha, she's in the life, but she's straight, she tells me she saw the duel."

"Mortay and the Jap?"

"Right on. In the basement. So I put it together, ask her how she got *into* the basement, dig? She says she and her man, they go downstairs from the main floor. Big metal spiral staircase. Everybody goes down that way, everybody goes out that way. Get it?"

"Yeah."

"One more thing, she says. This Spanish guy, she knows him too. Her man, Earl, he won't let none of his women anywhere *near* the Spanish guy. Word is he uses blood the way some freaks use Vaseline."

"I heard that too. Just today."

The Prof went on like he hadn't heard me. "But Tabitha, man, she thought that was funny. The Spanish guy, he don't want nothing to do with nothing that ain't white. No Puerto Ricans, no Chinese . . . nothing that's out there but white meat."

I drew on my smoke, watching Belle's face half hidden under the thatch of honey-taffy hair. Coming together.

"I'm out of here, Prof. It's coming down. I may not be back for a while."

"*What's* coming down, home?"

"A hard wind, brother. Hold tight to your alibi."

"You going to work solo? That ain't the way."

I bent close to him, lowering my voice even more. "What am I gonna do, wait till you're out of the hospital? Max is out of this—he has to be. I'm working on something . . . but I don't have it yet."

He tapped the end of my bandage. "That ain't much of a plan, man."

"That's the backup, not the plan. It all connects. Everything. But I can't call the shots. This is just in case he moves first."

The little man's eyes were hard, the yellowish cast gone. He was the Prophet again, the man who could see the future. "This freak feels froggy, he's gonna leap—I know you can't wait. But use your head, schoolboy. Pearl Harbor. When it comes to Nazis, the Mole don't play the role."

I squeezed his hand—his grip was hard as his eyes. Nothing more to say.

Belle bent to kiss him goodbye. "Remember what I told you, lady. Outside hell, blood don't tell."

"I'll remember."

When I looked back, he was pushing the button to call his nurse.

# 122

I WALKED Belle over to the Pontiac, let her in the passenger side.

"What happened to the Plymouth?"

"On vacation."

"I'm glad you didn't have to dump it. That's one fine machine."

"Yeah."

"What d'we do now?"

"Wait. There's stuff out there—I have to wait for a bite."

I drove back to Queens. Stopped at a deli in Forest Hills, waited in the car while Belle picked up some food. It was the first time I'd been to her house in the middle of the day. The street was quiet. Working people at work, kids at school. Belle saw me sweeping the street with my eyes.

"It's real quiet here until the summer. Once they start coming out to the water with their boats and all, it fills up."

"It'll all be over way before then."

"You're sure?"

I didn't answer her. I parked the Pontiac behind her Camaro. "That car's been moved since the last time."

"I took it down to the gas station. Changed the oil, front-end alignment."

I looked a question at her. "Just in case," she said.

"I don't need a driver on this, Belle."

This time she didn't answer me.

We brought the food inside. I called Mama. Nothing. Nobody looking for me. On the phone, anyway.

Belle made some sandwiches. Roast beef, boiled ham, lettuce and mustard. Opened a bottle of beer for herself, ginger ale for me. I opened the *Daily News*, scanned it quickly for any news of the Ghost Van. Nothing. I flipped to the race results out of habit, but I couldn't concentrate.

"Is it good?" she asked.

"What?"

"The *food*."

"Oh. Yeah. Great."

Her face went sad. "I'm not a good cook. Sissy was a *fine* cook. She was going to teach me. . . ."

"Who cares?"

"I thought you would. Remember when I cleaned your place? I did a good job, didn't I?"

"Perfect."

"Well . . ."

"Let it go, Belle. It was so important to me, I would have learned how to do it myself."

She pulled her chair next to me. "You can't do everything for yourself."

"Where's this going?"

She got up, moved in little circles. Like she was lost. "You're walking around with that ugly thing in your hand. . . . Maybe we won't have a little house with a white picket fence and all that . . . but I'm not gonna sit around and make plans for a funeral."

I slipped my hand around her waist, pulled her against me. "I know. But you got it wrong. I'm back on track now, I can feel it. This is just in case, like I told you. It's coming together. There's a way to take him down and walk away too. I need a couple more bits and pieces . . ."

"And you'll know where to look?"

"Yeah. In my head. I have to keep feeding stuff in, work it around. I can't go in the street and look for him—I have to figure it out. Where he is. This thing in my hand is only if he finds me first."

"What if you don't get any more information?"

"I *have* to. What I got, it's not enough. There's pieces missing. Maybe only one piece. I don't know yet. But if you don't feed the fire, it goes out. You get trapped."

She sat next to me again, her hand on my arm, watching me close.

"Trapped?"

"Patterns. Like I told you. I'm looking for a guy, right? I think he's holed up in a certain neighborhood. So I walk around, ask questions, leave notes. Sooner or later, he's looking for *me*."

# 123 | Late afternoon. I called Morelli.

"Anything?"

"Yeah. I'm not finished. Can't talk now—I gotta work the phones before the record rooms shut down for the day."

"Can I call you later?"

"I'll be here till nine."

"Eight-thirty," I said, hanging up.

Mama said it was all quiet. Asked me when I was coming around. I told her soon.

I put the phone down. "I got to get out of here."

"Why, baby?"

"I wasn't kidding about inertia, Belle. If there's an answer, it's in my head. No matter what kind of bites I get out there, I have to put it together. I can't work here. I need my stuff."

"Stuff?"

"In my files. It's not that I can't think here. I can think in a cell. But that stuff I've collected—it's like having a conversation. . . . I ask it questions, sometimes it talks back. Okay?"

"Okay," she said, opening her bureau drawers. "As long as I'm around when you have that talk."

**124** ‖ BELLE SAT in the front bucket seat of the Pontiac, watching the road. She giggled to herself.

"What's so funny."

"The Prof. I told him. About me. Not the whole thing, but enough. That's what he meant about blood only tells in hell."

"What's funny about that?"

"He said when the Lord made people He made them all the same for starters. But life marks people. If you know the way, you can read them like maps. He said the Lord made you so ugly for a test."

"What?"

"That's what he said. I told him I thought you were real good-looking. He said that was the test—I wasn't deep in love with you, I couldn't say such an outrageous lie."

"He should fucking talk."

"Burke! He *is* a handsome little man. I thought that nurse was gonna claw my eyes, she saw me with him." She giggled again. "He told me God only made one mistake. He said, you see a red-haired, blue-eyed nigger, you're looking at a stone killer."

"Sure, everybody knows that."

"Don't be crazy. He was just playing."

"Hell if he was. Every one I ever saw was a life-taker."

"That's ridiculous."

I shrugged.

The highway slipped by. Battery Tunnel coming into view.

"Burke?"

"What?"

"Why would the Prof call somebody a nigger?"

"It's just a word. Anybody can use words. I can't really explain it. . . . You say some words—say them the right way—they lose their power to hurt. The Prof, he'll say, 'That's my nigger,' he means that's his main man. Somebody *else* says the word, he's ready to rumble."

"But why . . ."

"I told you the truth. I really can't explain it. Maybe the Prof can, I never asked him, not really."

"Maybe I will, someday."

125 || THE OFFICE was quiet. Pansy was her usual sluggish self. She brightened a bit when I rolled the extra roast beef and ham into a fat ball and tossed it in the air for her.

Belle curled up on the couch with the newspapers. Pansy jumped up there too, growling. "What does she want?"

"Television."

"She wants to watch television?"

"Yeah. See if you can find pro wrestling; that's her favorite. But leave the sound on low, okay?"

Belle gave me one of her looks, hauled the portable over to the end of the couch. Pansy sat up, tail wagging. I went back to my work.

"Honey," Belle's voice broke through to me.

"What?"

"It's eight-thirty. Don't you have to make a call?"

I looked at my watch—I'd been out of it for three hours. I snatched the phone, hoping the hippies weren't discussing their latest dope deal. The line was quiet.

"Morelli."

"It's me."

"Come over to Paulo's tonight. Eleven. We'll have some supper."

I hung up quick. Looked over at the couch. Belle and Pansy were both watching me.

"Good girl," I said. Pansy came off the couch, strolled over to me. "I meant her," I told the beast, pointing at Belle. Pansy slammed a paw on the desk. "You too," I told her. I let Pansy out to her roof. Walked over to the couch, turned off the TV set.

"That's one strange dog, honey. She really does like pro wrestling. I thought dogs couldn't see TV. Something about their eyes."

"I don't know if that's true or not. Maybe she just likes the sound."

I lit a smoke. "Was I asleep?"

"I don't think so—I think you were somewhere else. Your eyes were closed some of the time. But you smoked a lot of cigarettes."

I rubbed my face, trying to go back. I gave it up—it'd come when it was ready.

"Burke, could I ask you something?"

"Sure."

"You know about this?" she said, pointing to a headline in the paper. I knew the story—it had been running for weeks. High-school cheerleader, sixteen years old. Father started raping her when she was eleven years old. While her mother was dying of cancer in the hospital. She finally told her boyfriend, he told somebody else. Ended up she hired another kid to kill her father. For five hundred bucks. Drilled the old man right in his driveway. Everybody pleaded guilty. The kid who did the shooting got a jackpot sentence, seven to twenty-one years. The radio talk shows took calls from freaks who said the little girl should have told the social workers—that is, if it "really" happened. Some people thought the father got what was coming to him. Not many. The judge sentenced her to a year in jail.

"Yeah. I know about it."

Her eyes burned. A little girl asking a priest if there really was a god. "Burke, do you think the little girl did anything wrong?"

"Yeah."

Belle's face twisted. "What?"

"She hired an amateur."

"The lawyer . . . the one who pleaded her guilty?"

"Not the lawyer. The shooter."

Her face calmed, but she was still struggling with it. "But he killed the guy. . . ."

"He wasn't a pro, Belle. Left a trail Ray Charles could follow. Talked about it to everyone who'd listen. Kept the gun. And he opened up when they popped him. You hire a killer, you buy silence too."

She took the cigarette from my mouth, pulled on it. "I'd like to break her out of that jail."

"Forget it, Belle. She wouldn't go. The kid's no outlaw. She's a nice middle-class girl. It wasn't simple for her—she didn't work it through. She still feels guilty about the guy getting killed. Incest, you don't just walk away from it like if a stranger raped you. That was her father. He's dead. Her mother's dead. She's gonna need a lot of help—she can't go on the run."

Tears spilled down her face. "My mother saved me from that."

"I know," I said, holding her.

**126** ‖ TEN-THIRTY. I put on a dark-gray suit, black felt hat. I hated to rip the sleeve, but I had to make the sacrifice. Belle did a neat, clean job. "I'll sew it back together later," she said, concentrating, the tip of her tongue sticking out the corner of her mouth.

"I'll be back in a couple of hours."

"I'll be here."

I kissed her. Her lips were soft. I slipped my fingers around her neck, pulling at the necklace, making it bounce against her chest, coaxing a smile.

"Me and Pansy, we'll have a beer, watch some TV."

**127** ‖ PAULO'S ISN'T one of those new restaurants in Little Italy. It was built when they were working on the third chapter of the Bible. When Morelli started working the police beat as a reporter, he would eat there every day. His mother came over, made sure her son was eating the right food. Marched right into the kitchen, told them what was what. They still have a couple of dishes on the menu named after her.

He was there when I walked in at eleven, sitting in a far corner. I started over to him. Two guys with cement-mixer eyes got in my way. I nodded over to Morelli's corner. One of the guys stayed planted in front of me; the other turned, caught the signal. They moved aside.

Morelli had a thick sheaf of papers next to him, glass of red wine half empty. I sat down. The waiter came over, looking at me like I was his parole officer.

"What?"

"Veal milanese. Side of spaghetti. Meat sauce. No cheese."

"No cheese?"

"No cheese."

"No wine?"

"No."

He moved off, mumbling something in Italian. When he came back, he had my food. Morelli had linguini with white clam sauce. The waiter said something to Morelli, moved off again.

I cut into the veal. It was perfect, light and sweet. We ate quietly, talking about the magazine he worked for, his kids, the neighborhood.

The waiter cleared the plates. "You want a hot fudge sundae?" he asked me.

"Tortoni," I said.

He bowed. I never saw a guy do that and sneer at the same time before.

When we finished, I lit a smoke, waiting. Morelli leaned forward. "We have a deal?"

I nodded.

He spoke quietly, one hand protectively guarding his papers. "You want the whole package or just the bottom line?"

"Bottom line."

His finger traced a path through the bread crumbs the waiter left behind on the white tablecloth. "Sally Lou," he said.

"Yeah."

"Adds up?"

"I think so."

Morelli sipped his espresso. "Burke, explain something to me. I grew up with these guys, I got no illusions. That dog you got . . . the Neapolitan? I know one of the old boys, has one just like yours. Keeps him in the back of the house. Every day he sends one of the kids to the pet store. Comes back with a couple of live white rabbits. The old man, he throws the rabbits over the fence. The dog catches them in the air, crunches them like a trash compactor. The old man, he thinks it's the funniest thing he ever saw." He took another sip of his espresso. "I know they put up with Sally 'cause he's a good earner. What I don't understand . . . where's the market?"

"You know where it is."

"No. I really don't. This whole porno business, most of it's bullshit. They make this triple-X film, tell the world it grossed fifty million dollars—it's just a laundry for dope money."

"So?"

"So why mess with the heavy stuff? Kiddie porn, stuff like that? The penalties are stiffer, they're taking all kinds of risks. There can't be *that* many freaks out there?"

Morelli's face was tight. Maybe having your own kids raises the stakes.

"There don't need to be that many," I told him. "Every one of them is a bottomless pit. It's not like dope—too much dope and you die, right? But these freaks, they can never get enough. One little piece of videotape, they can sell it again and again."

"Sally Lou, he's bent that way?"

"I don't think so. That's the hell of it—the market's so good, the wise guys are getting into it. It used to be just the freaks, making their own stuff. Mostly with their own kids. Now it's a business. The Postal Inspectors, they nail the end users. That's all. It's like when the DEA busts a bunch of mules—the processing plant keeps making the coke."

I ground out my smoke. "I'll let you know," I said.

His eyes held me. "Where do they get the kids? For the videos?"

"Same way they get anything else. Some they buy, some they steal."

"You going after Sally Lou?"

"No. He's not on my list."

"He's on mine," Morelli said.

# 128

THE PONTIAC didn't drive itself the way the Plymouth did. I poked it carefully through Little Italy, heading for home. Salvatore Lucastro. Sally Lou. A made man in one of the Manhattan families, but not a heavyweight. Years ago, he started moving in on the porno joints in Times Square. Nobody paid that much attention—he was operating with permission. It wasn't one mobster, it would be another. The sleaze-sellers paid off, the way they were supposed to. Then he went into business for himself, actually producing the peep-show loops, branching into full-length films, videos. Nobody had a good line on where his studio was. He was making so much money, the bosses let him run. The kiddie-porn stuff was recent, maybe last year. From what I heard around, it was his biggest grosser ever.

Sally Lou owned Sin City.

**129** I SWUNG by Mama's, parked in the back. I went into the kitchen, waited there while they brought her back. We went into the hall, near the entrance to the basement, standing by the bank of pay phones.

"I can't hang around, Mama."

"What is this with Flower?"

"Just give me a minute, okay? One call."

I dialed the Mole. Heard him pick up. "Go," I said. Hung up.

I turned to Mama. "It's complicated. There's a man wants to fight Max. Like a duel, understand?"

She watched my face, waiting.

"He made, like, this *public* challenge, okay? So it's all over the street. Max fights him, he has to kill him. And everybody knows. Big trouble."

Mama wasn't worried about Max killing someone. "Flower." It was all she had to say.

"This guy, he wanted to make *sure* Max would fight him. He said if Max didn't he'd kill the baby."

Mama's eyes were black marble. A fire flared; then it was gone. "Tell him Max here. Come any time."

"It won't work, Mama. It won't go down that easy. I've got it put together now. Just a few more days, maybe a little bit more. He couldn't find Max in Boston?"

She shook her head.

"I'll take care of it."

Mama bowed, showing respect. That I could bring it off. I turned to go, felt her hand on my arm.

"What name?"

"Mortay," I said. "Mor-tay."

"What that mean?"

"In Spanish, it means 'death.' "
Mama bowed again. "In Chinese, means 'dead man.' "
I bowed back. Goodbye.

**130** THE BACK staircase was quiet. I checked the pieces of tape I left behind. Still in place. The trip-wires were still attached in the hall. I let myself in. Pansy was at her post. "Where's Belle?" I asked her. The beast let out a halfhearted snarl. I bent to give her a pat. Her breath smelled like formaldehyde.

Belle was in the next room. On her back on the gym mat I keep there. Nude, covered with a sheen of sweat. "Twenty more," she said, her hands locked behind her head. She was doing killer sit-ups, up fast, down slow. Muscles rippled under the soft skin.

"How many do you do?"

"Two hundred a day, six days a week. The only difference between me and a fat pig is a small waist. I damn near killed myself to get *this* light, I'm not gonna be backsliding."

I lit a smoke, went back into the office room. Pansy didn't want to go out.

Belle came back inside, toweling herself off. "Pansy was watching me work out for a while—I guess she got bored."

"She heard the door."

"Oh." She slapped the outside of a thigh. "Only way I can get these any smaller is plastic surgery."

"They're perfect just the way they are."

She moved next to me. "I'm glad you said that."

"Because you weren't getting plastic surgery no matter what, right?"

"No, because I would if you wanted."

I gave her a kiss. "Help me off with this," I said, taking the pin from my jacket pocket. Belle slowly peeled back the bandage, working her way to the Velcro tab. "When I pull the tab, you wrap your hand around mine while I slip in the pin; my hand may be cramped."

Her forehead furrowed in concentration—her hands were steady. I popped the tab, squeezing the lever as hard as I could. My hand felt dead. Belle wrapped both of her hands around mine. Her knuckles were white. I slipped in the pin. "Let go," I said.

Her face was sweaty. "I can't."

"Come on, Belle. It's okay. Come on. . . ."

I watched her hands unlock slowly. Suddenly she pulled them away, closing her eyes. I grabbed the grenade in my right hand, slipped it into the desk drawer. My left hand was a claw.

"Go in the bathroom. Get me the little jar of Tiger Balm, okay?"

She opened her eyes. Went off without a word. Came back with the jar of red ointment. "Rub it into my hand. All over, hard as you can."

She worked my hand like she was rubbing oil into leather. I couldn't feel a thing. "Does it burn?" she asked.

"It'll get warm, that's all. Once you're done, I need to wrap it."

I sat on the couch. Belle came back with a towel. Sat down next to me on my left side, squirmed against me so my right arm was around her. She twisted sideways, took my left hand, and put it between her breasts. She pressed them together. "Pull the blanket over me," she said. I did it. In a few minutes, I could feel the heat. I wiggled my fingers, working the cramps out. "That stuff won't burn you," I promised. "Don't care if it does," she said, making sweet little sounds in her throat.

"How many beers did you give Pansy?"

"Just three."

"Damn! That's the most she's ever had. No wonder she looks glazed."

"I wanted her to like me."

"You can't buy stuff like that."

"I wasn't *buying* it. I just wanted to do something nice for her."

"Okay."

"You sleepy?"

"A little bit."

"Go to sleep, baby," she said.

I closed my eyes, my hand between her breasts, warm.

131 PANSY'S GROWL woke me up, her snout inches from my face. It wasn't an emergency; she just wanted to use her roof.

"All that beer, huh?" I asked her, disentangling myself from Belle.

When I came back inside, Belle was on the couch, the blanket pulled up to her chin.

"Where're we going to sleep?"

"You sleep right there. Go ahead, I got work to do."

"You going out?"

"No. I got to put things together," I said, working my left hand. It was fine. I stacked the news clips in a pile, started to sort through what I had so far. The street maps were still on the wall where Belle had tacked them. I started working. The Mole was going into the basement in Sin City—it had to be the last piece.

Pansy came downstairs, strolled to a corner, and closed her eyes. Belle threw off the blanket, came to where I was working at the desk.

"I want to help."

"You want to help, put some clothes on."

"Why?"

"Because you're distracting me. And because I told you to."

She leaned over the desk, her breasts against my face. "Do they smell like that Tiger stuff?"

"No."

"Take a deep breath," she said, pushing the back of my head to her.

"They smell like you."

"Still want me to put my clothes on?"

"Yeah."

She threw me a pout, switched her hips hard walking away. I heard the shower go on, went back to work.

I covered a yellow legal pad with scrawls, but the list was in my head. Ghost Van. Baby hookers. Mortay. Ramón. The dead man El Cañonero left in the Chelsea playground. Pain-for-gain. Ghost Van won't eat dark meat. Chilly menace like fog, working close to the ground. The peep-show token. Sin City. Church where they worship the ice god. Basement duel. And Sally Lou.

I felt a tap on my shoulder. Belle, a yellow sweatshirt covering her to her thighs. "You said I could help."

"Sit down," I said, patting the desk. "Listen to me play it out."

She planted herself on the desk, hands in her lap. Watchful.

"This all started with the Ghost Van, remember? Comes off the river, shoots some little girls. Marques doesn't care why; he just wants it off the streets. So he reaches out for me. I start looking around, and this Mortay shows up. Puts the Prof in the hospital. So he's linked to the van some kind of way."

She lit a cigarette, nodding to show me she was following along.

"Except that he's not just a bodyguard—he's a freak. Hitting dojos, challenging the leaders. We know he fought a duel with some Japanese *karateka*. In the Sin City basement. You ever work there?"

"No. You have to mix with the customers."

"Okay. The Ghost Van, it only hits young girls. And only white girls. The night I went out to meet Mortay, when I came back so scared? A guy got killed. The cops pulled his prints. One of them matched one they got from the switch-car for the Ghost Van. So this Mortay, he's not just linked, he's connected too."

I lit a smoke for myself. It was good to use two hands. Belle was listening so hard her shoulders shook.

"Mortay's stooge, this Ramón guy. With the diamond in his ear. He's a pain-junkie. Likes to hurt women, gets off on it. He's the gunman—Mortay only uses his hands. And now I find out that Sin

City's owned by this mob guy. Sally Lou. He's a sleaze-dealer. Hard-core stuff. Kiddie porn, snuff—you want it, he makes it."

"You think this Mortay works for the mob?"

"No. I looked in his eyes. He don't work for anyone. But that doesn't mean he wouldn't *do* stuff. . . ."

"Why would he . . . ?"

"I'm not sure. But it all adds up. Look at the maps. The Ghost Van has to have a place to land. Someplace close by where it hunts. Times Square. Sin City—the basement's big enough for hundreds of people to watch a duel. That's where it's got to be."

"I don't get it."

"Mortay has to be doing something for Sally Lou. If the Ghost Van's down there, then they're all hooked in. The reason the cops can't catch freaks, they don't know them. They don't ask people who do. Wasn't for informants, the *federales* couldn't find a donkey in Tijuana. Sex-death freaks, they love vans. I don't know why, but they do. And they feed each other—put two of them together, you got more than twice as much evil as two people could do on their own. Ramón loves pain, Mortay deals death. I don't know what the third guy was into. It doesn't matter. The Hillside Strangler—it was *two* freaks. That Green River Killer? The one who's been murdering all those street girls out in Washington State for years?"

She nodded.

"I think the cops are making a mistake. Looking for one guy. It sounds like a team to me. *Feels* that way."

Belle shuddered. I put my hand on her bare thigh. It was cold.

"People always think they know what to do," I told her. "Ever hear of chemical castration?"

"Arggh! It sounds disgusting."

"They get a chronic sex offender. One of those guys who's never going to stop, okay? Then they make him take these injections. Depo-Provera. Lowers the sex drive, so he won't be thinking about jumping on some little kid."

"Does it work?"

"Who knows? What's the difference? This one old freak, he was still raping little kids when he was seventy years old. Started on the shots years ago. He figured out how to beat the deal—got some bootleg doctor to shoot him up with hormones. And remember that baby-raper on the Coast? Instead of dumping him into prison, the judge made him post a sign on his house. Child Molester Inside—Kids Stay Away. Something like that."

"Yeah. Like a brand."

"Some brand. All the guy has to do is move to another neighborhood. Where they don't read English. Plenty of them around."

"It's so *sick*."

I grabbed her eyes. "You think your father was sick?"

"He's a dirty, evil man."

"They all are. It's their choice, Belle. Blood didn't make them that way. *You're* not that way."

"How do you know so much?"

"I never figured out what I was, but I figured out I was going to go the distance. Survive. Knowing is how you do it." I lit another smoke. "Mortay, he won't be living down there. Too risky. But Ramón, he'll lead me right to him."

"How you going to find out?"

"The Mole's going in. Tonight, tomorrow morning." I took a deep drag of my cigarette, thinking about the letters in my files from freaks. Always interested in the real thing. "I know what he's going to find."

"What?"

"I met this guy once. State senator. Spent so much time kissing ass, his face looked like it was split down the middle. But he told me something that was true. Where's the money? That's always the question. Where's the money? To the little whores on the street, the Ghost Van's a killer shark. But to Sally Lou, it's a money machine."

"How can he make money from shooting whores?"

"I got to wait for the Mole to be sure, but I think I see it. And if I'm right, I know how to do it."

My voice trailed off, tangled in my thoughts. Belle shifted her hips, sliding along the desk until she was right in front of me. "You're different now."

"How?"

"When you came to my house—shaking and all—you got past it. Whatever it was. And taping that grenade in your hand. Like you wanted to die. Just blow yourself up and go to a better place. But now . . . it's like you're getting cold inside. Like you're not scared anymore."

"I'm still scared. But I'm back to myself now. Whatever that is, that's where I am. It's true, I feel calm inside. But not dead. Just . . . centered, you know?"

"Yeah. It feels right."

"There's lot of things I can't do. I stopped feeling bad about them a long time ago."

"But you can do this?"

"I can do this."

**132** | BELLE CAME back inside, a glass of ice water in her hand. "Want some?"

I took the glass from her, sipped it slowly. "It's late, Belle. Go to sleep."

She bumped a rounded hip against my shoulder. "Come with me."

"I'm still putting it together."

"But you told me . . ."

"I *think* I know what it is. I have to play with it some more. Get it straight. We're playing for keeps now."

"Just lie down with me. Let me hold you. In my mouth. Like I did before. Until I fall asleep." Her eyes were sadness. "I'm so cold, honey."

I took her hand, led her to the back room.

**133** ┃ THE ROOM had a faint glow when I came around—the closest thing this joint gets to sunlight. Belle's head was against my chest, the gym mat hard against my back.

"I'm awake," she said, before I could ask her.

"How long?"

"I don't know. I've just been lying here. Thinking. Does Pansy always walk around at night?"

"Yeah."

"She's restless?"

"Pansy? She'd spend all her time sleeping and eating, it was up to her. She's just patrolling. Watching over me."

"I'm jealous of her."

"You're a dope."

She snuggled in against me, warm, smelling like soap. "Burke, can I ask you something?"

"Sure."

"Can you love two people? At the same time? Love them both?"

Flood came into my mind. Flash-images. Flood standing in a Times Square alley, facing three skells, her purse on the ground. Waving them in, daring them to come close enough. Blond hair flying. Chubby little hands that could chop or caress. The crosshatched scar on her face. Fire-scar on her butt. The duel to avenge her sister's baby. Flower. The name Max gave his child to honor the warrior-woman he'd never see again. I felt her spirit in me, sunburst smile covering my soul.

"I don't know," I said. "I don't know enough about love. It came so late to me."

"It's come again, darling. I asked the Prof."

"About what?"

"Love. He knows about love. Blood love. I remember what he said: Life ain't dice—they don't roll nice, you can roll 'em twice."

"What's that supposed to mean?"

"Nobody's stuck. Me and Sissy were walking back of the house one day. When I was just a little girl. This old coon was down by the water. Hunting. I saw he only had one front paw. Sissy told me he must have been caught in a trap. Bit his own paw off to get out. It costs something to be free." A tear welled, rolled down her cheek. "I didn't know what she meant then."

I kissed the tear track. She slid on top of me, reached down, fitted me inside. "The way people talk, it's not the truth," she whispered. "You can't *make* love. It's there or it isn't."

Her hips flicked against me, slow-sliding, one arm around my neck, her face buried against me. "I know it's there. You know it's there. Take it."

"Belle . . ."

"Take it!" Grinding hard, her teeth against my neck.

134 | BELLE WAS getting dressed. I was watching television with Pansy. The late-morning news. Some people tried to escape the Dominican Republic in an overloaded wooden boat, heading for Puerto Rico. The boat went down in shark-infested water. Another boat came alongside. Somebody had a video camera. The TV showed some of the footage. Living color. Blood thick in the water, like pus from a wound. Screams. Chunks torn out of humans. Sharks hitting again and again. Sound of shots fired. Belle stood behind me, hand on my shoulder.

"God! How can people watch something like that?"

Right then I knew. Why the Ghost Van hunted.

**135** WE WAITED until almost noon. "Ready to go?" I asked Belle. When she nodded, I took the grenade out of the drawer, rolled up my sleeve. "Come over here; give me a hand with this."

She took the grenade from the desk, bounced it up and down in her hand. "Let me hold it."

"Forget it."

"Listen to me . . . just for a minute?"

I said nothing, feeling the stone in my face.

"I'll carry it in my lap. Cover it with a scarf. You can carry your gun. If it happens . . . if he comes too soon . . . you get *two* chances."

"He's too fast, Belle. I'd probably never get a shot off. You want a gun, I'll give you one."

"I'm no good with a gun. Never shot one. I could stab him, but if he's too fast for you . . ."

"No."

"*Listen* to me! I'll get out of the way. He gets past the gun, puts his hands on you, I'll toss it."

"You'd toss it right at me? Blow me up too?"

"He gets to you, you're going to die anyway. I wouldn't let you go alone."

I watched her face. "You don't have the heart for it—you'd never pull the pin."

"I *would!*"

I lit a smoke. "Stay here, Belle. I'm going to the junkyard."

"I thought I was going with you."

"You *were* going with me. Not now. Stay here."

"You can't make me."

"Don't make me laugh."

"I'm telling the truth. You can't make me. You'd have to hurt me to do it. Really hurt me. And you can't do that."

I walked away from the desk. Belle stood, arms folded over her breasts. I snapped my fingers. Pansy's head came up. "Watch!" I said, pointing two fingers in front of me. I turned to the door. Belle stepped forward. Pansy bounded between us, an ugly snarl ripping from her throat, teeth snapping. "Pansy!" Belle said, like her feelings were hurt. "Don't try her," I warned.

The muscles stood out across Pansy's shoulders, hair rigid on the back of her neck. Belle snatched the grenade from the desk, cupped the blue handle, pulled the pin. She tossed the pin in a gentle arc over Pansy's head. I caught it in my hand. The beast never moved.

"I'll just hold this until you come back," she said, her voice quiet and steady.

I let out a breath, the pin in my hand.

"Pansy, jump!" She hit the ground. I snapped my fingers again, calling her to me. Gave her the command that everything was okay. She started to walk over to Belle. I held up my hand for her to stay.

I crossed the room, fast. "Hold it steady," I told her, slipping the pin back in. She put it on the desk, went in the back room, came out with a blue chiffon scarf. Wrapped it around the little metal bomb. "Let's go," she said.

I pushed her back against the desk, making her sit on it. Moved in so close her eyes were out of focus. "Swear on your mother," I said. "Swear on Sissy that you'll throw it if he gets to me."

"I swear."

I buried my hands in her thick hair, snatching a handful on either side of her face, pulling her nose against mine. "When we get back here . . ."

She licked my mouth, pushed her lips against me. I couldn't make out what she was saying.

**136** BELLE FOLLOWED me down the stairs into the garage. I snapped her seat belt in place for her, arranged a shawl over her lap. I worked my way through Lower Manhattan, grabbing the East Side Drive off Pearl Street. Belle was as good as gold, quiet and peaceful in the bucket seat, hands in her lap, little smile on her face. Like a kid who threw a successful tantrum—got her way and didn't want to brag about it.

"Call off the directions," I told her.

She was right on the money, every step of the way. I lit a smoke. "Me too," she said. I held the filter to her mouth.

"Don't get spoiled. It won't work every time."

"I know." Phony contrite tone in her voice, the Southern twang not softening it much.

"I'm not kidding."

"I *know*. Turn right up ahead."

I turned into Hunts Point, heading for the junkyard.

"You know something, Burke—you're not exactly what they call a well-rounded personality."

"Well-rounded's nice, long as you don't have to cut something."

She stuck out her tongue. A queen-sized brat. With a bomb in her lap.

I rolled the Pontiac up to the gates. "Will the dogs know it's a different car?" she asked.

"They won't care."

Simba made his move first. Sitting patiently while I rolled down the window. I talked to him, waiting for someone to come and let us through.

It was Terry, shoving his way through the pack just like the Mole. He saw who it was, stuck his head in the window.

"Hi, Belle!"

"Hi, good-looking. You gonna show this lug how to drive a car?"

The kid looked at me. I opened the door, climbed in the back seat. He piloted the Pontiac in an elaborate weave, showing off for Belle.

"Are you Burke's girlfriend?"

"Hey! The Mole teach you about asking questions?"

"I just . . ."

"Shut up, Burke. I sure am, sweetie. But if you were a few years older . . ."

"I'm *getting* older," the kid said, his voice squeaking, looking over at her.

She saw where he was looking. "I know you are, honey," she said, flashing a smile.

He pulled the car into a safe area. Jumped out, held the door for Belle. I lit a cigarette. The kid was so entranced he forgot to glom one off me.

"We don't need it here," I told Belle. "Hand it over."

She pulled the scarf from the grenade, put it in my hand. Terry paid no attention, chattering away, explaining all the features of the junkyard to Belle. I followed behind them.

The Mole was outside his bunker. He tilted his head. We all followed him downstairs, Belle's hand on my shoulder, Terry bringing up the rear. I hoped the view wouldn't stunt his growth.

The tunnel sloped, curved gently back and forth. Lights flicked on each time we came close to a curve. The Mole's living room was always the same. A thin concrete slab over hard-packed dirt, old throw-rugs on the floor. The walls are all bookshelves. Tables covered with electrical motors, lab beakers, other stuff I couldn't recognize. A tired old couch in the middle of the room, easy chairs from the same dump. All covered with white oilcloth. I caught the quiet whirr of the electric fans built into the ceiling, venting to the outside. It looked the same, but it felt different. The Mole built it to live underground—before Terry came along.

I sat on the couch, Belle next to me. The Mole pulled up a chair. Terry sat on the arm. Took his eyes off Belle long enough to ask me for a cigarette.

The Mole took off his glasses, rubbed them with a rag he pulled from his belt. No point asking him if he got into Sin City—he would have said so in front, if he hadn't.

"I found it," he said.

"You sure?"

His eyes were dim behind the heavy lenses, head solid on his stubby neck. "In the back, anchor holes. For a tripod. Video camera. Professional quality, heavy. Arc lights over the top. Cross-bolted brace. Beanbag rest."

"For the shooter."

"For the killer. The back doors work off a hydraulic valve. One switch—open and close."

"You understand what it is, Mole?"

"I understand. Killing machine. They go past the girls, hit the switch. Doors pop open. Killer shoots. Door closes." He took a breath. "And the camera is rolling. Taking the pictures."

"Snuff films," I said. "Live and up close. The real thing."

"Who does this?" Belle asked, her voice shaking. "What kind of freaks?"

The Mole pinned her with his eyes. "Nazis," he said. "They took pictures of us going into the ovens. Pictures of their evil. Treasures of filth."

"You find anything else?"

"Three more cars. Dark sedans. Another room. More cameras, lights. Drain in the floor."

That's where the baby pross they snatched off the street went. Down the drain.

I bit into the cigarette. I'd been ready for it, but red dots danced behind my eyes. I waited for the calm. For the hate to push out the fear.

"They have to go down, Mole. Can you get back inside?"

He didn't bother to answer me. Waiting.

"Can you wire it so it all goes up?"

He still waited—I hadn't asked him a question yet.

"Off a radio transmitter? So you push a button and . . ."

"How far away?"

"You tell me."

"It's all steel and concrete, that part of the city. The basement is deep. No more than four, five blocks to be sure. Easier to wire it to the ignition. They start the van . . ."

"That's no good. There's two freaks left who work the van. The shooter, and the man who wants Max. I think the driver's already dead. The van could sit there for weeks."

"Okay."

I got to my feet, stalking the underground bunker. Like they must have done in the Resistance a lifetime ago. "I got a plan. The shooter's bent—I think I can bring him in. Make him tell me where the other one is. Soon as I know, you can blow the basement."

"How long?"

"Couple of days—couple of weeks. I need more people," I said, catching his eye.

He knew what I meant. Didn't want to say Michelle's name in front of the kid. The Mole nodded again.

"I'll call you soon as I'm ready."

The Mole grabbed Terry's arm, pulled him around so the kid was facing him.

"Remember what I told you? About the Nazis? About our people?"

"Yes."

"Tonight," said the Mole, holding the boy's arms. "Tonight is Bar Mitzvah."

137 ‖ I BANKED the Pontiac across the on-ramp for the Triboro. Belle was quiet, smoking one cigarette after another, staring straight out the windshield.

"Go ahead," I told her. "Say it."

She turned in her seat. "You never gave me the grenade back."

"I know."

"You don't trust me?"

"I do trust you. I have to get out of the car, I'll hand it back to you." I glanced her way. "Okay?"

"Okay."

"Don't sulk."

"I'm not."

"Then you're a hell of an actress."

She tapped her fingers against one knee, keeping it under control. I lit a smoke for myself.

"What's the rest of it?"

She didn't answer me. Manhattan high-rises flew by on our right, river to our left. Mid-afternoon traffic still light.

"Burke, he's going to take that boy inside with him? Wire up a bunch of bombs?"

"Yeah."

"He's just a kid."

"It's his time. Like it was yours once."

"I wish . . ."

"Don't wish. It's a poison inside you."

"You don't wish for things?"

"Not anymore."

We were in midtown, heading for the Times Square cutoff. I rolled on past. Belle craned her neck, looking through the Pontiac's moon roof at the luxury apartments, balconies overlooking the river, high above it all.

"You think it's true? That it's lonely at the top?"

"I've never been there. All I know, it can be lonely at the bottom."

"But not always," she said, her left hand resting on my right thigh.

I covered her hand with mine. "Not always."

We passed under the Manhattan Bridge. I ignored the exit, taking it all the way downtown.

"Was the Prof really a shotgun bandit?"

"Where'd you hear that?"

"From him."

"I don't know if it's true or not. Ever since I've known him, he's been on the hustle. Maybe when he was younger, a long time ago. . . . Why'd he tell you?"

"I was telling him about me. That I was a driver. He said he used to cowboy liquor stores."

"Old as he is, he probably robbed stage coaches."

Belle giggled. "He's not so old."

"Anyone older than me is old."

"You don't feel old to me," she said, her hand shifting into my lap.

I grabbed her wrist, pulled her off. "Cut it out. Pay attention."

"I am."

"We got bigger things to think about."

"Bigger than this?" Grabbing me again.

I snarled at her. She giggled again. I turned off at the Brooklyn Bridge exit, took Centre Street to Worth, skirting the edge of Chinatown. I needed to make some calls, and I couldn't use the basement under Max's warehouse. Not now.

**138** I PULLED in behind Mama's. A black Buick sedan rolled across the entrance to the alley behind us, blocking us in. Its back doors opened. Three young Chinese jumped out. Long, shiny, swept-back black hair, red shirts under black leather jackets. They stepped into a triangle, using their car for cover. Two of them braced their elbows, locking their hands around automatics. The other crouched against the alley wall, an Uzi resting on one knee. No way out.

Belle caught it in the side mirror. "Burke!" she whispered.

"Don't move," I told her. I knew what it was.

The back door to the kitchen popped open. A monster walked out. He looked like a pair of sumo wrestlers. Shaved head, eyes buried in fat. He grabbed our car, shook it like a kid with a toy. He looked into my face.

"Mor-Tay?" It sounded like someone had taken his tonsils out with razor wire.

I put my hands on the dashboard, keeping my eyes on his face. "Burke," is all I said.

He shook the car again. Mama came out into the alley, said something to the monster. He let go, stepped aside. I motioned to Belle to get out. We followed Mama inside. Took my booth in the back. I lit a smoke. A waiter came up, a tureen of soup in his hands. When he leaned over, I could see the magnum under his arm.

"Where'd you find 'Zilla, Mama?"

"Always around. Good friend."

"I see you taught him some English."

Mama bowed. "Teach him everything." Most Orientals are fatalists—Mama was fatal.

I sipped the soup. Mama was serene. Greeted Belle, reached over, held her hand for a second. I left them there, went in the back to make some calls.

"Runaway Squad."

"McGowan. It's me. I got something. Can you meet me at the end of Maiden Lane, by the pier?"

"I can roll now."

"Make it in an hour."

"Right."

I tossed in another quarter, rang the private number for the phone-sex joint where Michelle worked.

"Yeah?"

"Michelle?"

"We got no Michelle here, pal."

"I know. Tell her to call Mama."

A sleepy woman's voice answered the next call.

"Put Marques on."

"He's not here."

"Right. Tell him Burke's going to call him. In two hours. Tell him to be in his car. In two hours, you got it?"

"I'm not sure . . ."

"This is Christina, right? You *be* sure. Two hours, I'll call him. Tell him to be in the car."

I hung up, not waiting for a whore's promise.

Back inside, Mama and Belle were huddled together, talking. I sat down across from them. Mama spooned some meat-stuffed dumplings onto my plate, still talking to Belle.

"Dim sum. Burke's favorite."

"How do you make them?"

Mama shrugged her shoulders—she wasn't a cook.

I ate slowly, one eye on my watch. The Maiden Lane pier was just a few minutes away.

"Mama, Michelle's going to call here. If she doesn't do it before we leave, make sure you get a number where I can reach her. Tonight. Very, very important, okay?"

"She help you. On this?"

"We'll see."

Mama bowed. More food came. Belle ate like Pansy, only with better table manners. I never felt so safe.

Finally, I pushed the plates away. Belle was still eating. "You hear from Mac?" I asked Mama.

She smiled. Made a gesture with her hands like a flower opening to the sun.

"Boston quiet?"

"Quiet soon. Max working."

I bowed. Held out my hand to Belle. She looked unhappy, not wanting to leave the warmth any more than I did.

Mama walked us out to the back. "I'll call later—check on Michelle."

The monster was still standing by the door. The Buick was still across the alley mouth, no gunners in sight. I backed up the Pontiac slowly, watching the Buick move out of the way in the rearview mirror. Pointed the car toward the pier.

**139** | BELLE WAS finishing off a last egg roll. She delicately wiped her mouth with the chiffon scarf, tossed it into the back seat.

"How come you call her Mama?"

"It's what she calls herself."

"Where're we going?"

"Meet some cops."

"Cops?"

"They're okay. For this, they're okay. They want him too." I handed her the grenade. "You stay in the car."

"But . . ."

"Shut up. I let you have your grenade, took you for a nice drive to the Bronx, gave you a nice meal. That's all the babying you're going to get today."

She reached into the back seat, put the greasy scarf in her lap, covering the grenade. I turned in to the pier and backed the Pontiac into an empty space, watching for McGowan. We were early.

"Burke?"

"What?"

"That huge guy . . . the one who came out the back door?"

"Yeah?"

"If he's Chinese, how come he has an Italian name. 'Zilla'?"

"It's not his name, just what people call him. Short for 'Godzilla.' "

"Oh. Why'd he say that name? Mor-Tay?"

"He was asking a question. That pimp, Marques. He wants to know about putting a bounty out on someone, he should talk to Mama."

**140** McGowan's car pulled up. I got out of the Pontiac, making sure he could see me, walking toward him, both hands in sight. His partner reached behind him; the back door popped open. I climbed in. His partner closed it behind me—no door handles on the inside.

"You know Morales?" McGowan asked.

"Yeah."

"He's with me on this. Understand?"

"Yeah."

"You called me out here."

I lit a smoke. "You sure you want your partner to hear this?"

They looked at each other. Morales said, "I need some cigarettes. Be right back. You need anything?"

McGowan shook his head. Morales stepped out.

"I found the Ghost Van."

"Where?"

"It's underground. There's three men in on the front end. One's the dead guy you found in the Chelsea playground. Two more left. I got a plan to trap one, work him until he shows me where the other one is."

"You saw the van?"

"Not with my eyes. I know where it is."

"That's enough for a warrant."

"The guy who saw it, he's not coming in. Neither am I. I got a deal. You interested?"

"Go."

"I need some things from you. Everything works out, I take this guy who wants Max. And the Ghost Van goes boom."

"What's mine?"

"The shooter," I said. "And Sally Lou."

McGowan knew the name. He puffed furiously on his cigar. I could see where they got the idea for smoked glass. "What do you need?"

"A massage parlor. In Times Square. And for the cops to stay away. A week, maybe two."

"Where am I gonna get a massage parlor?"

"McGowan, don't negotiate. I got no slack in my rope. You already *got* a couple of them. Maybe not you personally, but the cops have. That joint just off Forty-sixth—that was yours, right?"

"That was a sting. The tax boys. And it's all closed down now."

"But you got more. You've been after Sally Lou for years."

"There is one. But it's not ours."

"The *federales?*"

"Yeah."

"Tell them you need it. Couple of weeks. I'll staff it myself."

"With what?"

"Marques Dupree. He'll lend me some girls."

"He's in this?"

"It started with him. Like I told you. I'll be calling him in an hour. Get him over here. I want you to tell him it's okay."

"Now you want me to make a deal with a pimp."

"McGowan, you'd make a deal with the devil to drop Sally Lou."

"Spell it out—what do I get?"

"The shooter comes to the massage parlor. I talk to him. He turns over this other guy I want. We dump the shooter anyplace you say. The Ghost Van goes up in smoke. And you find everything you need to take Sally Lou down."

"This other guy . . . What if it doesn't work out?"

"I got one more deal. One more piece. You and me take a walk over to that brown Pontiac. The one I came out of. There's a girl sitting in the front seat. You take a good long look at her. Whatever happens, you make sure she walks away. In exchange, I leave you a letter. With everything in it. The Ghost Van, the shooter, this karate-freak, the shooting in the Chelsea playground, Sally Lou."

"And I let the girl walk?"

"She'll be the one mailing you the letter. Enough for a dozen cases."

"Let's take a look," he said.

**141** WE STROLLED to the Pontiac. I motioned for Belle to roll down her window.

"This is Detective McGowan, NYPD," I told her. She didn't take her hands out of her lap. "He's the one you're going to mail that letter to, okay?"

"Okay." No expression on her face.

We walked back to McGowan's car. Morales was halfway across the parking lot. McGowan waved him in.

"One more thing," I said.

"What now?"

"You know Morelli? The reporter?"

"Sure."

"He gets it first. Exclusive. He'll take care of you."

"And your people."

I nodded.

"Okay," he said.

Morales joined us. "Take a walk with me," McGowan said. "I'll fill you in."

I went back to the Pontiac, let myself in, watched McGowan and Morales standing by the pay phone on the pier.

"Good girl."

"What's in this letter I'm supposed to mail?"

"A free pass—I'll tell you later."

I watched McGowan pick up the phone. He talked for a couple of minutes. Stood where he was. Picked up the phone again. Talked some more. Waved.

"Be right back," I told Belle.

I walked up to McGowan. "Call the pimp," he said.

## 142 | MARQUES WAS on his car phone. Answered it himself.

"You know who this is?"

"Yeah, man. What . . . ?"

"The Maiden Lane pier. *Now*. It's coming down."

"I ain't walking into no . . ."

"This is a safe place, Marques. The *only* fucking safe place for you in the city, you don't show up."

I hung up.

McGowan stood on one side of me, Morales close on the other.

"You know Sadie's Sexsational?"

I laughed.

"What's so funny?"

"Girl got beat up there. Real bad, right? So bad the cops moved in, closed it down."

Morales turned to me. "You think *that's* funny?"

"I think *you're* funny," I said to McGowan. "You've been running the place ever since, right? That joint doesn't belong to the *federales*. You called One Police Plaza, not the FBI."

McGowan touched the brim of his hat. "What d'you care?"

"I don't. In fact, that joint is perfect."

"Why?"

"Good location," I told him, eyes flat.

Morales didn't like any of this. His eyes scanned the pier, waiting for the pimp.

"You guys know what to do?" I asked McGowan.

"We'll make it clear to him."

I lit a smoke.

"How you gonna get the shooter into this one massage parlor?" McGowan asked.

"I know what he wants."

## 143 ‖ THE ROLLS purred into the parking lot.

"That's him," I said.

"We know. Go and get him."

Marques was behind the wheel, Christina next to him.

"Thanks for showing."

"You didn't give me much motherfucking choice."

"Be cool, Marques. Be yourself—show your class. Walk over to the water with me."

"I don't like this."

I leaned in the window. "I wanted you off the count, you'd be in the morgue. You know it, I know it. This is legit. Come on."

He exchanged a look with Christina. Got out of the Rolls. We walked to the water. I couldn't see McGowan or his partner.

"I'm taking over a massage parlor," I said.

"You?"

"Me. And I need some girls. For a couple of weeks."

"You crazy, man."

"I got the van, Marques. I got it pinned to the wall. Start counting that bounty money; it'll be mine soon."

"What's that got to do with . . ."

"The van didn't move by itself. You wanted it off the street, you think I was gonna give it a flat tire?"

"Look, man . . ."

"I need the girls. Fill the joint up, make it look righteous. They can keep everything they score. The guy who did Sabrina? The pain-freak? He's the one—the lead to the van. I got to pull him in."

"My girls don't . . ."

"I *know* they don't. But you know some who do, right? I just need one. She takes the pain-tricks, your girls take the rest. You keep the cash. This one guy comes in, the show's over."

"My girls don't . . . Hey!"

McGowan stepped in behind me; I saw Morales roll up behind Marques.

"You know who this is?" I asked Marques.

"Yeah, man," he sneered. "Every player knows *Detective* McGowan."

"You don't want to know him better, you'll shut up and listen. He's here to tell you something."

McGowan leaned over my shoulder. "Nobody's going to bother Sadie's Sexsational for a couple of weeks, *Mister* Dupree. Nobody. Not the wise guys, not the heat. Got it?"

"I got it."

Morales pressed in against Marques. "Get *this*. You *go* along, you *get* along. You don't, I got a little girl. Says you tried to pull her. Says you had *mucho* coke in your ride. More than enough for a warrant. I toss your car, I find a couple of fucking kilos. Any fucking time I want."

Marques nodded. "I'm in. You got it."

McGowan spoke to him. "You got two days. Friday night, nine o'clock, you be there. With your girls."

"It's in the bank, man."

Morales pressed closer. "Or you're in the joint."

Marques walked back to his car alone. He didn't look back.

"I see your hand got better," McGowan said.

"I got more cards in it," I told him.

**144** ‖ I WAITED until McGowan and his partner pulled off before I went back to the Pontiac.

"What's going on?" Belle asked.

"It's coming together, little girl."

I drove a few feet to the pay phone, left the engine running, dialed Mama.

"It's me. Michelle call?"

"Yes. Come here tonight. Eleven."

**145** ‖ BACK IN the office, I let Pansy out, told Belle to stay where she was. I went down to the basement, came back with a big metal box. Belle watched as I laid the stuff out. I lit a smoke, left it smoldering on the edge of the desk while I worked. My hands were moving on the equipment, but I was watching a different picture in my mind. Seeing it happen.

I picked up the cigarette, took a last drag.

"Belle, honey, would you take off your top?"

She pulled it over her head.

"The bra too, okay?"

She unsnapped it, waited. Her breasts made a joke of gravity, the blue necklace falling just to the cleft. It wouldn't work like that. "Wait here," I told her.

I came back with a white T-shirt of mine. "Try this."

She slipped into it. Her breasts fought the thin material, the cleavage gone. No good.

"You have any real thin tops? Gauzy, maybe? The kind you can see through?"

"Like a nightgown?"

"That might work . . . if you have a real short one."

"I have a couple. Some teddies too."

"No. I need something that kind of opens down the middle. So your breasts stay separated."

"Why, baby? I can go buy anything you want."

I held up a pistol. From the side, it looked exactly like a Colt Python .357 magnum, even down to the ventilated rib across the top of the barrel. "You know what this is?"

"A gun."

"It's not, though. It's a gas gun. Works off $CO_2$ cartridges. It shoots these things," I said, showing her a handful of red plastic balls.

"What are they?"

"Paint pellets. Sixty-two-caliber. The survival-freaks use them when they play their little war games. The pellet hits you, it leaves a red splat, so you know who got hit."

"Do they hurt?"

"They sting. Especially up close. And you can feel them smack into you."

"What'd you want with it?"

"I got a plan, Belle. And part of it, I got to pretend to shoot you. Up close. Real close."

She pulled the T-shirt over her head. "Go ahead. Let me see how it feels."

"No. When it happens, you've got to feel it for the first time. You know it doesn't hurt, you won't act nervous enough."

"Honey . . ."

"You don't want to do it, say so."

"There's nothing I wouldn't do for you."

"I know," I said, holding her against me. I gave her a kiss. "Let me work now. I have to see it."

"See what?"

"See it happen. Like in karate, when they train you to punch. You don't punch *at* something, you punch *through* it. You have to see it happening, see your fist go right through the board. You don't see it, it doesn't happen. Something goes wrong in your head and it stops your hands. Okay?"

She nodded, solemn-faced.

I went back to work. The paint gun would need something that looked like a silencer. I fitted a piece of aluminum tubing, trying it out. Coming to it.

**146** ‖ WE PULLED into the alley behind Mama's just before eleven. Instant replay: the Buick rolling in behind us, the monster coming out the door. At least this time he didn't rattle the car.

Michelle was already inside, sitting in my booth. She looked pristine and elegant in a white double-breasted wool jacket, black blouse underneath. I let Belle in first. Michelle took Belle's face in her hands, turning it to catch the light.

"*Much* better. I think we could go for a little stronger look around the eyes. And your hair . . ."

"Michelle, we don't have a lot of time."

"You drag me down to this godforsaken neighborhood—no offense, Mama—right in the middle of my working hours, and *you're* in a hurry." She flashed her smile at Belle. "Men are always in a hurry, but they never have that much to do. That's a beautiful necklace," she cooed. Belle leaned forward so Michelle could hold it. "Burke bought it for me."

"Unbelievable. It's a beautiful thing, perfect for you. Maybe he's learning some class."

Belle was throwing off more wattage than the lights. Clothes weren't the only thing Michelle did right.

I got out of the booth. Bowed to Mama. "We can use the basement? Talk?"

She bowed.

The women followed me downstairs. "Very chic," said Michelle,
pointing at the wall of stainless-steel vats. "Is that high-tech?"

I ignored her. The basement is well lighted. The subbasement
isn't. Max keeps things down there. I never asked what.

Mama bowed again, leaving us alone. Michelle perched on a
wooden crate, crossed her silky legs. "You didn't bring me down here
to talk about our stock investments."

"No. It's the Ghost Van. We're all in it now. All that's left. I
have to pull a sting. Smoke out a freak. It's all worked out, but I need
you to run it."

"Tell me."

"There's a massage parlor in Times Square. Sadie's Sexsational,
it's called. You know it?"

"Nasty place."

"Yeah, it is. Our place, for the next couple of weeks. McGowan
cleared out the trash—nobody'll bother us."

"Us?"

"Marques Dupree; we're going to run his girls out of the place.
There's two guys left from the Ghost Van. The shooter, he's into pain.
Other people's pain. He's the one that tortured that girl before the
cops moved in to close the place. So we're opening up again. I want
to pull him in."

"I know Marques. His girls . . ."

"He's going to get one more. A free-lancer. She'll do all the whip-
jobs. The rest, we run it like a regular joint. Customers come in, say
what they want, pick a girl, pay the money. Guy comes in, asks for
some freak-fun, we turn him over to this other girl. I'll be there—it
won't get out of hand. But when this other guy comes, this guy we're
looking for, he gets Belle."

Michelle's eyes flicked to Belle, back to me. She took a long black
cigarette from her purse, tapped it on a fingernail.

"Belle takes him to the back. We'll have a place fixed up."

"What then?"

"Then he tells me where to find the other guy. And I go find him."

"There's no other way?"

"No. He walks back with Belle, I'm ready for him. We'll have it all worked out. You see this guy go back with Belle, you're gone. Just walk out. The other girls too."

"Who else is in on it?"

"The Mole. He found the van. I can talk him into it, he'll work the front desk."

Michelle's lovely face was serious, not playing now. "I always wanted to be a madam. Of course, I envisioned nicer surroundings, but . . . this'll do. I'm in charge?"

"You're in charge. The girls get to keep what they make, but pull the money at the front desk to make it look correct."

"You have pictures?"

"Pictures?"

"Of the girls. We need a book of pictures, show the johns when they come in. Let them pick the ones they want."

"I don't know."

"I'll take the pictures once they get in there. The Mole has the stuff. When does it happen?"

"Friday night we start. McGowan will put the word out. Sadie's Sexsational is the spot, you want to beat up a girl. It'll get around. We got two weeks tops. I'll be staying there. Once I go in, I can't go out. Can't take a chance of getting spotted. You bring food in with you every day. I'll be there until it's over."

"What if the freak doesn't bite?"

I shrugged. "I'm not thinking that way."

"Okay."

"We're playing for everything on the table, Michelle."

"I know. What if we need some operating cash?"

"Take it out of my share of the last score."

She dragged on her cigarette. "You worked with the Mole. . . . You see my boy?"

"He's fine," I assured her.

"A real doll," Belle chipped in.

Michelle smiled. Gave me a kiss. Kissed Belle. "I'll get a cab," she said.

**147** "TAKE EVERYTHING you're going to need," I told Belle. We were back in her cottage, two in the morning. She bustled around, filling two big suitcases.

"What about my car?"

"You follow me back to the city with it when we go in for the last time. Day after tomorrow. I'll stash the Pontiac on the street. We'll keep your car in the garage."

She was on her hands and knees, poking around in a corner near her bed. She came up with two handfuls of cash. "I've got about fifteen thousand here," she said.

"I'll show you where to hide it."

"You want . . . ?"

"No."

I walked out onto the deck, lighting a smoke. I felt Belle behind me. "How's this?"

I turned around. She was wearing a flimsy red wrapper, tied at the waist with a thin ribbon. Her breasts were barely veiled, slash of white skin down the middle.

"You'll freeze out here."

She moved into my arms. She was warm, soft. Her hips trembled against me. My hand slid to her butt.

"Doesn't this thing come with pants?"

"I'd just have to take them off," she said. "Come on."

**148** | I N   T H E  car heading back, Belle fiddled with the radio. Full-throated, late-night blues. "I'm a stranger, and afraid"—the singer well within himself, coming to grips, looking it in the eye.

"He's telling the truth," Belle whispered. "I've been both all my life."

I found her hand in the darkness.

The disc jockey broke in. "That was Johnny Adams, out of New Orleans. Singing a new Doc Pomus tune, 'A World I Never Made.' You all remember Doc Pomus, the man who gave us 'Save the Last Dance for Me,' 'Little Sister,' and so many other monster hits. Doc's one of the world's great bluesmen. Now here's the flip side. Down and dirty. Like they don't do anymore."

Rattling soft piano, sinuous spiking guitar notes dancing on the top, teasing. Johnny Adams, making his promises, bragging his brag. "I'm your body and fender man, let me pound out your dents." In case anyone listening had maple syrup for brains, he spelled it out:

> *I don't care if your body's brand new*
> *Or it's been knocked around . . .*
> *I swear they're all the same, babe,*
> *When you turn them upside down.*

"He's off the mark there," Belle said.

"No, he's right. There's no such thing as a golden snapper—the difference is in here," I said, tapping my chest.

"Here," she said, pulling my hand to her breast.

I lit a smoke. Doc Pomus on the radio again. Like that night I left my basement. Full circle.

**149** THE PONTIAC slipped into the garage. I showed Belle the circuit-breaker panel in the back corner. "You know what this is?"

"Sure. Like a fuse box."

"Watch." I punched the switch marked Hall. Then Lobby. Then Second Floor. The box popped open, flat plate inside. I used a thumbnail to open the setscrews. Behind it was a deep, lead-lined box. A revolver rested on a neat stack of bills. "Put your money in there."

"That's neat. It has wires running from it and everything."

"The wires run to the house current. Electromagnetic switches. Like a combination lock. You remember?"

"Hall, lobby, second floor."

I patted her butt. "Good girl."

"If I tell you again, will you pat me some more?"

"Upstairs."

**150** "YOU READY to go over it again?"

"Honey, I got it down pat."

"One more time—it's got to be perfect."

"Okay," she sighed.

I took the handcuffs from the drawer, hooked one cuff to her right wrist, the other to the back of a chair. She took the long-handled speed key from the desk, holding it in her left hand.

"Go!"

She twisted her wrist, exposing the key slot, slammed the speed key home, twisted it, pulled free.

"Beautiful."

She stood up. "I am. A beautiful young girl. Like you taught me."

**151** | LATE THAT night. Belle on her knees in front of me, her head bent between my legs. Licking me like a cat cleans her kittens. Thick thatch of hair falling. I felt the beads of the necklace lapping against my thigh.

Her head came up. Whispering in the dark. "You think it's too much?"

"What?"

"This. The way I am. I'm just like this with you. I swear it."

"What're you talking about?"

"I want your hands on me—I want you inside me. All the time. Everyplace inside me. When you just pat me on the bottom, I get wet."

"It's your way of dealing with it. Everybody's lying but you and me, Belle. To each other. This all started out with a lie. Some punk lawyer, chumping me off, he thought. And Marques, with his fifty-grand bounty. He probably collected a hundred. Maybe made a side bet about taking the van off the street. I lied to Max to get him out of the way. Mama helped me. McGowan trying to tell me the *federales* had the massage parlor. Me telling him I'm going to give him the van, and Sally Lou too. There's no letter for him—there never will be. The Mole, he could never tell Michelle he's made a Nazi-hunter out of the boy. Morelli, he thinks there's a story in this for him. Mortay. He's the only one who told the truth."

His name hung over us in the dark. I could see it. Neon-red, dripping.

"I looked in his eyes. He wasn't lying. He's earned his name. Scared me *past* death. Till I came out the other side. My old friend's there. On the other side. Hate. It didn't save my basement, but it saved my life. Plenty of times. You got your way, I got mine."

"Will it stop? When it's over?"

"It might for you," I told her. "It won't for me."

**152** I CALLED Mama at seven the next morning.

"Anything?"

"Nobody call."

"Good."

"Nobody come either," she said. "Too bad."

I left Belle a note, telling her I'd be back soon with something to eat. Took my time about it. Fresh rolls, big slab of cream cheese, two six-packs of beer, pineapple juice, seltzer. I grabbed a copy of the *Daily News*. Bob Herbert's column came out on Thursdays—he'd been pounding the cops about the Ghost Van, the only one writing about it.

When I got back to the office, Pansy let me in, a distracted look on her face. She sniffed the food. "You been out?" I asked her.

"She sure has." Belle's voice from the back room. "Come on back here, you nasty old thing, let's finish this."

Pansy loped off. Belle was on her hands and knees, wearing just a bra and pants. Pansy ran over to her, lowering her head like a charging bull. They butted each other back and forth, going nose to nose. Belle was bigger and heavier, but Pansy wouldn't budge an inch, snarling happily.

"Are you nuts? What if she snaps at you?"

"She won't do that—this is a fair fight."

They pushed at each other, faces pressed together, Belle making grunting sounds of her own. Finally she dropped to the floor, face-down. Pansy sniffed the back of her neck. "You win," Belle muttered.

I put the food together. "What was that all about?"

"I told her I didn't mind her threatening me before, but if she messed with me again, I was gonna kick her ass."

"You're out of your mind."

"It was fun. You want to try?"

"Not this year. With either of you."

Belle went into the shower. I mixed the pineapple juice and seltzer, added some ice. Then I stuffed a roll full of cream cheese and gave it to Pansy. Belle came out, wrapped in a towel. Helped herself to the food.

"Beer for breakfast?"

"Save it for later. And don't give Pansy any."

Belle dropped to her knees, hands in front of her like a dog's paws. "Just one?"

Pansy stood next to her, watching me closely.

"Yeah, all right. I give up."

Belle's laugh was sweetness on the morning.

## 153

PANSY PROWLED the floor, sniffing the corners, snarling at nothing in particular. Our last night in the cottage. Belle was stuffing another pair of suitcases.

"Why'd you bring that old dog anyway?"

"I wanted to get her used to sleeping outside the office—she's going to be at the massage parlor with us."

"In case somebody wants something special?"

I didn't answer her. I dialed the Runaway Squad. They told me McGowan was in the street—they'd take a message. I hung up. Mama had nothing to tell me. I had nothing to tell the Mole.

"Don't make it look like you moved out," I warned Belle.

"I'm just taking a few things. The rent's paid till the end of the month, and I got two months security down. I'll throw another money order in the mail to the landlord. People mind their own business out here."

I went out on the deck, minding mine. Pansy trotted along next to me. She jumped up on her hind legs, hooking her front paws to the railing. I scratched the back of her neck. "You want to see the junkyard, girl? Meet a few new guys?" She made a happy rumble in her throat. The sound rippled across the water. I smoked a couple of cigarettes, calm inside. Once you jump off the bridge, everything's smooth until you hit the water.

It was past midnight when we came back inside. Belle was wearing a gauzy blue nightgown, her face fresh-scrubbed and clean. Ready for bed. She took a bottle of beer from the refrigerator, poured herself a glass. Pansy made a pitiful moaning noise, brushing her head against Belle's thigh.

"Oh! *Now* you wanna be pals, huh?"

She found a cereal bowl, another bottle of beer. Took them both into a far corner. Bent from the waist and filled it up. Pansy got about half of it, the floor got the rest.

I lit a cigarette. "You taught me something."

"What, honey?"

"The poison-proofing I did with her . . . so she won't take food unless she hears the right word?"

"Yes?"

"I'm a jerk. I never thought about liquids. She'll drink any goddamned thing."

"Can't you . . . ?"

"Yeah. You take the time, the patience, you can train a dog like Pansy to do just about anything. I didn't do it. And I just figured out why."

Belle was next to me, my arm around her waist, listening like I was saying something important.

"There's no way to throw liquid under a door. She wouldn't take it anyway—not unless it was in a bowl, or in a pool. I never figured on anyone being *inside*, you understand?"

"I'm inside," she said softly.

"Yeah, you are. Let's go to sleep."

She gently twirled away from me. Turned off the lights. "Not yet, honey. Sit in the chair. This is our last night here. Until it's over. I want to say my prayers."

She knelt before the bed, hands clasped in front of her. Her skin glowed under the nightgown. Blue light.

Belle looked over her shoulder. She played with the sash at her waist. The nightgown floated to the floor.

"Rescue me," she whispered.

**154** ‖ IT WAS still dark when I watched Belle slip the Camaro into my garage. I stashed the Pontiac a few blocks away, in a safe spot near the river.

I didn't like the walk back to the garage. Pinprick tingles all across my back. But it was quiet—my fear was just picking up long-distance signals.

The garage was dark when I stepped inside. I headed for the stairs, sending Pansy ahead, Belle right behind me. She pulled at my arm. "Wait."

She stood before the circuit-breaker box. Punched the three buttons in the right sequence, puffing out her chest like a proud little girl when the box popped open. If little girls looked like that when they got a question right, I might have stayed in school. She slipped off the necklace, holding the blue glow in her hands. I watched her, one foot on the first rung of the stairs.

"I can't do it," she said. Slamming the box closed. "It don't seem right to wear it inside a whorehouse, but . . ." She patted the front of her thigh. Where her mother's gravestone was etched in her flesh.

**155** | Upstairs, I dialed McGowan again. This time he was around.

"It's me. Everything okay?"

"It's empty right now. There's an alley running behind it. Room for three cars, four if they're packed tight. Chain-link fence, barbed wire on the top. They used to keep a German shepherd out there."

"Okay. I'm rolling."

"Wait. There's one more thing. The joint next to it. The video store. That's ours too. You can walk in, go down to the basement, and walk through. We punched a tunnel through. You can go in and out."

"Thanks, McGowan."

"I should've been straight with you." His honey-Irish voice was soft around the edges. "Square it up, now."

"For all of them," I promised, hanging up.

I called the Mole, gave him the word. Whoever was listening at the other end hung up when I was finished.

Belle was unpacking her clothes, laying them across the couch, bumping Pansy out of the way with her hip.

I called Mama.

"I'm going in. You know where everything is. Max knows the rest. I'm putting it all down. In a letter. To the Jersey box."

Mama said something in Cantonese.

"What was that?"

"If the letter come, I fix everything."

"I know. Goodbye, Mama."

She hung up. A sadness-shudder passed through me, leaving me chilled. I lit a cigarette and started to write.

**156** FRIDAY NIGHT. Eight o'clock. I followed Pansy down the back stairs, a heavy suitcase in each hand. Belle behind me, carrying two more. I left her in the garage with all the stuff, snapped the lead on Pansy, and went for a walk.

Electric fear-jolts danced through me. Pansy felt it. Her massive head swung back and forth, pinning everyone she saw. Her teeth snapped together in little clicks, kill noises slipping through. Her eyes were ice cubes.

A yuppie couple approached, her hand through his arm. They crossed the street. A wino was propped against the car right next to the Pontiac. I tightened the leash. Pansy lunged, snarling. He sobered up, moved off. I opened the door, put Pansy in the back seat.

Belle was ready when I pulled up in front of the garage. I popped the trunk; we threw the suitcases inside and moved off.

West Side Highway to Tenth Avenue. Across 30th down to Twelfth. And then a right turn back into what the tour guides would call the heart of Times Square.

The fear-jolts were spiking inside me. Pansy prowled the back seat, side to side; her face loomed at the windows.

"Jump!" I snapped at her. Nobody'd remember the Pontiac, but nobody'd forget Pansy. She went down, snarling her hate for whatever was frightening me.

I found the alley, nosed the car in, creeping forward, driving with my left hand, the pistol cocked in my right. The fenced-off section was where McGowan said it would be—huge padlock in place. I stopped the car, popped the door for Pansy, calling to her. "Watch!"

I walked to the fence, the gun in front, poking its way through the darkness.

A flashlight beam behind the fence. I hit the ground, leveling the pistol as Pansy charged past me, throwing herself at the chain links. "Don't shoot—it's me." The Mole's voice. I called Pansy off, met him at the fence. He reached through, opened the padlock, swung the gate open. I pulled the Pontiac inside, between a white panel truck with the name of some kosher butcher shop on the side and a dark station wagon. "All ours?" I asked the Mole.

"Sure," he said.

**157** WE FOLLOWED him inside. Big room, dim lights, cartons stacked against the walls, steel shelving loaded with video cassettes.

"Basement," the Mole said.

"You know about the video store next door? Like I told you over the phone?"

The Mole barely kept the sneer from his voice. "I was in last night." He held up a ring of keys. We could go visit the cops, but they couldn't come see us.

Upstairs, we walked through the place. The front door was between two windows, one a little square patch of glass, the other running down the length of the place. All the glass was blacked out except for the little square near the door. Lights flashed outside.

"One-way glass," the Mole explained.

The joint was a long hall, L-shaped at the far end. Rooms opened off the corridor. Tiny hook-and-eye locks inside. Vinyl massage tables set up for quick-change sheets. Wood benches in some, leather chairs in others. They all had tables in a corner, bottles of lotions, perfumes, air fresheners. Tiny sinks against the wall. Heavy mats on the walls. All class. The L-shaped area was much larger. Bathrooms off to the side. Big ones, complete with glassed-in stall showers. Partitions made a private office in one corner. Red leather executive's chair, blond wood desk, red leather couch, white two-line phone. Even had a view—dirt-streaked window, thick bars running the full width across.

I walked back through the place, the Mole behind me. Wall-to-wall industrial-grade carpeting that had once been pink covered every square inch of floor. Recessed lighting ran the length of the hall. A desk was set up against the wall right across from the door. A wood railing made two gates—one to the desk, one to the corridor. Huge blowup pictures covered the walls of the entryway. Only two chairs, both against the left-hand wall. No Waiting. A giant round mirror was in the upper right-hand corner, cocked at the angle formed by the wall and the ceiling. I sat at the desk, looked up. You could see the length of the corridor.

"We need a . . ."

"Periscope," the Mole stepped on my lines. "You stay in the back room, see every face that comes in."

"Okay. What's that?" I asked, pointing to a light on the desk.

"Switch in every room. Girl has trouble, she pushes it."

The phone on the desk rang. I picked it up. "Yeah?"

"It's me." McGowan's voice. "I'm next door. I see you managed to get in."

"We're in." I looked around. "One more thing. I can't work the bouncer job in here. Got to stay out of sight. I'm going to have some boys sent over."

"What kind of boys?"

"Chinese boys."

"No way! That's all I need. Can you rig up a buzzer? Between us? Your man hits it, we'll have someone through the basement in a minute."

I looked at the Mole. He nodded. Rigging a buzzer wasn't going to overload his brain cells.

"Okay, we'll take care of it right away."

"Hey, Burke?"

"What?"

"Tell your man to leave the door open, okay?"

I hung up on him.

**158** ‖ MICHELLE showed a little later. You could see her through the square piece of glass. The Mole buzzed her inside. She was wearing a scarlet pants suit over a white turtleneck sweater, black spikes on her feet. The Mole and I stayed out of her way as she stalked the length of the corridor. Me smoking, watching the door, the Mole starting to set up the periscope.

Michelle came back to the front room, hands on hips. "This place is the pits. Mole, I need everything out of the first room. That'll be my office. And put that disgusting tool belt someplace—you're supposed to be the manager, not the janitor."

"I have to fix things," the Mole said, mildly.

"Well, go ahead and *fix* things. I'll go out tomorrow, get you some decent clothes."

"Michelle . . ."

"Don't you *Michelle* me. I work my beautiful butt off to keep my kid in nice clothes, and every time I see him he looks more like *you*, God forbid."

"He's my boy too."

"Sure. Next thing, you'll want him Bar Mitzvahed."

The Mole said nothing—even a lunatic knows the limit.

I left them to fight over who was going to go back to the junkyard every morning to check on the kid.

**159** BELLE AND Pansy were in the back. Pansy was stretched out on the couch, Belle in the chair. "You okay?" I asked her.

"I'm fine, baby."

I gave her a kiss. Heard the buzzer. Female noises, Michelle's voice cutting through the chatter. I heard someone coming back, stepped outside into the big room. It was Michelle.

"I have to have a meeting with my girls. And take some pictures. It's gonna be a while—you both just stay back here, keep it quiet."

I nodded, putting my finger to my lips. Pansy closed her eyes.

A couple of minutes later, I heard Michelle bossing the Mole, telling him where she wanted the light stands, not to get his greasy hands on the lens. One day she was going to push him over the edge.

The room filled with girls. Pansy's face wrinkled at the overpowering smells. Michelle's voice:

"Okay, now, I understand you ladies have not worked inside before. Which one of you is Christina?"

"Marques says Miss Bitch don't have to do this. Just us."

Murmur of voices.

"Well, girls, it seems to me that opportunity is knocking. Here's the way we work it: the trick pays thirty bucks—he gets fifteen minutes. Straight massage, that's a handshake. He wants something more, *anything* more, that's an extra, got it? The trick pays at the front desk; whatever he tips, that's up to you."

"How much for the extras?" one girl asked.

"You decide. Set your own list. And don't do anything you don't *want* to do, got it? You turn over your tips to Marques, you don't turn them over, it's not my problem."

"But Marques . . ."

"Marques isn't running this show. I am. And I run it my way. Now, which one of you turns the hard tricks?"

"That's me." A husky grown-woman's voice.

"What's your name, honey?"

"Bambi."

"Okay, Bambi. You set your prices, you keep the coin. And listen to me, girl. This is a no-risk gig, you follow me? There's a button in each of your rooms—I'll show you where it is. You hit the button, and we have some nasty men to take care of any problem."

"The guy with the tool belt?" one of them giggled.

Michelle's voice went from sweet cream to barbed wire without missing a beat. "That man with the tool belt, honey, he makes people *disappear*. You watch your smart mouth, bitch. Your idea of a hard guy's some half-ass nigger pimp with a coat hanger in his hands."

"Hey!"

"You want to get down, go for it. Right now."

The room went quiet.

Michelle let the silence hang. Then she sheathed her claws. "Honey, I've been around longer than this sweet young face shows. Now, I want to treat all of you like the *ladies* you are. Nobody's going to mistreat you while you work for me. Nobody's going to disrespect you. You work your shift, you mind your business, and you make some nice money. We're just moving the stroll indoors for a couple of weeks, that's all. But anyone gets the idea they can fuck with my friends, they go back to work without a face."

The room was quiet again.

"Okay?"

The girls stepped on themselves agreeing with her.

"Fine. Now, the next thing, we have to put together some portfolios for each of you."

"Like models?"

"Of *course*, like models. Isn't that what we are? Are we any different from those walking sticks in the magazines? A john comes in, he comes to the desk. We show him the book. Pictures of each of you. He picks the one he wants."

"We don't have to line up?"

"This isn't the precinct, honey. A trick wants to see live skin, he puts his money down. Now, there's five girls, we got nine rooms. The first one, the one near the desk, that's mine. Leave the last two empty, the ones right across from here. You divide the rest the way you want—Bambi, you take the one furthest back. And no fighting! To-morrow I'll go out and get some decent furnishings. Okay? Now, we are *not* open for business tonight. You come back, one at a time, we'll put the portfolios together. When we're done, you can hang around or you can split. Be back tomorrow. Four o'clock. We'll work twelve-hour shifts; you leave at four in the morning. Any questions?"

Nobody said a word.

"One more thing. This place is under *heavy* protection. You'll never see a cop in here. You play this right, it's a working girl's dream."

## 160

"WHAT'S YOUR name, honey?" Michelle asked.

"MaryAnne."

"Let's lose the black stockings, honey. Your legs are already so nice and slim—the black won't show them off."

"Okay."

"And just a touch more rouge . . . there! Brings out your color. Now, sit straight in the chair. Cross your legs. *Elegant!*"

"Michelle?"

"Yes, honey?"

"The guy with the tool belt? The one out front? Boy, you were right about him. He had this jar of water on the desk, fiddling with some locks. Marcy flashed her ass at him, sat on the desk. Asked him if he ever sampled the merchandise. He drops a key in the glass of water, and it *disappeared!*"

"I told you not to play with him."

"I *won't*. Does he ever . . ."

"He's not for hire," Michelle snapped. "Now, flash me a smile."

## 161

BAMBI WAS the last one in. "Any special way you want this?" Michelle asked her.

"I've got my own handcuffs. I can twist right out of them if I have to. Can I loop them around the back of this chair?"

"Sure, honey. Go ahead. Bend forward. More. Give your butt a little shake. Beautiful."

Sound of handcuffs clicking. "You don't put me down for it?"

"Why should I?"

"Some of the other girls . . ."

"You got a pimp?"

"No."

"So who's the masochist?"

Bambi laughed.

## 162

THE GIRLS were gone by one in the morning. "You're next," she told Belle.

I snapped the lead on Pansy, taking her to the basement. The Mole followed me down, shining his flash. "All fixed," he said.

"Okay, Mole. We roll tomorrow for real. Any way I can get Pansy down here without going past the other rooms?"

"Only to the basement, not outside."

"We'll do it that way. Over in that corner," I said, pointing. "Watch where you step from now on."

We went back upstairs. "Try the buzzer," I told him. He hit the switch. I counted in my head. Thirty-five seconds, Morales burst through the door, gun in his hand. "Which way?" he snapped.

"Just testing it," I said.

"Next time make it real. I'm looking forward to it."

**163** IN THE back room. Michelle was still working on Belle's face. Cat's-eye makeup, pancaked cheeks, slash of red across her mouth. It didn't look like her. "This is mousse—it'll wash right out," said Michelle, spraying it over Belle's hair, working it through with her fingers. "Let's see. . . . You'll turn over your right shoulder"—pancaking that side of her face. "Try it."

Belle peeked over her right shoulder. Her hair was dark, face a stranger's mask.

"Okay, let's do it."

Belle unhooked her bra, knelt before the chair, hands on either side. Michelle wrapped a black scarf around each hand. "Slide further back to me," she said. "Let them swing free. Turn your head. . . . Not so much."

She went over to Belle, pulling the big girl's panties over her rump. Belle lifted a leg to help her get them off.

"Leave them that way—like they've just been pulled down—it'll work better."

Michelle went back to the camera. "Okay, turn your head again. Just a little bit. Can you look a little scared? Oh, forget it —I'll open the lens, blur your face. Nobody'd look past that ass anyway."

Belle giggled. Twin dimples at the top of her butt, strip of black cloth around her thighs. The shutter clicked. Again. She shook her butt at the camera.

"Got it," Michelle said, then snapped off the lights, carried the camera out to the front.

The cigarette burned my mouth. I ground the tip out in the ashtray. Belle was still on her knees, watching me.

"Make you think of something good?" she asked, wiggling again. Then she saw my face. "What's wrong, honey?"

I walked over to her, took the loops off her hands. She put her arms around my neck. I stood up, hauling her to her feet. Reached behind me, pulled the panties back into place.

"Go wash that crap off your face."

"You're mad at me?"

I held her against me. "I'm not mad at you."

"I'm sorry, sweetheart. Truly sorry. I thought it would be a turn-on for you."

"It made me sick to look at it."

Her tears against my face. "I'm sorry. . . . I'm sorry. . . ."

I squeezed her rear with both hands. "Shut up," I said, quietly.

164 ‖ THE JOINT was open and rolling the next afternoon. Michelle was there by eleven in the morning, her arms full of bags. She and Belle worked like maniacs cleaning. The dump even smelled clean when they were done.

I stayed in the back room. The Mole would buzz me if any Hispanic male came in, anyone that could come within a half-mile of Ramón. I checked the periscope a few times on the little TV screen the Mole put on the desk. It worked perfectly.

I spent my time checking my tools. Supermarket shopping cart full of empty plastic one-liter bottles. The kind street bums collect from garbage cans—turn them in for a nickel apiece. I ran a few copies of the *Daily News* through a paper shredder. Packed a half-dozen of the bottles with the paper. I filed the front sight off the long-barreled .38. A couple of tiny slits with a razor blade and the barrel fit deep into the mouth of a bottle of Coke. I felt an ugly smile inside me—the real thing. I wrapped duct tape around the mouth of the bottle, sealing the pistol barrel inside. Pointed it at the wall, holding the bottle in my left hand. Pulled the trigger. It made a sound like snapping fingers. Plaster flew off the wall.

I lined up twelve bullets. Mole specials—super-speed hot loads, mercury tips. Any one of them would total whatever it hit. Six bullets went into the long-barreled .38, another six into the two-inch revolver next to it.

The guns were ice-cold, brand-new. No serial numbers.

A pair of the fragmentation grenades sat on the desk, the blue handles winking at me.

The Mole stashed a new car for me every morning. All along the river, one block apart. We had four cars now. I fingered the ignition key—it would work in all of them.

A tattered khaki raincoat hung on a hook. It would reach well past my knees. A long blond wig was on top of the hook. Straight hair. A blue golf hat, wine-stained. An old pair of white running shoes. Baggy black pants. Black sweatshirt with a hood. Black gloves. A slap-on mustache.

I clipped two nails on my left hand at a sharp angle. A drop of Permabond under each one. I held the razor-filed steel slivers in place against each nail, waiting for the super-glue to dry. It only took a few minutes. I brushed my left hand against a piece of paper. It fell into three pieces.

I slid back the lid on a flat metal box, looked at the colorless paste inside. I'd pass the razors through the paste before I hit the street. Mortay had to get his hands on me to kill me—one scratch, and I wouldn't go alone.

Belle watched me work, cat's-eye makeup on her face.

**165** BUSINESS BOOMED. Men got buzzed in, looked through the book. Came and went.

We cleaned up Sunday's business at five in the morning. The Mole was wearing a black silk shirt, red suspenders, cream-colored suit. Dark glasses on his face. Michelle counted a wad of cash and credit-card slips. "You look like death," she told me.

"Good," I said.

**166** MONDAY, BAMBI turned her first hard trick. The Mole buzzed me—the video screen showed a middle-aged white male, blobby face, light-colored sport coat. Not Ramón. I heard the slash of the belt, cutting through the soundproofed walls.

Later that night, one of the tricks got off the wall. I don't know what he did. I heard Morales' voice in the corridor. "How do *you* like it, motherfucker?" Metal slamming into a face. I heard whining, Morales' voice cutting harsh through it. "Whatever you want here, we got it, see? But we got different girls for different stuff. You want hard stuff, you ask for Bambi, understand? *Bambi*."

It got quiet after that.

**167** ‖ HE CAME Wednesday evening. Seven o'clock. The buzzer sounded. Ramón's face on the screen. I hit the switch. The light would glow on the Mole's desk.

"It's time," I said to Belle.

She was covered with body makeup head to toe. Fishnet stockings, black spike heels, black panties. She slipped into the red gown, belted it at her waist. A stranger—her face a hard mask.

I watched the screen. Ramón. Wearing a black leather bomber jacket, looking through the book. There was no sound on the screen.

"Monique!" the Mole called.

Belle walked past me into the corridor.

I held the sawed-off shotgun in my left hand, the paint pistol with the phony silencer in my right. Waiting.

I heard them come back. Belle's voice. "I get an extra hundred for hard stuff, honey."

Ramón's voice—couldn't make out the words.

The door to the last room closed.

I sucked air in through my nose, filling my stomach. Let it out, expanding my chest. Stepped into the corridor.

I couldn't hear through the door. The hook-and-eye lock was held in with paste. Every square inch of the room was burning in my mind. I slipped the pistol into a side pocket, cut deep enough to hold the silencer. Counted to five. I hit the door with my shoulder, stepping inside, sweeping the scattergun corner to corner. Belle was on the couch to my right, the red nightgown hiked over her hips. Ramón froze, a thick leather belt dangling from his hand.

The snout of the scattergun froze his balls down to dots. His hands shot into the air, belt still dangling. I stepped to him, the gun leveled at his gut. Five feet away.

"Drop it. Slow."

"Hey, man . . ."

"One more word, I'll blow you all over the walls."

The belt dropped from his hand.

His leather jacket was hanging from a hook in the corner. I could see the shoulder rig inside.

"Got any more guns on you, Ramón?"

He shook his head no.

"Take off your clothes. Real, *real* slow. I want to see for myself."

Belle's voice from the side of the room. "Mister . . ."

"Shut up, bitch!" I snapped at her.

Ramón dropped his pants. Black bikini briefs. Very macho. "Those too," I said. "Watch your hands."

He pulled off his cowboy boots, one at a time, standing on one leg, never taking his eyes from me.

"Sit on the couch," I said quietly. "Next to the cunt."

He sat down. I pulled the handcuffs off my belt, flipped them into Belle's lap. "Put them on. One cuff on your wrist, one on his. Now!"

Belle snapped the cuff on Ramón first, her hands shaking. Her left hand slid to the back of the couch cushion.

I took out the paint pistol. Slowly, letting Ramón get a good look. He didn't want one.

"You know what this is, shooter?"

"I know what it is." His voice shaking like Belle's hands.

"You got two choices. You live. Or you die. Pick one."

"I want to live, man." Thin, weak, soft voice. If he recognized me, he was keeping it to himself. Holding that card.

"Your pal Mortay, he stepped in some shit, understand? Sally Lou's decided to take him off the count."

"But . . ."

"That's the way it plays. I got my money, I got to come back with a head. His head. One more don't mean a thing to me. I'm gonna waste him. Tonight. You tell me what I want to know, you take that fucking diamond out of your ear, and you make tracks. Got it?"

"Man, I don't know where he lives!"

"You're going to meet him. Tonight. Where?"

"He'll *kill* me."

"Ramón, he's a dead man. I don't find him tonight, I find him some other time. But you don't tell me what I want to know, he won't get a chance to kill you."

"Man, I don't know where he is. I'm *serious!*"

"So am I," I said, leveling the pistol at Belle's chest. I pulled the trigger. *Splat!* Belle slammed back against the couch, a red stain running between her breasts. I aimed the gun at Ramón—he never looked at Belle. The sound I made cocking it was the loudest thing he ever heard.

"Where?"

"Under the New York Times clock! Between Seventh and Eighth! On Forty-third! *Don't!*"

"What time?"

"Ten-thirty!" Piss flowed down his legs.

"Who gets there first?"

"He does, man. He *always* does. . . ."

Belle's left hand flashed, plunging the hypo deep into his thigh, her thumb driving the plunger home as I fired a paint ball into his face.

"I . . ." and he was out. Belle rammed the speed key home, unsnapping her cuff. I pulled his free arm behind his back, locked the other cuff. Belle jumped off the couch, rubbing her breasts. I kicked Ramón onto the floor.

"Go get the Mole," I told her.

**168** MICHELLE AND the Mole stood on either side of me. Ramón was in the corner, breathing deeply, out.

"The joint is closed," I told Michelle. "How many of the girls have customers?"

"Just MaryAnne."

"When he's finished, let him out. Tell the girls the show's over—the cops are going to hit in an hour. Get them out the door. You have any trouble, you hit the buzzer, they'll come from next door. Then take off yourself."

She kissed me. "Call as soon as it's over."

"I will."

She went out the door. I knelt down, pulled Ramón over my shoulder by one of his arms, positioned his weight. "The basement," I said to the Mole. Fuck McGowan and his deals—I wasn't going to leave a body around for the cops to hang me with.

He led the way. Pansy met us at the bottom of the steps. "Speak!" I told her, tossed a slab of steak through the air. She caught it on the fly.

"Is the panel truck ours?"

"Yes."

"I'm going to throw this garbage in the back. That shot'll keep him out for hours. You get stopped, it's not a murder beef. He won't testify."

"Where should I dump him?"

"He's the shooter, Mole. One of the Nazis."

He nodded.

"Take Pansy too."

"She won't . . ."

"Yes, she will. That last piece of meat I gave her was laced. She should be asleep by now. Keep her with you—lock her up in one of the sheds. Leave water for her. I'll be back in the junkyard sometime late tonight. Belle will get there before me. Your piece is done."

"The basement?"

"Eleven o'clock. You can do it?"

"Yes. Me and the boy."

"He's a good boy, Mole. You should be proud."

"You too."

"Yeah. Look, Mole. If I don't come back, do something for me. Tell Belle I love her."

He nodded.

"And Pansy, let her loose. Let her run with your pack. Let her and Simba-witz make puppies."

I dumped Ramón's body in the back of the panel truck. The Mole snapped a heavy padlock across the back.

I went back for Pansy. I scooped her up in my arms, carried her to the truck. "Open the front door," I told the Mole. "I don't want her to ride with garbage."

I laid her gently across the front seat. Kissed her snout. "See you soon, girl."

The Mole wrapped his stubby arms around me, squeezed hard. "*Sei Gesund*," he said. Go with God.

## 169

MICHELLE WAS pushing the girls out the door when I slipped back upstairs. It sounded like sorority girls saying goodbye for the summer.

Belle was in the back room, toweling herself off, the cat's-eye mask still on her face.

"You were perfect," I said, holding her close.

"I was scared."

"I still am. It's almost over. Get out of here. Take the Pontiac. Don't leave the office until past midnight. I'll see you at the junkyard."

"Where's Pansy?"

"She's with the Mole. It's okay. Go."

"What'd you do with the freak?"

"He's gone."

"But you're working with the cops, right? They're right next door. He's not dead—why don't you just leave him for them?"

I cupped her chin, making her watch my face. "I'm not working with the cops, Belle. A cop sees me doing my work on the street tonight, I'm going down. McGowan, he can't call off the whole fucking force. He wouldn't do it if he could. I'm not leaving that freak around to tell his story."

I felt a pulse in her throat, just under her chin. Steady beat.

"We're outlaws, little girl. We can step over the line to the other side, but we're not welcome there. We can't stay. The next cop I see, he'll be trying to stop me from coming home."

She nodded, knowing it was the truth. "Burke, it's not even eight o'clock. You have until ten-thirty. Let me wait here with you."

"No."

"I knew you'd say that."

"It's all right, Belle. Smooth as silk. I'll meet this Mortay at ten-thirty, I'll be in one of the cars by eleven. That's when the Ghost Van goes. I'll be with you soon."

"And you'll never leave."

"And I'll never leave."

I lit a smoke, watching her dress.

"Burke?"

"You're going, Belle."

"I know. I will, promise. Remember when you came back to me? After you met that man?"

"Yeah."

"I want you inside me. To keep with me until I see you again. I want my smell on you when you kill him."



170 I CARRIED two of the suitcases out to the back. Tossed in the scat-tergun. Closed the trunk. I held her next to me.

"Belle . . ."

"Don't you say it! Whatever you're going to say, don't say it. Tell me tonight."

I kissed her. There was blood in my heart.

When she drove away, I was alone.

**171** || In the back room, I put it all together. Cut two fingertips off the black gloves. Buried the plastic bottle in the cart, pistol handle sticking up, wrapped in black tape. I put on the black pants, the black sweatshirt. Worked the blond wig over my hair, stuck on the mustache. The blue golf cap was a tight fit. The black pants had cargo pockets— I put a grenade in each one. The two-inch pistol in my belt.

Pain plucked at me. Fear. I climbed down into my center. Stayed there, feeling the calm.

Mortay wanted what was mine.

If you can't stand to read the weight, you don't climb on the scales.

Ten o'clock. I pulled on the gloves, ran the two razor-tipped nails through the poison paste.

It was a struggle getting the shopping cart down the stairs.

Then I was in the street. All my people safe behind me. Whatever happened.

I reached down, deep as I could go. Telling myself it would be over soon. I'd be Home Free.

But I knew. Knew why I was pushing a shopping cart filled with homicide through Times Square. No home is free.

**172** || I pushed my shopping cart along, smoking a cigarette, mumbling to myself. The clock in the package store on 43rd said ten-twenty. I slowed my pace.

Three kids came up the street toward me, wearing matching red silk jackets. I watched their eyes, praying they wouldn't think it was funny to tip over my cart. They went on by.

I turned the corner. Moving slow, checking doorways for bottles, picking one up, tossing it into my cart.

The Times clock was a round light in the distance. I pushed the cart ahead of me, one hand on the pistol.

He was standing under the clock. A long white vertical ribbon in the dark doorway. The clock said ten-twenty-eight. I kept rolling.

A hundred feet away. Mortay saw me. A used-up bum, collecting empties.

Fifty feet. I saw his hands hanging loose in front of him. Head turning, scanning the street. Almost home.

I looked him full in the face. Pushed my cart into his life. Felt the chill. His eyes flicked past me, over my shoulder. I pulled the gun loose, snapped off a shot at his chest, the bottle popping off the front of the pistol. A piece of his coat flew as he spun to the side, moving right at me. I kicked the cart toward him, fired again. The gun cracked alive. Missed. Mortay spun in his tracks, shoulder-rolled against the wall. I leveled the gun. He took off, running the other way.

I jumped past the cart and took off after him. Four shots left. Humans jumped off the sidewalk. He wasn't used to running—all his speed was short-range. I was forty feet behind him at the corner of 43rd and Eighth. Mortay glanced west, gave it up, charged across 44th for the Playbill Bar. I was right behind him, the long-barreled pistol looking for his back. He chopped through people, heading for the side door. I fired another shot to clear the way, coming through. The street was clogged. He couldn't lose me.

A cop was on the corner of Eighth and 46th. Mortay took him out with one chop. I jumped over the body, holding the pistol high to clear the street, locked on him.

At 48th I was close enough. He felt it, dodging behind cars, weaving through humans. He was running out of gas. When he turned . . .

Construction site at 49th, high chain-link fence. Mortay ripped his way over the top, white coat flying as I missed another shot.

Couldn't follow him. I raced along Eighth until I found an opening, stepped through, gun up.

I dropped about five feet—they must have started the excavation. No lights. Street noises over my head. Quiet. No sirens.

I was safe there. Scared to be safe. He couldn't come up on me without getting blown away. But if he got out . . .

It was like being back in Biafra. Focus on the sounds, separate the jungle-noises from the man-noises. Breathe shallow. Don't fight the fear.

I heard him, moving west, toward Ninth Avenue. Machine-gun thoughts ripping at me. Did he know how to do this?

Something moved—flash of white in the night. I fired at the sound. The gun barked—the bullet whined close to the ground, disappointed. I heard him move again.

I got to my feet, running right at the sounds he made, cracking off another shot. One left.

Quiet now. I cocked the pistol. Man-sounds to my right.

"I'm still here, pussy." Snake voice hissing out of the night. He wasn't in a hurry.

I dropped to my knees, crawling forward toward the voice. Another flash of white. I fired. Another crack. Then a dry, audible *click!* I pulled the trigger again. Nothing.

I felt my guts lock. "Fuck!" Letting him smell my fear, throwing the empty pistol as hard as I could in the direction of the noise.

"My turn!" he screamed, coming for me.

I ran for my life, pulling the little backup pistol from my belt. I dived for the ground, rolled onto my back, pushed myself backward by driving my legs into the dirt. Making panic sounds. Leaving a blood-spoor.

Begging him to come in my mind.

He flew out of the darkness in a twisting, spinning series of kick-thrusts, a ghost target if I had a knife. I came to my knees, holding the pistol in both hands. He saw the gun, threw himself flat, already tucking his shoulder under to kick upward when the hollow-point slug caught him in the chest, pinning him to the ground.

The noise from the tiny gun was deafening; the dirt bowl we were in made it sound like a cannon. The street noises all seemed to stop at once. I walked slowly toward Mortay. He was choking on his own blood—the slug must have caught a lung.

I stood over him, legs shaking. His eyes were ice-pick dots under the shelf of bone, holding me the way the slug held him.

"You can't kill me," he whispered. Stone-carved ice. "Death can't die."

"You still want Max?" I asked, cocking the gun.

He launched himself off the ground, the knife edge of his hand extended. I fired twice more, blowing him off his feet.

I heard a siren in the distance. Mortay was on his side. I dropped to my knees next to him. Blood bubbled from his mouth, killing his last words. I pumped two more shots into his chest. His body jumped. I turned him over with my foot. His eyes were open. I fired again, right into the ridge of bone that covered his eyebrows. His eyes wouldn't close.

The sirens were closer. More than one now. I pocketed the gun, pulled the pin from one of the grenades, holding it tightly in my hand. I slammed the metal ball hard into his face, cracking past his teeth, holding it there. With my other hand, I folded his hands so they were on either side of his face.

I let go of the lever and ran toward Ninth Avenue. Passed a white coat, swinging gently from a steel girder. The target Mortay had left while he moved in on me. I was almost to the fence on 50th when I heard the explosion. I hit the fence, sirens screaming to my right. Dropped over the top, feeling the breath burst out of my lungs. I popped the pin on the last grenade, side-armed it back over the fence, crouching in the dark. The sirens shrieked at each other—wolf-pack sounds, telling each other the prey was dangerous. The grenade exploded, buying me a little time.

I ran up 50th, the pistol in my hand, driving my knees up to my chest, trying for a burst of speed that wouldn't come. I crossed Ninth, heading for the river, still blocks away from any of the cars we had stashed. Tires shrieked behind me. Cops? I dropped to one knee, leveling the gun. Back over the line—me or them. Belle's Camaro smoked to a stop.

"Come on, brother!" The Prof.

I ran for the car, diving headfirst into the window. Belle stomped the gas, charging for the river. She shot through red lights, standing on the brakes to make the car squat at Twelfth, nailed it again, power-sliding around the corner. She pulled off at 45th, right behind the black Cadillac the Mole had left for me. I jumped out, scooping up the Prof. His legs were still bolted together in casts, the scattergun steady in his hands. I unlocked the door, threw him in the back.

Blue lights flashed on 45th, couple of blocks away and moving in.

I started the engine. Looked over my shoulder. Where was she? "Belle! Let's go!" I yelled at her.

The Camaro's engine roared an answer as she peeled out. Right up 45th.

The blue lights came closer. A phalanx of squad cars screaming down the block, at least three deep, spread out to block the way. I wheeled the Cadillac across the highway after her. The Camaro's taillights blazed—she was flying at the cop cars. Head on. I heard her little-girl voice, singing hard-edged in my head. Calling to the cops. "Come on!"

The Camaro was a red rocket.

"Hit the brakes! She ain't gonna stop," the Prof yelled.

The Camaro shot right down the middle of the street, going the wrong way. The police car in the lead charged to meet her.

Time stopped. The squad car swerved at the last second. Too late. It fireballed against a row of cars on the left as the Camaro shot past. Gunfire cut through the siren's song, a roadblock of wreckage in its wake.

"They'll never catch that girl," the Prof whispered. A prayer.

I threw a U-turn and headed for the junkyard.

**173** ON THE West Side Highway I tried to light a cigarette. My hands wouldn't work.

"I can light one for you, bro', but I can't drive the car."

I straightened the wheel. Reached for the smoke he handed me. "What happened?"

"Girl walks in my hospital room, shotgun in her hand. Comes right in my room. 'What's this?' the doc asks her. 'Jailbreak,' she says. Throws me over one shoulder like a sack of cement, carries me down in the elevator, walks right out the front door. Puts me in that red car. 'Burke needs us,' that's all she said."

Nothing in the rearview mirror.

"She knew I needed it too," the Prof said, hands on the scattergun. "He took something from me. She was giving me a chance to get it back. Said you were going to take out that motherfucker—our job was the cops."

I dragged on the cigarette, seeing the fireball.

The Prof read my thoughts. "Ain't nothing God or the devil put on this earth gonna catch Belle, brother. She's coming home."

**174** I WHEELED the Caddy into the junkyard. The gate swung open. Terry jumped in, steered us through.

"Belle?" I asked him.

"Not yet," the kid said, his mouth hard.

The Mole was waiting. "Where's Ramón?" I asked him.

He pointed at the wolf pack. Fighting over what was left.

I lit a smoke. Carried the Prof out of the Caddy, put him on top of an oil drum. I stood with my people.

"Mortay's dead."

"You make sure?" the Prof asked.

"They'll need a microscope for the autopsy. It's over. You blow the basement?" I asked the Mole.

"You didn't hear it?" Terry said.

"No."

"It'll be on the news," the Mole said.

I looked at the Prof. "She was well away. They weren't looking for her. Why didn't she just run?"

His eyes shone in the fire. "Why didn't you?"

I couldn't answer him. Fists clenched so tight my arms ached.

The little man dragged on his smoke. "Her dice, brother. Hers to hold, hers to roll."

**175** TORTURED rubber screamed on concrete.

"Belle. The back way!" the kid shouted, taking off. We ran to the fence. The Camaro shot through, skidding past us. It stopped where the Prof was sitting. Belle didn't get out.

I ran back to her. Bullet holes stitched the driver's door. I wrenched it open. Belle fell into my arms. The Mole reached past me, unsnapped the seat belt. I carried her to the bunker. "Don't talk," I said, lowering her to the ground.

Her gray sweatshirt was one big dark stain. The Mole cut it away. She was torn to pieces, the blue necklace around her neck. "Get the medical kit," he said to Terry.

I bent close to her. "Hold on, Belle. You'll be okay in just a minute."

Her eyes were closed. They flicked open. "Burke?"

"You're home now, Belle. It's all right."

Her voice was soft. "My race is run, honey. I'm done."

"Shut up! Save your strength."

"Tell me."

"I love you, Belle."

"I'll be waiting for you," she said. Her eyes closed. The Mole shouldered me out of the way, plunged a needle into her chest, his fingers at her neck. I was on my knees, watching him work, begging in my mind.

He turned to me. "She's gone."

## 176 THEY LEFT me alone with her then.

I couldn't hold it in me—screaming curses at the night. The dogs went quiet.

I lay down next to her, wrapping her in my arms. Tears on blood.

## 177 THE SKY was getting light when they came back. The Mole. Terry. The Prof, riding a wheelchair.

I stood next to the little man, my hand on his shoulder. Felt his hand on mine.

"Pull it together, brother. The way she'd want it. She's with the Lord now. And He's one lucky son of a bitch."

The Mole covered her with a prayer rug.

I gripped my brother's hand, and said goodbye to my Blue Belle.

## A NOTE ON THE TYPE

This book was set in a digitized version of Granjon,
a type named in compliment to Robert Granjon, a
type cutter and printer active in Antwerp, Lyons,
Rome, and Paris from 1523 to 1590. Granjon, the
boldest and most original designer of his time, was
one of the first to practice the trade of type founder
apart from that of printer.

Linotype Granjon was designed by George W.
Jones, who based his drawings on a face used by
Claude Garamond (ca. 1480–1561) in his beautiful
French books. Granjon more closely resembles
Garamond's own type than does any of the various
modern faces that bear his name.

Composed by PennSet, Inc.,
Bloomsburg, Pennsylvania

Printed and bound by R. R. Donnelley & Sons,
Harrisonburg, Virginia

*Designed by Marysarah Quinn*